"My death wins you nothing but more suffering. Another will take my place, and another should he fall. Seventy-seven mages will hunt for you until the desert turns red with your blood. Do you hear them coming, Spellslinger?"

Beneath his bravado and contempt was a terrible sadness, as though he were watching all his dreams of being a great mage—dreams I had once shared—collapse like castles made of sand. His sorrow filled me with shame for what I was about to do next, but I did it anyway. I grabbed his shoulders and squeezed until he winced in pain. "Tell me what happened to Ferius Parfax. You said you killed her. Was it a lie?"

His lips twitched and I wasn't even sure if he'd heard me. Then he spat out a ragged laugh that brought more blood with it. "Did I say I killed her? Perhaps she escaped. Perhaps I never found her at all. Beg me for the truth and I might remember."

I shook him again. "Please! Just tell me if she's—"

My enemy met death with a soft exhalation of breath that carried with it his last words: "Suffer, shadowblack."

Praise for

Spellslinger

"Told with the conviction of Ursula Le Guin and the dash of Alexandre Dumas." —*New Statesman*

"A fast, fun, often funny fantasy series." —*B&N Sci-Fi and Fantasy Blog*

"An intriguing system of magic, wry humor, and a twisting plot make for an entertaining series debut." —*Kirkus*

"A bucket-load of tension is offset with humour, power struggles, lots of magic and some great characters. Fantasy junkies will devour with relish." —*Guardian*

"*Spellslinger* is the start of something truly special. Sebastien de Castell is a master of breakneck pacing, dagger-sharp dialogue, and twists you didn't see coming—and this series has it all." —Nicholas Eames, author of *Kings of the Wyld*

"This book is dangerously addictive. It has it all: compelling world-building, breathtaking plot-twists, a page-turning pace, and characters who soon feel like old friends. I can't wait for the next one!" —Melissa Caruso, author of *The Tethered Mage*

"Exotic, original and gripping from the get-go, *Spellslinger* is a must-read." —Jonathan Stroud, author of the Lockwood and Co series

"A tremendously fun read full of wit and action." —James Islington, author of *The Shadow of What Was Lost*

By Sebastien de Castell

SOULBINDER

Spellslinger: Book Four

SEBASTIEN DE CASTELL

www.orbitbooks.net

Copyright © 2018 by Sebastien de Castell
Excerpt from *Queenslayer* copyright © 2018 by Sebastien de Castell
Excerpt from *The Fifth Ward: First Watch* copyright © 2017 by Dale Lucas

Author photograph by Pink Monkey Studios
Cover design by Lauren Panepinto
Cover art by Shutterstock
Cover copyright © 2018 by Hachette Book Group, Inc.

Orbit
Hachette Book Group
1290 Avenue of the Americas
New York, NY 10104
orbitbooks.net

Originally published in 2018 by Hot Key Books in Great Britain
First U.S. Edition: December 2018

Orbit is an imprint of Hachette Book Group.
The Orbit name and logo are trademarks of Little, Brown Book Group Limited.

The publisher is not responsible for websites (or their content) that are not owned by the publisher.

The Hachette Speakers Bureau provides a wide range of authors for speaking events. To find out more, go to www.hachettespeakersbureau.com or call (866) 376-6591.

Library of Congress Control Number: 2018957255

ISBNs: 978-0-316-52587-9 (trade paperback), 978-0-316-52586-2 (ebook)

Printed in the United States of America

LSC-C

10 9 8 7 6 5 4 3 2 1

When I was seven years old, my parents unexpectedly picked my brother and me up from school. I figured something terrible had happened, but instead they presented us with two puppies. We named them Lady and Tramp, after the greatest movie of all time. In the strange way of these things, Tramp became 'mine' (or rather, I became his). I guess loads of people have had similar experiences, and I don't know why they mean so much to us, but they do. They mean everything.

Hope is a wondrous island upon whose shores we all wish to tread. Be wary though, that when you find your eyes drawn to that distant horizon, you remember to look down once in a while . . .

—Stupid Argosi proverb

1

The Problem with Sand

The desert is a liar.

Oh, sure, from a distance that endless expanse of golden sand *looks* inviting. Standing at the top of a sand dune, warm breezes soothe the scorching sun above, beckoning you to the wonders awaiting below. Whatever you desire—treasure beyond imagining, escape from your enemies, or maybe even a cure for the twisting black lines that won't stop growing around your left eye—some fool will swear it's waiting for you across the desert. *A dangerous journey? Perhaps, but the rewards, boy! Think of the rewards . . .*

Look closer, though—I mean, really close—say, an inch or so from the sand itself. This is easy to do when you're face down in it waiting to die of thirst. See how each and every grain of sand is unique? Different shapes, sizes, colours . . . That seamless perfection you saw before was just an illusion. Up close the desert is dirty, ugly and mean.

Like I said: it's a stinking liar.

"*You're* a stinking liar," Reichis grumbled.

My head jerked up with a start. I hadn't even realised I'd spoken out loud. With considerable effort I turned my head to see how my so-called business partner was faring. I didn't get very far. Lack of food and water had taken their toll on me. The bloody bruises inflicted by the spells of a recently deceased mage whose foul-smelling corpse was rotting in the heat a few feet away didn't help either. So was I going to waste what life I had left to me just to glare at the ill-tempered, two-foot-tall squirrel cat dying by my side?

"*You* stink," I replied.

"Heh," he chuckled. Squirrel cats don't have a very good sense of their own mortality. They do, however, have an acute penchant for assigning blame. "This is all your fault," he chittered.

I rolled over, hoping to ease the stiffness in my spine, only for the wounds on my back to scream in protest. The pain drew a rasping moan from my parched throat.

"Don't try to deny it," Reichis said.

"I didn't say anything."

"Yes, you did. You whimpered and I heard, 'But, Reichis, how could I possibly have known that I was leading us into a death trap set by my own people? I mean, sure, you warned me that this talk of a secret monastery in the desert where monks could cure me of the shadowblack was a scam, but you know me: I'm an idiot. An idiot who never listens to his smarter and much better-looking business partner.'"

In case you've never seen a squirrel cat, picture an angry feline face, slightly tubby body, unruly bushy tail and strange furry flaps connecting their front and back limbs that enable them to glide down from treetops to massacre their prey. "Good-looking" isn't exactly the phrase that comes to mind.

"You got all that from a whimper?" I asked.

A pause. "Squirrel cats are very intuitive."

I drew a ragged breath, the heat off the sand burning the air in my lungs. How long had the two of us been lying here? A day? Two days? My hand reached for the last of our water skins, dragging it closer. I steeled myself for the fact that I'd have to share what was left with Reichis. People say you can live three days without water, but that's not factoring in the way the desert robs the moisture from you like a ... *like a damned squirrel cat!* The water skin was bone-dry. "You drank the last of our water?"

Reichis replied testily, "I asked first."

"When?"

Another pause. "While you were asleep."

Apparently the desert wasn't the only liar I had to contend with.

Seventeen years old, exiled by my people, hunted by every hex-tracker and bounty mage with two spells and a bad attitude, and the last of my water had just been stolen by the closest thing I had to a friend out here.

My name is Kellen Argos. Once I was a promising student of magic and the son of one of the most powerful families in the Jan'Tep territories. Then the twisting black markings of a mystical curse known as the shadowblack appeared around my left eye. Now people call me outlaw, traitor, exile—and that's when they're being polite.

The one thing they never call me is lucky.

"Sure, I know the place," the old scout had said, her mismatched hazel and green eyes glued to the dusty leather bag of copper and silver trinkets on the table between us. We had the ground floor of the travellers' saloon to ourselves, with the exception of a couple of passed-out drunks in the far corner and one sad fellow who sat on the floor by himself, rolling a pair of dice over and over as he sobbed into his ale about having the worst luck in the whole world.

Shows what you know, buddy.

"Can you take me to it? This monastery," I asked, placing a card face up on the table.

The scout picked up the card and squinted at the shadowy towers

5

depicted on its surface. "Nice work," she observed. "You paint this yourself?"

I nodded. For the past six months, Reichis and I had crossed half a continent in search of a cure for the shadowblack. We'd pick up clues here and there, brief scrawls in the margins of obscure texts referring to a secret sanctuary, rumours repeated endlessly by drunks in taverns like this one. The Argosi paint cards of important people and places, imbuing them with whatever scraps of information they collect in hopes that the resulting images will reveal otherwise hidden meanings. I'd taken to painting my own. If I died in my search for a cure, there was always a chance the cards would find their way into Argosi hands, and then to Ferius Parfax, so she'd know not to bother looking for me.

The old scout tossed the card back down on the table as if she were placing a bet. "The place you're looking for is called the Ebony Abbey, and yeah, I *could* take you there . . . if I were so inclined." Her smile pinched the crags of sun-browned skin on her forehead and around her eyes, her face like a map of some long-forgotten country. She had to be well into her sixties, but her sleeveless leather jerkin revealed rope-like muscles on her shoulders and arms. Those, along with the assortment of knives sheathed to a bandolier across her chest and the crossbow strapped to her back, told me she could probably handle herself just fine in a fight. The way she kept staring at the bag of trinkets on the table without paying much attention to me made it plain that I hadn't made a similar impression on her.

Searching for a miracle cure hadn't been a particularly profitable enterprise so far. Every coin I earned as a spellslinger during my travels had been wasted on snake-oil salesmen peddling putrid concoctions that left me sick and vomiting for days at a time. Now my travel-worn linen shirt hung loose on my skinny frame. My face and chest still showed the bruises and scars from my last encounter with a pair of Jan'Tep bounty mages. So I could understand why the sight of me didn't exactly fill the scout with trepidation.

"She's thinking of beating you up and taking our money," Reichis said, sniffing the air from his perch on my shoulder.

"That thing ain't rabid, is it?" the scout asked, sparing him a wary glance.

Other people don't understand the chitters, snarls and occasional farts Reichis uses to communicate. "I'm still trying to figure that out," I replied.

The squirrel cat gave a low growl. "You know I can just rip your eyeballs right out of their sockets and eat them while you sleep, right?" He hopped off my shoulder and headed towards the two drunks passed out in the corner, no doubt to see if he could pick their pockets.

"Ask them that know the tales," the old scout began in a sing-song voice. "They'll tell you naught but seven outsiders have ever been inside the Ebony Abbey's walls. Five of them are dead. One's a dream-weed addict who couldn't find his own nose with both hands, never mind a secret monastery hidden in the desert." She reached for the little bag that contained everything I still had of any value. "Then there's me."

I got to the bag first. I may not look like much, but I've got fast hands. "We haven't agreed terms yet."

For the first time the old scout's mismatched eyes locked on mine. I tried to match her glare, but it's unnerving to have two different-coloured eyes staring back at you. "Why you want to mess with them Black Binders anyway?" she asked. Her gaze went to my left eye, and I could tell she'd picked up on the slight discolouration where the edges of the skin-coloured mesdet paste met the top of my cheekbone. "You ain't got the shadowblack, do ya?"

"Shadow-what?" I asked. "Never heard of it."

"Well, I hear there's a posse of Jan'Tep spellcasters who'll pay plenty for one o' them demon-cursed. There's a particular fellow they've been hunting a while now, or so I hear."

"I wouldn't know about that," I said, trying to lend my words a hint of a threat. "Like I told you before, I'm just writing a book about obscure desert monks."

"Lot of money for that bounty. Maybe more than what's in that bag of yours."

I removed my hands from the bag and let my fingers drift down to open the tops of the pouches attached to either side of my belt. Inside were the red and black powders I used for the one spell I knew that always left an impression. "You know what?" I asked casually. "Now that you mention it, I think maybe I *have* heard about this shadowblack bounty you mention. Word is, a lot of dangerous folk have tried to collect on it. Have to wonder what happened to all of them."

One corner of the scout's mouth rose to a smirk. Her own hands, I saw now, had managed to make a pair of hooked knives appear. "Met plenty of dangerous men in my time. None of them impressed me much. What makes you any different?"

I returned her smile. "Look behind you."

She didn't, instead angling one of her knives just a touch until the blade caught the reflection of a certain squirrel cat who'd surreptitiously made his way up to the top of the coat rack behind her and was now waiting for the cue to pounce.

Yeah, the little bugger makes himself useful sometimes.

I counted three full breaths before the old scout slowly set her knives down on the table. "Sounds like a mighty fine book you're writing, my young friend." She snatched up my bag of trinkets and rose from the table. "Best we load up on supplies in town before we make the trip."

I waited a while longer, doing my best to make it appear as if I hadn't decided whether to hire her as my guide or blast her into ashes. Truthfully though, I was waiting for my heart to stop racing. "How far away is this abbey?" I asked.

She adjusted the strap of her crossbow and slid her knives into their sheathes. "A long ways, as these things go, but don't worry; you'll enjoy the journey."

"Really?"

She grinned. "Folks say the Golden Passage is the gentlest, most beautiful place you'll ever see."

2

The Virtue of Corpses

Faint scratching sounds returned me to my current predicament. I opened one eye a fraction, groggily expecting to be blinded by the reflection of sunlight against the shimmering golden sand. Instead I was greeted by twilight and a bitter chill. You'd think a place as blisteringly hot during the day as the Golden Passage would be temperate at night. But no, the temperature goes from scorching to freezing with barely an hour of warmth in between. I shivered and tried to go back to sleep.

The scratching continued though—so close that for a second I batted at my ear, fearful that some insect was burrowing inside. When that failed to solve the problem, I forced my head up enough to turn towards the source of the incessant noise. Reichis was wearily dragging himself along the sand.

He's trying to get to me, I thought.

Fondness broke through the cold and despair. For all our quarreling, the squirrel cat and I had saved each other's lives more times than either of us could count; now he wanted to die beside me.

I reached out a hand, only to discover he wasn't getting any closer. He was actually crawling *away* from me.

Have I mentioned that squirrel cats are ungrateful little wretches? My so-called business partner hadn't been expending his last ounce of strength so that we could meet our end together; this wasn't some final moment of friendship between us. No, instead the furry monster was slowly working his way to the war mage's corpse.

"What are you doing?" I asked.

No reply. Reichis just kept crawling inch by inch to his destination. When he finally lay next to the corpse's head, panting and exhausted, I worried that perhaps the squirrel cat's mind was so far gone from thirst that he'd mistaken the dead man for me. With a trembling paw, he reached for the mage's unblinking eyes that stared blindly up at the darkening sky. That's when I finally understood what Reichis was up to.

"Oh, for the sake of all my dead ancestors," I swore, "tell me you're not planning to—"

With the deftness that comes from practice—a *lot* of practice— Reichis used one of his claws to dig out the man's eyeball. He then opened his jaws wide, dropped the disgusting, squishy sphere into his maw, and bit down. "Oh…" he said, moaning rapturously, "that's tasty."

"You're repugnant, you know that?" I'm not sure the words actually came out of my mouth. At that precise moment I was using what little strength of will I had left to keep myself from vomiting.

"Yummy," he mumbled between chews, then swallowed noisily.

What few people know about squirrel cats is that the only thing more revolting than the way they devour their food is their insistence on rhapsodising about it afterwards. "You know," he began with a contented sigh, "you worry that it'll be overcooked, on account of this guy's face having caught fire and all, but it turned out perfect. A little crispy on the outside; soft and warm on the inside." He reached a paw over to the other side of the dead mage's face. "You want the left one?" he asked, adding a slight snarl to convey that the offer wasn't entirely sincere.

"I'll pass. Doesn't it just make you more thirsty? We're likely to die from lack of water a lot sooner than we'll expire from hunger."

"Good point." Reichis hauled himself closer to the mage's chest, where a massive wound from our duel had left a pool of blood. The squirrel cat began lapping it up. He paused when he caught me staring at him in horror. "You should probably drink some too, Kellen. Must have *some* water in it, right?"

"I am *not* drinking blood. I am *not* eating eyeballs."

The squirrel cat served up a sarcastic growl. "Oh, right, because your culinary hang-ups are so much more important than our survival."

I couldn't think of a suitable retort. He might've been right, for all I knew, though I had no idea if human beings could actually get enough moisture from blood to make a difference, or if it would just make me sick. Either way, I couldn't bring myself to find out, so I just lay there for a few minutes with nothing to do but listen to the sound of Reichis's enthusiastic slurping. When he was finally done, he lay back down on his side and called to me. "Kellen?"

"Yeah?"

"I know this is kind of a sensitive topic, but..."

"What?"

"Well, when you're dead, is it okay if I eat your corpse?" Hastily he added, "I mean, it's better if one of us lives, right?"

With what little strength I had left, I rolled away from him onto my back, ignoring the pain that exploded from my injuries. I didn't want the last thing I saw in this world to be the blood-soaked face of a squirrel cat as he pondered which to eat first, my eyeballs or my ears.

High above, beyond the petty concerns of mortals, the stars began to appear, thousands of tiny sparks coming to life. Though the Golden Passage was an arid, unlivable hellhole, the night sky out here could really put on a show. I took in a breath, only to have my throat spasm painfully—a reflex that I guess must be the result of going too long without water.

I'm going to die here. The words invaded my thoughts as suddenly and as forcefully as an iron binding spell. *I'm really going to die tonight, killed by some arsehole Jan'Tep bounty hunter and my own stupidity.* I felt myself starting to cry, and with trembling fingers reached up to wipe at tears that weren't there.

I must've let out a sob, because Reichis groaned. "Oh, great, cos bawling your eyes out is really going to help conserve water." Squirrel cats aren't exactly known for their compassion.

Usually when I get myself into trouble, my survival depends on the timely arrival of a certain curly red-haired gambler by the name of Ferius Parfax. There I'll be, on my knees, begging some lunatic who happens to have a thing against shadowblacks, waiting for the blade (or mace, or crossbow, ember spell, or... you get the idea) to come crashing down on me, when all of a sudden *she'll* turn up.

"Well now, don't you two look as fussy as two feisty ferrets fightin' over a fern," she'll say. Actually, she's never used those exact words, but it's usually something equally nonsensical.

"Do not dare interfere, Argosi," the mage (or soldier, assassin or random irritated person) will shout back.

Ferius will push that frontier hat of hers a half-inch higher on her brow, reach into her waistcoat to pull out a smoking reed, and say, "Far be it from me to interfere, friend, but I've grown somewhat accustomed to that skinny fella you seem intent on carvin' up. Gonna have to ask you to kindly back off."

After that? Well, fight-fight-fight, clever remark, certain death, near-impossible daring feat, enemy goes down, one last clever remark—usually at my expense—and then I'm saved. That's how it's been ever since I left my homeland on my sixteenth birthday.

Only now everything's different. Six months ago I'd abandoned Ferius, my mentor in the ways of the Argosi, and Nephenia, the charmcaster I once loved, on account of I'd learned that my people were never going to stop hunting me and anyone with me, so long as I had the shadowblack. Since the swirling black marks around my left eye showed no sign of fading away, that meant leaving the two people I was closest to behind or risk them being killed by enemies intent on getting to me. As painful as my departure had been, at least it had felt kind of noble.

For about six minutes.

The problem with being noble and self-sacrificing is that when you get into a jam—say, like, when the tattooed metallic bands on a Jan'Tep hextracker's arms are glowing from all the magic he's summoned to kill you—there's nobody to get you out of it.

"Hey, Kellen...?" Reichis asked with an uncharacteristic hesitation in his voice.

"Yes, you can eat me when I'm dead. Happy now?"

Silence for a moment, then, "No, I was just wondering if you think that mage was telling the truth."

"About what?"

"When he said he killed Ferius."

3

The Trouble with Spells

I'd suspected the old scout would betray us the minute she had us in the desert and away from any prying eyes. Reichis and I took turns watching her, day and night, as we trudged up and down one sand dune after another. Our vigilance proved to be misplaced, however, because although she really was leading us into a trap, it wasn't one she'd set herself.

Among the many ways the desert messes with you is the way light reflecting off the sand plays tricks with your eyes. Sometimes you'll see a shimmer in the distance that looks just like a Jan'Tep shield spell. You'll get ready for the fight of your life, only to have your mean-spirited guide mock you for being "as jumpy as a tadpuddler."

I have no idea what "tadpuddlers" are. Apparently they're quite jumpy.

Every time I freaked out over a mirage, the old scout would ride up to the glistening haze, holding her hooked knives aloft and shouting, "Have at thee, foul patch of empty air!" She found it all terribly funny, right up until one of those blurry shimmers fired a bolt of ember magic that blasted her into ashes.

Reichis and I were so exhausted by then that we barely had time to drop to the ground before another bolt came after us. Turned out we weren't even the target: the ember spell was aimed at our horses.

They died a mercifully quick death. Unfortunately, with them went the supplies we needed to survive another week in the desert.

"How many?" the broad-shouldered mage asked as he stepped out from his obscurement spell. As cloaking conjurations go, it wasn't particularly impressive, which gave me hope this guy might be relying on a charm and wasn't particularly powerful himself. Maybe he was just a one-bander like me.

"How many what?" I asked, rising to my feet and casually reaching for my powders.

"How many of my fellow mages have you killed, shadowblack? How many of our people have died trying to bring you to justice?"

I considered the question. "Nine," I lied, then corrected myself. "Actually, ten now." I tossed the red and black powders into the air in front of me. Just before they collided, I formed the somatic shape with my hands: index and middle fingers pointed towards my target, in the sign of guidance; ring and little fingers pressed into my palm, the gesture of restraint, and thumbs to the sky, the closest I ever get to a prayer to my ancestors for help. "*Carath,*" I intoned.

The explosion shattered the air between us. Twin red and black flames intertwined around each other like snakes as they roared out after my enemy. An instant later, the flames were gone, broken against his shield spell.

Guess this guy's sparked more than one band.

"Did you really expect that to work?" he asked.

"No, but I'm ready for you now, and you can't cast another ember blast without dropping your shield." I let my hands drift back down the pouches at my sides. "Care to see who draws faster?"

"Heh," Reichis chuckled.

"What?" I asked.

"Nothing. It's just funny when you try to sound tough."

"Not helpful."

My opponent watched me closely, taking my measure as I took his. He was young, as mages go, not much older than twenty. Usually that means I can count on them to take up my challenge, but he didn't bother with another ember spell. Instead he flicked copper-coloured hair out of his eyes and kept up the somatic gesture for his shield with one hand while raising the other so I could see that one of his fingers had an unnaturally elongated nail. With a slow, deliberate motion, he pushed the nail into the skin of his wrist and drew a sinewy line about six inches long, leaving behind a trail of crimson.

Reichis sat up on his haunches, licking his lips. "Isn't making him bleed supposed to be our job?"

"Blood magic," I whispered, cursing my lousy luck. "Why did it have to be blood magic?"

If the guy had been Berabesq, I might've confused him with one of their crazy faith warriors who use their own blood to conjure shields, but he was Jan'Tep, like me, which meant this was something much worse.

"Would you like to know how I found you, shadowblack?" he asked.

Definitely Jan'Tep. My people always feel a burning compulsion to talk you to death before they actually kill you. "I must be sparking the sigils for sand magic," I replied, "because I'm having this premonition that you're about to tell me."

"We heard rumours of an outlaw spellslinger travelling the length and breadth of the continent in search of a cure, which is ridiculous, of course, since everyone knows there's no cure for the shadowblack. But I was positive the fool in question was none other than Kellen of the House of Ke, the most notorious traitor in our people's history."

That hardly seemed fair. I couldn't have been more than the

second or third most notorious. "So you figured you'd get your own name in the history books?"

"It wasn't easy." He gestured towards the silver glyphs around the brim of my black frontier hat. "Those veiling charms are remarkably effective."

Well, that was good to know. I'd stolen the hat from a fellow spellslinger named Dexan Videris as partial compensation for his having tried to kill me. I was never sure how reliably it warded off tracking spells.

The mage tapped a finger on his temple. "Then it occurred to me: an exiled shadowblack fleeing Jan'Tep justice, knowing his luck had to run out sooner or later—could desperation lead such a one in search of that preposterous old legend about an 'Ebony Abbey'?" He laughed at the name. "Didn't it ever occur to you that if such a place had ever existed our people would have long ago destroyed it?" He glanced at the dusty yellow desert all around us. "Well, you've found your mythical sanctuary. This is where so-called 'scouts' bring the afflicted. They slit their throats and leave them here to die so that their flesh will be consumed by scavengers, their bones scoured clean by the wind, sinking into the sand to make room for the next poor fool."

"What did I tell you?" Reichis growled at me, then muttered, "Gullible moron."

Still maintaining the somatic form for his shield with one arm, the mage turned over the other and squeezed his fist until drops of blood fell to the ground, turning the golden sand at his feet a deep crimson.

"What's he doing?" Reichis asked.

"I think he's summoning a blood-shaping," I replied.

"That sounds bad. How do we fight it?"

"I'm working on a plan."

The squirrel cat's fur changed to match the red of the sand spreading towards us, making him blend in with our surroundings. The muscles on his hindquarters bunched. "So I should probably run away?"

"Yeah."

Reichis took off as fast as his legs would take him. I didn't resent him for it. As he frequently reminds me, it's inevitable that one day our luck will run out. No point in both of us getting killed. I would've run too, but by then the mage's blood had gone deep into the sand. With a few esoteric syllables, he completed his invocation. The spell came to life and so did the desert all around me.

The bloodshaper—because that's definitely what he was—raised his bleeding arm and reached out for me. Thousands of pounds of sand rose up from the ground, taking the exact same shape as his arm only about a hundred times larger. As his fingers grasped the air in front of him, his sand form mirrored the gesture, grabbing me and lifting me ten feet above the ground.

The mage sauntered towards me with the sort of casual self-assurance of one whose carefully planned ambush has now reached its conclusion. "That's odd," he said, glancing around theatrically. "Shouldn't a certain Argosi meddler be coming to your rescue right about now?"

"Give her a minute," I said. A bluff couldn't hurt at this point. "When we saw your pathetically obvious obscurement spell, Ferius went to get the rest of her Argosi friends. Apparently they're playing a hand of poker to decide who gets to kick your arse first."

The mage reached into the folds of his robes with his free hand and pulled out a playing card. Dark red lines flowed elegantly along the painted surface: a hand with seven thorns in its palm. I recognised this instantly as one of Ferius's debt cards—the ones she keeps as reminders of each of the obligations she's accrued over the years. Only this one was marred by splotches of something darker. "The Argosi's blood made my little souvenir terribly sticky. I'm afraid the rest of the deck was ruined entirely."

"You're bluffing," I said, struggling in vain to free myself from the giant sand fist holding me prisoner. "Ferius Parfax is way too smart to get caught by a stupid—"

The mage cut me off with a tut-tut sound. "Don't be so hard on your dead friend's memory. Not even she could be expected to out-wit all seventy-seven of us."

"*Seventy-seven…*" That number stole the breath from me. Or maybe it was just the sand fist crushing my lungs.

The mage gazed up at me triumphantly. "Tribulators. Chaincast-ers. Lightshapers. War mages. Sightblinders. Seventy-seven of us, Kellen. A true war coven." He smirked. "Though I think the Argosi called it… What was that funny little name she gave us? A 'posse'?"

Posse was exactly the kind of word Ferius would've used. "Now I know you're lying," I said. "There hasn't been a war coven in three hundred years. No clan prince has the influence to…" Even as I began to say it, I knew I was wrong. While getting Jan'Tep mages to agree on anything is like herding a bunch of angry, spell-wielding cats, there was one person who could probably pull it off: the newly ascended prince of my own clan; the one man whose scheming and manipulations might just be enough to unite seventy-seven lords magi to his cause.

The bloodshaper must've caught the awakening despair in my expression. "Ke'heops," he confirmed, "Lord of the House of Ke. Your father." A thin-lipped chuckle. "You really have been a terribly disobedient son, haven't you?"

"He wouldn't do this! Not just to kill me!"

"What's the old saying? 'A father's love is only ever exceeded by his wrath.'"

I'd never heard the quote, but it described Ke'heops perfectly.

"If it makes you feel better," the bloodshaper went on, "this isn't just about you. Lord Ke'heops petitioned the clans to name him mage sovereign of our entire people, but they are, as yet, unresolved on the matter. So he asked for seventy-seven mages to join him on a great quest. He seeks to prove his worth by hunting down every remaining shadowblack on the continent." The bloodshaper raised a finger, and part of the massive hand construct reached up to gently touch the black markings around my left eye. "Starting with his own son."

He kept looking at me, as if waiting for some reply, but when I tried to speak he closed his fist a fraction tighter and the breath fled me. "You should be proud of him, Kellen! Not since we rid the world of the infestation of the Mahdek tribes have our people been so united." The mage paused before adding, "Well, I suppose we missed one or two stragglers here and there."

Ferius, I thought. *He knows Ferius is Mahdek!*

"She died for you," the bloodshaper said softly, almost soothingly. "A dozen of us spread word that you'd been captured not far from here and that members of your clan were gathering to hold a trial for your execution. The Argosi reasoned that she had to free you before the others arrived. She walked right into our trap. That's how we captured her, Kellen. That's why her corpse lies rotting even now. Unburied. Awaiting the carrion eaters to rid the world of her stench." He came close and flicked the card at me. It struck my cheek before falling to the ground. "A clever trick, wouldn't you agree, shadowblack?"

Futile rage rose up inside me, and like a fool I struggled even harder against the unbreakable grip of his sand shape. *Stop*, I told myself. *Anger won't do any good now. Think, damn it! Think!*

Unfortunately I'm not the only one with anger issues. Reichis's outraged howl split the air. "Lousy Jan'Tep skinbag!"

21

In the periphery of my vision I saw him leap out at the mage, fangs and claws poised to tear into our enemy. But the bloodshaper was smart—and prepared. He must've known about Reichis, just as he'd known about Ferius, so he'd been waiting for the squirrel cat's attack. His hand opened wide, causing his sand shape to do likewise and sending me tumbling to the ground. With a casual slap of the air, the shape struck Reichis hard, hurling him some twenty feet before the squirrel cat landed in an unconscious heap. Before I could get to my powders, the mage reached out to me and closed his hand again. Once more I was immobilised.

"Nine mages," he said, venom thick in his voice as he squeezed my ribcage to what felt like breaking point. "Nine good men and women brought low, all because you didn't have the courage to meet your destiny."

"In my defence," I groaned, struggling for breath, "it wasn't an especially appealing fate."

He laughed, coming closer, his sandy grip easing just a fraction. "I have to admire an opponent who makes jokes right up until the moment of his death. Ferius Parfax did that too."

"Yeah?" I asked, struggling to shift my hands just enough to flip open the tops of the pouches at my sides. I had no hope of tossing the powders into the air—never mind forming the somatic shape to guide them—but a new plan was coming to me now. It was dirty and underhanded and even cruel. That only made it more appealing. "You should've been there when I blasted those nine mages, because that was *really* funny."

His mouth twisted into an ugly grimace. He lifted the hand up high for an instant and then brought it back down, throwing me to the ground and knocking the wind out of me. "You would mock the deaths of your own countrymen?" he demanded. "Cannot even an exile like yourself understand how few true mages exist among us? How numerous our enemies?" Shaking in righteous fury, he willed the sand into a massive fist and brought it down on me like a hammer.

I should've died then, but the form wasn't as durable as before. The sand shape broke against my shoulders, falling apart and half burying me. The blow hurt like hell, but it revealed that my opponent's concentration was fallible.

I spat out sand. "They aren't *my* countrymen. They're a bunch of thugs who hide behind spells because they're too cowardly to get their hands dirty."

"Filthy shadowblack!" he shouted, and back-fisted me with about two tons of sand. Once again, though, the shape fell apart before it could do any serious damage. In the meantime, most of the powder in my pouches had fallen into the remains of his shaping.

I staggered unsteadily back to my feet and gave the mage my biggest, most slap-worthy smile. "Don't look now, friend, but it looks like your precious spell is falling to pieces."

He smirked right back at me. "Is that what you believe? That you can goad me into losing control of my own magic? Allow me to show you the difference between an amateur spellslinger and a true mage." He held out his hand, palm up, and the sand rose up in the air to take the shape he willed. Slowly he began to close his fingers, watching me as I waited for death. But waiting for death has never been my style. In fact I was waiting for something else entirely.

Come on, I begged silently. *Show me how tough you are. Make a nice big fist to smite me with.*

The metallic red and grey tattooed bands on his forearm, signifying blood and iron, shone brightly as he focused his will, closing his fist ever tighter, the sand shape become more and more densely packed as he prepared to bring it down on my head. "Any last words?" he asked.

I would've liked to have replied, "Just one, arsehole," but that would have risked mistiming my spell. I kept my mouth shut and watched for the sign. When it didn't immediately come, I was afraid that the powders had become too diluted in the sand to ignite. But then I saw it: the first beautiful sparks rising up out of the sand as the powders trapped inside came into contact. "*Carath*," I said.

The mage's eyes went wide as he too noticed the flash of light and saw the somatic gestures my hands were making. Twin fires, red and black and carrying all the fury of a hundred hells, bore down on him, swirling all around him. Reflex made him abandon his blood spell as he tried desperately to form the somatic shapes for a shield. Too late though, because by then the sand was exploding all around us. I felt the heat as the blast of air sent me flying.

I'm pretty sure I lost consciousness for a second or two, because when I opened my eyes I was face down on the ground. Unable to get to my feet, I crawled on all fours towards my enemy, following the stench as much as my blurred vision.

When I finally reached him I was surprised to see that he actually *had* managed to cast a shield. Unfortunately for him, the spell had only partially manifested when the flames hit. Instead of being fried to a crisp, his body was now a patchwork of untouched skin next to tracts of burnt flesh the colour of ash. A wound on his chest bled profusely, too fast for me or anyone else to have stopped it. "Ten," he said, spitting blood with the word. "Ten of your own people. Does it make you proud?"

"Almost never," I replied.

He chuckled, even as tears came to his eyes, belying the curse he uttered next. "My death wins you nothing but more suffering. Another will take my place, and another should he fall. Seventy-seven mages will hunt for you until the desert turns red with your blood. Do you hear them coming, Spellslinger?"

Beneath his bravado and contempt was a terrible sadness, as though he were watching all his dreams of being a great mage—dreams I had once shared—collapse like castles made of sand. His sorrow filled me with shame for what I was about to do next, but I did it anyway. I grabbed his shoulders and squeezed until he winced in pain. "Tell me what happened to Ferius Parfax. You said you killed her. Was it a lie?"

His lips twitched and I wasn't even sure if he'd heard me. Then he spat out a ragged laugh that brought more blood with it. "Did I say I killed her? Perhaps she escaped. Perhaps I never found her at all. Beg me for the truth and I might remember."

I shook him again. "Please! Just tell me if she's—"

My enemy met death with a soft exhalation of breath that carried with it his last words: "Suffer, shadowblack."

4

The Dilemma of Dying

A day and a night went by before either Reichis or I could manage to crawl a few more feet without passing out from the pain. The pair of us were exhausted and half dead. Being stuck out in the desert with no guide and no supplies would soon take care of the other half.

"You know what I was thinking?" Reichis asked, rousing me from my steady drift into a sleep from which I was unlikely to awake.

I forced my eyes open. The first blush of orange dawn was pushing back against the darkness. It would start getting hot again soon. "What's that?"

"When that mage asked if you had any last words? You should've said, 'Just one,' and *then* blasted him."

I lay until I could get enough breath in my lungs to waste it on a reply. "Good note. I'll remember that for next time."

As the first rays of morning light brushed my cheek, numbness began to seep through the rest of me. This was it. This was *really* it. In another hour, maybe two, I was going to die.

With the last dregs of strength of will left to me, I slowly inched towards Reichis.

"What are you doing?" he asked suspiciously.

I collapsed a couple of feet away from him and reached out a hand to lay it against his fur.

"Kellen?" He figured out what I was doing. "Get that stinkin' paw of yours off o' me!"

"No," I said, watching as his coat slowly changed colour. He was trying to make it go black with dark red stripes the way he does when he wants to look threatening, but he was too weak now. Instead it turned a pale grey. I stroked it gently. "If we're going to die out here, then I'm going to say what I have to say. And you're going to listen."

The squirrel cat tried to squirm away, but he didn't have the strength for it. "Get off me, skinbag! I'm not your kin. I'm not even your friend! This was strictly a business arrangement!"

"Reichis," I said, ignoring his protests, "you were mean and irritable. A thief, a liar, a..."

"A murderer," he added.

"Right. That too. But despite all that, you were...Reichis, I want you to know that I lo—"

He cut me off with a snarl, scrambling to try and get his legs under him. "Idiot skinbag! All your moanin' and talkin' kept us from hearin' them!"

"Hearing who?" But then I heard it too: the quiet plod of footsteps on sand. I managed to roll onto my back, not that it would do me any good. My fingers were so numb that if I tried to cast the carath spell all I'd do was blow my own hands off.

Two hooded figures stood over us, the rising sun at their backs hiding them in shadow. Gradually I made out the long black leather coats they wore, nothing like the brightly coloured silks of a Jan'Tep mage, but far more functional. They knelt down and began to drag me onto a litter made of woven reeds.

"Well, what do you know?" I said to Reichis. "That scout wasn't lying about taking us to the Ebony Abbey."

"Yeah," he growled softly, "only she left something out."

Squirrel cats have better eyesight than humans, which is why he noticed what was wrong before I did: underneath his hood, the face of the monk nearest me was covered in twisting black lines that moved as though alive when I stared at them.

"Well, crap," I muttered as consciousness slipped away from me.

Despite all the trials and tribulations in our way, we'd found our mythical monastery in the desert, or rather, it had found us. Problem was, it hadn't gotten its name because they had a cure for the shadowblack.

They called it the Ebony Abbey because the monks who lived there embraced it.

5

The Downside of Dreams

My people hate dreams.

Can't stand them.

Awful things.

The most fundamental demand magic makes of a mage's mind is clarity: complete awareness of your surroundings and absolute discipline over your thoughts. You can't exert dominion over the six esoteric forces of reality if your brain is busy telling you that you're bouncing atop the back of a floating snake, surrounded by white bears who keep whistling in your ears.

So, yeah, my people have no use for dreams.

Neither do outlaws, by the way. Hard to get yourself out of a jam while hallucinating something that—in retrospect—probably isn't much worse than what's actually about to happen to you.

"White bears!" I screamed, struggling to escape my bonds. As if the bears weren't enough, a slick, oily sea creature was swallowing my legs. I was already halfway down the monster's throat, the disgusting slackness of its outer flesh smothering me in its wet, icy grip. The more I tried to kick it away, the tighter the foul thing's grasp became, until at last my highly trained Jan'Tep mind took control.

You're tangled in your blankets, moron. And they're only wet because you've been sweating in them.

With considerable effort I unwrapped the heavy coverings from my legs and threw them off. I regretted it immediately. Wherever I was, it must be night because it was damned cold. And dark. I shook my head until I felt fully awake and then slapped myself a couple of times just to make sure. Dreams are tricky that way; they fool you into *thinking* you're awake, and then a few seconds later, sure enough, more whistling white bears come to eat you.

As my eyes slowly adjusted to the darkness, I found myself in some sort of tent constructed from three poles joined at the top by leather straps, the entire affair draped in thick canvas. I was still wearing my own clothes, which was bad, because like the blankets they were soaked through with fever sweat. Shivering uncontrollably, I nonetheless got myself up to a sitting position and looked around for something to use as a weapon. I almost never wake up in a strange place without somebody planning to kill me.

I found the remains of my pack nearby—at least what hadn't been burned to a crisp in the desert by that Jan'Tep bloodshaper. Most of the contents were destroyed, but I still had a half-deck of Ferius's razor-sharp steel cards. I put those aside before remembering to run a hand along the bottom seam of my shirt. My fingertips found the distinctive shapes of the five castradazi coins hidden inside a secret fold sewn into the fabric so that Reichis wouldn't steal them when I slept. My chest unclenched a little. A bunch of cards and a few coins might not seem all that impressive, but at times like these you take what you can get.

I peered around the rest of the tent, looking for...Yes! A couple of feet away my belt was waiting for me, coiled up, the pouches still attached. They'd be almost empty of course, since I'd used up most of the powders on that damned bloodshaper, but even a pinch or two can mean the difference between escape and execution.

I put on the belt and placed the steel cards in a leather case I'd had sewn onto the right leg of my trousers by a tailor who'd found the idea ridiculous but had been happy to take my money.

Okay, I thought. *I've got all my stuff. Now where's—*

"So. You're awake."

The voice that had nearly given me a heart attack had spoken in Daroman, but the accent made me suspect he was Berabesq. A face whose sharp features confirmed as much appeared at the opening of the tent. He was younger than I expected—maybe a year older than me—and didn't look like any monk I'd ever seen. His hair was chestnut brown and came down nearly to his shoulders. Instead of robes he wore a long, sleeveless black leather coat that showed off both the lean muscles of his arms and the twisting black lines that wound around them. What *wasn't* there was just as surprising.

"You don't have any bands," I said, my voice creaking like the hinges on a rusty gate.

He rolled his eyes. "Typical Jan'Tep. Probably raised to believe only mages can get the shadowblack, right?" He flexed one of his arms. The markings writhed around the skin. "Just one more lie your people tell." He sat back on his heels. "My name is Tournam, and in case you're wondering, I'm the one who saved you from dying in the desert. Don't get all weepy with gratitude." He held out a silver bowl to me. "There's food, if you're hungry."

"I'm…" *Starving*, I realised. *Absolutely starving. I'd eat my own arm if there was enough meat left on it.*

"I could eat, I suppose," I replied, shivering because he was letting in the cold air.

Inside the bowl was a fairly disgusting-looking mixture of dried

31

grasses topped with bits of cooked meat from something unidentifiable and probably equally disgusting. I practically tore the bowl out of his hand.

So good . . . I thought, only tasting the food because a few particles of the meat still remained on my tongue once the rest had already slid down my throat.

"You shouldn't eat so quickly," he advised. "You'll make yourself—"

"More!" I demanded, showing him the empty bowl.

He crossed his arms over his chest, flexing the muscles, which—unnervingly—caused his shadowblack markings to writhe like snakes. "Later, once your stomach has adjusted to the food."

"Now," I rasped, my voice still too raw for such extended conversations.

Generally speaking, it's not advisable to make demands of your hosts—or kidnappers—but I'd been pretty much starving even before they'd taken me, and at least a couple of days must have passed since then. Also, it's possible that my table manners had become a little less refined after spending too much time around a certain two-foot-tall furry glutton.

Wait, I thought. *How was I even able to get three bites without him stealing them?*

"Where's Reichis?" I asked.

My benefactor stared back at me quizzically. "I don't know any place with that name. This is—"

"The squirrel cat! The animal that was with me when you found me."

He chuckled, which the Berabesq manage to do with an accent. "Ah, the animal."

"'Ah' what?" I asked, a sudden cold creeping into my belly.

The young monk knelt down and sat back on his heels. "The

32

abbot ordered us to bring you, not anyone else. The abbey has no use for animals." He nodded to the bowl in my hand. "Except as food, of course."

There wasn't much powder in my pouches, so I only got a pinch in each hand before I blasted the son of a bitch.

6

White Sand

My spell doesn't work the same as regular fire. The twin red and black flames react differently depending on how much powder I use and the precise way I angle my fingers. The effect can range from being hit with a very large tree to having rapacious fiery apparitions tear your flesh apart. With the tiny pinch of powders I'd used in this particular case, and with the index and middle fingers of each hand aimed just a touch away from each other, the result was like taking a very hot cooking pan and slamming it into Tournam's chest. Very, very hard.

He was knocked back several feet, so I took advantage of his momentary disorientation to scramble out of the tent. Soon I was a dozen yards away from him, fleeing into the night.

He's lying about Reichis, I told myself over and over. Even injured, the squirrel cat would've got away before they could catch him. With his ability to change the colour of his fur to match his environment, he could have disappeared into the golden sands.

And then what?

Even if Reichis had been able to get away, I'd left him alone in the desert, wounds festering, dying of thirst...

"Reichis!" I shouted.

The slapping of sandalled feet close behind. Someone was already on my tail.

Have to keep moving. The damned cold was already getting to me though. I looked down and discovered that the one thing they'd removed from me had been my boots, and that the sand here was white. It chilled the bottoms of my feet and had an oddly smooth quality to it that I wasn't at all accustomed to. Just how far had they taken me?

"Reichis!"

I listened for his voice. A growl, a moan—hells, even an insult would've been welcome. My stomach clenched, whether from fear or the cold or because, perhaps, squirrel cat meat didn't agree with me.

Ancestors, if you've let me eat my business partner, I swear I will get myself two full pouches of red and black powders and meet you in the grey passage where I'll pay my respects in a most discourteous fashion.

"Stop!" shouted my pursuer. "You can't go out there!"

I glanced back. *Two monks. The Berabesq and another guy.*

Evidently I hadn't done enough damage to keep Tournam out of the fight. His companion was bigger, wearing a coat with sleeves that covered his arms, but the light from the moon above illuminated a shaved head covered in twisting shadowblack lines that ended in three teardrop-shaped markings below his left eye that almost made it look as if he were crying.

I kept running, my eyes searching for a weapon in this damned white desert with its cold wind chilling me to my bones.

"Heed us, you fool," the big monk yelled. "You're racing towards your own your death!"

They were catching up to me already, which meant my odds of outrunning them were not good. Fortunately I've had plenty of practice being chased.

I reached into my pocket for the steel cards. Stopping suddenly, I spun on my heels to face my pursuers even as I slid backwards in the slippery white sand. I flicked two cards at the approaching monks.

I should point out here that when I say "flicked," what I really mean is that I sent a pair of razor-sharp rectangular steel blades spinning at a speed that's almost impossible to dodge and which would slice into my opponents' flesh as deeply as any throwing knife.

The monks didn't even have time to get their arms up to cover their faces as the cards sailed through the air towards them. They didn't need to. The instant before the blades could reach their target, Tournam's shadowblack markings unwound themselves from his arms, dancing in the air like ribbons of black ink strewn from a pen, and swatted the cards aside.

I watched in horrified fascination as the sinuous lines returned their master, wrapping around his limbs to settle once more into the design they'd had before.

Whenever *my* shadowblack acts up, it's either to show me horrible visions of people turning into monstrous apparitions of themselves, or to smother me in darkness. Life is so unfair sometimes.

"Wait where you are, idiot!" Tournam shouted. The front of his leather coat was burned through where my flames had hit, but the skin beneath was so covered in black markings that I couldn't tell if I'd even hurt him. I considered trying my spell again, but I was low on powders, which meant I'd need to scrape the sides and bottoms of the pouches for enough to fire the spell properly—something I didn't have time for. That just left running some more.

In situations like this, I have exactly five weapons I can use. The first is my powder spell, which requires, you know—powder. The second are the steel cards, which had proven useless against these guys. The third is a wind spirit called a *sasutzei* that lives in my right eye and who never—and I mean *never*—helps when I want her to.

The fourth are the castradazi coins in my shirt, which I hadn't yet learned how to use. And the final weapon in my deadly arsenal? A two-foot tall squirrel cat with a bad attitude.

This would have been an excellent time for him to make an appearance.

He didn't.

"Look, you fool!" the big bald-headed monk called out. "Look where you're standing!"

That turned out to be sound advice as I had just reached the edge of a cliff. The confusion of all that empty space below me made my vision blur and my legs go wobbly.

Who stuck a mountain in the middle of a desert?

A whole bunch of things suddenly made sense—such as why I couldn't feel my feet any more, why the sand crunched as I ran on it, and why I was shivering. Oh, and also why I'd been dreaming of whistling white bears.

If this all makes me sound kind of dumb, I should point out that never in my life had I seen snow before. Neither had I been expecting to, since you don't usually find snow in a desert.

Where the hell am I?

"Do not move one more inch!" the bald monk shouted.

How long had these guys kept me unconscious?

"Stay back!" I said, scraping my fingertips into the crevices of my pouches to get at what little of the black and red powders I had left. At the very least it might distract them.

"Don't you even *think* about using that spell on me a second time!" Tournam warned, the ribbons on his bare arms unwinding themselves.

Well, of course he'd say that. I fired the spell anyway. It made a pretty satisfying booming sound that split the air between us and sent the two monks dropping to the frosty ground.

Okay, I thought. *Now where do I go from here?*

This last question became moot because it turns out there's another property of snow that no one warns you about when you live in a hot climate. I'd read about snow in books of course, and knew lots of terms like ice frost, blizzard, and even a particularly funny-sounding one: avalanche.

I couldn't recall at first what that last one meant, but the question was soon solved when the ground beneath my feet gave way. The ear-splitting crack of the cliff edge coming apart was like being trapped inside thunder itself. Too late I tried lurching back towards my pursuers.

The monks ran towards me, arms outstretched in what I now knew would be a futile attempt to catch me. The last thing I saw was the two of them shaking their heads at me as I tumbled to the abyss below.

There are seven different Jan'Tep spells that allow a mage to fly, float, levitate or otherwise defy gravity.

I couldn't cast any of them.

7

Black Snow

The first part of the fall wasn't nearly so bad as I expected. I dropped around twenty feet before sinking into a soft snow bank on an outcropping. Then that broke as well. I slid another hundred feet or so down the mountainside, scrambling to grab hold of anything I could find. Turns out snow makes a poor handhold.

The sequence of whooshing along then plummeting a short way only to land on another snow bank was oddly pleasant. For about three seconds. I tumbled another fifty feet before I approached the next steep drop and saw that what awaited me below was not another pillowy carpet of snow but jagged rocks.

"Use your shadow, you fool!" one of the monk's voices echoed down the mountainside. I swear the sound of it sent even more snow and ice crumbling down towards me.

Use my shadow how, *exactly?* Unlike these guys', my shadowblack had never done anything but torment me. I dug the soles of my feet into the snow in an attempt to slow my descent, but found myself flipping head over heels. *Great, now I can land on my head when I hit the rocks.* A moment later I was sailing through the open air.

Please, I thought, begging the black markings around my eye, *just once, help me!*

Snow from the avalanche drifted all around me as I fell, the flakes like tiny butterflies dancing in the air.

I clawed at the empty space around me—a reflex I couldn't control even though I knew it would do no good. In desperation I redoubled my efforts to awaken the shadowblack markings around my left eye. It felt a bit like trying to give yourself a headache.

Ancestors, I'm going to die. Shattered against the rocks, surrounded by all this ugly black snow.

Wait . . . Black snow?

In my defence, becoming lost in shadow is a disorienting experience. Everything goes pitch black, and yet you can see perfectly clearly, as if what normally appears to be the absence of colour actually comes a thousand shades of obsidian.

I was still falling, but slower now, almost gently, like a leaf carried by the breeze. I was able to right myself and a moment later my feet touched the ground. Gone were the jagged grey rocks I'd seen during my fall, replaced by onyx sands as far as the eye could see.

I did it! I thought. *I shifted into shadow!*

Of course, that raised an important and troubling question: every other time I'd been lost in shadow, my spirit alone had come to this place, while the rest of me remained in the real world. So either I'd gotten very, very lucky and something was different this time, or else my physical body now lay broken and bloody against the rocks at the bottom of the mountain. But if that were so, did that mean my spirit was trapped forever in the shadowblack?

8

Onyx Shards

I stood upon a wide plain, the ground beneath my feet covered in tiny shards of onyx and the sky above my head filled with ebony clouds. If those two sound like the same colour, well, they might be in our world, but not in this place of endless shadows. For that matter, the obsidian ocean in the distance was distinct from the flakes of soot-coloured snow that still fell all around me. Oh, and while there was no sun and thus no way to tell the time, I was fairly sure it was always midnight here.

"Hello?" I called out.

Nothing.

Whenever I'd been lost in shadow before, my friends had been nearby. I'd seen shades of them made from the secrets they kept. Maybe that's what the shadowblack was all about: our darkest fears given physical form. If so, I wondered what mine were.

Maybe it's being trapped alone for eternity.

I shouted again, as loud as I could, "Hello? Anyone?"

My voice sounded strange. Too close—as though I were whispering in my own ears. The effect made me feel more alone than ever.

Damn it, Reichis! Why aren't you here to bite me and call me a coward?

"Kellen?" The faint chitter drifted across the barren black landscape, so faint it could easily have been my imagination.

"Reichis?"

Silence for a few seconds, then even more faintly, "Kellen, where are you? I'm hurt, Kellen. I keep trying to get up, but I—"

Reichis's voice was cut off. Even in the silence I somehow knew he'd slipped and fallen in the sand. But how did I know he was still in the desert? His voice came again, softer than ever. "I'm tired, Kellen. Gonna sleep for a whi—"

"Reichis, I'm coming!" I shouted into the endless black land-scape. Off in the distance, probably more than a hundred miles away, the twin silhouettes of what might have been the mountain pass that led into the Golden Passage appeared. Waiting for me. Taunting me. It was too far of course, but I didn't care. I tore off towards them, my feet slapping silently against the onyx shards. Maybe space wasn't the same here as in the real world. Maybe if I ran fast enough, held Reichis's image clearly in my mind, I could—

The squirrel cat's voice echoed once again, barely more than a whisper on the breeze. "Can't wait for you, Kellen. Sorry I never said..."

Again the broken, chittering voice drifted away. "No!" I screamed. "No, Reichis, hold on!" I kept running, but the mountains were receding further and further into the distance. The ground moved under me, but I never seemed to get any closer. Was none of this real? Was my body lying shattered against the rocks at the foot of the mountain and this was nothing more than the last vestigial thoughts as the blood slipped out of my veins and my brain was starved of oxygen?

No, I thought. *This is real.*

I don't know how I knew, but I did. Reichis *was* out there, at the edge of the desert. And I knew more. One of his legs was broken, wounded in a fight with a creature that had attacked when he'd tried to steal one of its eggs for food. He was starving. He'd dragged himself miles and miles, trying to follow my tracks. Now he was dying. Alone. And I couldn't get to him!

"Please!" I shouted up at the sky. "Someone help me!"

If the gods of earth and air that the borderlands folk pray to could hear me, if the ancestors my people worshipped knew of my plight, if the damned Berabesq's six-faced god was listening, none of them gave a sign.

"Damn you all! Why are you doing this to me? Why do you make my life so..." *No. Stop. This isn't helping Reichis.*

If Ferius was here, she'd say, "Ain't nobody doin' nothin' to you, kid. Best you start doin' something for somebody else for a change." She'd be right too. Reichis was a mean little cuss, but he was my business partner. He'd saved my life a dozen times, because that's how it worked between us: we'd fight and argue and insult each other, but when the chips were down, he was there for me. Always. Now I had to find a way to be there for him.

Squirrel cats were hardy creatures, and Reichis was more bloody-minded than most. Could he last another day out there, wounded and starving in the desert, dying of thirst? A proper Jan'Tep mage could've used blood and sand magic to lend him the strength to survive a little longer. But I'd only sparked the tattooed metallic band for breath magic before my parents had counter-banded the rest. If I'd been powerful like my sister, Shalla, I could've devised some kind of spell to—*Wait... Shalla.*

She could do it. She'd sparked all six of her bands. Moreover, she was a genius at concocting new spells. I just needed to get a message to her. I looked around me at this place that wasn't really a place at all, but something different—something that was both separate and yet attached to the physical world.

"Shalla?" I called out.

Could it really be that easy? Was I about to finally find a use for the cursed black marks around my left eye?

Nothing. Not a word, not a sound. I closed my eyes and willed myself closer to her, hoping that would somehow manipulate the ethereal physics of shadow to reach out to her. Nothing happened.

It made sense, in a way. I loved my sister, but the world doesn't give a damn about love. Reichis and I shared a *bond*. All his little growls and chitters became words in my mind. Whatever made that connection work, I didn't have it with anyone else.

A soft, wheezing sound reached my ears. It was Reichis's ragged breathing. I could feel him out there, far from this damnable mountain where those bloody monks had dragged me, waiting to die.

I pushed panic aside. I may never be an Argosi like Ferius, but I'd follow their unrelenting Way of Stone if that's what it took. What I needed was a spell like the one Shalla had used to communicate with me back when I was travelling through the Seven Sands. Sometimes her face would appear in a patch of sand or a bowl of water and she'd start berating me over one thing or another. Once she even appeared in the clouds overhead. *That* had been particularly unsettling.

Focus, idiot.

I couldn't cast a spell like Shalla's, but maybe I didn't need to. I knelt down on the ground, my hands smoothing the tiny onyx shards. Shalla had only had to cast her spell the one time, and afterwards could awaken it through will alone whenever she wanted to talk to me. The magic had weakened over time, but the ethereal threads might still be there. One of those threads was made from breath magic. I stared down at the pale blue metallic band around my right forearm, sending my will through it, urging it to spark. If I could activate even that small part of Shalla's spell, maybe she'd notice and use her own considerably greater powers to do the rest.

The breath band shimmered, its blue light pushing back against the black of the shadow lands. I passed my hand over the shards of onyx and filled my mind with Shalla's essence. People aren't just a name or a voice or a face. They're not just memories either. They're bigger than all of that—so big that it's almost impossible to conceive of a human being in their entirety. Yet that's precisely what I had to do. With a finger I traced the line of Shalla's face in the shards, pulling more and more breath magic through my band. It stung like hell, which wasn't usual for me. I ignored it and kept drawing Shalla's features, the slant of her eyes when she's looking at me like I'm an idiot, the hint of a smile when she's gotten the better of me. The pain got worse and worse, becoming almost unbearable. But I'd been in pain before, and besides, I knew however much it hurt, it was nothing compared to what Reichis was—*Stop. Pity and despair won't help.*

I turned my thoughts back to my sister: the precocious girl, more talented than any other member of our clan, even our father. The sister who always believed I could be better, even if that meant trying to kill me. The...*No, you have to see all of her, not just the good parts.*

Shalla was a temptress. She loved the way all the boys in our clan looked at her, tried to impress her. She cared about me, sure, but she'd betrayed me more than once. She was every good and bad thing you can imagine in a person, but more than anything else, she was complicated. *Too damn complicated!*

The wind was swirling all around me now, whisking away the shards I was so carefully trying to compose into her features. It was as if the air itself was resisting me. A sudden pinch in my band drew my gaze. I was bleeding drops of black blood. The pain was making me lose hold of Shalla in my mind.

No. Whatever you are, you won't beat me. I will walk the Way of Stone. I will not bend. I will not break.

I closed my eyes, drawing Shalla's face in shards once more, this time from memory. I let thoughts of her fill me up, allowing my feelings about her to overwhelm everything else. I loved my sister. I hated her. I admired her. I resented her. I *needed* her.

"Kellen?"

I opened my eyes. "Shalla?"

The winds had only gotten worse, but though the onyx shards were swirling all around me, trying to cut into my flesh, there, on the ground, thousands of them resisted, taking on the shape of my sister's face. The eyes narrowed as if squinting up at me. "Kellen? Where are you?"

"Shalla, I need your help! Reichis is hurt. You've got to—"

The shards making up her left eyebrow rose. "The nekhek? You interrupted my studies to prattle about that foul *nekhek?*"

Nekhek meant "servant of demons." It was the word my people used for squirrel cats.

"Shalla, please! He's in a desert on the southern edge of the Berabesq lands called the Golden Passage. He's hurt bad. You need to cast a spell to heal him. Try to get word to Ferius Parfax. She'll go there and find him. Please, sister, you've got to—"

"I won't be doing anything of the sort until you at least tell me where you are, Kellen." The shape of her eyes in the shards shifted left and right as she looked around. "What is that place?"

"It's…I don't know exactly. I was searching for the Ebony Abbey when—"

"The *Ebony Abbey?* Oh, Kellen, how could you believe in such nonsense? Everyone knows the abbey is a myth."

"It's real, damn it! Or at least the monks are, since two of them found me in the desert and now they're taking me to some mountain."

Her features changed, becoming deadly serious. "Kellen, if that's true, then I must tell Father right away. The war coven must be dispatched to destroy that abomination before—"

She wasn't listening. All she cared about was the glory of our people, and most of all of our family. I poured all the *arta siva*—the Argosi talent of persuasion—into my words. "Sister, you're going to listen to me now. Reichis is dying and you're the only one in the whole world who can help him. If you love me at all, if you ever want to call me brother again and have it mean more than a sick joke, then you're going to save him. You're going to save my friend."

She stared back at me from the onyx shards, but then sighed. "Very well. Describe the place where you left him and perhaps I can—"

"I've got him!" a deep, angry voice called out from the sky above me. It was one of the monks. "The damned fool tried to slip into shadow!" Black ribbons appeared out of the clouds, wrapping around my wrists, twisting over and over and tightening their grip. They began to tug at me, pulling me away from Shalla.

"No!" I shouted. "Let me go!"

More whirling strips of shadowblack appeared, winding themselves around my chest. I felt them tugging at my ankles. Suddenly I was being pulled into the air, yanked up like a fish on a line. I screamed and cursed, pulling against the ribbons until it felt as if my shoulders would tear from their sockets.

"Kellen? What's happening? I need you to tell me how to find the nek—"

I never heard the end of that sentence. The hard ground slammed into me. Cold ran up my back. Above me the sky was now grey, shedding tiny flakes of white snow that melted into tears when they touched my skin.

The monks had pulled me out of shadow before I could tell Shalla how to find Reichis.

9

The Fool

The word "fool" is notable for having more than one meaning regardless of which language you're speaking. Whether in Jan'Tep, Berabesq, Gitabrian, Daroman or any number of other tongues, a fool is one deficient in judgement or prudence, someone who's been taken advantage of, a deranged person lacking powers of understanding or a chilled dessert made from mixed fruits. You'd think that last one would appear only in one language, but in fact there are several that use the word "fool" to refer to a frozen fruity treat.

When my captors referred to me as a fool—which they did often over the next day—I'm pretty sure they meant all the assorted meanings simultaneously.

Except the fruit one, though I couldn't exclude that either, come to think of it.

"The fool is freezing to death," Tournam said.

The harshness of his tone stirred me from my slumber. I turned my head and saw what I'd been seeing every day since they'd pulled me from the shadows: snow, ice, rocks, mountain. In my weakened state the trip would have been far too arduous, were it not for the fact that I was pretty much just floating along, held aloft by Tournam's shadow ribbons wrapped around my torso and legs while the monks marched up the mountainside.

I'd learned that the one with the shaved head and teardrop markings beneath his eye was named Butelios. "Of course he's freezing. It's cold."

That made me chuckle, and like him more than Tournam.

"And he is obviously weak," Butelios added. "Both in mind and in body."

Okay, maybe Tournam was my favourite of the two. It didn't really matter. I wasn't planning on being in their company much longer.

"I should feed him to my demon," the Berabesq said, fussing at the burnt patch on the front of his leather coat. "What use is he going to be to the order?" The young man looked down at me, a big smile on his face. *No, wait, I'm seeing him upside down. That's a glower.* "Nearly dragged me right over the cliff with you. I should've let you shatter your spine on those rocks. Your death would've been as unpleasant as it is deserved."

My life hasn't exactly been a bowl of fool either, you know. I giggled at my own cleverness, which set me to shivering. I really *was* freezing. In addition to all my other injuries and ailments, my brief venture into shadow had left me with some kind of fever.

"Why did you flee from us?" Butelios asked. His back was to me as he slogged patiently up the mountainside.

"My friend," I said—or, rather, croaked. The thought of Reichis spurred me on though. "I need to help my friend."

"The animal?" Tournam laughed. "Didn't I tell you already? Animals are for food, not companionship."

His jibe reminded me that he'd tried to make me believe I'd been eating Reichis. "How're those burns on your chest?" I asked pleasantly.

From my vantage point looking up at him, his snarl looked impressively menacing. "Your pet was already dying when we took you from the Golden Passage. By now his corpse has been picked over by buzzards and jackals."

"You're wrong!" My attempt to shout produced barely more than a hoarse whisper. "I *heard* him speak to me, when I was in shadow. He's still alive."

"You weren't *in* shadow, moron," Tournam countered. "You were just falling to the rocks when my ribbons caught you."

Liar, I thought. *I saw the black snow. I heard Reichis call to me, and I spoke to my sister. She said she'd help him!*

Only...That would've taken a long time, wouldn't it? Several minutes at least. Falling off a cliff takes only seconds. My clothes were still soaked in sweat, my skin clammy. Had I been so feverish and desperate to save Reichis that I'd imagined the whole thing?

"Look. Now he's weeping," Tournam said. "Over a worthless animal."

Butelios came and stood over me, the shadowblack markings on his cheeks making him look oddly sympathetic. "Forgive Tournam. He cannot see the sharp blade of grief twisting inside your heart. We will arrive at the abbey in three days' time. Until then, sleep." A shadowy liquid appeared at the corners of his eyes. Black tears drifted down his cheeks and fell onto my forehead and into my eyes. I tried to shake them off, but I was suddenly so tired that it was all I could do to hold on to consciousness long enough to hear Butelios say, "Poor fool."

10

The Sleeper

I drifted in and out of sleep, with only brief snatches of consciousness in which to plan my escape. I had no idea what awaited me inside the Ebony Abbey, but I no longer had any intention of finding out. Either Reichis was alive, waiting back in the desert for me to save him, or he was dead. I could snivel and whine about it, or I could toughen up; choose to believe that squirrel cats were as unkillable as he always claimed and go find him. I knew which decision Reichis would make.

Actually, he'd probably assume I was dead and go find some other sucker to steal from.

"Doesn't matter," I mumbled aloud.

"What's that?" Tournam asked, his shadowblack ribbons bobbing in the air as he turned to look at me. "Butelios, dose him again."

No, I thought. *Don't let him.*

The strange thing was, some part of me was actually starting to crave the blissful, dreamless oblivion his tears brought on. Maybe being cried on with shadowblack is addictive. "Leave me alone," I said, when the big monk slowed in his march up the mountain pass to look down on me. Had Nephenia been here, she would've given him a proper thrashing. Sleep spells really piss her off.

"Rest will ease your wounds," Butelios said gently. "Both those we can see and those we can't."

"Shut up," I replied groggily. "'M'tryin' to sleep." With that I closed my eyes and let my head flop to the side. I'm not sure if he bought the act or if he just wasn't comfortable with the idea of forcing his will on me, but he didn't try again.

Okay, I thought, that minuscule victory spurring my brain to work a little faster. *Now what?*

I wasn't in great shape for an escape attempt, but if I waited until Tournam and Butelios got me inside the Ebony Abbey, it would be too late. Who knew how many monks they'd have in there? Or if the entire place might be some kind of prison? No, I'd have to make a run for it just *before* they got me to the abbey.

Why wait that long? Why not try sooner rather than later? Because in the outlaw business, timing is everything.

When Ferius was teaching me gambling, she said an amateur plays their cards, an expert plays their opponent's, and a master plays the space in between. Yeah, it didn't make sense to me at first either. But I think what she meant was that the cards don't matter nearly as much as the psychology of the players themselves. Let's say you've got a good hand, but you think your opponent has a better one: your cards no longer matter. Even if your opponent has a terrific hand but thinks yours might be better, then—again—his cards don't matter. It's all about expectation and anticipation.

Right now my captors were wary because they knew my strength was slowly returning. Once inside the abbey, someone would no doubt be taking steps to keep me there. But what about *near* the abbey? What about those precious five or ten minutes before we arrived? Tournam and Butelios would begin to feel safe—after all, we'd be close to the end of the journey. Their minds would turn to better food and shelter and whatever else awaited them in their home. They'd figure their mission was over and the danger had passed. If I made my move, say, a few hundred yards from the abbey entrance, then my two escorts would be stuck: they'd be tired from carting me all this way, and while there might be any number of other monks to help them at the abbey, getting those people would require running in the opposite direction to where I was headed. So they'd probably have to split up, which would make my job a lot easier.

Because in life, as in poker, the real game happens in the space between your cards and theirs.

Nope. Still doesn't make sense.

Regardless, it was as good a strategy as I could come up with. Now I just needed a plan. And some rest. I couldn't recall ever being so...

No, wait! Don't fall back aslee—

11

The Stall

The slight jarring sensation of being set down on the snowy ground roused me again.

Okay, now where was I? Oh, right: a plan.

A successful getaway plan depends on three elements: the stall, the break and the twist.

The stall is the diversion you set up to draw your captors' attention so that you can escape whatever cage, chains or noose they're using to keep you prisoner. The measure of a good stall comes down to how distracting it is and how long it lasts. Usually my powder spell can produce a big enough explosion to give me a decent head start, but scraping at the insides of my pouches every chance I got only produced enough for one or two decent blasts.. Once that was used up, I'd be dry. I had my castradazi coins sewn into the hem of my shirt, but I still didn't know what each one did; I'd only worked out a couple of decent tricks—neither of which would hold off Tournam and Butelios long enough. So I'd have to look for something else.

Then, of course, comes the break—that's where you get free of your bonds. Tournam's shadowblack ribbons enabled him to both carry me and hold me immobile at the same time, so I'd need to somehow disable him. I had a couple of ideas, but neither could be tested in advance, so that was a problem too.

Even if I could come up with a decent stall and then break away from the monks, they'd simply follow my tracks until they could hunt me down. That's why the third part of any solid getaway plan is the twist. I had to come up with a way to send Tournam and Butelios on the wrong trail. Normally the twist is the hardest part of the plan to come up with, but in my case I already had it worked out. See, even if I could get away, I didn't have the supplies or equipment to get myself back down the mountain and away from this territory. So I'd either fall to my death or starve along the way. The good news was that since "escape" is supposed to mean getting away from something, Tournam and Butelios would be expecting me to make a run for it.

That's why I'd do the opposite.

"Almost there," Butelios said, stopping to lean against an outcropping of rock.

"Thank God for that," Tournam said, pressing his palms to his lower back as his shadowblack ribbons wound themselves back around his arms. "Carrying this moron has been giving me a headache for days."

I *had* noticed that my ride had been getting a little bumpier today. *Good to know.*

"How far?" I asked, then, to cover my enthusiasm, added, "Will there be decent food there?"

Tournam chuckled. "If there was, do you think we'd waste it on some Jan'Tep sand rat who's already caused us more grief than he's worth?"

Guess not.

"Just over that ridge," Butelios replied, pointing along the path to a sharp elevation in the distance. I looked off to where he'd gestured. My best guess was a mile or so.

"I need to piss," I said, rising unsteadily to my feet. "And the other thing."

"The other thing?" Tournam asked. "You mean take a shit?"

I nodded.

Fast as whips, his ribbons lashed themselves around my arms. "Well, you can wait. It won't be more than half an hour."

I squirmed against the shadowy restraints. "Then it'll be a half-hour of you smelling something very unpleasant."

"Stop that!" Tournam said, wincing in response to my twisting and wriggling.

He's exhausted, I realised then. Which both made this the perfect time for me to attempt my stall and also made it much, much more dangerous.

"Just give me two minutes," I begged. "I'm dying here."

"I'll show you dying," Tournam grumbled, but finally he relaxed the muscles of his arms and the black ribbons let me go, but not before lifting me a foot in the air to drop me unceremoniously to the snowy ground.

I got up again and made a show of looking around. To our right, a sparse forest of evergreens spread out across the mountainous terrain. To our left was the edge of a cliff even more sheer than the one I'd fallen off a few days ago. I started for the trees, and made it all of two feet before one of Tournam's ribbons grabbed at my wrist. "Over there," he said, turning me around and pointing to the cliff's edge. "That way we can keep an eye on you."

I did my best to look annoyed and embarrassed. I was neither actually. I hadn't for one second thought they'd let me wander off into the forest. So I sauntered over to the cliff's edge and stood there a moment, looking down at what had to be a good two-thousand-foot drop.

"Well? Are you going to get on with it?" Tournam asked.

"Is he really dead?"

"What?"

"My friend. Do you think he's really dead? Was it just the fever that made me think I'd slipped into shadow and spoken to him? Or could it have been real? Maybe I really can fall into shadow."

Butelios's heavy footsteps were quickly followed by his hands grabbing onto my shoulders. "Do not even think of jumping again, my friend. I fear Tournam may not save you a second time. Learning that there's a Jan'Tep war coven out there intent on seeing us all dead has done nothing to improve his already uncongenial disposition."

"He likes you though, right? I mean, you're friends?"

"I suppose."

"Good."

I dropped down, using my weight to break free from Butelios's grip. Instinctively he tried to grab me again, but now I was under him and his those big arms of his caught nothing but air. With the monk already off balance, I drove my shoulder deep into his stomach. The breath fled his lungs as he folded over the top of me. I grabbed hold of the back of his robes and pushed against the rocky ground with every ounce of strength in my legs. Butelios was a lot heavier than me, but Ferius had taught me a thing or two about leverage—specifically how to throw someone bigger over your shoulder.

The whole thing had taken less than two seconds, far too fast for Tournam to react. By then Butelios was hurtling over the edge. The brief look of confusion that passed over his features was enough to make even an outlaw feel guilty.

Sorry, friend. For both our sakes, I hope Tournam likes you more than he hates me.

12

The Break

Ferius says you should never kill someone if there's an alternative, and there's *always* an alternative.

Ferius doesn't have the shadowblack though, and while she certainly annoys people enough to make them homicidal, it's rare that anyone actually tries to murder her. Furthermore, crazy monks who *do* have the shadowblack don't tend to take her prisoner in order to feed her to their demons.

So I was prepared to treat Butelios's imminent demise as an unavoidable consequence of his having captured me. That said, I really did hope Tournam would save him. In fact, I was counting on it.

"Butelios!" he shouted as he ran to the edge. With a look of agonised concentration, his brow furrowed and the shadowblack markings on his arms spun off into ribbons that darted down the cliff to wind themselves around the bigger man's ankles. Tournam grunted from the intense effort, swaying as he tipped dangerously close to the edge himself. I grabbed hold of his torso and hauled him back a foot or so until he caught his balance. After all, I'm not a monster. Yet.

I looked over the ledge. Butelios had dropped a good two hundred feet before Tournam's ribbons had caught him, but the enfeebled tendrils were struggling to keep him from falling further into the abyss. The bald monk grabbed at uncertain handholds in the rock face, straining to climb back up even with the support of the ribbons.

I patted Tournam on the shoulder. "Looks slippery down there. You'd best hold on tight."

The glare he shot me could've frozen the sun right out of the sky. "You little bastard. You *want* me to save him so we'll both be too weak to pursue you."

I ran back to fill my pack with what few supplies I could find. "Sorry about that, but you shouldn't've made me leave my business partner behind."

"A squirrel cat? A God-damned squirrel cat? For the sake of some filthy rodent you're going to make enemies of the Ebony Abbey?"

I shouldered my pack. "You know something, friend? Most of the world already insists on trying to kill me. They would've finished the job too, if it hadn't been for that particular rodent." I headed off, away from the cliff. "So what's a few more enemies?"

Tournam kept yelling at me. I'm pretty sure he would've killed me then and there if he weren't desperately hanging on to Butelios. I can't say my step felt light as I entered the forest, but at least I was free. It would take a long while before my captors would be able to begin searching for me.

That, friends, is what we call a break.

I spent the next hour trudging through the snowy trees, stopping every dozen yards or so to go back and set false trails going in all different directions, the way I'd seen Ferius do when we'd been on the run in places that, while not snow-covered, had enough in common that I figured the same techniques would work. Eventually I decided it was time to head for my true destination.

Having against all odds managed to pull off a decent stall and a solid break, it was time for the twist.

I felt it was a safe bet that once Tournam had gotten Butelios back up the cliff, they wouldn't even try to come after me. Instead they'd walk to the abbey to get help. While I had no idea how populated the Ebony Abbey was, I doubted anyone builds a monastery at the top of a mountain just to house a couple of monks. So pretty soon the passes would be filled with shadowblack brethren, seeking to hunt me down before I could find my way back to the Golden Passage. They'd be searching a long time.

Despite appearances (and history, I suppose), I'm not a complete idiot. There was no way I could outrun a bunch of crazed monks—especially if they knew where I was headed. Since they likely knew all the paths down the mountain and I didn't, I needed to head for the one place they would least expect me to go: the abbey itself.

Once the bulk of the monks had cleared out to hunt for me, I'd sneak inside, steal enough supplies for my journey and then follow my pursuers from a safe distance. Since the bottom of a mountain is obviously bigger than the top, the lower we got, the more places there would be for me to hide until I could make a break for it. Eventually I'd find somewhere to buy or steal a horse and then make the trek back to the Golden Passage. My enemies would not only have failed to catch me, they'd have shown me the way off this ancestors-damned mountain and provided me with the supplies for my journey.

See? That's why the third part of a successful escape is called the twist.

13

The Twist

I once asked Ferius if there was ever a fourth stage to a getaway plan. She responded by taking a puff from her smoking reed and blowing it out her nose. "Three's plenty for any proper escape, kid. You find yourself needin' a fourth, it means you're in deep trouble."

By the time I got my first look at the Ebony Abbey, I had no doubt whatsoever that a fourth step was going to be required.

This being the top of a mountain, I'd been expecting some kind of loose collection of log cabins or huts or something. Instead, from my precarious vantage point swaying atop the tallest and sturdiest tree I could find at the edge of the forest, what I saw took my breath away. Seven gleaming obsidian towers rose more than a hundred feet above the curtain wall, itself over fifteen feet high and travelling a good mile around the circumference of the abbey. Onyx pathways traversed three separate courtyards and linked enough two- and three-storey buildings to house an entire village. Outside the front gates, a glossy black stone path stretched out like a snake's tongue, inviting you to come inside.

How had anyone been able to engineer such a colossal edifice in secret? Where had they quarried so much black stone? Who had lugged it all the way up this mountain, and how did they supply themselves with enough grain, meat, timber and other provisions?

I climbed back down the tree—which turned out to be harder than climbing up—and, once I'd caught my breath, resumed my painfully slow trek to the abbey. I was lucky that the forest was thick enough to give me cover as I walked all the way around. Ferius says castles are like horses: majestic from the front, but vastly less appealing from the rear. That's because any large enclosed space filled with people produces a lot of waste (not unlike the rear end of a horse), and it has to come out somewhere. Regrettably, that somewhere is usually the best avenue for sneaking in and out.

An hour of casing the abbey rewarded me with the entrance to a remarkably well-built sewage tunnel opening out over the side of a cliff not unlike the one where I'd stranded Tournam and Butelios. I stashed my supplies in the snowy underbrush and proceeded to climb down twelve feet of rocky outcropping without the benefit of a rope to land unsteadily at the edge of the tunnel. From there, I made a very unpleasant journey in darkness.

It turns out that the defecation of holy people smells at least as bad—and possibly slightly worse—as that of the profane. Eventually, though, I passed beneath the abbey's curtain wall and found myself in a network of less disgusting tunnels that connected the various towers and buildings to the sewer. I walked along, periodically looking up through gratings to stare into storage rooms, kitchens and two separate libraries. It wasn't until I got to a grating that must have been near the centre of the abbey grounds that I saw any people.

Actually, I didn't see *them* so much as notice the pools of their blood pouring down the grating in front of me. That's when I started hearing the screams.

The soles of boots and sandals slapped frantically against the ground above my tunnel. Men and women fled, shouting words I didn't recognise. There was just enough light in the tunnel for me to make out another grating some fifteen feet along a smaller duct to my right, with an iron ladder leading up to it. I ran there and climbed up. The grate was attached to hinges, and despite the fact that a sane person usually runs in the other direction from such things, perverse curiosity made me want to discover what was causing all this chaos.

When I pushed up the metal grille enough to poke my head above ground, I saw a dozen men and women dressed in black robes, their shadowblack markings winding out in ribbons as they wrapped themselves around the limbs of a thing so mammoth in size and horrifying in appearance that I couldn't tear myself away.

The creature had horns on its head, but instead of one or two horns, like on the old Mahdek masks that used to terrify my own people, it had six. In a hideous symmetry, six limbs extended from its torso: four arms and two legs. The enormous chest heaved like a bellows and its enormous jaws tore into the flesh of a dying man who, despite his clearly mortal wounds, was struggling to free himself. Judging by the pile of at least a dozen dead behind the creature, I doubted he'd have much success.

My people believe the shadowblack to be a conduit by which demons will one day manifest themselves into our world and use the power of the mages they've infected to bring untold horrors upon us all. Ferius considers that nothing more than folk tale and superstition.

Turns out Ferius doesn't know squat.

14

The Fourth Step

My education on the subject of battling demonic forces had up till then been limited to three sources: Jan'Tep theories on the nature of cross-planar entities, borderland folk tales shared by tavern drunks eager to keep you refilling their cups, and my own natural aptitude for deductive reasoning. All three were telling me to run like hell.

I felt certain I was on solid ground with this conclusion; I had no relationship to any of the abbey folk, with the possible exceptions of Tournam and Butelios who weren't exactly fond of me. Furthermore, my entire plan had involved using chaos and confusion to facilitate my escape. Even I had to admit that a monstrous, six-limbed demon eating everyone in sight was a more effective distraction than pushing some guy off a cliff.

I turned to head back down the tunnels beneath the curtain walls and away from the demon's roars and the screams of the dying and soon-to-be-dead, determined not to join them. It was only when I heard a third sound that I stopped in my tracks. A crying child.

Who the hell brings a kid to a place like this?

I took a step back and glanced up through the grating to find a pale, skinny leg. A boy of maybe five or six stood there, his limbs trembling so hard it made the grate creak against its hinges. He didn't run though, just kept shaking uncontrollably. I recognised that particular impediment, having experienced it myself many times. The boy was frozen with fear.

"Kid, run!" I shouted.

He didn't respond. Well, not with words anyway. A cloying, caustic smell reached my nostrils just before a stream of urine came down the boy's leg and through the grate. He was pissing himself. I jumped back and shouted at the top of my lungs, "Don't just stand there! Run!"

"Oh no," the boy moaned. "Oh no."

It wasn't immediately clear whether it was fear of imminent demise or shame at the loss of bladder control that had prompted his words. I've pissed myself on several occasions and I can't recall which was the stronger impulse.

"Boy!" I called out again, this time in an impression of the clear, commanding voice my father had always used with me when he wanted to force my body to act even if my brain wouldn't. "You will turn around and run from this courtyard. *Now!*"

Either he didn't hear me, or I didn't sound very threatening, because he just kept standing there, urine trickling down his leg. The shrieks and shouts from the courtyard were getting louder, which meant the monks were losing and it was past time for me to go.

So why wasn't I running as fast my legs would carry me?

Damn. Damn. Damn.

I started back up the ladder. Annoying bloody Ferius Parfax. "*Nobody gets to choose their cards, kid,*" I imagined her scolding even over the din, "*Only thing to do is decide how to play the ones you got.*"

The latch keeping the grate shut was on the outside. Fortunately the last few months hadn't exactly been a time of frequent feasting for me, so my forearms were skinny enough to slip through. I slid the bolt and started pushing on the grate. The kid was still standing on it, but he was small and light enough that he just tumbled over. I climbed up until my waist was at ground level, tried not to look at the carnage or hear the screams and grabbed hold of the boy. He screamed and kicked at me of course.

"It's going to be okay," I promised him. "I'll get you out of here!"

He was clawing with his hands at the ground, trying to keep me from pulling him into the sewer. I was afraid he'd break his own fingers. "Let go!" I yelled. "I'm trying to help you!"

Then he sobbed something that made my day much, much worse. "What about the others?"

"The others?" Only then did I hear the lighter, higher voices among those screaming for mercy. I turned to see the demon towering over black robes stained red from the dead at his feet, then watched as the creature took its first step towards an alcove on the far side of the courtyard where a dozen boys and girls huddled together, holding on to each other, waiting for the end.

15

The Epitaph

I pushed myself up and out of the sewer entrance, then grabbed hold of the kid, forcing him to let go, and lowered him down. He landed poorly and gave a yelp that meant he'd sprained his ankle. A more capable rescuer would've done the job without injuring the person I was supposed to be saving, but I didn't have much practice at being heroic. "Stay down!" I ordered him, then turned to face the enemy.

What in the name of all my lousy ancestors am I doing? This thing is twelve feet tall and clearly unimpressed by the bevy of monks who've already died trying to stop it. What's my grand plan?

In the Jan'Tep tales of my childhood heroes never bothered with plans, because by the time the brave young mage faced his enemy, he or she had already learned the fantastical spell along the way that just happened to be the perfect way to destroy the monster. So far all I'd gotten on this trip was a nasty cold.

My list of demon-fighting strategies being rather limited, I opted for the tactic best suited to both my skills and temperament: distraction followed by a very speedy retreat. Taking a run towards the demon, I popped open the leather case attached to my trouser leg. First up was a little slicing and dicing. I drew a half-dozen of the razor-sharp metal cards and sent them spinning at the demon's head. For such light objects, they fly remarkably well. The first three missed—one bouncing off the edge of the alcove and actually hitting the foot of one of the poor kids huddling against the wall. He stared back at me with an expression that somehow managed to convey both abject terror and being mildly pissed off at me. Hey, *you* try throwing a card at a demon's head when your arms are shaking and your legs are desperately trying to convince you to go in the other direction.

Thankfully the next three hit their mark and bit deep into the back of the demon's skull. A steel card embedded in your enemy's flesh makes for a perversely satisfying sight. Too bad I didn't get more time to enjoy it.

The demon let out a growl that I was pretty sure came from annoyance rather than actual pain. As the massive blackened skull turned towards me, I ran around the other side. With only a couple of pinches of powder left in my pouches, I'd have to pick my target carefully. You might expect that would be the demon's eyes or mouth, but trust me, most creatures do a pretty good job of shielding those especially vulnerable parts of the body. Besides, my priority here was enraging the beast enough to make it lose interest in the kids and focus his ire on . . . Well, I'd figure that part out later.

This close, I could see the thick carpet of short, almost viscous hairs that covered the demon's body, which made it impossible to ascertain if it even *had* the particular bodily apparatus required for my next trick. With neither time nor desire to investigate thoroughly, I aimed for where the target ought to be and left the rest to hope. I tossed the powders up in the air, formed the somatic shapes for the spell and uttered the incantation. "*Carath*," I said, enunciating the word more heavily than necessary. Then again, the one thing you do *not* want to do when casting a spell is stutter.

The explosion thundered through the courtyard as the twin red and black fires followed the line of my fingers to their destination.

I heard a scream then; a howl that carried with it all the infernal depths of a demon's fury. Turned out the creature *did* have the requisite body parts.

Ancestors, I thought, as the monster spun around to find me with what appeared to be five angry red eyes. *If I'm about to die, let my epitaph be this: "Kellen, son of Ke'heops, exile of the Jan'Tep, outlaw and spellslinger. He once blasted a demon in the testicles."*

16

The Shadows

First came the roar, a ground-shaking thunder that carried with it the most noxious scent ever to assault my nostrils—and I've slept next to a squirrel cat after he's eaten too many butter biscuits following on from a dinner of two-day-old rabbit carcass. Trust me, demon's breath smells even worse. Though perhaps it was the bits of dead monk inside its jaws that were to blame.

The lashing of tails came next. That's right, *tails*. The grotesque creature had not one but three. Now I'm no expert in either demons or zoology, but I really feel it's unfair for any beast to have a triad of separately prehensile barbed appendages, each one sharp enough and powerful enough that when they struck the onyx flagstones of the courtyard, shards of black stone went flying.

I leaped out of the way as best I could, my cheek feeling the wind as a tail's spiky end nearly took off my right ear. Ferius performs these remarkable shoulder rolls that not only get her out of danger but also manage to propel her into the perfect position for a counter-attack. Me? I bashed the top of my head on the ground and flopped onto my back before rolling onto my belly and pushing myself to my feet.

I hate this. I hate this. I hate this.

The children, apparently having completed their assessment

of my heroic abilities, unleashed ear-splitting screams that did me no good whatsoever. Those monks who weren't yet dead staggered around in dazed confusion, their shadowblack markings looking soft, almost withered. They kept their distance, content to let me take the brunt of the monster's ire for now, prudently reasoning that allowing the creature to tear me apart would give them extra time to recover their strength.

As for the demon, he (though I didn't know demon anatomy well enough to be sure—I inferred the "he" from the now-charred dangling bits between his legs) had thus far demonstrated only one virtue: he was slow. Not *oh-I'll-just-race-around-him-throwing-cards-into-his-weak-spots* sort of slow. More *oh-I'll-really-see-it-coming-when-he-eats-me* slow. I was dodging pretty quickly, all things considered, but doubted I could keep it up for long. I was going to need a little help.

"Suzy," I whispered.

It's actually quite hard to whisper while your lungs are pumping and you're running this way and that, trying to keep from being crushed. But whisper magic requires a kind of patient emotional focus that you can't get from shouting.

"Suzy," I said again, speaking to the wind spirit—or sasutzei, as they're properly called—that lives in my right eye. "If you're not too busy, I could really use a hand right now."

Most days she was only good for showing me hidden paths or blasting my eyeball with cold air whenever I did something that offended her moral sensibilities. A few months ago, though, she'd saved my life by fighting back against my own shadowblack. If I could rouse her now, there was a chance she'd take a dislike to this particular demon before it ground my skull underfoot. If not, she'd have to find a new eyeball to hang out in. In the meantime, my daring counter-attack amounted to not much more than running maniacally around the courtyard.

"Anytime now, Suzy," I said. Well, I said a lot more than that. Whisper magic is strange that way: there aren't any specific incantations; it's more that you let your feelings intermix with your breath, like flowery, poetic pleading. It's actually pretty embarrassing.

One of the demon's left arms swept low along the ground as he tried to swat me. I was now faced with the rather difficult decision of whether to duck beneath it or try to jump over it. I chose the latter. Poorly. Another couple of inches and the thing's massive black forearm would've sailed beneath my feet. As it was, he caught the edge of my toes. I went head over heels in the air, and only by chance did I happen to land back on my feet. To someone watching, I imagine I'd have looked fairly athletic in that moment, but it was luck and nothing more.

The demon tried a different approach this time, spreading his huge hands out in preparation for squashing me like a bug.

"Suzy, it's now or never," I whispered.

No answer. Never count on wind spirits.

The whoosh of the monster's massive hands coming for me told me my time was up. I tried to shut my eyes—there being no evidence that facing death head-on made it any more pleasant—but my right wouldn't close. Instead a sudden blast of white cloud emerged from it, the sensation bitterly cold and unsettling. The view wasn't much better. The sasutzei billowed out from my eye, growing larger and larger as it rose up to face the demon. She unleashed a whistling shriek that sent the monster rearing back. I couldn't be sure if this was due to some innate fear of wind spirits or because he just found it weird to see a cloud coming out of some insignificant human's face.

The demon roared a challenge at the sasutzei. Suzy roared right back with the high-pitched scream of a hurricane blowing through canyon walls. I was left staggering from the sheer force of her winds. Other noises followed: shouts and cries and boot heels slamming against the flagstones.

"Quickly," a young woman called out. "While the stygian's distracted!"

I didn't know what a stygian was, but I hoped she meant the creature and not my wind spirit. My vision was kind of blurry on account of Suzy's cloud, but I could just make out the newcomers rushing towards us. There were six of them—teenagers, from what I could see—spreading out next to me to surround the demon. They all had the shadowblack, but unlike the other monks, they wore long coats of black, accented with reds or dark blues or silvers instead of traditional robes. Those coats were uncomfortably reminiscent of the ones worn by the two guys I'd only recently escaped.

"That wind spirit won't hold the stygian for long," said the girl— well, young woman, really. It's hard to call someone a girl when they're waging war against a demon. "Let's show the bastard what we can do!"

The sight of red curls and a fierce, wild grin gave me a sudden shock. For an instant I could've sworn a young Ferius Parfax had take up a position next to me, weaving her arms in the air with a fluid grace that looked more like she was dancing in front of an audience than facing off with a monster. Of course it *wasn't* Ferius. Now that I saw her more clearly, this girl didn't even look like her, apart from the hair. I guess I just missed my mentor.

"I'm Kellen," I said, though this seemed a remarkably inappropriate time for introductions.

"Diadera," she replied, close enough now that I noted the sun-bronzed skin of her cheeks was covered in tiny dark freckles. Her eyes narrowed in concentration and suddenly the markings came alive, launching into the air like a swarm of gleaming black fireflies. They darted into the demon's five eyes, stinging them repeatedly. When the monster batted at them, Diadera reeled back as if she'd been the one struck. "Are you planning to help anytime soon or are you just going to keep standing around looking pretty?"

"How?" I asked.

She gave me a wink. "Sort of medium pretty, I suppose. Maybe if we got you cleaned up I could reassess. In the meantime, use your bloody shadowblack to help me kill that thing!"

The demon clapped two of his massive hands together, crushing the swarm of her freckles between them. They drifted to the ground like dead ashes. Diadera groaned and fell to her knees, but she soon got back up and reached out with her hands, commanding the black fireflies back up into the air.

"You're wasting your time if you think this moron's going to be any use, Diadera," an angry—and all too familiar—voice on my left replied. Shoulder-length brown hair and a pretentious sleeveless black leather coat confirmed it. "I'm going to kill you when this is over, Jan'Tep," Tournam said.

"First hold the stygian," a deeper voice rumbled, taking Diadera's place when she fell back from the demon's onslaught. The shaved head and facial markings ending in black teardrops beneath his eyes made him known to me as well.

"Oh, hey, Butelios," I said. "Sorry about pushing you off that cliff."

I'm not sure if he found my apology sufficiently sincere, because right then the entire courtyard shuddered as the demon slammed all four of his fists down on the flagstones. I looked up, wondering why neither I nor any of the others was dead yet. It was Suzy, wrapping her white clouds around the monster's head, blinding him. The demon smashed his foot down, close enough to Tournam that he fell back, the black bands from his arms unwinding from the demon's limbs.

"Everybody, keep up the pressure," Diadera said, once again sending the ebony fireflies of her shadowblack freckles to assail the demon.

There were almost a dozen of us now trying to hold the creature back, though in fairness I was mostly just acting as a kind of vessel for the sasutzei. One girl half my size dropped to her knees and opened her hands, palm down, on the ground. Black vines from her fingers burrowed into the flagstones, only to erupt several feet away to tangle themselves around the demon's legs . Butelios shed ebony tears into his hands and hurled them at the creature, not so much attacking it as making it hesitate, as though the beast were suddenly drunk on sorrow. My amazement at how these people were capable of using their markings in such remarkable ways was overshadowed by the realisation that we were losing. The creature tore through the black vines and swept his forelimbs at us, forcing everyone to fall back as he tried his best to find anything soft and fleshy to grab on to.

Diadera grabbed my arm. "Kellen, the others are tiring. Use that cloud of yours to hold the stygian!"

"She can't!" I shouted back. Suzy's cloud had faded to a pale fog that was rapidly dissipating under the demon's assault.

"Just a little longer," Diadera urged. "He's almost here!"

"Who?" I asked, then realised that it didn't matter since in about three seconds we'd all be dead. I grabbed the rest of my steel cards from the pack strapped to my leg and threw them one after another at the creature's eyes. Most just bounced off his hide, but one stuck dead centre. That won me a howl of pain and outrage along with a couple of seconds' reprieve. "That's it," I said. "I'm all out of tricks."

The demon lumbered towards us. I tried to shield Diadera with my body. It wouldn't do any good of course, but I figured it couldn't hurt for my ancestors to think I'd performed at least one noble act when they judged me in the grey passage after my death.

The slap of sandals on flagstones was followed by a bellowing voice. "Hey, arsehole, you want a fight? *I'll* give you a fight."

I turned to see a tall man racing into the courtyard. Loose curls of ash-blond hair framed as square a jaw as I'd ever seen. The lines on his forehead and around his grey eyes marked him as middle-aged, but he had the broad chest and lean muscles of a younger man. Also, he was naked, now that he'd torn off his robes. What should have been pale skin was covered almost head to toe in a twisting web of shadowblack. He stopped before the demon, spread his arms wide and squeezed his fists so tight the knuckles went white. Every muscle on him clenched at once, and his body gave a shudder as the ebony markings burst from his skin. They struck the demon like a wave breaking on the shore, enveloping his body. Suzy gave her own scream, fleeing back into my eye, but the demon got it worse.

The creature was utterly drenched in the newcomer's shadows, as though a thousand barrels of oil had been poured over him. Snarling with rage, the beast clawed this unwanted shroud, desperately tearing at it to no avail. All three of his tails stabbed at the oily covering, but none of them could pierce it.

The black fluid solidified as it began to contract, tightening around the demon, crushing him. He kept fighting though, and the naked man's expression contorted with pain, as if every one of the demon's blows were striking him. Slowly, inexorably, the shroud became smaller and smaller, until the demon was crushed inside, leaving nothing but a twisted heap of shattered bones and ravaged flesh in a pool of black oil upon the ground.

A couple of the others ran to the blond man, but he pushed them away. He stumbled alone into the centre of the black oil. "I'm ready," he said, but it seemed as if he were talking to himself. The oil started to slide onto the tops of his feet, up his calves, twisting around his legs and over the rest of his body. When it was done, he was once again covered in the winding markings of the shadowblack.

Diadera walked over and handed him his robe. He took it from her and slipped it over his head. The children who'd been cowering in the alcove ran to him, cheering as they tried to take his hand. He gave them smiles and pats on the head but soon shooed them away.

"Who is he?" I asked Diadera, who seemed to both know him and be entranced by him.

Her reply was filled with a level of awe usually only seen in Berabesq clerics talking about their six-faced god. "That's the abbot."

The abbot walked around the courtyard, stopping to kneel by each of the dead monks. Then he came over to me, his blue eyes locking on mine. He was just standing there, watching me. So was everyone else. Finding the silence uncomfortable, I extended a hand and tried to introduce myself. "My name is—"

He cut me off. "I know exactly who you are, Kellen." He was silent again for a second before a wry smile appeared at the corner of his mouth. "Boy, have you ever come to the wrong place."

Cages have bars and everyone knows you're supposed to escape a cage, but houses have walls and people lock themselves inside to feel safe. You ask me, it's a lot easier to break out of a cage than a house.

—What Passes for Squirrel Cat Wisdom

17

The Abbot

I disliked the abbot almost immediately, and not just because he opened negotiations with, "Are there any Jan'Tep funerary rites you'd like us to perform on your corpse?"

He'd said this while leading me into one of the abbey's immense towers and then up enough flights of stairs to remind me that I wasn't sufficiently recovered from my assorted injuries and exertions to get into another fight. By the time we reached the top floor, I was dripping with sweat and trying to hide the fact that I was gasping for breath.

"In here," he said, motioning for me to accompany him into a darkened room about eight feet square, whose only light came from a window nearly as tall as I was but far too narrow for me to fit through, should negotiations go poorly.

"You first," I replied.

Following him into the tower might have been a mistake, but I had a better chance of fighting him alone in here than I would surrounded by his fawning acolytes in the courtyard. One way or another though, I was leaving this bizarre abbey with its freakish monks and even less pleasant demonic manifestations.

I needed to get off this mountain, and from there to the nearest village or town where I could steal a horse and ride for the Golden

Passage. Assuming I could find either of course. I had no way of knowing whether I was still near the Berabesq border or somewhere north of the Seven Sands. I couldn't even say for sure how many days it had taken to get to this place. All I could do was hang on to the hope that Reichis had survived his wounds and found water. It wasn't impossible. The squirrel cat was tough. If Shalla had worked up a spell to keep him alive, if she'd found a way to send word to Nephenia and Ferius…If…If…If…

The abbot pushed past me and entered the small room, slumping down into a chair behind a small writing desk. "Accept the inevitable, Kellen. You're going to die."

My hands drifted inside the sagging, depleted pouches at my sides. "People keep telling me that. Want me to show you where I buried their corpses?"

My *arta valar*—what the Argosi call "daring" but Ferius refers to as "swagger"—would've been more impressive if my fingertips could've scraped more than a pinch of red and black powders from the bottom of my pouches. Might be enough to slam the abbot into the rear wall and knock him unconscious if my timing was perfect. And if I were a lot luckier than usual.

The abbot paid no attention to what I'd said or any potential danger I might present. Instead he rummaged through heaps of papers and shoved aside books strewn across his desk. Jan'Tep sigils adorned two of the cracked, leather-bound covers. No spellmaster would ever allow such texts to leave their sanctums, which meant they were stolen. Something rolled out from underneath a stack of documents that put a broad smile on the abbot's face as he snatched it up. "Now I have you, you little bastard! Thought you could escape, didn't you?"

I was halfway to blasting him when he stuck the object in his mouth and leaned back in the chair. The golden-brown tube was roughly the length of his hand and the thickness of his thumb, wrapped in some kind of gauzy cloth or parchment. The abbot rummaged around the desk some more before sighing disconsolately. He looked up at me expectantly and tapped the end of the tube as he gestured to the pouches at my sides. "Help out a fellow demon-cursed fugitive, would you?"

"Is that some kind of smoking reed?"

Ferius Parfax was the only person I knew who smoked, and her reeds were just little things, almost as thin as the stem of a flower.

"It's called a *cigar*," the abbot replied. "It's like a smoking reed but for civilised people."

He tossed back a lock of ash-blond hair from his brow, exuding that casual self-assurance that only the truly handsome possess, making me feel small and petty all at once. Small, because he was big, muscular man with a square jaw and a smile that suggested he knew things I didn't. Petty, because, well, worrying about someone else's looks is just petty.

I didn't trust handsome people though. My father was handsome, and he'd counter-banded me so that I'd never be able to fulfil my magical potential. My one-time best friend Panahsi—now called Pan'erath—was handsome, and he'd tried to kill me. Twice. Dexan Videris, a fellow spellslinger, was so good-looking even Reichis had thought he was cool. Dexan turned out to be the biggest arsehole of them all.

So, yeah, I don't get along with the undeservedly attractive.

The abbot grinned up at me, white teeth biting onto the cigar to hold it in place. "Come on, kid. Don't leave me hanging. Show me what you got." He leaned back in his chair, hands behind his head and eyes slowly closing.

He was practically daring me to attack him. Did he know I was almost out of powder? Or was he so confident in his own abilities that he simply wasn't worried about what I could do?

I let the pinch of powder slip back into the pouches and only kept a few grains on my fingertips. I flicked them into the air between us. My hands formed the somatic shapes to strike my target.

Considerable skill is required to channel an explosion of flame into such a tiny, precise area. I'd be more likely to set the silvery blond bristles of the abbot's chin on fire than hit the end of his cigar. "*Carath*," I intoned, and a pencil-thin, somewhat anaemic belch of red and black flame ignited the end of the cigar.

The abbot showed no sign of being impressed at my skill with the powders. He was grateful though. "Oh, thank the mountains and oceans," he moaned, taking long drags. "Thought for sure I'd be dead before I got another taste of these beauties." Puffs of pungent grey smoke filled the space between us.

"Speaking of impending death…" I began.

The abbot opened one eye and looked at me as if he'd long ago forgotten I was still here. "Hmm? Oh, right." Reluctantly he removed the cigar from his mouth. "Don't take it personally. I say that to all the newcomers. 'You're going to die' is practically how we say hello around here."

"Some would say that's a dangerous way to greet strangers," I observed, right hand slipping into the leather pocket attached to the leg of my trousers. I'd only had time to pick up two of my steel cards after the fight with the demon, but in an enclosed space like this, I wasn't likely to miss.

"Shadowblacks don't exactly age well, Kellen," the abbot replied, holding his cigar out the narrow window and tapping it on the ledge. Ash drifted down to the courtyard below. "That stygian monstrosity you helped me fight? That was brother Caleb." The abbot's prior good mood seemed to collapse in on itself. "He was a good man. Always thought Caleb would outlast the rest of us."

"I'm sorry," I said, more out of reflex than from sincerity. No matter how kind or decent these people pretended to be, I had to remind myself that for all intents and purposes they'd kidnapped me and most likely planned to keep me prisoner here. I couldn't allow that. Not with my business partner waiting for me to rescue him.

The abbot took my words at face value. "Thanks. And thanks for helping me put an end to him. His...change came on quickly. None of us expected him to lose the fight so soon."

Those words spawned a thousand questions for me. *What fight? How does the transformation from human being into demonic manifestation work? And if that's what happens to us, is my father right? Is it better to kill us all before we become a danger to everyone around us?* But what I asked was, "Since you're feeling grateful, how about you let me leave this place and we'll call it even?"

"You really want to go back to that lousy desert where we found you? With a posse of seventy-seven lords magi on the hunt for shadowblacks?"

"Beats hiding out here in the mountains," I replied. "Though I suppose it must be easier than facing enemies who are probably younger, stronger and smarter than you are."

He met my challenge with a smile. "'Younger, stronger and smarter'? That's one of those Argosi tricks, right? You want to get me off balance, so you bring up everything from my age to my ability to my intellect just to see if being diminished will trigger a reaction?"

Pretty much spot-on, but his confidence really bugged me. "No, you just seem old and tired and kind of dumb."

He snorted out a laugh that caused the cigar to fall out of his mouth and onto his robes. He brushed it off before it could set them on fire. "That's a real charming personality you've got there, Kellen.

Am I going to have to keep Tournam and Butelios from trying to kill you?"

"Only if you reckon you haven't lost enough monks for one day."

The sudden flash of anger in the abbot's eyes told me I'd pushed him too far. He got himself under control pretty quick though. "You do not go out of your way to be liked, do you?"

"Would it get me out of here faster? Look, I'm sure your abbey is a nice place and all, but judging by how covered you are in shadowblack markings, I'm guessing you don't have a cure, and I have business elsewhere."

He gave a chuckle and stubbed out the cigar on his palm. "So go. Only reason I sent my boys out to get you in the first place was because Butelios's tears sometimes lead him to shadowblacks in distress. Since you seem to think you were doing just fine on your own, go on and see how well you fare against a posse of war mages with nothing but some flashy powders and that big mouth of yours."

"Really? You'll let me—"

"Just one thing," he said, rising from his chair. "Come up to the roof with me first."

I felt that prickly feeling on my skin that comes right before a conversation that began with "Are there any Jan'Tep funerary rites you'd like us to perform on your corpse?" ends with someone pushing you off the top of a tower. "Why should I?" I asked.

With a firm hand the abbot shoved me out the door and up a set of black stone stairs leading up to the top of the tower. "Simple. Because you have no idea where you are right now."

18

The Tower

The rooftop's chill conspired with my lack of warm clothes to make me shiver as I stared out over the abbey's strange and wondrous architecture. The tower on which I stood was crowned with a circular battlement, the crenellations rising almost to the height of my chest. Upon four separate raised promontories, which I guessed matched the cardinal points of a compass, stood rotating brass fixtures, each holding a rectangular piece of curved black crystal roughly two feet wide. I was surprised when I looked through the nearest one to discover they were a kind of magnifying glass, enabling me to see for the first time that each of the abbey's seven towers bore their own unique design.

Opposite us, across the courtyard, a thin minaret perhaps fifteen feet across rose up like a spear, topped in a smooth, curved structure like a black candle flame. Narrow vertical slits spaced evenly along its circumference allowed those inside to see out and, I assumed, aim weapons at potential invaders. A third tower was even more eccentric, the top shaped like a giant hand reaching up to snatch the sun from the sky. I was about to ask how the monks had come to create such singular buildings when the abbot made it clear that he'd be the one asking the questions.

Even though I'd been half expecting some kind of attack, he

surprised me with his speed, grabbing me by the jaw and hauling me towards the edge of the tower before I could reach for my weapons.

"Who sent you to my abbey?" he demanded.

My feet struggled to keep their balance as he pushed me nearer and nearer to the ledge. "Nobody! Your idiot monks dragged me here against my will!" I tried without success to pull out of his grip. Hells, but this guy was strong.

"Nice try, but you were already searching for the abbey before Tournam and Butelios found you. Now you want to leave? There's a war coven out there that would pay a hefty reward to find this place. A spy might try to discover the abbey's location, learn its defences so he could report back to his Jan'Tep masters." He leaned in closer, the smell of his cigar heavy on his breath. "Those markings of yours are way too smooth and precise to be natural." The thumb of his other hand rubbed the twisting black lines around my eye, so hard I feared the skin would come off.

I drove the palm of my hand under his elbow, pushing it up until it forced him to release my jaw. Chances were he'd follow up with a roundhouse punch, so I readied myself to duck a blow that never came. The abbot just stood there, examining his thumb for signs that my markings had come off. "Doesn't prove anything," he said, more to himself than to me.

I fought the urge to call him an idiot and remind him that I'd probably been hunted by more bounty mages than anyone living inside this abbey. Ferius's first lesson in the art of persuasion was to remember that the simplest truth usually gets you further than the grandest deception. "My grandmother," I said. "She banded me in shadow. That's why the markings look the way they do."

"Impossible," he snapped, but then he came closer to peer into my eye. This time he didn't try to grab me. "Son of a bitch," he breathed. "Or, I guess, grandson of a bitch in this case." He stepped back. "Show me what you can do."

"I can't do anything. I don't have abilities like you or Tournam or the others. I get headaches! And horrible visions of people becoming monstrous versions of themselves. I get lost in shadow sometimes, and when I do, even my friends start to forget me. I was a baby, and my own grandmother stole my future from me without ever telling me why!"

The abbot was silent, as though weighing my words for evidence of deception. "Something about this stinks. Despite the nonsense your people believe, the shadowblack isn't some poison or disease. You can't just infect someone with it. I need to consult my books," he said finally. "If some crazy old Jan'Tep really did band you in shadow, then I need to figure out how she did it and why. We'll talk more tomorrow once I've—"

"No," I said.

"No?"

"I told you, I have a business partner who's dying out in the damned desert. While I'm wasting time here with you, he's waiting for me to come and save him!"

The abbot tensed. Even through his robes I could see the muscles in his arms and shoulders bunching. He wanted to hit me. Badly. "Have you forgotten here's a Jan'Tep war coven out there hunting us? My boys risked all our lives bringing you here, and all you can do is whine at me about some lost pet. Where's your damned sense of duty to your fellow shadowblacks?"

Before I could reply, he waved me off. "No, forget it. Even if I didn't need to understand what those markings around your eye signify, I can't take a chance on you getting captured and revealing the location of the abbey. There are too many lives at stake."

Fear gave way to a cold certainty in my guts. I reached for the castradazi coins sewn into the bottom of my shirt, tearing the thread holding them even as a half-dozen very bad plans for escape came to mind. "You won't be the first person who tried to lock me up."

The abbot gave a weary chuckle and put up his hands. "I surrender, spellslinger or Argosi or whatever the hell it is you think you are." He retrieved the stub of his cigar from his robes and stuck it unlit in his mouth. "I swear, never have I grown so damned sick of someone I only just met."

I backed away, moving slowly towards the door that led down. From there I'd have to move quickly in case he changed his mind and sounded the alarm.

"You know, I always heard the Argosi have an uncanny knack for knowing exactly where they are. Guess they never taught you that particular talent, eh?"

I spun around, a sick feeling in my guts even before I ran up to one of the black lenses housed in its rotating brass fitting atop one of the crenellations. I caught a glance of the mountains in the distance, appearing so close it was as if you could reach out and touch them. There was just one problem: these weren't any mountains I recognised. I ran to the next magnifier, aiming it in the opposite direction, only to again be presented with a vista that bore no resemblance to anywhere I'd been in my travels across the continent. It was when I looked through the fourth slab of curved black glass—the one facing east—that a feeling almost like vertigo overtook me. What I saw in the distance wasn't land, but water. An ocean's worth. "Ancestors, where have you brought me?"

The abbot came to join me at the magnifier. "Haven't you wondered why this place wasn't overrun with bounty mages years ago?" He took hold of the sides of the brass frame holding the magnifier and swivelled it downward. "You want to leave, Kellen? Just follow that road until it takes you to the foot of the mountain. About three days' walk south you'll reach a village, and a hundred miles past that you'll hit the coast. Wait out the winter and, if you're very lucky, you might just find a ship willing to sail a thousand leagues to the south-east." He clapped me on the back. "Welcome to the continent of Obscaria, Kellen. The weather's cold, the food is terrible, and the reason those who come to the abbey never leave is because we're a long, long way from home."

19

The Firefly

I stumbled down the stairs, the abbot's parting words ringing in my ears. An initiate in Jan'Tep magic doesn't spend a lot of time studying road travel or sea voyages, but a year of riding with Ferius had taught me enough to come up with a rough calculation: it would take me six months to get back to my own continent and return to the Golden Passage.

Six months.

I ran a hand across my chin. I wasn't one for beards, but even so, there was only a week or two's worth of stubble. How on earth had Tournam and Butelios gotten me here in that time?

"Guess you got the speech, huh?" a voice asked.

Even before I saw her, I recognised Diadera's voice, which was odd since we'd only met briefly and most of that time was spent fighting a demon. She was just around the bend in the stairs, leaning against the curved stone wall, apparently waiting for me. A tumble of red curls framed green eyes and the hint of a lazy smile occupied one corner of her mouth. It says something that it was her smile that caught my attention rather than the filigree of tiny intricate black markings across her cheeks and chin.

It might sound hypocritical, but the sight of the shadowblack makes my stomach churn. I'd grown up in a society that considered it to be the most disgusting disease imaginable. Healthy Jan'Tep had a responsibility to shun those afflicted so as not to let the condition spread. Mages had a duty to kill them. So even though I had it myself and had come to learn that the shadowblack wasn't precisely what I'd always been taught, seeing the markings on someone else—someone standing so very close to me—was profoundly disconcerting.

"Don't like what you see?" she asked, and though her light tone of voice tried to mask any animosity, I had the sudden feeling I was in more danger now than I had been with the abbot.

It's not like I hadn't been this close to someone else's markings before. Seneira had them, though hers turned out to be something completely different. Maybe on some deeper level I'd sensed it, which was why she hadn't produced the same reaction in me as this girl did.

Or maybe it was taking me a second to understand exactly *what* I was feeling.

Diadera's reaction, on the other hand, was entirely different. She peered at the markings around my left eye, tracing them with her gaze, looking so deep it was as if there was something written there that I'd missed in all the hours I'd spent staring in the mirror. She reached out a finger and touched the ridge of my eye. *Cool*, she said.

No. Wait. She hadn't said it. She'd *thought* it.

"What the hell is going on?" I asked, pulling away.

"Our shadows," she replied, coming closer, not showing the least trace of anger or embarrassment at my awkwardness. "They're both connected to Umbra Arcanta—that's one of the ethereal planes. I've never met anyone whose shadows are so close to my own." She tapped the freckles on her left cheek. "Are you an inspiritor like me? Can you make your markings come to li—"

"Stop it!" I said, my voice rising in both volume and pitch. "I've never heard of this 'Umbra Arcanta.' I haven't a clue what an 'inspiritor' does."

Ancestors, why am I even talking to her? I might not be a prisoner here, but I'm not free either. I don't know these people and I don't want to know them. If I'd just fought back when they took me, maybe I could've stayed with Reichis and died with my frie—

"Shh…" Diadera said. She took my hand and, more slowly than before, as though I were a frightened rabbit, she brought my fingertips to the freckles on her cheek.

I'm sorry I was so forward before, she said without speaking. *I just wasn't expecting this.*

"I still don't kn—"

She put her other finger on my lips. *Just think it.*

I tried to settle myself, but it was hard. It wasn't just her words I could hear. When she touched my markings, it was as if all my senses became overwhelmed by her presence. Her smell. The texture of her hair. The way she—

Focus, she thought to me. Even without looking at her face I could sense her grinning. *We hardly know each other.*

Once again I tried to get control of myself. I'd never properly learned *arta precis*—the Argosi talent for perception—but I knew something was up.

Tell me what's happening, I thought back to the red-haired girl. *You're not just sending words into my mind. You're messing with my head.*

She nodded. Well, she didn't, but in my thoughts she did. *Let's start at the beginning. You probably think the shadowblack is this big evil plague, right?*

Isn't it?

Oh, definitely. That stuff about demons taking us over? Well, you saw the stygian in the courtyard, so you know it happens. But it's a lot more complicated than you've probably been told. The black markings on our skin are a kind of . . . portal . . . for energies between our plane of existence and ones far outside our own.

Portals?

Her finger tapped one of the tattooed bands on my forearm . . . No, again, she hadn't. She'd just *sent* that touch to me. *Your Jan'Tep bands connect to six esoteric planes, which you call things like "sand," "silk" and "fire," right?*

Ember, I corrected.

Whatever. Anyway, think of the shadowblack kind of like your bands only it connects to one of dozens, maybe hundreds, of different ethereal planes. Most people's markings come from one of a dozen or so lower planes. When their shadows touch or, like I'm doing now, they touch skin to the other's markings, their minds share a connection on that plane. Does that make sense?

Hardly at all, I replied.

She took my fingers away from her cheek and smiled at me. "What's my name?"

"Diadera. You told me before, in the courtyard."

"My full name."

"Diadera dan Hestria," I replied. "Wait . . . How did I—"

"What's my favourite colour?"

I answered without even having to think. "Green and silver. You can never decide between them."

Somehow I knew more about her than I did most of the people I'd grown up with. Dozens of little details. Likes and dislikes. Fears and desires. A few scattered memories, though I knew she'd kept most of those to herself. I also knew she hadn't taken any from me. What I knew from her had been a gesture. An offering of friendship.

"And your markings are from the same plane as mine? This 'Umbra Arcanta'?"

95

She nodded. "It's supposed to be one of the hardest to control, but I've always been able to bring my shadows to life."

"Because you're an . . . 'inspiritor'?"

"Exactly." She touched a finger to my own markings again. *Now we just need to figure out what you can do, Kellen of the Jan'Tep.*

It was getting easier to share thoughts with her. *Well, I get splitting headaches and have horrible visions. Does that count?*

Show me.

I shook my head. *No. The things I see are . . . I don't go looking for them.*

Too bad. We have a Jan'Tep girl here named Suta'rei who's an alacratist. That means her markings let her reach into the past and reveal it for us. Is that what happens to you?

Not unless the past is a lot uglier than anyone remembers.

Diadera's finger began tracing the lines around my eye. *Your markings are strange. Almost like the wheels of a lock. Maybe you're an enigmatist.*

What can they do?

Nobody knows. Outside of a couple of brief mentions in one of the abbot's books, no one's ever met one. She took her finger away, leaving me feeling oddly alone. "Come on," she said, turning to the stairs that led back down the tower. "I'll show you around."

I didn't budge. My conversation with the abbot came crashing back down on me, reminding me that I was as much a prisoner here as if they'd locked me in a cell. "I think I've seen enough of the abbey for one day."

She stopped, and turned back to me, sliding her fingers between mine as if we'd known each other forever. "Everybody gets the speech, Kellen." Her face contorted to a deeply serious expression clearly not suited to her features. " 'You're going to die, you know?

You'll fight it, you'll think you've mastered it, but the shadowblack will still take you, my son. You'll die. Die. Die. Die.'"

Despite how hard I tried not to, I couldn't help but break out laughing. And when I did, I couldn't stop—not even when the laughter turned to useless tears and racking sobs so bad I slipped and found myself on my butt, a sharp pain in my back where I had struck one of the stairs. Even then I couldn't stop myself. Reichis was dead. I'd left him behind. In a lifetime of feeling useless, I'd never felt as helpless as I did now.

Diadera grabbed on to me, kneeling awkwardly next to me. "It's all right, Kellen. I know. I know what this feels like. But I promise, it's all going to be different for you now."

"Different how?"

She took my hand and put it against her cheek, my fingertips touching her markings, that strange connection between us igniting once again. Then she looked at me with those pale green eyes of hers, and I swear she could've said just about anything and I would've believed her, even if the words she chose hadn't been the ones I'd most wanted to hear since the day I'd left the Jan'Tep territories. "You're home now, Kellen."

20

The Invitation

Diadera led me by the hand down the tower's winding stairs. At the end of a curved hallway on the third landing she pointed out a half-open door. "There's a room there for guests of the abbey," she said, adding, "if you want to sleep."

I could've sworn I'd heard a slight rise in her voice at the end, like she'd asked a question. For a fraction of a second the corner of her mouth had twisted up into a smile. Or had it? I was so exhausted and bleary-eyed by this point I might've just imagined it.

Spend enough nights in travellers' saloons, though, and you come to learn that when someone says, "If you want to sleep," sometimes they're asking if you're tired and other times they're asking whether you'd like to sleep *with them*. My people consider innuendo to be the province of poets, actors and other undesirables, which has left me kind of bad at it.

Ferius Parfax had once demonstrated to me how a simple greeting such as "Well, hello there" could convey as many as twelve different insinuations, ranging from mild disinterest to outright salaciousness. So which was it now?

"Kellen?" Diadera asked.

Damn, but she was beautiful. Even her shadowblack freckles drew my gaze—the way they adorned her cheeks down to her jaw line, with just a few trailing down that perfect neck, the last ones hiding just beneath the collar of her long leather coat.

"*If you want to sleep . . . ?*"

No, she hadn't said it like that. Not exactly. And why would Diadera be interested in me anyway? We'd only just met. It was ridiculous. The question had been perfectly innocent. Only, my palms were slick. My breathing was unusually fast. There were other signs of my interest in her too, though it felt very, very important to ignore those ones.

If only I could be sure what she'd meant. Had Reichis been here, he'd've sniffed her leg and then informed me she was expecting me to kiss her and then suggested elaborate—and highly inappropriate—mating rituals. Ferius, on the other hand, would've advised responding with the most innocent answer possible, but delivering it with a saucy wink.

"I *am* very tired," I replied, remembering to wink about a second too late. Then I wasn't sure if I even *had* winked properly, so I did the thing one should never do in such situations: I winked again.

Diadera looked back at me, head tilted. "Are you all right? You have a twitch in your eye."

"I'm fine . . . I just . . . you know . . ."

Oh, ancestors, did I just wink again?

I suddenly missed Nephenia so much my chest hurt. I never had to put on airs around her. She would've responded to my pathetic attempts at romantic subtlety by telling me that playing coy in the hope that the other person will make the decision for you is both selfish and cowardly. Then she would've smiled at me in that way that said, without words and yet with perfect clarity, "*It's okay, Kellen. You're allowed to be bad at this,*" and everything would've been okay again.

Reichis. Ferius. Nephenia. How was I supposed to stop missing them when I couldn't get them out of my head?

"Kellen?" Diadera asked. She appeared genuinely concerned about me by this point.

I started to reach out to her. Maybe if my fingers touched her markings, the way hers had touched mine, we'd share that connection again and this would stop being so complicated. My hand moved slowly, tentatively, then stopped.

No. Not like this. Not in the way of a boy trying to steal a slice of cake.

An odd sense of calm came over me. I had made a decision. Regardless of what Diadera had or had not implied by her question, I was not going to fall into bed with a girl I'd just met out of some desperate desire to escape my grief. I'd take my pain and my loss like a man. Whatever that meant.

I was about to say goodnight when I noticed she seemed to be getting taller. A dull ache was coming to the back of my head too. That's when I realised I'd fallen back against the wall and was now slumping down to the floor. Diadera ran over and grabbed me, pulling my arm over her shoulder and supporting me as she led me into the tower's small guest room.

She managed to get me over to the bed. I said, "Diadera, I've decided not to…"

"Idiot."

"What did I—"

She gently set me down on what turned out to be a remarkably comfortable mattress. "Not you, me. I should've realised you're not used to this altitude. The air's thinner up here. No wonder you've been staring at me like some half-witted village oaf. And you're obviously exhausted. It's a wonder you've survived any of this." She tossed a thick blanket over me. "You'll be better in the morning. For now, sleep."

Sleep. The word alone was enough to make my eyes heavy. But I pushed the blankets aside nonetheless. "We have to...set traps," I mumbled.

Ferius always set up a perimeter when we bunked down for the night—whether in some stray patch of forest in the middle of nowhere or inside a wealthy merchant's palace. I fumbled in the pockets of my shirt and trousers. Where had I left the strings with the bells and the foot spikes?

"Kellen, stop." Diadera pushed me gently back down. "You'll hurt yourself. It's safe here, I promise. Rest."

"Can't," I said, my attempts to rise failing utterly. "Never bed down without settin' yer tra—"

I felt that strange connection again. When I looked up, some of her shadowblack freckles were drifting from her face to mine. They fluttered against the markings of my left eye like the wings of a butterfly.

Rest.

I lost consciousness after that.

21

The Dreamer

I dreamed of those I'd left behind.

Ferius Parfax was dancing with two other women in flowing silk garments. They spun and twirled along a marble floor like graceful planets orbiting her sun, their arms swaying out to touch her shoulder or her cheeks. It felt wrong, watching the dance unfold. It was too intimate, too...

Wait. They're not dancing. Ferius calls it dancing, but to everyone else it's fighting.

The women were attacking her. Their hands whipped out, and tiny knives appeared out of nowhere. The Argosi batted them away with fanned-out steel cards in one hand and her extensible steel rod in the other. She was tired though, and as she spun to keep her attackers in view, droplets of blood were flung from a half-dozen wounds on her face and arms.

Ferius! Ferius, hold on! I'm coming!

She turned and looked at me over her shoulder. "Don't talk crazy, kid. You're nowhere near here. You left, remember?"

I didn't mean to . . . I was trying to keep you safe from—

"Don't waste time wrastlin' problems you can't fix." She whirled just in time to dodge a short, thin blade thrust at her face. Then she said, "This isn't a dream, Kellen."

Wait, what? What do you mean, this isn't—

She was gone. So were the two assassins.

The sound of hoofs thundered in my ears. Nephenia was riding a fast horse along a grey dusty road, coming towards me. Ishak, her hyena familiar, balanced atop the horse's neck, barked something I couldn't understand.

Nephenia, where are you going? Who's chasing you?

"There's no time!" she shouted. "He's all alone out there!"

Who's alone, Nephenia? Who are you—

The horse was almost upon me now. "Kellen, look out!" she shouted, seeing me for the first time. "This isn't a dream!" The horse reared up, its hoofs—

Sand.

Nothing but sand now, deep underfoot and swirling in the air. A squirrel cat reared up, hackles rising, coat turning pure crimson with black stripes, gliding flaps stretched out to make itself appear larger. It was Reichis. He growled and hissed and snarled at someone behind me. I tried to turn my head to see who it was, but I couldn't. Reichis began to circle his enemy. The squirrel cat was hurt, dragging his front leg. His eyes were unfocused, blinking away the sand as he struggled to see his opponent. I heard laughter, and the sound of ember fires igniting the air.

Reichis, run! Don't fight a mage without me! We have to be smart, do this together, like we always do. We'll kill him, Reichis. We'll kill him for trying to hurt you. We'll—

Reichis chittered. "Don't be stupid, Kellen. You're a thousand miles away. You can't help me. I'm doing this for you."

Fear and frustration took hold of me. I could feel my body struggling against the blankets I'd gotten myself wrapped up in. *It's a dream*, I told myself. *A meaningless hallucination. It's all just pain and bad memories and all the wasted—*

But then Reichis looked up at me, the fur of his muzzle so close I could've reached out and touched it. "Stop saying that, Kellen," he growled, voice thick with irritation. "I keep telling you, this isn't a dream."

My hands gripped at the blankets, tearing them off me. I tried to rise, to force my eyes open...

"No, dummy," a new voice said. It didn't belong to Ferius or Nephenia or Reichis, but to someone just as familiar. "This only works if you're unconscious. Calm down and listen to me, Kellen. This is *not* a dream!"

It was all gone now. The marble floor, the dusty road, the desert sand. I was standing inside a vast heptagonal room, barefoot. The floor was cool, but not unpleasant. When I looked down I saw it was made from silver, polished and gleaming. Seven columns held up a domed roof of dusky glass through which pinpoints of starlight stretched down to glisten in the silky white smoke of a brazier set in the centre of the room.

"Hello?" I called out.

A feminine form strode through the haze towards me, robed in silks that shimmered softly through every colour imaginable, anchored only by the sun-golden hair that framed her face and the cuts on her hands that dripped blood onto the silver floor. "Finally," she said. "I thought you were going to make me stand here and bleed to death before you'd stop filling my head with all your inane thoughts."

I hate it when my sister does this.

22

The Sanctum

I've heard that when you're not sure if what you're seeing is real or a dream, pinching yourself is a good way to—

"Don't," Shalla warned, and held up her bleeding hands. "If you wake up now, all this will have been for nothing."

"Why are you using blood magic?" I asked, and turned—more slowly this time—to take in the massive sanctum. "And where is this place?"

My sister grunted in annoyance, a somewhat childish mannerism at odds with the unworldly scene she'd conjured. "We're in my mind, obviously," she replied, then added, "Yours is exactly as much of a mess as I would've expected. Why on earth do you allow all those terrible thoughts of death and dying into your dreams?"

"You think I have a choice?"

She gave me a raised eyebrow by way of reply.

"Shalla, you're telling me you've learned how to control your dreams?"

"Of course. I've been doing it since I was ten." She gestured to the serenity of her imaginary—at least my jealousy made me hope it was imaginary—mage's sanctum. "I spend my nights here. I find it very practical."

"Practical?"

She walked over to the nearest column and touched its surface. The marble coating seemed to dissolve, revealing shelves holding countless vials and glass boxes with all manner of stones and powders inside them. She picked up something that looked like a piece of jade and tossed it onto the brazier in the middle of the room. The smoke took on a green hue, and the room came into sharper focus. "That's better," she said, coming back to me. "I'm sure some people enjoy bizarre night terrors or perverse fantasies, but I prefer to use my sleeping time for experimentation."

"Experimentation…" I said.

She looked at me quizzically. "Are you drifting away again? You keep repeating the last thing I said. Anyway…" She aimed a finger at the silver floor and traced a circle in the air. Yellow sparks appeared, forming a perfect spell circle. "See? If you establish the rules of your dream world accurately, you can work out all number of esoteric geometries while designing new spells."

I walked over and took her wrist, holding up her bleeding hand. "Too bad you can't envision it without all the blood."

"Don't be silly, Kellen. I told you—this isn't a dream. I'm just using this place to give you focus so you don't regain consciousness and break this very complex and taxing silk spell." She took her hand away. "The blood magic was the only way I could create a connection between us. Now, can we get down to business?"

She gestured behind me. I turned and watched as part of the silver floor turned liquid, rising up like a fountain. When it had reached about two feet, it slowed, the molten silver taking on the shape of a rather elegant chair. Knowing Shalla's propensity for obstinacy—especially after she's taken pains to be impressive—I sat down. "Good," she said, taking a seat upon her own somewhat more regal silver throne. She looked down at the blood from her hands already pooling on the wide arms. "I suppose we'd best be quick. If I pass out from blood loss, it's unlikely anyone will find me in time."

Any concerns I might have had that this *was* just a dream were banished by Shalla's unbearable and all too familiar self-assurance. That this was real gave me a small sliver of hope. "Did you do it? Did you get help to Reichis?"

"Who? Oh, the nekhek." She leaned back on her silver throne. "Really, Kellen, I wish you'd just get a proper familiar, or at least a less offensive pet. Father should've dest—"

"Shalla," I said, cutting her off. I considered my next words carefully. Despite all the complicated machinations and deceits between us, despite the way she'd always treated me as an inferior, and one who—no matter the horrors our parents had tried to inflict on me—always needed to be reminded of my duty to our house, I still loved her. She had saved me as many times as she'd nearly gotten me killed. She was my sister, and she would always be precious to me. But she was talking about my business partner. "Finish that sentence, and, dream or no dream, I will make you regret it."

She stared at me, her smile easy, everything in her posture relaxed. I knew it for an act. She was scared. And hurt. I'd just hurt my little sister. She held on to the pretence regardless. "My, my. Outlaw life has changed you, brother."

"Having people try to kill you all the time tends to clarify things. Where is Reichis?"

"Clarify things such as...?"

I couldn't afford to let up. Shalla has a kind of addiction for control. When it gets the best of her, she follows what the Argosi call the Way of Stone. "Such as who you're willing to die for, and, sometimes, who you're willing to kill. Now tell me what happened to Reichis."

"What if I told you I forgot all about the rodent? What if I told you I had better things to do with my time—and my spells—than search out a filthy nekhek and try to save its life? Would you kill me, brother?"

"I…"

I was going about this all wrong. Ferius wouldn't use arta valar against someone as obstinate as Shalla. Daring would only harden her. A better path was arta precis. Perception. My sister wouldn't go to all this trouble to contact me if it weren't important. Chances are, she wouldn't do so just to tell me she'd saved Reichis either.

She wants something.

Arta siva, the talent of persuasion, is not so much about coaxing an opponent as it is about reframing their context. "I'm sorry, Shalla. I shouldn't have frightened you. I'd never hurt you for failing to help Reichis. I'm only half the mage you are, but I can't imagine how difficult those spells would be."

Frightened. Hurt. Failing. That should do the trick.

An angry flush came to her cheeks. "*Half* the mage I am?" In fact, Shalla was ten times the spellcaster I would ever be. The idea that I considered myself anywhere in her league was intolerable. "I've cast more complex spells in my sleep. Literally."

"I've upset you, sister. Again, I apologise." I rose from my chair. "You and Father have probably been right all along. I should never have bonded with a nekhek. All he ever did was steal my stuff and bite me."

Shalla's not so easily fooled. "After all your bleating about the squirrel cat, now you don't care?"

Arta tuco, the talent of subtlety—or gambling, as Ferius calls it—has many facets. The simplest one is reducing the value of your own stakes, and thus raising those of your opponent. "Your hands are still bleeding, Shalla. This spell is dangerous." I walked past her, to the door at the far end of the room. "I'm going to go now. I've found a new home, a new place in the world far from the things that once seemed so important. You should rest. I hope we get to speak again soon."

I had no idea what would happen if I passed through that door, but before I reached it, Shalla called out, "Kellen, stop!"

I turned. "Sister?"

She came to stand before me, looking considerably less certain than she had before. "I need information."

"About what?"

"The Ebony Abbey. You said two men were taking you there. Was that true? Is it real?"

Now that was an interesting question. I would've thought someone with Shalla's abilities—not to mention my father's, since I had no doubt he was the one who wanted to know—could've stolen the thoughts from my mind. So either I was too far away or something about this place prevented them from using scrying spells to track me. "Tell me what happened to Reichis."

"Oh, for the sake of the Ancestors! I helped him, all right? I helped your filthy squirrel cat. Happy now?"

It took every ounce of arta valar for me not to break down crying with relief. Instead I hugged her. "Thank you, Shalla."

She pushed me away. "I said 'helped' him, Kellen. I didn't say I saved him."

"What does that mean?"

She shook her head. "No, now you answer *my* questions." Stepping aside, she motioned to the door. "Or go ahead and walk out of here. The spell will be broken and you'll wake up in whatever little shadowblack hovel you've found yourself in this time."

She was bluffing, I was sure of it, and yet I couldn't risk it. Turns out some people can learn arta tuco without ever meeting an Argosi. "What do you want to know?"

The slight smile on her face was a reminder of the hundreds of battles of wits I'd lost against her. "Everything, beginning with the abbey's location."

That part she'd almost certainly figured out already. "Far away, on another continent across the ocean."

She nodded. "Most likely Inkrissa, in the South Sea."

Obscaria, actually, about three thousand miles north of Inkrissa, but I didn't see any reason to share that with Shalla and thus my father's posse.

"How many shadowblack mages do they have?" she went on, rattling off questions one after another. "How many demons do they command? What kind of defences do they—"

"Shalla, stop! These people aren't warriors. They're monks and students trying to keep the shadowblack from swallowing them up. There are families here! Children! They're no threat to the Jan'Tep."

My sister gave a soft snort, then reached out a hand to pat my cheek. "Apparently being an outlaw hasn't lessened your naivety, brother. The 'monks' of this abbey are no doubt shadowmasters, bent on bringing back the forbidden magics for summoning demons. Now, tell me how they plan to—"

"Sister, please."

"What?"

It took me a moment to figure out what to say. Should I tell her that the people here are the first to suffer when the shadowblack goes astray? That all they want is to live some small part of their lives free from the terror of being hunted down like dogs by Jan'Tep war mages?

No. None of that would work on her any more than it would my father. So instead I asked, "Why does it have to always be this way?"

Her eyes narrowed. She thought I was playing a game. "What way?"

It was a question I could answer honestly, because it was one I'd been asking myself for months. "Why is it that the Jan'Tep have the most wondrous magic anywhere in the world, but all we seem to use it for is to plot and scheme and kill our enemies?"

Without missing a beat, as if it were the most obvious thing in the world, she replied, "We have a duty to protect our people, just as you and I have a duty to protect our house."

I took her hands in mine. Even in this dream state I could feel the warmth of the blood on her palms against my skin. "Shalla, you're the most powerful mage of our generation. One day you'll surpass everyone, even Father. You'll be the one to rule our people. All our lives you've shown such promise, and yet you wield your power without an ounce of compassion. If you can't... If you of all people can't find a way to use your magic for something more than just causing more pain and destruction, then what hope is there for any of us?"

She didn't answer. She just stood there, looking down at my hands around hers. I could feel something waver in her. "What would you have me do, brother?"

I felt a bit like a character in one of those frontier tales who finds a magic candle that can't be lit by any flame, but if you breathe on it just right your heart's desire will be fulfilled. But Shalla is, above all else, devoted to our family. Ask her to go against my father's wishes and I'd lose her. Loyalty is the one thing we both understand. "Can you save Reichis?"

She didn't look surprised. "And if I do? If I risk myself for your disgusting pet, will you think better of me, Kellen? When we see each other, will you tell me you love me for who I am, and not always in spite of it?"

"I..." I probably should've lied, but I couldn't. Not when she was letting me in like this. "I hope so. I want to, Shalla. I swear I do."

She gave me a small, fragile smile. "I guess that will have to be enough for now, brother." She took in a long, slow breath. "The squirrel cat is still in the Golden Passage. I was able to keep him alive awhile, but the spell fades too quickly."

"There must be some—"

"That's why I met you like this, Kellen." She glanced around, reflexively, as though she worried someone were listening. "I promised Father I'd get information from you about this Ebony Abbey, but I also summoned you because I think there's a way we can heal the squirrel cat's wounds and give him the strength to get himself out of the desert."

"How?"

She gently prised my hands apart and went to one of her columns. Again she passed her fingertips along its surface and the marble dissolved, to reveal yet more shelves filled with jars and boxes. When she came back she was holding a single gleaming blue grain of sand. She gestured and spoke a word. The grain bobbed in the air between us. "Do you remember the saret'kaveth?"

"The floating compass spell? That's barely more than a cantrip."

"All breath spells are weak, Kellen—you should know that better than anyone." The old Shalla was back. "Saret'kaveth lets you float an object along the winds. That's why I need you: send me something that Reichis has touched. Then I can use that connection to send enough healing magic to save him."

"Shalla, saret'kaveth sends a pebble on the breeze. I can't make it fly an object halfway around the world."

"Of course not," she said, clearly irritated even by the possibility that I could accomplish something on that scale—something she herself couldn't do. "But what if it wasn't made from normal matter? And what if it wasn't moving across natural space?"

"You mean like a thought? Isn't that what we're doing now?"

She shook her head. "No, a thought can't hold a binding. I'm talking about something else. Something only you can do." She reached up and touched a finger to the markings around my left eye. Even in the dream world I flinched.

"You want me to slip into shadow?"

She nodded. "Like you did before. Distance doesn't seem to mean the same thing there as it does in the normal world, and shadow matter doesn't have any inherent physical weight. But it *does* carry spiritual resonance. So if you were to touch an object there—even a grain of that bizarre black sand—to something Reichis has touched..."

"Then I might be able to float it to you through the spell you've created between us."

The esoteric geometries behind what she proposed were insanely complicated. I couldn't begin to calculate how it all...But that didn't matter. Shadow never seemed to obey the usual rules of magic. It operated more on instinct than on a mage's focused will.

"I don't even know if I can force myself into shadow," I said. "Most times it was just a fluke that I was able to—"

Shalla rolled her eyes. "Oh, for goodness sake, brother. Think of where you are. How hard can it be to enter shadow when you're already in a place with so much of it around?"

She had a point. "Okay. Okay. Let's try this. How do we start?"

Shalla walked over to the door and held it open for me. "Just walk through there and you'll wake up. Try not to forget that this wasn't a dream."

That hardly seemed an issue at this point. I headed towards the doorway, but stopped for a moment to look back at her. "Thank you, sister. This means...This means everything to me."

A weary sadness came to her gaze. "Oh, Kellen. Sometimes I wonder how you survive out there, so utterly alone."

23

The Compass

I opened my eyes in darkness, no idea how long had passed since Diadera had brought me to the guest room. I was still exhausted though, and found myself drifting back into sleep, wondering if I'd have more of those odd dreams about...

Crap. Shalla was right. I nearly forgot it was real.

I forced myself out of the bed, despite my desperate desire for its comforts. The floor was cold, which helped keep me awake, aided by the fact that I was barefoot. More precisely, I was naked.

I had no recollection of taking off my clothes. So either I'd done it in my sleep, or Diadera had...

Focus, idiot. Save being embarrassed for later.

I closed my eyes and breathed deeply, attuning my senses to the black markings around my left eye. Most of the time I ignore the chill they give me, but now I embraced it.

All right, you useless, foul thing. You've made my life hell more times than I can count. Now it's time for a little payba—

Something was wrong. I'd expected the usual strain of the shadowblack awakening, followed by the burning agony it sent through the markings. But though I felt none of that, I knew something had changed.

114

I opened my eyes. The room was gone.

"Wow," I said aloud, though my words had that distant, echoing quality they always had in this strange place. My feet no longer felt the stone of the floor. Instead I stood upon a carpet of tiny onyx shards. What I'd thought of as darkness in the room before hadn't been, not really, as there had still been a little light from out the window. Here, though, the world was painted in a thousand different shades of black. It shouldn't have been possible to see, yet I saw with more clarity than I ever did in my own world. Not wanting to press my luck, I set to work.

The saret'kaveth is made up of the same five components as any other Jan'Tep spell: envisioning the specific esoteric geometry, forming the somatic shape, uttering the invocation, summoning power through the appropriate band and sending it into the anchor. Shalla had said I needed to send her something touched by Reichis, which was going to be a problem.

The little monster had all kinds of baubles and precious items he'd stolen from one poor sap or another in our travels. Often the sap in question was me. But I didn't have his little bag of treasures. Even if I did, I couldn't bring it into shadow with me. Then I realised that I did have a number of things that the squirrel cat had touched: the scars from all his bites.

I knelt down and picked up a tiny shard of onyx from the ground. I bore the marks of a few different bites on me, but the most recent was on the back of my right hand. One night, in my sleep, I'd accidentally touched Reichis's fur. He assumed I was trying to pet him and delivered his response with all his customary affection for "skin-bags who think squirrel cats make good pets."

I pushed the onyx shard into the scar. It hurt, but in an odd, almost emotional, way rather than physically. I took this as a good sign. When I held up the shard, its particular shade of black had changed, glistening somehow. I might've just been imagining it, but what else was I supposed to do?

Most breath magic takes two hands, so I tossed the shard into the air. As it came down, I formed the somatic shapes. They're actually kind of tricky: middle and ring fingers pressed together in the sign of binding, thumbs pointed down for grounding, and index and little fingers fluttering like the wings of a bird. It's that last part that's really hard. Try it. You'll see.

"*Saret'kaveth,*" I intoned, pouring all my will into the word, struggling to hold both the esoteric geometry of the spell and Shalla's essence in my mind. I heard a scream along the wind as the tiny shard sliced through the air, flying with more speed and force than I'd ever seen with the floating compass spell before.

I had no idea if this would work—if my little shard would somehow pass through shadow to find my sister, or if the bond from a squirrel cat's bite would be enough for Shalla to reach him with her healing spells. But it might, and that gave me something I'd been sorely lacking for a while now: hope.

Reichis, for all his thieving and scheming, for all the bites and insults he'd inflicted upon me, was the best friend I'd ever had. I'd felt helpless since the moment we'd been sep- arated. Everything I'd done so far had failed, only taking me further away from him. There was nothing more to try, no one else to fight, nothing left to sacrifice. If anyone could help him now, it was Shalla.

I hope this works, Reichis. I hope I get to see you again, if not in this world, then in whichever hell you and me are both bound to wind up in one day.

Fatigue overtook me then, far more than such a simple cantrip should cause. I fell backwards, slipping out of shadow. My body hit the mattress, which was nice, and my head hit the wall behind it, which was not. I wormed my way under the coverings and leaned back on the small pillow to sleep.

Traps, I remembered, hauling myself out of bed. *Can't go back to sleep without setting the traps.*

Before I could take my first step, four twisting bands of shadow wrapped themselves around my wrists and ankles. I was being lassoed like an errant calf found crossing onto the wrong herder's land. The next thing I knew, I was being lifted up into the air several feet above the bed. "Using Jan'Tep breath spells to report to your people?" a voice in the darkness asked. "Should've known you for a spy the moment I laid eyes on you."

Before I could argue, a fifth ribbon slipped over my head. *Not a ribbon*, I realised too late, clawing at the shadows helplessly. *It's a noose.*

Three rules every outlaw needs to live by: don't trust any place that doesn't charge you rent, don't go to bed before setting your traps, and never, ever forget about the guy you pushed over a cliff. I would've apologised for that last one, but the shadows around my neck had begun to tighten.

24

The Interrogation

My hand slapped at my right thigh, searching in vain for my leather case of steel throwing cards and finding only my own skin, because of course the fourth rule of being an outlaw is: never go to bed naked. Now, in addition to having none of my weapons, I also had to wonder if maybe Diadera had set me up.

"Looking for these?" Tournam asked, stepping into the dim light shed by the window at the back of the room. He wore his long leather coat, the sleeves cut off to show the taut muscles of his shoulders and reminding me I was outmatched physically as well as magically. Also sartorially, since I wasn't wearing any clothes. My trousers dangled into view, held aloft by a shadowblack ribbon. The leather case sewn onto one leg was tantalisingly close yet impossible for me to reach with my hands bound. "No fancy throwing cards now," Tournam said, that insufferable Berabesq accent of his vibrating along the shadowblack noose wrapped around my neck. Another tendril appeared, this one waving my belt with the pouches on either side. "No magic powders either." A third tendril quivered, setting off a clinking sound. "I even found the little coins sewn into your shirt."

My odds had just gone from dicey to downright lousy. As unpleasant as it is to be ambushed by a smug, self-righteous arsehole convinced of his own innate superiority, it's much more perilous to be taken captive my an enemy who respects you enough to keep track of your weapons. I opened my mouth wide, visibly struggling to breathe.

"Something you want to confess, spy?" Tournam asked.

His fingers twitched, and the noose loosened enough for me to gasp in a tiny mouthful of air. Tournam watched me, no doubt expecting me to either beg for mercy or taunt him with insults. I did consider bringing up the fact that as it was Butelios I'd pushed off a cliff, not him, why was he the one coming after me? But I had better things to do with my breath.

I parted my lips, allowing the air to trickle out as I silently whispered my need, sending each desperate plea like a paper boat floating down a river until my lungs were empty.

Okay, Suzy, I thought. *You're up.*

I felt a cold chill in my right eye, but the soft shrieking sound that usually signalled her emergence had barely begun before it faded away again.

Tournam leaned closer, straining to hear what I'd said. "Is that whisper magic?" he asked. "Because I read up on that cloud in your eye. The abbey has an extensive library of occult works. According to the most authoritative book I could find on the subject, manifesting on our physical plane the way your wind spirit did yesterday comes at a terrible cost. It often takes them days or even weeks to recover." He reached a finger and tapped the ridge just above my right eye. "No sasutzei to save you today, cloud boy."

I guess that explained why I wasn't getting the usual chill on my eye that accompanied her awakening. I started shivering, and not from the cold air. Being helpless does that to you.

No. Maybe you can't move or fight, but that's different from being helpless. Whenever Ferius got into trouble, her first gambit was to talk her way out of it. *Arta loquit*. Eloquence. Talk to a person in their own language and you can build bridges to understanding and peace.

"You're a child," I wheezed, then added, "and a coward." I finished by spitting in his face.

To the untrained observer, it might seem as if I hadn't quite mastered my lessons in arta loquit. However, the purpose of eloquence isn't to make friends with your opponent; it's to speak to them in a way they truly understand—to use words and ideas that reach deep inside them. Now, inwardly, the Berabesq culture is considered rich and vibrant, full of traditions and contradictions, devout faith and philosophical questioning. I'd never really gotten to know that part of their people though, because the face their religious leaders show to the rest of the world is zealous, dogmatic and arrogant as all hell. *That* was the language I'd chosen to speak.

The Berabesq view the passage into adulthood even more seriously than the Jan'Tep. When I'd called Tournam a child, I'd implied he'd failed to make that sacred transition. Next I'd impugned his courage. Bravery is considered by the Berabesq to be the fundamental distinction between themselves and foreigners, so naming him a coward was akin to saying he wasn't Berabesq at all. Finally, Tournam's people live surrounded by desert and pride themselves on being able to survive without water for days at a time whenever they go on their holy pilgrimages. To spit at a Berabesq is to imply that they need the water more than you do.

See? Arta loquit. No problem.

The bands around my limbs tightened, squeezing so hard I feared the small bones in my wrists and ankles would shatter. "What did you say to me, Jan'Tep?" Tournam hissed. He gestured at the floor, and his shadowblack bands forced me to my knees. "Look at you," he said, towering over me. "Feeble. Helpless. No real shadowblack abilities of your own—just a few tricks easily evaded by taking away your toys. You're a spy, Kellen, and that means I can do anything I want to you." He knelt down until his lips were practically touching the lobe of my ear. "Let me hear you say it."

For a guy who wanted me to speak, he wasn't making it easy. The noose around my neck was making it harder and harder to get any air into my lungs, and my heart was beating so rapidly that I was convinced I had only seconds before I'd pass out. That's why I didn't waste what little breath I had left on trying to deny I was a spy. Instead I forced out a single word: "Duel."

I've never seen someone's eyes go that wide so quickly.

Yeah, I thought. *That got you, didn't it?*

I'd accused him of being a coward and a child. Now I was offering him the chance to prove me wrong, which is always more satisfying than beating up a helpless victim. Unless he turned out to be a lunatic who got off on murder, at which point I was in serious trouble.

Tournam stepped back a few feet. His shadows lifted me up until I was floating a foot off the ground. "You really think you could take me, Jan'Tep?"

I nodded.

He snapped his fingers. All of a sudden the ribbons let go and I fell gasping to the floor. I ignored the jolt to my knees in favour of rubbing desperately at my wrists to get the feeling back into them.

"Oh, this is going to be fun," Tournam said.

No, it's not, you moron. You're an arrogant, privileged arsehole. I'm a gods-damned outlaw spellslinger who's faced guys a lot tougher than you. I'm going to beat you silly.

When I was reasonably sure I wouldn't fall down, I rose to my feet and reached out for my trousers and powder belt, only to have

Tournam's ribbons yank them away. "That's not how shadowcasters duel, Kellen." He gave me as close to a friendly smile as that smug mouth of his was capable of producing. "This is the Ebony Abbey. The rules are a little different here."

Okay, so this might be a problem after all.

25

The Duel

"Everyone at the abbey's been wondering what your shadowblack abilities are," Tournam said. "Diadera says she thinks you're an enigmatist." Another pair of black ribbons unwound from his arms to sway in the air between us. "So come on, mystery boy. Show me what you've got."

Hearing that Diadera had talked to him about me put a sour taste in my mouth. I set that aside though, because regardless of what she thought, I was no more an enigmatist—whatever that was—than I was a lord magus. "Give me back my cards, Tournam. Make it a fair fight and I'll—"

"Fair?" Tournam practically spat the word. "Are you sure you didn't just paint those markings around your eye? No one cursed with the shadowblack still thinks the world is fair."

One of his ribbons cracked like a whip at my cheek. I'd seen it coming, but my limbs were still so numb from having been constricted that I couldn't risk any of Ferius's fancy evasion techniques. Instead I threw myself out of the way. The room was narrow, and I misjudged how hard to push with my legs. I ended up slamming against the wall like a bird flying into a closed window.

"So much for those Argosi martial arts I've heard so much about,"

Tournam said. He sounded almost disappointed. "Use your mark-ings, Kellen. Fight me like a proper shadowblack."

"I can't!" I yelled back at him. That proved a mistake. He'd been goading me, and now took advantage of my lack of focus to lash out at me with a second ribbon. This time I moved too slowly, and my cheek stung as if I'd been struck with a leather belt. Tournam was toying with me.

"*This* is who I risked my life to carry back from that barren desert? A simpering boy who can't even conjure an ounce of shadow?" Two of his shadowblack tendrils reared up, then sliced down in opposing diagonal cuts to my face. I got my arms up in time to block them, but the pain was worse than being flogged. Tournam's attacks were becoming rapidly more violent. I couldn't take much more of this.

"Fight back!" he demanded.

I spun around in an old Daroman dancing turn that Ferius had taught me to use as a whirling kick. My foot stopped an inch from Tournam's face, caught by one of his ribbons. Before I could recover, it wrapped around my leg and hurled me backwards with enough force that I knew I'd either wind up knocked unconscious against the stone wall or break my neck. I arched my back the way you do in a Gitabrian tango dip, transferring my momentum into a back-flip. Oh, how I wished I'd spent more time practising those damned tangos with Ferius. By some miracle I managed to turn in the air and get my feet back under me. Before I could attack again though, I saw that I'd landed right inside the loop of one of Tournam's shadow-black ribbons. When he twisted his right hand, the lasso tightened and my legs were jammed together.

"No more games," he said. "Show that you can cast shadows, Kel-len. Prove to me that you belong here."

I couldn't cast shadows of course, or do any of the other things these people did. The markings around my left eye only ever brought me pain and misery. *Damn you, Seren'tia. Why did you do this to me? How could you band your own grandson in shadow?*

The bitterness and anger hit me even worse than the pain of Tournam's lashing black ribbons. "I never asked to come to this damned abbey!" I shouted at him. "I just want to leave and find my friend!"

My outrage only seemed to spur his indignation. "Shadowblacks don't have friends. We only have each other. You're either one of us or you're one of them." His voice went quiet, calm. *No, not calm. Cold.* "If you're one of them, Kellen, if you're an agent of the Jan'Tep, I'll kill you."

"I'm not a spy!"

"Prove it." He flicked a hand and one of his ribbons wrapped itself around my forehead, forcing it back. A second one began probing the winding black lines around my left eye, poking at them like a surgeon's knife preparing to make an incision. "Awaken your shadowblack," Tournam said. "Use the markings to save your life before it's too late."

The tip of his ribbon pushed against the skin above my eye like a needle. I could feel the flesh about to part from the pressure. "Stop!" I screamed. "My shadowblack doesn't work like yours! It doesn't do anything except make my life hell!" I struggled to pull away, but more and more of Tournam's ribbons were wrapping themselves around my body, entombing me like a mummified corpse.

"I know you're a spy," he murmured. Something about the way he repeated it over and over was odd, as if he weren't so much trying to get me to confess as to convince himself.

Ancestors, damn me for a fool. I'd completely misread this situation. Underneath Tournam's bravado, he was afraid. Panicked. The idea that there was a Jan'Tep spy in the abbey terrified him. But he wasn't a murderer. So he'd tried to goad me—to push me until

I put him in a situation where he'd have no choice but to kill me in self-defence. Even though I'd failed to present a genuine threat, he'd come too far now to stop. Tournam was working up the nerve to finish me off.

A terrible resolve rose up inside me, and I prepared myself for what I would have to do next.

I'm sorry, Ferius, I thought.

As much as I'd tried to study her gentler ways, I'd learned just as much about fighting from Reichis. Squirrel cats, for all their big talk, are small animals. Fragile. Like me. The only reason they survive against larger predators is because they've adapted to seek out the perfect moment to strike, and when it comes, they do so without mercy. The Way of Thunder, the Argosi call it. That was the path I was going to have to walk now.

I watched Tournam's eyes, thinking through what I would need to say next, what final trick would get him to lose his grip on me. When that moment came, there'd be no more of Ferius's clever movements. No more dancing. I would press my fingers together to form a striking surface and then I'd drive it straight into the ball of Tournam's throat.

"There!" he said, pointing at me as if I'd just uttered a confession. "I can see it in your eyes! That same look you had when you pushed Butelios over a cliff." He came closer. "When you tried to kill him."

Well, he sort of had a point there, and I doubted I could convince him otherwise. In a second it wouldn't matter though, because he'd become so focused on my face that the band around my right wrist was almost loose enough for me to work my hand free. I choked down the feeling of guilt crawling up my belly. This is the Way of Thunder, I told myself. This is how it has to be.

"Kellen only pushed me over that cliff because he knew you'd use your shadowblack to save me," a deeper voice said, surprising us both. The slow plod of sandals against the stone floor preceded Butelios pushing open the door to the room.

Light from the hallway trailed him into the room, the faint morning sun from windows on the other side reflecting orange off those parts of the big man's shaved head that weren't covered in black markings. He offered us both a hint of a smile. "I may have forgotten to thank him for that."

"Thank me later," Tournam said. "I'm about to save your life a second time, and the lives of everyone else at the abbey."

Butelios put a hand on his shoulder. "No, I don't think you will."

"How do you plan to stop me? Drown me in those shadowblack tears of yours? Get out of here, you oversized child. You've never been a fighter."

Before he could respond, before I could bring my now-freed hand back in preparation for driving it into Tournam's throat the instant he turned back to me, a new voice broke the silence.

"But I am." It was Diadera.

She stepped inside the room and my heart jumped from one too many shocks for any sane person to endure. Just a minute ago I'd thought Tournam was going to kill me, then I'd committed to murdering him first, then Butelios had tried to calm things down only that hadn't looked like it would work. Now Diadera had entered the picture.

An unexpected sensation came over me. Not relief or lust, but mortification. I glanced down. *Yep. Still naked.* Tournam's ribbons hadn't even had the decency to cover up the important parts.

"Did you boys throw a party and forget to invite me?" Diadera asked without a trace of awkwardness. Her gaze travelled all the way from my feet to the top of my head via all points in between. "Why, Tournam," she said lightly, "I never knew you were into bondage games. Think of the fun we've missed."

Tournam's cheeks went red, either from outrage or humiliation. "Get out of here, Diadera. You were supposed to kill him, not bed him."

"I changed my mind," she said, though now she refused to meet my gaze.

Great. The one person I thought might not hate me had been planning on killing me.

For his part, Tournam now seemed angrier with her than with me. "Then I guess it's a damned good thing I'm leader of the shadowcasters and not you."

Diadera batted her eyelashes innocently up at him. "You mean because you're the biggest, baddest, toughest shadowblack of us all?"

"Damned right."

She sauntered over to stand between us before spinning to face him. "The thing is, Tournam dear—and I don't mean to brag now—but I can be big and bad too. So maybe it's time I took over the shadowcasters."

Tournam's whole body was shaking with barely contained frustration and humiliation. Diadera had pushed him too far, misjudging him as badly as I had. "You think you can best me, girl?"

"Oh, definitely." Suddenly she grinned and tossed her red curls back. "But then I'd have to bruise that beautiful face of yours, and we couldn't have that, could we?" Without warning she stretched up on her toes and kissed him full on the lips. Without giving him time to react, she came back down and walked right past him, stopping at the door to give us all a wink. "Playtime's ended now, boys. We're due in the training square."

I fully expected Tournam to use her departure as an opportunity to renew his attacks on me. Instead he just stared after her, fingers brushing his lips where hers had been. How long he stood there, how long he left me waiting to see if this was still going to end in one of us dying, I couldn't say, but the next thing I knew, his ribbons released me, and without so much as a stern look back he followed Diadera out of the room.

I steadied myself against the wall, taking long, deep breaths as I tried to slow my heart rate. I couldn't decide if I should be jealous, or relieved, or whose gender I should be the most disappointed in. "You people are insane," I murmured.

Butelios offered me my clothes and a deep-throated chuckle. "Don't look at me, friend. Attraction to the opposite sex has always struck me as a little perverse. You should get dressed. Brother Dyem is training us today and his lessons can be somewhat...distressing at first."

"Distressing?" My hands shook as I struggled to get my trousers on. "What's distressing is that I'm a thousand miles from my homeland, trapped inside a madhouse where the inmates can't decide between murdering strangers or seducing them."

The big man shrugged. "Most of us are young, Kellen." His index finger traced the pattern on his face that ended in three black teardrops. "If the shadowblack does not kill me before I am twenty, then surely those who hate me for having it will. The others here will likely suffer the same fate. Is it any wonder our impulses tend to be...pronounced?" I was still buttoning up my shirt when he threw an arm around my shoulder and led me out of the room. "Welcome to the Ebony Abbey, Kellen of the Jan'Tep. A place of respite from a world that despises us. Here's hoping you survive the experience."

26

People and Places

Diadera was at the end of the hall, engaged in deep conversation with Tournam, their voices too quiet for me to hear. When she saw Butelios and me approaching, those pale green eyes of hers followed my every step without ever meeting my gaze. Had she set me up last night, using her shadowblack to put me to sleep, knowing full well Tournam was waiting to ambush me? Or had she genuinely not known? Come to think of it, given Tournam's earlier threats, I really shouldn't have needed any warning.

At times like these it's impossible not to imagine Shalla giving me one of those disapproving sighs of hers. *You're too trusting, brother. You always have been. So desperate for love and acceptance that you gift your enemies with the means to get the better of you.*

"You'll be happy to hear that Tournam has agreed to desist in his attempts to execute you as a spy," Diadera said brightly. "Until he finds some... Now what was that word we were using a moment ago, Tournam?" She prodded him in the chest before answering her own question. "Oh, that's right. *Evidence.*"

He tried and failed to meet her challenging stare. "Have it your way. Cloud boy's your responsibility now." He turned on his heel and set off down the stairs.

Diadera gave an exasperated sigh before following him. "Believe it or not, Tournam really does grow on you after a while."

"So does gangrene," I muttered to myself. "That's why its better to cut it off sooner rather than later."

Butelios chuckled behind me. "'So does gangrene.' Good one." He gave me a gentle nudge towards the stairs. "I can sense already that we're all going to be great friends, Kellen of the Jan'Tep."

Somehow I doubted that.

Round and round the four of us went, descending the winding tower stairs in silence. Diadera's steps were quick and assured, almost playful, reminding me that this place that loomed so dark and ominous to me meant something completely different to her. Safety. Sanctuary. Home.

Had Ferius been there she might've opined—in that frontier drawl of hers—*You can learn a lot about a person's relationship to a place by watching the way their body moves inside it.* She'd never said those exact words, but they certainly *sounded* like the kind of thing she'd say. Maybe I was now stumbling across new Argosi insights all by myself.

Tournam reached the wide double doors at the base of the tower first, pushing them open to reveal the early morning sun reflecting off a narrow black path that led back to the main courtyard.

"Is this some kind of volcanic glass?" I asked, noting a similar quality to the abbey's towers and other buildings.

"Sounds about right," he replied, clearly never having given the question any thought.

He led us along a covered cloister, his heavy stride a sharp contrast to Diadera's light-hearted steps. Unlike her, he walked not so much with a sense of confidence, but rather importance. Ownership.

He never paused or stepped aside for the people we passed along the way—monks walking silently with their hands joined beneath the long sleeves of their robes, craftspeople and labourers, children trudging after their parents. Tournam surveyed them all with a benevolent half-smile and the gaze of a prince who saw himself ruling these people one day, rather than merely living among them.

Butelios caught my gaze. "Argosi?" he asked.

It took me a second to understand what he meant. "Not really. Just spent a lot of time around one. Why do you ask?"

"I met an Argosi wanderer once. She surveyed the world around her much the way you do."

"What was her name?"

He replied with a kind of amused reverence. "The Path of Skyward Oaks. A great big woman she was, almost as big as I am now. Strangest person I ever met."

"How so?" I prompted, figuring I may as well learn whatever I could about him in case he, like everyone else here, decided at some point to try to kill me.

"You must understand, Kellen, my city lies in the far northern reaches beyond Darome, a place too cold in winter for foreigners to travel. Yet this woman laughed at the frozen winds assailing our lands. Called them her truest friends." He shook his head wistfully. "The skills that woman displayed! I begged her to allow me to become her student, her *tey*...*tey*... You know, I can't remember the word now."

"*Teysan*," I replied, mindful that pretending not to remember something is a good way to probe someone else for what they know. "And did she agree?"

"She politely informed me that the way of the Argosi isn't about tricks, which was all she saw in my desire to emulate her."

Those words struck a chord. How many times had Ferius made

that same accusation of me—that all I wanted were the Argosi abilities rather than the commitment to follow a path? And yet, she'd let me stay with her and kept teaching me anyway. Until that moment I hadn't fully realised how precious a gift I'd given up when I'd left her.

"You're fooling yourself," Tournam said, not bothering to look back at us. "The Argosi are spies and infiltrators. She was probably there to kill you for being shadowblack, only once she caught sight of those black baby tears on your cheek she decided you weren't a danger to anyone."

Butelios gave a soft chuckle, more to himself than anyone else. Yet his chin was low to his chest, and it seemed to me he was closing in on himself a little. I couldn't quite make sense of his reaction. The big man looked like he could've picked up Tournam with one hand and chucked him over the abbey's walls if he wanted. Instead he suffered the jibes without ever pushing back. "You think everyone is a spy," I said to Tournam. "Have you considered that you might just be paranoid?"

Diadera laughed, a light, tinkling melody, like when the arbiter of a game taps their bell to ascribe a point to one side. Tournam didn't seem happy with the referee's decision. He gestured ahead, through an archway that led into the main courtyard. "Tell me again how paranoid I am?"

The demon's corpse was gone, but the bodies of dead monks still littered the ground, their blood being cleaned away by their brethren while others stood by, whispering or chanting prayers of one sort or another. Ordinary men, women and children—relatives, I presumed—performed various rituals upon the deceased. Some anointed pale dead flesh with oils or used coloured paints to adorn it with words and symbols of various religions. The bodies of others were placed upon mounds of wood and then covered in kindling

133

in preparation for a funeral pyre. *They're all from different places*, I realised. *Different cultures, different religions, different burial practices.* The only thing these victims had in common was that they were all dead.

From the opposite side of the courtyard, a child came running, soon followed by a man and a woman shouting after him. It was only when I noticed his limping gait that I recognised him as the boy I'd set down in the sewer yesterday.

Guess I really did sprain the poor kid's ankle.

"You're Kellen," he said in a strong Gitabrian accent I hadn't noticed before. "The Argosi!"

I shook my head. "I'm no Argosi, just a—"

"You fought the demon for me. I saw you." He started gesturing wildly with his hands in what I guessed was a child's approxima‑ tion of me throwing cards. After a few seconds of that, he pranced around in what I feared was an extremely accurate portrayal of my *arta eres*—the Argosi fighting ways. Finally he stopped, out of breath. "You outsmarted the monster." He tapped a finger on his forehead. "Like a contraptioneer, but with fighting!"

The couple, who I assumed were the boy's parents, caught up to us. "Forgive him," the woman said. "He wanted to make sure you had these." She handed me the four steel cards I'd left in the court‑ yard the day before.

"Thank you," I said, relieved to have them back, and silently scolding myself for having left them there in the first place.

The mother smiled. "He talks of nothing but 'The Argosi! The Argosi!' ever since you saved him."

"Well, I had plenty of help," I said graciously. "For example, Tournam here…" I let the words drift off. "What was it exactly you accomplished yesterday, oh wise and powerful shadowcaster?" I probably shouldn't have been goading someone who less than an hour before had nearly killed me, but hey, I don't get a lot of chances for revenge.

"You got lucky yesterday," Tournam said. "How do you suppose you'll fare the next time, when that little cloud in your eye is too tired to fight your battles for you."

"Every Argosi knows a thousand tricks," the boy told him with rather greater authority than the situation warranted. "Next time he will use a different one."

"Get the child out of here," Tournam said, ignoring the kid entirely to glare at his parents. They shied away, pulling their son with them, but the boy broke free and ran back to me, grabbing at my leg, trying to pull me down to his level. I knelt and looked him in the eye.

"My friend Joggo says the posse is coming for us," he said quietly. "But I said, if they came, Kellen Argos would beat them all."

If I'd known all it took to become a hero was to let some kid pee on you through the grate above a sewer, I'd've...Actually, no, I'd still rather be a disgraced outlaw than be urinated on. "Tell Joggo the abbot will look after you. That's his job, isn't it?"

The boy grabbed me around the shoulders. I thought he was hugging me, but he whispered in my ear. "No. Only the Argosi can protect us."

Before I could ask what he meant, the boy's parents had caught him again. His father hauled him up into his arms and took him away, murmuring the shy, apologetic noises one makes at a time like this. I wanted to stop him, to ask why the boy—who'd no doubt seen what the abbot could do—would think I would have more luck staving off an army of mages than someone with that much power.

"Hey, hero," Diadera said, pulling at my arm. "If you're done preening for your adoring audience?"

"I wasn't preening," I said. Despite her urging that we move on,

135

I couldn't stop myself from gazing back at proceedings in the court-yard, perversely entranced by the carnage left behind. What must it be like for a child to witness such violence? No wonder he was desperate for someone new to pin his hopes on.

"Don't," Diadera warned. "You'll make it worse."

"Make what worse?"

She tapped one of the shadowblack freckles on her cheek. "The things on the other side, the ones like the stygian, they can sense the work of their kind. It excites them. Don't you feel it?"

It might have been my imagination, but I could've sworn the markings around my left eye were prickling me. My pulse was defi-nitely quickening.

The sound of a wooden cart rolling past us caught me by sur-prise. It carried the body of one of the monks. The fellow pulling it whispered some sort of mantra or prayer. Was it for the soul of the dead, or for his own? The sight was oddly compelling. Captivating. I couldn't tear my eyes away.

A sharp slap knocked me back a step, shaking me from my reverie.

"You hit me!" I accused Diadera.

"You were feeding your demon," she replied, without a trace of apology. "A physical shock is one of the most reliable ways of break-ing contact."

I jerked a thumb to the monk pushing the corpse cart. "What about the guys dealing with the bodies?"

"They are trained in a discipline we have not mastered," Bute-lios explained. "It enables them to be close to the destruction left behind by the stygian without channelling any emotional energy to their own demons."

Diadera led us to a second covered walkway, outside the main courtyard and beyond the abbey's main hive of towers. "The training is why we're all here, Kellen: to give us the means to control the shadowblack so that it can't be used to hurt others."

"What about the ones you don't find until it's too late? Or maybe don't want to be recruited into this 'training' you and the abbot keep talking about?" I asked, noticing for the first time how the long leather coats that Diadera, Butelios and Tournam wore gave them the appearance of soldiers rather than monks.

It was Tournam who answered. "We take care of our own." His eyes locked on mine, and his expression made it clear that no matter what Diadera said, he still considered me a threat. "When a shadowblack becomes a danger to this abbey or to the world outside, we hunt them down and kill them."

27

Training and Tribulation

I'd always understood monasteries to be secluded religious communes where reverent brothers and sisters sat around praying, chanting or otherwise wasting a great deal of time. The only appeal I could envision in such aesthetic pursuits was the possibility of living in quiet—and, above all, peaceful—solitude. That impression changed the moment Diadera left me alone at the edge of abbey's training grounds, where four onyx spires connected by gleaming black walls demarcated an area large enough to hold a Daroman jousting tournament.

"Gonna kill you good this time, boy!" a pale-skinned girl with strangely braided hair and blackened lips shouted at her prey. She couldn't have been more than thirteen years old, far too young to be chasing Tournam, who grinned as he spun to face her. A half-dozen shadowblack ribbons lashed out, striking at her like serpents.

Far from being afraid, the girl opened her mouth wide, revealing white teeth that gleamed like stars against the endless night of her throat. Smoke erupted from her mouth, a wafting black vapour that seemed to vibrate in the air as it encompassed Tournam's snake-like ribbons. He laughed at first, but when he tried to retract his tendrils, he found them caught inside the black fog. "Beg for mercy, boy, and maybe I let you keep one of them arms."

There were others in the training square practising with their own shadowblack, their abilities as varied as their colouring and clothing. It seemed exiles from every corner of the world found themselves at the abbey.

There were regular folk too—those not cursed with the markings. They fenced with regular weapons, from battered steel swords and iron-shod staves to crossbows and even a pair of twelve-foot-high trebuchets that required three people working in concert. Many of them were older men and women in their sunset years. Most of the rest were just kids of ten or twelve. I even saw a few younger ones playing with wooden practice swords and shouting bizarre challenges at each other. The abbey struck me as a terrible place to raise kids, though at least these ones had the sense not to face off against Tournam.

The Berabesq's brow was furrowed in concentration. His ribbons whipped and tugged, but only became more ensnared in the girl's shadowblack cloud as it became more and more solid. "That's enough, Ghilla," he said. "Release me before I grow cross with you."

"'Cross'?" she mocked. "Oh, spirits in the earth and spirits in the sky, whatever shall I do? The boy is threatening to be 'cross' with me!"

She should've taken the threat more seriously, because Tournam had been wise enough not to use all his ribbons in his first attack. While she laughed at his apparent torment, another black tendril unwound itself from his arms and slithered across the ground unnoticed, making its way underneath her feet. But it was the look in his eyes that made me worry for her. "Watch out!" I shouted at her.

Look, I'm not stupid. I know interfering in the fights of others is a sure-fire way to make enemies. I just hadn't expected the pair of them to gang up on me.

"What you think you doin', interferin' in our game, boy? You think you some kind of hero?" the girl demanded. She paused what I felt sure would be a lengthy tirade to suck the shadowblack vapours back into her mouth.

Tournam, now freed from Ghilla's cloud, decided to be chivalrous for a change and save her the trouble of berating me further. "Don't be silly, Ghilla. Kellen here just wants his turn in the ring." He sent two of his ribbons weaving through the air to wrap themselves around my wrists. They tightened until I could feel a prickly, numbing sensation in my fingertips.

"Making friends already, I see," a deep voice said from behind me. Abruptly Tournam's ribbons released me. I turned to find the abbot standing behind me, arms folded across his broad chest as he took a wide stance. "Since everyone's feeling frisky, who wants to go a few rounds with the old man?"

Tournam and Ghilla managed to disappear faster than a sightbinder who'd just sparked his silk band. The abbot looked mildly disappointed in all of us, but me most of all. "You really have a remarkable talent for pissing people off, don't you?"

I shrugged. "It just takes practice. I'm sure even you could learn if you tried hard enough."

I'm not sure why antagonising the abbot came so effortlessly to me. Maybe it was all that intelligence, strength and self- assurance exuding off him like a bad smell. He gestured to a small, squat building at the far end of the training grounds. "How about you come with me and we'll see if we can find you a more practical skill?"

The structure wasn't much bigger than a cottage of the kind you might find in any village, but its outer stone walls were curved like a miniature tower and its roof was a dome made from dozens of individual panes of black glass.

"What's in there?" I asked. I've learned to be suspicious of any place that looks like it could serve as a particularly secure prison cell or possibly a ritualistic torture chamber.

"We call it the cauldron," he said. The name didn't strike me as being even remotely reassuring. The abbot gave me a shove in the direction of the iron-gated front door. "Time to see what you're made of, kid."

28

Revelation and Regret

"Try to relax," the abbot said.

This is precisely the sort of thing people tell you right before they do something that, despite the old adage, hurts you much more than it does them.

He'd had me sit on a stiff wooden chair behind an apparatus made up of a dozen brass-fitted glass discs of various sizes and thicknesses, each one suspended on its own metal arm. These the abbot moved about in different configurations as he peered through the lenses at the shadowblack markings of my left eye.

"Stay still now," he warned. He repeated that every few minutes when he paused to make sketches in a little notebook that he'd return to the pocket of his robes before readjusting the lenses on the apparatus.

With nothing else to do but await either the diagnosis or— more likely—some form of intolerable agony, I watched the abbot at work. He was a strange man to look at; shadowblack markings covered more of his body than anyone I'd ever met. Not only that, his markings seemed...deeper, somehow, almost etched into his flesh. And yet, his markings also had a kind of flow to them. A balance. Maybe I was getting used to the sight of people who shared my disease, but still, he wasn't nearly as disgusting to look at as I would've expected.

"Enjoying the view?" he asked.

His smirk reminded me of Diadera. So did the way he paraded his self-confidence to make me feel awkward. "Just trying to decide if you're ugly and slow because having so much shadowblack ruins one's features and intellect, or whether it all happened naturally."

He laughed at that, even as he continued adjusting and repositioning the many lenses of his apparatus. "You know, Kellen, eventually you're going to realise that I was on your side the whole time. One day you might even miss me."

I started to rise. "How about you let me go so we can test that theory?"

He pushed me back into the chair. "Quit wriggling around."

"What are you looking for anyway?"

He brought one of the lenses—a very thin one, barely the size of a small coin—right up to my cheek just below my eye, so close I could feel the coolness of the glass. "Have you ever looked really closely at the shadowblack?"

"Only every day."

"I don't mean stared at it blankly in the mirror while moping about how unfair life is."

"There's a different way to do it?"

"Funny. Think you'll ever find a way to use that wit to make people like you instead of wanting to punch you in the face?" He held up a hand. "No, don't answer that. Just listen for a change. To the untrained eye, the shadowblack looks like a sinister, unnatural discolouration of the skin. Almost like bruises or burns that have turned black from the necrotising flesh underneath."

"Can't imagine why anyone would mope about that."

"What matters is that we're so horrified by the sight of shadowblack that our minds don't allow us to truly see how much more is there."

"What do you see?" I asked.

He answered with an almost hushed reverence. "I see a fluid grace in the lines, Kellen. I see complex patterns in the markings. Words in each swirl. I see a language written in shadow."

"Language? What does it say?"

He smiled. "That, my friend, is what I've spent my life trying to figure out. Best I can guess, when we become infected with the shadowblack, the specific rules of whichever esoteric realm our markings are bound to compose a unique pattern of lines on our skin. Those markings define our particular connection to shadow."

"So that's what gives some people their abilities?"

"Near as I can tell, what looks to us like just a bunch of black scribbles is actually a kind of... Well, to a Jan'Tep like you, it might seem like a spell. To me, though, it's a kind of poetry."

Poems. Just what I needed.

"And what does mine say?" I nevertheless asked. I was sitting up straighter in my chair. For all that I didn't trust the abbot—or anyone else here—the possibility that my shadowblack might be something more than a curse was too compelling a proposition to resist.

"That's what's so strange," he replied. "What your grandmother did to you—it's not supposed to be possible. I've read every book and scroll ever written on the subject of the shadowblack—some of which cost me a small fortune to have translated. Over the centuries, mages and natural philosophers have tried everything to decode the way in which the markings operate. Some performed experiments attempting to intentionally imprint shadow onto another human being."

"Why?" I demanded, suddenly feeling the knot in my belly. "Why would anyone do that?"

He shrugged, unconcerned by either the question or my anger. "People sometimes do awful things in the name of discovery, Kellen. They want so badly to understand how the universe works that they'll commit any act, no matter how dark or soulless, to find answers to the questions that haunt them."

People like my own grandmother apparently.

Was it worth it, Seren'tia? I wondered. *Ruining my life, just to satisfy some arcane curiosity?*

"Strange," the abbot said, peering at me through one of his lenses.

"What is?" I asked.

He leaned back and reached for another of the metal arms and swung a mirror into place so I could see what had captured his attention. "Look at the three innermost circles of your markings. See how the lines intersect, closing on themselves like rings?"

I stared into the mirror, tracing the markings of my shadowblack with my gaze, but the more closely I followed the lines, the more I seemed to get lost, returning to where I'd started over and over again.

"You've got to focus," the abbot urged. "Our eyes aren't really meant to peer into shadow, so our minds get foggy when we try. Keep your attention on the line of the marking and don't let yourself become distracted."

It was harder than he made it sound. Harder than should have been possible, in fact. Eventually though—and at the cost of a sudden, massive headache that felt like a spike coming out of my eye—I saw what he was talking about. "They're not rings," I said. "I mean, they're shaped like rings, but the word feels wrong for what I'm seeing."

"Tell me," he said, his own eye appearing inhumanly large as he watched me through one of his lenses. "Don't look for the precise word so much as the metaphor."

But neither would come. It was as if my mind was resisting, fighting to keep me from describing what I was seeing. It was like trying to untie an incredibly complicated knot inside my own head... as if the shadowblack itself was a mind chain keeping me from uttering the words. Then it came to me—something Diadera had silently conveyed to me when she'd touched my markings in the abbot's tower, and that let me break through. "A lock," I said, gasping for breath. "The rings are like the rotating discs of a combination lock!"

The abbot pulled the mirror away and then the various glass lenses he'd positioned around me. "Yeah, kid. That's what I see too."

Something in the way he said it made me uneasy. "What's wrong?" I asked. "Diadera thought I might be... I think the word she used was *enigmatist*."

"A seer of hidden truths," the abbot said wistfully. "One who looks into shadow and witnesses the secrets locked in the hearts and minds of others. I've always hoped to meet an enigmatist one day. The gods know we could use one at the abbey." He looked at me with more sympathy than I could stand. "But it isn't secrets that you see, is it?"

What I saw, when the attacks came, were distorted nightmares. I saw the very worst in people. But even if I wasn't an enigmatist, one truth was becoming clear to me. My fingers reached up to touch the closed rings around my left eye. "It's because of how she banded me, isn't it?"

He looked uncomfortable, only replying when he saw I wouldn't let the matter go. "When your grandmother fashioned those closed rings around your eye, those locks, as you called them, she bound the shadowblack inside you. She made it so you wouldn't be able to draw on its abilities."

"Why?" I pleaded. "Why would she do this to me?"

I guess the look on my face must've been pathetic enough to

elicit the truth, because this time he didn't hesitate. "I think she found a way to use you as a source of power."

"Like an oasis," I said numbly. "My grandmother was turning me into her own personal oasis."

I sat on that hard, uncomfortable chair, surrounded by bits of metal and glass, being watched—*touched*—by this stranger. I recognised the look of pity in his expression as the same one I'd had for fellow initiates back among my people when they learned they were Sha'Tep and would never be mages. The sounds outside the building grew louder in my ears. Diadera. Tournam. Butelios. All of them training together, applauding each other's accomplishments, learning to use their shadowblack abilities to protect themselves and the people they cared about.

"I'm truly sorry, Kellen," the abbot said, making one last drawing in his notebook before moving his equipment out of the way. "I'll keep trying to find a way to unlock your bands, I promise." He sighed, and placed a hand on my shoulder. "I can't imagine why anyone would do this to their own kin."

Ever since the day the black markings had first appeared on my face, I'd been asking myself why my grandmother had banded me in shadow, what I could possibly have done to make her do this to me. But the answer was so obvious now, so eminently logical, that I wondered how I hadn't known it all along. Seren'tia had been my father's mother. A true and proper mage of the Jan'Tep people. I felt almost relieved when I said, "She used me because that's what family is for."

29

Introductions and Interventions

The second-to-last thing I needed to see right then was Diadera waiting for me outside the cauldron with a sly grin. "Have a fine time in there, did you?"

She was leaning against one of the thin black columns supporting the cloister, arms folded across her chest and one hip jutting in a way that even in my morbid state threatened to awaken a desire for something other than revenge against my family. Too bad I couldn't trust her any more than I could them. "What do you want, Diadera? Here to play another round of 'seduce or slay'?"

She brushed aside my rudeness without seeming to even notice it, much less be offended. "The abbot said, when the two of you were done, I should introduce you to the rest of the shadowcasters properly."

That was the absolute last thing I needed. "Maybe some other time."

"Have other plans, do you?" she asked, sauntering up to me.

"Nothing much," I admitted. "Breaking out of this hole, climbing down a mountain, stealing a ship—learning how to sail, of course—and then making my way home."

She tapped a finger on my chest. "Sounds like a lot of work, and something that can as easily be started *after* I fulfil my sacred duty to make polite introductions." She gestured behind her to the training grounds. "Besides, everyone's dying to meet the deadly Argosi wanderer who kills—well, *threatens* to kill—just about everyone who dares look cross-eyed at him."

"I'm not an Argosi," I said reflexively, but my attention was taken up with the five people standing in the centre of the grounds waiting for me. Butelios I already knew of course, along with Tournam and the girl he'd called Ghilla. There were two others as well. A skinny boy who was younger, maybe thirteen or so, and a tall girl closer to my age. "Why are you all teenagers?"

Diadera shrugged. "That's when the shadowblack first appears for most of us. These first few years we can learn to control it without having to devote ourselves body and soul to suppressing it the way most of the monks do. The discipline that requires is...severe." She touched a finger to my bottom lip. "All the more reason to fool around while you can, Kellen."

Despite knowing this was a tactic with her, my mouth went dry and I could feel my cheeks flush.

Ancestors. What flaw in my breeding makes obvious ploys like this work so well on me?

For her part, Diadera wore a painted-on expression of wide-eyed innocence, waiting for my response. Anything I tried to say would come out in a childlike stammer. My voice would probably break—as it generally does in these situations—and she would then chuckle at my naive awkwardness. Only I was tired of people messing with my head.

I may be no more an Argosi than Butelios, but I've studied a little of the four ways and even more of the seven talents. In particular, Ferius made sure I learned how to—as she called it—"be handsome." Rather than say anything, I straightened my back, imagining a wall behind me and aligning my head, shoulders and butt to it, then made myself relax in that pose.

Stupid, I know, but it works.

Ferius also taught me how to smile, which she referred to as "listening with your eyes." I looked at Diadera, not trying to stare her down or outfox her, but simply listening to what her eyes told me. You don't force the smile itself—that comes naturally. Ferius claimed this was because you're finding the beauty in another person, and witnessing true beauty always leads to the best smiles.

Hogwash of course.

"Wow," Diadera said.

I tilted my head, but didn't speak. The first part of arta loquit is quiet. Let the other person be the notes in the music. You play the silences.

I think Diadera realised she'd been staring at me too long, because she reached up and pinched my cheek between her thumb and forefinger. "You have an interesting face, you know that? For a Jan'Tep, I mean."

I ignored the jibe, partly because I knew it for what it was—an attempt to reassert control by getting a rise out of me—but also because it invited the question that had been poking at the back of my mind since I'd first met her. "I know Tournam is Berabesq, and Butelios is a northerner, but you still haven't let on where you're from."

She slipped into her performance so smoothly it was like watching an actress step out onto the stage. "Can't you tell a proper Daroman court girl when you meet one?" She gave me a graceful, almost florid curtsy, the movements nimble and fluid. Rehearsed. When she'd touched my shadowblack markings up in the tower, she'd shared details about herself and her life with me, but this one thing she'd kept secret.

You're no more Daroman than I am, Diadera. So why are you lying?

"No more stalling," she said, taking my hand and leading me towards the waiting crowd. "Time for you to make friends."

Yeah. That was not going to happen.

I've never been comfortable in groups. When you're a Jan'Tep initiate, the rules are simple: the more talented you are at magic, the more allies you have. In my clan, everyone knew who was who and what they could do. Now I was facing strangers who looked entirely too comfortable around each other, and altogether too suspicious of me. The last time I'd been in a situation like this had been at the Academy of the Seven Sands. There I'd used Ferius's tricks to ingratiate me with Seneira's classmates. At the time it had seemed a challenge as complex to navigate as the most esoteric spells and rituals. By comparison, this was much, much worse.

"Ready for a proper duel then, cloud boy?" Tournam asked. Evidently the abbot's earlier intervention had only meant a temporary reprieve.

This guy's never going to stop, I realised then. *He's just going to keep finding excuses to go after me until one of us gets hurt.* If Reichis were here, he'd've chittered about how there's no shame in getting beat up, just so long as the other guy gets it worse. Squirrel cat wisdom was starting to grow on me.

"Stop right there," Diadera said, her tone making it clear she had a grand plan for all of this. "Now, we're all going to play a little game I call 'nobody kills anybody else.' Anyone need me to explain the rules?"

The tall girl I hadn't yet met came closer. "Why does Tournam call you 'cloud boy'?" Auburn hair hung down to her jaw, framing high cheekbones and a heart-shaped face. Her chin was soft but the line of her mouth was sharp. So were the shadowblack markings that traced the ridges of her eyes like a harlequin's mask. Even without seeing her tattooed bands beneath the sleeves of the long leather coat she wore, I could tell she was Jan'Tep. My people have a certain stand-offish quality that's hard to disguise.

"That's Suta'rei," Diadera said quietly to me. "Just because she's one of your people, doesn't mean she'll take kindly to you, so be polite."

It's not like any of the other Jan'Tep I'd encountered recently had been friendly. Nonetheless, I accepted the advice and gave a straight answer for once. Tapping my right cheek just below the eye, I said, "He means the sasutzei I carry around with me. It's a type of wind spirit."

The younger girl, Ghilla, came at me fast as a rattlesnake. "You talkin' 'bout whisper magic, boy? Who taught you that?"

Her accent and sing-song manner of speaking were reminiscent of Mamma Whispers. So was the fact that she kept calling me "boy," even though she was at least three years younger than me. Remembering my visit to the swamps outside Teleidos, I put a finger to my lips. "Shh. The spirits, they like to keep their secrets."

"You mockin' my tongue, boy?" she asked, blackened lips pursed.

"Probably best you not antagonise Ghilla either," Diadera murmured. "Actually, if you could see your way to not annoying any of them, that would be best."

See? This is the problem with groups. How was I supposed to know whether following Diadera's advice would make my life easier, or if showing weakness would in fact make me a target? I didn't like the look of these people. Underneath the stylish coats and posed self-confidence, there was a feral quality to the way they stood there. The air around them practically thrummed with barely contained animosity.

"I be mockin' your tongue," I said to Ghilla, "but only cos I don't know you so well. Maybe later I'll find other things to laugh at."

The girl took in a long, deep breath, and I could already see the wisps of smoke coming from the edges of her lips. Evidently Diadera really *was* going to have to explain the rules to "nobody kills anybody else." "You lookin' to play with me, boy?" Ghilla asked.

"Watch out," Tournam said, jostling her out of the way. "That spirit in his eye did some nasty business to the stygian." His smile was more a sneer than anything else. "Guess that's your real ability, eh? Wait for your little sasutzei girlfriend to come and fight for you?"

Another snide remark. Another attempt to get a rise out of me. I fully recognised that I was putting myself at needless risk by taking his bait, but I couldn't seem to make myself care any more. Still, I wouldn't give him the satisfaction of attacking first.

From the moment I'd met him, I'd recognised both his colouring and accent as Berabesq. Now, though, I recalled that "Tournam" was one of the twelve names given to the sons of high clerics. That, along with his jibe about women—a sentiment not shared outside their religious orthodoxy—told me a lot about him.

"You trying to stare me down, Jan'Tep?" he asked.

His ribbons started to come for me, but Diadera got between us. "Step back, Tournam."

He did as she bade him, using the opportunity to grin back at the others. "Look, he's using his special power already!"

There were some chuckles and snorts. Ghilla scowled at him. So did the younger boy I hadn't met yet. None of them said anything though.

Tournam turned back to me. "Well? Is that how it works? Your mouth gets you into trouble; then you wait for a girl to protect you?"

"Almost always," I replied. The others chuckled—more at him than at me. I should've left it there, but I was piecing together a few details about him in my mind and I've always been too much of a smart-ass to keep my mouth shut. "They must've loved you back home, Tournam," I nodded at the markings around his arms. "Tell me, when they chased you from the temples, was it your dad leading the pack or did the whole family get involved?"

Diadera flashed me an angry glare. "Are you trying to make this difficult?"

I was, in fact. I should've been scared, and I guess I was, at some level. But some deeper part of me *wanted* Tournam to attack me. It didn't take long for him to oblige me either. Before Diadera could react, three of his ribbons lashed out, knocking her aside and wrapping around my arms and my neck.

"You should let me go," I said, not even trying to sound calm, some perverse part of me delighting in the thought that this was going to end with blood spilled. *His* blood.

"And why would I want to release you, spy?"

"Because I'm very weak. You should never pick on the weak, Tournam. When a weak man fights back, he knows there can be only two outcomes." I didn't even bother to resist the tug of his ribbons on my arms as Tournam yanked me closer. "Now, see, if I were a proper Jan'Tep mage, I might use any number of spells to shatter your little shadows."

"If you had any real magic, you'd've—"

"—shown it before, I know. You're absolutely right. I can barely manage a little breath magic here and there. So no ember spells to blast your ribbons apart, no silk magic to addle your mind into releasing me. I can't use shadows like you do either. Hell—" I gave a gentle tug against his ribbons—"I'm not even strong enough to keep you from dragging me around the length and breadth of this training yard to put on a show for your friends."

He smiled. "It's good that we see eye to eye on some things then."

I shook my head. "No, you idiot. There's a difference between being weak and being helpless, and I already have plenty of enemies,

Tournam. Walk away now, or I'll be more than happy to rid myself of one permanently."

I was pretty much out of powders and had no clue how I'd beat him, but I didn't care. I'd taken on deadlier opponents than this smug bastard. My steel cards were in the leather case sewn to my trouser leg, and I still had my castradazi coins. If that didn't work, I'd just grab him and rip his throat out with my—

"Leave him be," Butelios said, pushing us apart.

"You should back away, big man," Tournam warned him. "Do what you do best. Give the new boy a hug and cry about all his pain."

"Don't be a blind fool, Tournam!" he said, more firmly than I'd heard him speak before. "Kellen's going to kill you. He doesn't even understand why, but he'll do it just the same. He can't stop himself."

All of the others stared at me, even Diadera, a sudden tension in their expressions as though I was transforming into a demon before their eyes.

"It's not the shadowblack," Butelios said. He came and stood so close to me that I had to tilt my head back to lock eyes with him.

"You should step back," I warned. "Or Tournam will be right and you *will* be crying."

The strangest thing happened then. Butelios *did* cry. Black, oily tears dripped down his cheeks. I'd seen him do this before, but this time he reminded me of Cressia back in Gitabria, when she'd been suffering the attacks of the obsidian worm in her eye. This was different of course. Butelios wasn't under the control of some faraway mage. Something else was guiding his actions.

Diadera put a hand on his arm. "What are you seeing, Butelios? What are the shadows showing you?"

"It's Reichis," he said.

Just the fact that he had the gall to say that name after he and Tournam had dragged me here against my will, forcing me to abandon my business partner, was enough to make me reach for my steel cards. Before I could, Butelios grabbed my shoulders. He wasn't squeezing, but even if I hadn't still been trapped in Tournam's ribbons, I couldn't have freed myself. "Your friend's shadow is upon you. I think you...you feel his bond slipping away, don't you?"

The truth of those words hit me harder than any physical blow. The air left my lungs and all I could do was nod my assent.

"That's why you're so angry now, Kellen. The further Reichis's soul is from you, the more you take on his spirit. This isn't who you are."

"Stop talking as if you know anything about me," I said, straining against Tournam's ribbons now. Butelios was right. Something was very wrong with me. I was...bloodthirsty. I wanted to fight something. No. *Kill* something.

The big man suddenly doubled over, his forehead smashing into my chin and knocking me back.

For an instant I thought he'd attacked me. Tournam's ribbons had loosened their grip, so my right hand reached for my throwing cards. Only then did I notice Butelios grunting in pain.

"Forgive me," he said, looking up and offering a wan smile as the oily black tears floated from his cheeks and drifted outwards, forming a line like tiny signal fires that went far away from the abbey, past the mountaintop and into the clouds in the distance.

"Looks like we have business to take care of," Tournam said. Abruptly all his ribbons let go of me. He gestured to the younger boy who'd scowled at him earlier. "Come on, Azir. Let's get a move on."

The boy knelt down and removed his boots and socks. His feet were covered in the shadowblack. He stood back up and closed his eyes, forehead furrowing as he stamped his heel on the ground.

What looked at first to be flakes of charred skin slid from the tops of his feet. The pieces grew, thickened, even as they arranged themselves like an elaborate puzzle, becoming a road of pure onyx that traced the path of Butelios's tears before fading a dozen yards away into a dark fog.

"We'll have to leave the rest of the introductions for later," Diadera said to me, the lopsided smile almost, but not quite, hiding the slight tremor in her voice.

"What's happening? Where are you going?" I asked.

The smile faded, as if it took too much energy to keep up the pretence. "This is what we do, Kellen—what we're trained for. Butelios can sense when a shadowblack loses themselves to their demon. Azir builds a bridge. The rest of us go and…deal with it."

I stared at the black road heading off into empty air. "Wait, you mean he can—"

"How do you think we got you here, all the way from the other continent?" Tournam asked.

Ancestors, but I was a fool. I'd been so exhausted and disoriented when I got to the abbey, hit with one horrible revelation after another, that it never even occurred to me to wonder how they'd gotten me to this mountain in the first place. The boy, Azir, had the ability to move through shadow. Not the idiotic, pointless wanderings I'd made, but actual travel across vast distances.

"Look," Tournam said with a chuckle. "He's finally figured it out."

Despite his casual tone, I could hear the edge to his voice. The tension in all of them was almost palpable. Butelios had recovered from the initial attack, but the pain in his expression had turned to sadness. Suta'rei, the Jan'Tep girl, appeared lost in thought, but I recognised that, too, as a tell-tale sign of anxiousness among my people. In each of their faces I saw concern over what they were about to do, Tournam even more than the others.

That was my opening—the weakness in the bars of the cage that kept me locked away in this foreign land. Before Diadera could stop me, I reached out and patted Tournam's cheek, the way you might a child being sent off to school. "Have fun playing heroes. Try not to piss yourself."

I really think he would've killed me then, but Diadera grabbed his arm. "We've got a mission, remember?"

His gaze locked on me. "It's easy to talk tough when you're here, safe and sound behind these walls. You wouldn't last ten seconds against the threats we face to keep those walls from coming down."

I shrugged. "Oh, I don't know. I'm willing to bet I've gotten out of worse scrapes with nothing more than half a deck of cards and— unlike some people—a little more than half a brain."

His shadowblack ribbons reached for me. "Maybe I should bring you along and see how well you fare against the enemy."

"No!" Diadera said. "The abbot would never allow it!" She glanced back at me. "Kellen, whatever the hell is wrong with you, get it under control before it gets you killed!"

As it happened, for practically the first time since I'd come to this place, I was perfectly in control of myself. Now it was my turn to laugh. "I thought Tournam here was supposed to be leader of your precious shadowcasters. So who does he take orders from? The abbot, or you?"

Tournam shrugged off Diadera's hand and turned to Butelios. "What can you tell me about our quarry?"

"He's tough," the big man replied. "As bad as we've ever faced. The shadows tell me he's a mage of considerable power in his own right, and now his demon has overcome his sanity."

"There, see?" Tournam said, smiling at the others. "Maybe what our little troop has *really* been missing all this time is someone who talks their way out of trouble instead of fighting." He turned back to me. "Let's see what you're good for, cloud boy."

He gave a signal and Azir took off at a run along the black path, seemingly unperturbed that he was heading straight off the edge of the cliff. He kept going though, continuing until he vanished into the black fog. Ghilla went after him, then Butelios, Suta'rei and finally Tournam.

Diadera looked at me, and for once there was none of her usual flippancy or flirtation in those pale green eyes. "Stay close to me. Stay on the road, and when we get to the other side, for everyone's sakes, stay out of our way."

I nodded, showing just enough trepidation to make it convincing. She needn't have worried. I had no intention of being in the way. In fact, I had no intention of being there at all. I let Diadera lead me up to the edge of the black road.

Hang on just a little while longer, Reichis. I'm coming.

Grieve not the dead. The dead trade the weakness of flesh for spirit boundless and eternal.

Weep not for lost love. When we weep too long, the light of their memory becomes dimmed by sorrow.

Laugh. Love. Rejoice. Only then can their spirits shine so bright that, even in the darkest night, they can never be lost to us.

—*Completely useless folk saying*

30

The Path of Onyx

"Have you passed through shadow before?" Diadera asked gently.

My first step onto the onyx road hadn't filled me with confidence. Though it felt solid enough beneath the heels of my boots, my eyes told me a different story: instead of strong, dependable stone, up close the two-foot-wide path appeared as if cobbled together from panes of broken black glass. Hundreds of misshapen fragments, cleverly arranged to create a track that floated a few inches above the ground. Roughly two yards ahead, the fractured road continued past the edge of the cliff, heading off into thin air, where it eventually disappeared into an ebony fog through which the others had already passed.

"Kellen?" Diadera was staring at me now. She looked about as confident in my courage as I felt about the reliability of the black road.

"I'm fine. Just... give me a second."

I took another step on Azir's onyx path, then a third and a fourth. I was now standing over empty space, which would have been less disconcerting had the ground thousands of feet below not been visible through the glass-like panes of shadow. They swayed a little in the breeze, making the whole thing feel less like a road than a precariously assembled rope bridge.

"Almost there," Diadera said, prodding me. "Just walk into the fog now."

Just walk into the fog.

Staring into shadow—somebody else's shadow, no less—is a chilling experience. My first few times entering that hazy netherworld on my own had left me confused and traumatised. The longer I'd spent there, the more even my closest friends seemed to forget me. Lately it had become easier and easier to slip into shadow, and the landscape there was becoming more and more real to me, begging the question, would I one day enter only to find myself unable to leave?

And was today that day?

Diadera glanced into the fog. "I'm sorry, Kellen, but I've got to go help the others. It's okay if you want to stay behind. The rest of us have had a lot more practice at this. No one expects you to—"

"I said, I'm fine."

Reichis would've already been leaping up into the air, those furry flaps between his front and back legs catching the breeze so that he could glide into danger with a feral grin on his little face, all the while bragging about how even demons feared the deadly fangs of squirrel cats.

Or maybe he would've run off in the opposite direction, reckoning this was a fool's mission and there was no sense in us both dying. He'd be doing *something*, anyway, not just standing there frozen as a rabbit staring into a crocodile's maw.

"I'm fine," I lied, for the third time, before I took a deep breath and strode through the fog and into shadow once more.

The only thing more unsettling than having your entire world disappear is to have it replaced with a much stranger one. The late morning sun over the mountains to the east was gone. In its place a huge black disk hung in the sky, casting a thousand shades of darkness on the landscape below. The unnatural physics of this place meant we could see perfectly, which made the shifting terrain around us all the more unnerving.

"Cool, isn't it?" Diadera asked as she walked purposefully ahead of me.

With every step the bizarre scenery transformed, as though we were in a horse-drawn carriage looking out through the window at paintings hung so close together you could barely make out one before another took its place. One second we were striding through a shrouded valley, the next a forest thick with ebony trees stretched more than a hundred feet above us. Shimmering flakes of black snow drifted down beside us for a few moments, only to disappear as we found ourselves walking beside a roaring jet-black river. The only thing that remained constant was Azir's road, which cut straight as an arrow through the shadow lands like one of those famed Daroman Imperial highways of old.

"What happens if we step off the path?" I asked.

"Oh, you might wind up lost in a canyon somewhere in Gitabria," Diadera replied lightly, "or trapped inside ice caves in the frozen north. You could find yourself floating alone in the middle of the ocean, or tumbling head first into a live volcano." She spread her arms wide, untroubled by her own ominous warnings. "The geography here doesn't map to that of normal space. Azir's the only one of us who can navigate it to reach the destinations he wants."

"What's there to navigate? The road is perfectly straight."

"It only looks straight to us. Our minds can't deal with all the multidimensional geometry involved." She glanced back and gave me a grin. "Don't overthink it, Kellen. Enjoy the ride while it lasts."

"And Azir is the only one of you who can do this?"

"There's a little girl back at the abbey who shows promise, but the abbot says she isn't ready yet. We all suspect he can do it a little too.

Not even he can travel as far or bring as many people through safely as Azir can though."

The boy's miraculous ability filled me with bitter jealousy. My own journeys into shadow had twisted and turned drunkenly, leaving me more confused and paranoid the longer I remained inside. Think of all the places you could go if you could conjure roads like this one? Imagine travelling wherever you wanted to, leaving your enemies behind, having the entire world at your feet. My fingers reached up to trace the twisting black lines around my left eye. *And what did you curse me with, Grandmother? A set of ugly markings that offer nothing but headaches and bad dreams, all so you could use me as your personal oasis one day.*

"We'd better pick up the pace," Diadera said, breaking into a light jog.

"What's wrong?"

"Look behind you."

I did, and quickly sped up to match Diadera's pace. Behind us, the road's fragments of glassy onyx were beginning to fade, slowly breaking apart into a hissing black mist that evaporated into the empty space they left behind.

"The road only lasts a little while once Azir's left it," Diadera explained.

A few dozen yards ahead, a patch of fog much like the one we'd entered before awaited us. The closer we got, the more we heard the echoes coming out of it. Shouts. Screams.

Diadera's shadowblack freckles left her cheeks, swarming in the air above her. "Sounds like an even worse one than Butelios expected. We have to hurry now."

"An even worse *what?*" I asked, but by then she was already leaping into the fog.

I pulled up short at the edge of the cloud and drew a half-dozen steel throwing cards from the case sewn onto the right leg of my trousers, unsure of what kind of monstrosity awaited us on the other side, but quite certain I wasn't going to be happy to make its acquaintance.

Which was fine, because I had no intention of doing so.

Diadera and the rest of them thought I'd come along out of some perverse competition with Tournam, but one of the first lessons you learn as an outlaw is that being tough is nowhere near as useful as being alive. Now that I was back on my home continent, all I had to do was make a run for it; find the nearest town and figure out where I was, steal a horse and set off for the Golden Passage. It wasn't the most tactically ingenious plan I'd ever come up with, but it was all I had right now.

So why was I hesitating?

The screams and shouts from the fog were growing louder and I could just about make out murky shapes through the black haze. Two quick steps would take me through.

You don't owe these people anything, I reminded myself. *They're not your friends. They're strangers.*

I guess Butelios had been nice enough, considering I'd pushed him off a cliff. Maybe he was just more cunning than Tournam though, delaying his revenge until the perfect opportunity presented itself. As for Diadera? Well, yeah, there was a connection between us that tugged at me even now, but the second lesson you learn as an outlaw is that the more appealing a person is, the worse they usually turn out to be.

The world's a lot less complicated if you just remember how rotten it is.

I'd just about set aside my qualms and was about to step through the fog to make my escape when I heard Diadera shouting my name. "Kellen, turn back! It's a tra—"

Ah, crap.

31

The Fork in the Road

I backed away from the fog just in time, but the pieces of shadow upon which I stood had already begun to disintegrate under my heels. Spiderweb cracks appeared as the glassy surface hissed, warning me it would soon disappear into mist like the rest of Azir's road. Given Diadera's earlier warning about what might happen if I stepped off the road, whatever demon or mage or other monstrosity they were fighting must be pretty awful.

Okay, so what now?

On either side of the road I could make out two completely different environments. On the right a snow-covered forest, on the left a swampy marshland. Either looked pretty good right about now.

I couldn't hear Diadera's voice any more. In her place, someone else had taken to shouting my name, along with words like "bastard," "coward" and "I knew he was a spy!" I'm pretty sure that came from Tournam.

People say a lot of nasty things about outlaws. We're criminals. Con men. Duplicitous double-dealing two-faced thieves who can't be counted on for anything except betrayal. And okay, sure, that's all true, but there's something to be said for a little judicious treachery now and then. No doubt my failure to meet their fate alongside them would prove to everyone that Tournam had been right about me all along. Meanwhile, I wouldn't be dead.

So, really, win-win.

Another shimmer in the onyx, and I could feel the road splintering beneath me. I had maybe five seconds before it faded away completely. If I fell through, would I just keep falling through shadow forever, or would I crash into whichever hell is reserved for craven tricksters who abandon their comrades?

Four seconds...

This was stupid. I didn't even know these people, and what little I *did* know didn't exactly endear them to me. That bastard Tournam had been ready to kill me. How long would it be until he found an excuse to finish the job?

Three...

The marshland to the left of the road was looking real good now. I'm no expert on geography, but I could've sworn I'd seen something just like it in the eastern region of the Seven Sands. I had friends in the borderlands. Friends who might be willing to supply me with a horse and enough money and supplies to make my way south to the Golden Passage.

Two...

I jumped across to the last two panes of shadow. The sounds from the other side of the fog had grown quiet. Maybe Diadera and the others had won. Maybe they were dead.

One...

An eerie, inhuman voice cackled triumphantly through the fog.

Guess that settles who won the fight.

I was just about to leap into the marsh when an entirely different voice stopped me short. This one wasn't coming through the fog though. It was in my head, and all too familiar; that irritating, unrelenting frontier drawl that had a tendency to buzz through my skull at times like these. *"The path ain't just a destination, kid,"* Ferius was saying. *"The path is who you are and who you aim to be."*

Just as my feet left the onyx road, my body twisted awkwardly in mid-air, sending me not to the welcoming safety of the marshland, but through the fog to whatever awaited me beyond. It occurred to me in that moment that my Argosi mentor seemed to be intruding on my decisions a lot more now than she ever had when we'd travelled together.

Sometimes I hate you, Ferius.

32

The Mad Mage

They hung in the air, their wrists bound painfully aloft by twisting black vines. Diadera, Tournam, Butelios, Suta'rei, Azir and Ghilla swayed back and forth like cornstalks on a windy day, trussed up with shadowblack tethers thick as ropes and textured like spiked tree roots. Trickles of blood dribbled down the captives' arms where the thorns pressed into tender flesh.

The man—if you could call the jeering, screaming lunatic who danced around his prisoners while tearing strips from his own skin that—taunted them in giddy delight.

"Thought you could hunt down Tas'diem, eh?" he cooed melodiously. Fingers with blackened nails too long and sharp to be human dug into his own cheeks. A thick, ebony sludge seeped from the wounds, spreading over the contours of his face. "But Tas'diem is too fast for you, children! Too clever! Too powerful!" As if to emphasise his point, the tattooed metallic bands around his forearms began to spark and shimmer.

Figures this jerk would be Jan'Tep.

He hadn't noticed me yet, clearly too occupied with the very important work of announcing his infinite superiority while ripping himself apart. Diadera tried to get my attention with her eyes, signalling for me to get away. That was a very bad sign. Usually when people are in trouble, they expect you to try to help them, not flee. She mouthed a word to me: *rabbit*.

No, wait, that couldn't be right.

Cabbage?

She rolled her eyes at me and mouthed the word again. This time I got it: *abbot*.

Sure. All I had to do was flee this place—with no idea where I was since the only landmarks consisted of dried-out greenery that withered more and more each time the dancing madman gouged his own flesh—and somehow get back to the Ebony Abbey to find the abbot. That should take only about, oh, say, forever, since the kid who'd brought me here was hanging from his wrists and no doubt soon to die. Sometimes other people's plans are even worse than mine.

Not by much though.

"Hey, moron," I called out to the lunatic.

He turned. It took a moment for his wildly shifting eyes to locate me. Streaming tendrils of his shadowblack darted out at me, the ends splitting apart like the mouths of snakes, hissing an ebony mist into the air in front of me.

"Diadera, now!" I shouted. "The binding spell!"

The mage spun, his hands coming up to form a defensive somatic form. He muttered the incantation and the Jan'Tep bands around his forearms sparked briefly as he tried to summon the magics of iron and sand. But the glyphs didn't produce the grey and gold light that they should have. Instead the sparks turned black.

So when the shadowblack takes over, it blocks Jan'Tep bands from drawing on the other forms of magic. That might be useful information some day. If I survive today.

I sent a pair of steel cards spinning through the air at Tas'diem. One caught him in the chest, embedding itself for just a moment before falling to the ground. More of the black ichor seeped from the wound.

This must be how the demon takes over, I realised then. *The shadow-black turns the body's internal fluids into some kind of etheric essence that reshapes flesh and bone.*

My second card had struck him in the forehead, and that's when I noticed the three protrusions pushing through his sallow skin. He screamed in pain, yet continued—as under an irresistible compulsion—to tear at himself.

His tendrils came for me a second time and I dived forward, rolling under them and bashing my shoulder on the hard, knobby ground in the process. I wished I'd kept up with my dancing practice after I'd left Ferius. I came back up just a couple of feet from Tas'diem, jumped up and then kicked out with both legs. He went stumbling backwards, but soon regained his balance, shaking his head in disbelief. "You think you can defeat a lord magus with tumbler's tricks?"

Okay, so arta eres wasn't going to get me anywhere. Screw it. For all the Ferius's training, I'd never been much better with my fists than with magic. I'd always, however, been an outstanding liar.

I put my hands up, palms out in what any Jan'Tep mage would recognise as a gesture of submission. "I just needed to get your attention, My Lord Magus. Are you calm now, Tas'diem? I can't help you otherwise."

The mage looked at me as though I were the insane one. Diadera was giving me the same look. Actually so was everyone else.

"I have what you need right here," I continued. Very slowly I reached into the pouch at my right side, scraping the crevice in the leather with my fingernails. My ancestors must've been smiling down at me because a pinch worth of the black powder slid out from one of the folds. I held up a few grains to show Tas'diem.

"What is that? Why would I want it?" He spread his arms wide.

"I will soon be more powerful than any mage in the history of this world!"

"I know, my lord, but the pain...It must be beyond belief."

That right there was one of the foundations of my hastily constructed plan: the assumption that screaming and insane gesticulations were evidence that whatever was happening to Tas'diem was, at the very least, uncomfortable.

"You can blunt the torment?" he asked. "I thought it was impossible...My own spells have proven ineffect—"

"It's not your fault," I said. "The Black Blessing grants us a thousand wonders, but each comes with its price. That's why I'm here, to help you as you join—" I paused dramatically for a count of three— "the Order of Onyx."

Tas'diem stared back at me through narrowed eyes almost as full of suspicion as they were of black ichor. I was making up the stuff about onyx orders and the black blessings and, well, all of it. Here's the thing though: in all my travels I've never found anyone other than the abbot who knew much of anything about the shadowblack, so who's to say I wasn't right? Maybe there really *was* some kind of brotherhood of shadowblack demons. Either way, someone going mad from agony is going to be highly predisposed to believing there might be a remedy for their suffering. I say this as someone who's spent six months being suckered by every snake-oil salesman on the continent flogging cures for the shadowblack.

"Show me," Tas'diem commanded, his ebony tendrils swaying as they reached out to me.

I gave a small bow. "Of course, my lord."

Time to peddle my own miracle cure.

33

The Miracle Cure

The three protrusions on Tas'diem's forehead were beginning to push through his skin. A trickle of black ichor slithered its way down from the wounds, dripping into his eyes. He blinked furiously, anxiously holding my gaze with a hunger that only someone in agony who realises they haven't even begun to hit the limits of their pain can convey.

"Give me the cure," he groaned, punctuating his words with a sob. Tendrils of shadowblack erupted from his chest and arms, then split apart into even more threadlike appendages. They reached out for the grains of powder in my palm.

Here's the secret to a good grift: it's not about confidence like you might hear in the shouts of market hawkers trying to fleece their marks with curative ointments and virility potions. You don't even need the near-religious exuberance peddled by roadside preachers swearing that *their* stash of finger bones will bring salvation in the afterlife and increased virility in this one (don't ask me why, but virility is pretty much always part of the package). No, the real key to a successful flimflam job—as I'd learned over the many months of being swindled out of my hard-earned coins—is denial.

I closed my hand over the paltry pinch of black powder. "Forgive me, My Lord Magus. I see now that I was in error. The sacred dust is not for you."

Tas'diem's upper lip curled, showing his teeth like a dog about to bite, but his eyes betrayed his desperate longing. "You would refuse me?"

I nodded sadly. "It is too powerful, my lord. In your present weaken—" I cut myself off. A touch theatrical perhaps, but screw it. As Reichis generously said to me once, some skinbags are even more gullible than I am. "The transformation is especially difficult... for some."

The mage let out a howl of pain as the middle protuberance pushed further out from his skull. "Give it to me!" he screamed. The tendrils of his shadowblack wound around my wrist. They dragged me off my feet towards him. I kept my hand tightly closed. "Lord Magus, no! The sacred dust will kill you! The only way to survive is to... But no, it is too dangerous."

The shadows holding my wrist snapped upwards, yanking me into the air and holding me there by one arm. It hurt a lot more than I'd've expected. "Tell me!" the mage howled.

"The dust relies on the shadowblack itself to turn the torment into pleasure. You must draw the energies back into your body and *then* swallow the powder."

See how I threw the word "pleasure" in there? Why sell someone a fake cottage when you can offer them a make- believe mansion instead?

For all his pain, Tas'diem wasn't an idiot. His eyes narrowed. He glanced up at Diadera and the others, hanging in the air by the tendrils of his shadowblack. "You seek to trick me into freeing them?" He jabbed a thumb against his chest, the claw at the end piercing his robes and the skin beneath to wound himself further each time.

"I am the trickster here! I am the one who skilfully deceived the war coven!"

"Clever indeed, My Lo—I'm sorry, deceived the who now?"

He twirled around, enthralled by his own cleverness and, evidently, the presence of an audience. "That fool Ke'heops called me his finest hunter! All the while I hid deep within the very army of mages that crosses this continent executing lesser shadowblacks!" He proudly displayed his arms, the skin bloated from the black fluid underneath. "Each time I stay behind to drain the dead, taking their shadows from them as I ascend step by step to perfection!" He stopped whirling when he came back round to me. "But you think Tas'diem a fool, don't you? Luring me in with false promises to get me to free the black binders?"

How on earth had this nutjob tricked my father and the entire Jan'Tep war coven?

I shook my head vigorously. "No, my lord. I was sent from the Onyx Order to infiltrate the Ebony Abbey and uncover its location. Soon my brethren will be swarming their lair, destroying each and every one of them. We will make of their foul monastery a grand temple for ourselves." I gestured to the others. "I only came here because I feared these few, weak and dull-witted as they are, might catch you unawares. But now I see you are fine, so I should go back and—"

"I am not fine!" Tas'diem bellowed. The bones of his shoulders were starting to stick out, the jagged edges piercing his robes. "The pain, it is too much!"

Considering how badly my arm was hurting from just hanging in the air, I could almost sympathise.

Almost.

"I have an idea, my lord! What if you were to bring *most* of your shadow back into your body, and use only what you must to keep these enemies bound? If we are lucky, you'll have still have enough within you to endure the sacred dust."

The tendril attached to my wrist lowered me back to the ground. "And you say this will turn the pain into pleasure?"

"Most assuredly, my lord. I have seen it used by others, and I am told the feelings are wondrous." I glanced around. "Though it would be better if there were a tavern or village nearby."

"Why?"

"Because..." I did my best to look sheepish. "My brethren tell me that one of the effects of the sacred dust is a pronounced increase in...sexual desire and potency."

You would think that someone in agony being offered a release to their pain wouldn't care about such things, but, like I said, increased virility is pretty much a necessity in any miracle cure. Tas'diem grinned with fiendish excitement. The tendril holding me unwound itself from my wrist. "Yes. Yes! Give it to me!"

I reached into the pouch of black powder and took out every last speck that remained. "Here, my lord. Quickly. I see your time of change is almost upon you. Draw the energies back into yourself and place the dust on your tongue."

His brow—what was left of it that wasn't flaking off to reveal the horns on either side rising up to join the one at the centre of his forehead—furrowed with deep concentration. The rope-like shadows withered as they slithered back into his body. The tendrils holding Diadera and the others shrivelled and faded, though there was still enough there to hold them captive no matter how much they struggled against their bonds. Tournam, who I guess didn't have much faith in my abilities as a con artist, shook his head as if to say, "See? You failed, dummy."

Tas'diem approached me, his movements stiff and jerky, as if his muscles hadn't yet learned how to make sense of his changing bones. He started to reach for the powder in my hand. Then he stopped.

And smiled.

"You first," he said.

Remember what I said about denial? "No, my lord...I must not. The dust is sacred—not to be used until the appropriate time. You can see my own shadow markings are too small and weak. The dust would have no effect on me."

"Then you shouldn't be afraid to swallow some."

Having been caught in his unassailable logic, I gave a small bow. "As you command, my lord." I took about half the powder from my palm and placed it on my tongue.

Then I swallowed.

Everyone—I mean, *everyone*—was staring at me, waiting for me to fall dead or grow horns or something equally horrific.

Morons.

The only consequence of swallowing the black powder is a bad case of constipation. "You'll need to place the sacred dust on your tongue, my lord," I told Tas'diem as I held the rest of it out to him.

With remarkable restraint he'd held out against the pain a long time. Now that he saw the grains on my palm though, apparently safe and so close, he could resist no longer. He grabbed at my wrist and licked my palm clean. Disgusting.

"Good, my lord," I said soothingly. "Now, don't swallow. Keep the sacred dust there on your tongue as you utter the incantation—hold it as long as you can!"

He stared at me, confused.

I slapped my right hand against my forehead. "Forgive my stupidity, Lord Magus. The incantation is the first shadow syllable. Allow it to vibrate from your throat."

Again he looked at me blankly, no doubt wondering what the hell a "shadow syllable" was.

"It's 'ah,' my lord." I gestured with my right hand to beckon him to speak.

"Ah?" he said tentatively.

I nodded, waving my hand even more. "Open wide and say, 'Ah.'" Somewhat surprisingly, he did. "Aaaaahhhhh," he intoned.

"Just hold that a second longer, my lord." The reason I'd been using my right hand to gesticulate whenever possible was so that he wouldn't notice my left, that was now in my other pouch, scraping for every grain of red powder I could find. I tossed it all into the air, then, with both hands formed the somatic shapes: ring and little fingers pressed into my palms—the sign of restraint. Thumbs pointed to the sky, for whatever that was for, and middle and forefinger aimed straight at the crazy bastard's wide open mouth. "*Carath*," I said.

Normally I let the powders collide and then channel the explosion at my enemy, but I can guide anything light enough through the air—there just isn't much force behind it. Fortunately that didn't matter right now. Propelled by my spell, the red grains of powder flew right into Tas'diem's mouth, where they met up with the black powders. The push of breath magic sent the mixture deep down into his gullet.

The shadowblack mage stared at me in surprise and confusion, but only for a fraction of a second, because then the twin powders exploded and blew out his throat.

What remained of the shadowblack tendrils holding Diadera and the others were quickly pulled back into Tas'diem, no doubt trying to preserve what was left of the mage's body from being destroyed. His captives fell to the ground. The six shadowcasters quickly recovered their footing and came to stand next to me, staring in amazement down at the soundlessly screaming Tas'diem, who even now continued his transformation into the demonic form that had been waiting to emerge.

I looked over at them. "Any time now," I said.

Tournam stared at me. "Any time wha—Oh, right."

Despite my revulsion—and the not inconsiderable fear that Tas'diem might still kill me—I grinned. It was kind of nice to be the one who knew what the hell he was doing for a change.

The shadowcasters turned their remarkable abilities against the mage. Tournam's ribbons grabbed hold of his arms and legs, pulling them in opposite directions even as they lifted him up into the air as he'd done to them. Diadera's markings flew from her cheeks to swarm around the dying mage's head, tearing apart what remained of his face. The others joined in, their combined assault making resistance impossible. Only Butelios held back, either because his powers weren't suited to violence or because he knew it was no longer necessary. There was nothing left of the mighty Tas'diem but a mound of bones and broken flesh, all covered in a thick black oil. I wondered if I'd end up much the same way one day.

The others rubbed at numb limbs, huffing and puffing even as they leered down at the dead mage like a pack of wolves searching for any sign that some shred of life remained in their prey, waiting to be torn apart.

"I wonder what he was like," I said, feeling as if someone had to speak up for the poor wretch. "Maybe he wasn't such a bad person before this happened to him."

The shadowcasters—all of them, even Diadera—looked back at me as if they now wanted to kill me even more than Tas'diem. "*Maybe he wasn't such a bad person?*" Suta'rei repeated, the growl in her voice reminiscent of Reichis after a fresh kill. "Did you not hear him brag about what he did to those the war coven sent him to hunt?" Her eyes fluttered, the black markings of her lids like the wings of an angry butterfly. She looked past me at the muddy track of road behind us. Abruptly she strode over, grabbed my arm and starting hauling me down the road.

"What are you doing?" I asked, trying to pull away.

Whether because she was remarkably strong or simply out of her raw fury, she didn't let go. "Come, fool," she said. "I will show you what kind of man he was."

34

What Kind of Man

There were a dozen of them, waiting for us outside the small village, all of them bearing shadowblack markings on their faces or limbs. They stood unclothed, stiff as withered trees stripped of their bark. Dead eyes stared out from grey faces. Blackened tongues lolled from open mouths like dogs waiting on scraps of food. You might have mistaken these for signs of life, were it not for the smell.

"Why are they still standing?" I asked, though it came out as a strangled whisper.

Suta'rei strode over to the nearest victim. What must have once been a heavyset frame now looked...hollowed. She spoke quietly to herself, almost as if in prayer, which was impossible since she was Jan'Tep like me. When she was finished she gave the man a gentle push. He tipped backwards like a tree felled by an axe, his body perfectly rigid until it hit the ground and shattered into fragments that looked like shards of glass.

"Tell the boy how it works," Ghilla said. I hadn't realised until then that the others had followed, but they were all there, still as the dead, quiet witnesses to horrors I had yet to comprehend.

Suta'rei gestured to the victims. "You see the runes on their chests?" she asked in our language. It seemed an odd thing to do, since it meant the others likely wouldn't understand. Again my eyes went to her forearms to see which bands she'd sparked, but they were still covered by the sleeves of her coat. "Breath, blood and ember," she said, noting my gaze. "Not that it will matter much once the black takes me." She turned to look back in the direction we'd come, to where we'd left the remains of Tas'diem. "I'll become just like him one day."

Butelios came to stand beside her. "Keep faith. The monks of the abbey resist its influence. So will you."

Why would a northerner learn to speak Jan'Tep?

Suta'rei caught my eye. "He understands our language, but not our people. None of them do. They aren't like us."

Because of our shared heritage, I immediately knew what she meant, and the thought sent a shudder through me. For centuries our people had valued nothing so highly as magic. Even I—even after all this time in exile—still found myself at night dreaming of spells at night. Spells to protect myself. Spells to enact my will on the world. Spells to . . . just to feel the movement of magic inside me. We Jan'Tep were born addicts, our every impulse urging us to pursue power at any cost.

"Tas'diem was a lord magus," she said, not needing to add that you don't become one without an indomitable will, and yet he'd succumbed utterly to the shadowblack's seductive promise of power. If resisting the effects of the shadowblack meant overcoming those urges, then Suta'rei was right, and we were both screwed.

"You said something about runes?" I asked, desperate to leave that particularly awful thought behind.

She led me closer to the bodies, eleven of which still waited there. She pointed a slim finger at an elderly woman's chest. "Look, here."

Like the others, this one was naked. Averting my gaze at a time like this seemed futile, not to mention craven, so I examined her with as much dispassion as I could summon. There, beginning just below her collarbone, was a circular design etched into her flesh that went all the way down to just below her navel. It was hard to make out at first because it was simply more black on black, but the texture was smoother, less shrivelled, than her own flesh. Within the circumference were inscribed a dozen sigils, each one intricately etched with the same smooth black texture. "Why would he mark her with a spell circle?" I asked.

Suta'rei held my gaze. "Do they perform abnegation rituals in your clan?"

"No. Never." A chill came to my bones at the mere thought of it. My people—my clan at least—only practise what are called the tactical high magics. We consider elaborate rituals full of intricate chants and the imbibing of elixirs and such nonsense to be beneath us.

Suta'rei considered me for a moment. "Among my clan, we sometimes punish those guilty of capital crimes by imprinting abnegations on their flesh." She pointed to the dead woman's eyes. "See how empty they are? Not simply lacking in life, but devoid of will. The abnegation cripples the spirit, making the victim nothing more than a vessel for the whims of others. Soulbinding, we call it. Even Sha'Tep servants can command such a one to do anything they require. For Tas'diem, however, it served a different purpose."

The circular designs on the blackened flesh of the victims' torsos were easier for me to spot now. In fact, they fairly gleamed at me as a burning itch emanated from the markings around my left eye. *Soulbinding*, Suta'rei had called it. What had Tas'diem sought to accomplish with these abnegations? Was it simply to create a small army of slaves to watch over him? Wait, no, he'd said something about staying behind after the war coven so he could drain the dead...

"They were just vessels to him," I murmured. "So he could..." I couldn't finish the sentence. Saying the words out loud would have felt like giving the atrocity that had been committed here new life.

"The lord magus used the abnegation ritual to loosen the shadowblack from their spirits, drawing it into himself," Suta'rei finished for me. "To increase his power."

Was this what you'd planned for me, Grandmother? To wait until I was old enough and then use me as Tas'diem used these poor souls?

The itching in my eye went away as a darker realisation infected my thoughts: some clans were even worse than my own. Some mages more avaricious for power than my father. Some crimes worse than simply killing those who got in your way. "Maybe the war coven have it right. If this is what we can become? If we're capable of—"

"It's not their choice to make!" Tournam shouted. He started pushing the bodies down one after another. "If something must be done, then *we'll* do it. Not some Jan'Tep posse who do it for the greater glory of their would-be king!" The corpses shattered into fragments of desiccated flesh when they hit the ground, leaving behind glassy shards black as onyx.

Diadera came closer, eyes watching me. "What are you saying, Kellen? That we should stand by and let the war coven do its work? Should we let them hunt *us* down as well?"

"I don't know," I replied. "I don't know anything any more."

In my travels I'd grown accustomed—no, *comforted*—by the belief that I'd already seen the worst the world had to offer. But in the past few days I'd seen my first demon, and then a man who longed so much to become one that he'd commit the atrocities to which we now bore witness. In that light, it was hard to convince myself that I wouldn't find even worse things out there someday soon.

I missed Nephenia right then—missed the way she'd get that steel in her eye at times like these, determined neither to bend nor break in the face of people's infinite capacity for malice. I missed

Ferius and how she could stare down the darkness and laugh at everything hidden inside it. Most of all, I wished Reichis were here to bare his teeth and promise a thousand punishments he'd inflict on all the mages like Tas'diem, even if most of his schemes involved eating eyeballs.

"Are you all right?" Butelios asked, jostling me.

"I'm fine, what do you—"

He spoke quietly. "You were growling."

"I was just...It's nothing."

The big man leaned in closer. "Next time do it in private. Among us, such outbursts could easily be misinterpreted."

The others were staring at me, watching as though looking for signs I might... *They're wondering if the shadowblack is taking me—if I'm becoming like Tas'diem. If they might have to kill me.*

My world, it seemed, was becoming more precarious by the minute.

"We should leave this place," Suta'rei said, switching back from Jan'Tep to the more common Daroman that everyone else spoke.

Tournam took the boy, Azir, by the shoulder, pulling him from his incessant staring at the fallen dead with the hideous abnegation marks carved into their corpses. "Shake it off, runt, and shadow us up a way home."

Azir nodded and stamped his bare foot down hard on the ground. The black markings on his feet stretched out before him into the distance. He stepped forward and the others lined up behind him. I was about to follow when I felt a sudden chill in my right eye—the one inhabited by the sasutzei. I felt the wind pick up around me, swirling the leaves and bringing with it a sound so soft I thought at first I was imagining it. "What is it, Suzy?" I asked in a whisper.

Again the wind blew, and I heard the sound louder this time. *Weeping.*

"There's someone else here," I said.

Tournam looked back at me. "I doubt it. Your countryman won't have left anyone alive. They never do."

I ignored the jibe and took off at a run into the village.

"Hey!" he shouted. "Don't think we won't leave you here, cloud boy!"

"Kellen!" Diadera called out. "Where are you going?"

I followed the whimpers and sobs, spurred on by Suzy, who not only enabled me to hear them but lent the cries an urgency with her own blasts of freezing air in my eye. I heard the others following, Tournam demanding to know what I was doing.

I must've run through the entire village before I found the crowd of men, women and children huddled together—at least fifty of them. A few of them had the shadowblack marks, most didn't. But they all had one thing in common. Around each of their necks wound a single strand of gleaming copper wire, going from one to the other, linking them all together. A young boy was trying desperately to run away, held in check by a man who looked to be his father. The other adults were hissing furiously for the boy to stop. "You'll kill us all, you little fool!" a woman said in a thickly accented borderlands tongue, her own fingers grasping desperately at the strand of wire cutting into the skin of her neck.

"A blood noose," Suta'rei said, catching up to me.

I'd never seen one up close before, but I understood the principle. Spelled copper wire wrapped around each of their necks would choke them all if even one dared to move away from the centre of the spell. "Can you break the binding?" I asked. "You've sparked your blood band. If you—"

She shook her head. "It's more complicated than that. I'd need to have sparked iron too. Probably sand as well."

"You Jan'Tep," Tournam said, extending his arms out towards the mass of bodies. "Always looking to your feeble little spells instead of your faith."

The ribbons of shadow unwound from his arms and stretched out towards the crowd. "No!" Suta'rei shouted, knocking him aside.

He looked up with rage in his eyes, and his shadowblack ribbons reared at her. "Have you lost your mind?"

"If your bands touch the wire you'll trigger the constriction portion of the spell. You could've cut all their heads off, you idiot!"

"Then how are we supposed to remove it? We can't just leave them like this!"

Tournam was right. The air was chill, and it would grow colder as the sun went down. From the looks of them, the villagers had been out here a long while already. Tas'diem must have needed to perform the abnegation ritual on one person at a time, keeping the rest penned up together like livestock. That raised an important question. "How was Tas'diem freeing them when he wanted to take one?"

Suta'rei pointed to the centre of the crowd. "The ends of the copper wire meet in a knot that functions as a kind of lock. With iron and blood magic you can manipulate the lock to release one victim at a time."

I turned to face Tournam, who was rising to his feet. "Can you use your shadow ribbons to get into the centre of the crowd and untie the knot?"

He shook his head. "They're packed together too tight. I can't control something I can't see."

A soft caress of air on my right eyeball told me Suzy was trying to get my attention. "I know," I whispered back to her.

"What is it, boy?" Ghilla asked, watching me closely. "What's the spirit sayin'?"

My fingers went to the bottom of my shirt where my coins were sewn inside a folded hem. "I have an idea," I said.

Her eyes narrowed. "Is it a good one?"

The people crowded together stared at me, evidently wondering the same thing. What I intended to do would require a level of dexterity I'd never attempted before with the sotocastra coin. If I got it wrong, I'd end up killing each and every one of the captives.

Arta precis, I reminded myself. Persuasion. Ferius excelled at it, but I'd never shown much promise. "Don't worry," I told the villagers. "I've got this completely under control."

35

The Lock and the Key

In Gitabria, the coin dancers, or castradazi as they're called, are either beloved folk heroes or a reviled criminal underclass, depending on who you ask. In the old days, they could perform all manner of feats and tricks with their special coins. But where there were once twenty-one different *castragenzia* or "beautiful coins," now you'd be hard-pressed to find a coin dancer who possessed more than two or three.

I had five.

As gifts from strangers went, the coins were pretty great. The only problem was that I didn't know how most of them worked. Fortunately, one of them was a sotocastra—a warden's coin—and I'd had some experience with that one.

I felt around in the sewn fold of my shirt and retrieved the smallest coin. Silver and black, one side depicting a lock, the other a key. Its most intriguing property was the ability to manipulate locking mechanisms. You can kind of see why Gitabria's secret police weren't fond of this particular *castragenzé*. I flipped the coin in the air a few times, partly to get the feel for it again and partly to calm my nerves.

"What are you planning to do with that?" Tournam asked. His

tone of voice made it clear he had exactly zero confidence in my abilities.

Guys like Tournam always bring out the worst in me. "Break the dead mage's spell and save all these people from a horrible death. In other words, do what you clearly can't do."

He grabbed my shoulder, nearly sending the coin flying. Before I could even think of doing something about it, Butelios picked him up and gently moved him a couple of feet away. "Let him try."

Suta'rei came to stand next to me. "For an outcast, you don't go out of your way to make friends."

"I'm not opposed to it," I replied. "I'm just not very good at it lately."

She watched the way I flipped the coin in the air and how it sometimes would float for a fraction of a second before spinning on its axis and falling back down into my hand. Jan'Tep are particularly watchful for the subtleties of somatic gestures. "The coin responds to the force and direction of your throws, generating some kind of contrary motion from the—"

"Nah," I said. "That's all just Jan'Tep nonsense. The coin's just dancing is all."

Once I had a feel for the coin, I balanced it on the side of my index finger between the nail and the first knuckle. The way the warden's coin works is that you find the right position and axis to match the mechanism of the lock you're trying to open, almost like how a sympathy spell creates a bond between two different objects. Only with a spell, your mind and will define the connection, whereas with a sotocastra it's all done by feel.

Dancing, I reminded myself.

What made this particularly difficult was that there wasn't any actual lock. Instead, in the centre of the prisoners, the two ends of the copper wire that wound its way around all their necks came together into a knot. I needed to use the warden's coin to connect to that knot, and then carefully untie it without triggering the part of Tas'diem's spell that would slice off all their heads.

I felt the coin vibrate against my finger, threatening to fall off. I adjusted my hand to keep it in place. This was more than just a slight tilt here or there. I needed to kind of weave my hand in a sort of figure-of-eight pattern and then subtly adjust the position of my finger to get the coin to manipulate the ends of the copper wire. It was strange to not see something and yet be able to feel the precise way in which the wire was tied together.

"Intriguing," Butelios said, watching me. "I never thought I'd meet a true castradazi."

I'd never even heard of the castradazi until a few months ago, I thought, *so how come you're familiar with them?* I set that question aside to deal with my more pressing problems, starting with the fact that I *wasn't* really a coin dancer. I only knew a couple of tricks with this coin and one of the others. The rest was mostly experimentation and dumb luck—which was kind of the story of my life.

Among the Jan'Tep I'd never really been a proper mage. I hadn't learned enough of the Argosi ways to be like Ferius either. Despite the sasutzei spirit in my right eye, I understood only the rudiments of whisper magic. Hell, I barely had enough tricks to call myself a spellslinger, and now I was trying to be a coin dancer too? Was that what my whole life was going to be? An amateur at everything, master of nothing?

"You're losing it," Suta'rei warned.

She was right in more ways than one. *Breathe in emptiness*, I reminded myself. It was one of those stupid things Ferius would advise periodically that I had no idea what it meant. It made me laugh—a uniquely inappropriate time for that, given fifty people whose lives depended on me not screwing this up were watching me, desperately hoping I was a lot more competent than I looked. Strangely though, my ill-timed mirth gave me control over the warden's coin again, and thus the copper wire.

"By the Ancestors..." Suta'rei breathed, "I think the coin has taken hold of the lock."

Sweat was dripping down my forehead from the effort of keeping the coin so precariously balanced on my finger while I used it to manipulate the ends of the wire. I felt the last loop of the knot beginning to come undone just as Suta'rei figured out something I really should have thought of ahead of time.

"What about the recoil?" she asked.

Oh, hells. I'd completely forgotten about how the spell for a blood noose is structured. Creating the sympathy between the wire and the bodies is only part of the issue: the mage also needs to give it the intrinsic force to slice through its victims. So first the wire is imbued with iron magic to cause it to tighten when triggered. Once the knot was undone, the sympathetic connection would be removed, but the iron magic would still be there and would cause it to wind itself up like a spring. That would mean a lot of dead people.

"I need you reach into the folded part of the hem of my shirt and take out one of the other coins," I said. Already the precarious balance of the warden's coin was threatening to slip away. That's why they call it coin *dancing* and not coin *standing-there-waiting-for-you-to-do-something.*

She hesitated. "I prefer not to touch—"

"It's kind of important."

"Spirits of earth and air," Ghilla swore, and came over to reach a hand into the fold of my shirt. "Which one, boy?" she asked, digging around with a finger. It was incredibly distracting.

"It's one of the bigger ones. Eight sides."

"I think I have it." She managed to remove it and held it up for me to see. The bluish metal glinted in the fading light. How long had I been at this? I felt like my legs were stiff and my shoulders were too tense.

"That's the one," I said, still weaving my right hand back and forth. "Put it in my left palm."

She did. I didn't know this one's proper name, but I'd taken to calling it the fugitive. Like my warden's coin, it could find a connection to another metallic object if I flipped it just the right way. Doing this with my left hand while my right was still using the warden's coin to manipulate the copper wire was murderously difficult. *Just keep it together a little while longer. You're almost there . . .*

Ghilla watched me work. They all did. The men, women and children bound by the wire. Diadera. Tournam. Azir. Everyone. I don't think I'd make a very good performer because I found myself with a sudden case of stage fright. "Everybody, close your eyes!" I said.

"Is that necessary for the coin magic?" Suta'rei asked. Her own eyes were narrowed. She wasn't even *trying* to look as if she believed me.

"Of course it is. I'm a castradazi, remember? This is how our great and ancient art works. Now, everybody, please shut up and do as I say!"

They did, but slowly. Even the people whose lives I was trying to save hesitated as if worried this was all some trick so that I could pick their pockets. I don't seem to inspire a lot of trust. Finally, though, everyone's eyes were closed and I got myself ready for the final act.

My request that people not stare at me hadn't been from nerves or vanity. The thing was, I needed everyone to remain perfectly still for this next part, otherwise, well, otherwise it would go badly. I kept the fugitive coin in my left hand flipping in the air over and over, fractionally adjusting angle and force each time until I felt a tingle when the coin landed on my thumb that signalled I'd found an etheric connection to the copper wire. With a sudden flip of my right hand, I untied the last twist of the knot joining the two ends of the wire. Before the warden's coin had even begun to fall to the ground, I hurled the fugitive coin high up into the air.

The reason I came up with that particular name was because of a peculiar property I'd discovered by accident: any object bonded to the fugitive would pursue it wherever it went. In this case, the entire length of the copper wire flew fifteen feet above the heads of the crowd as it chased the fugitive coin, even as the iron magic in it caused it to wind itself together with tremendous force.

I was the only one with my eyes open, so I was the only one who saw how close they all came to being cut to shreds. As it was, people screamed at the shock of sharp wire suddenly whipping past them. But they all kept their heads.

The fugitive coin fell to the ground, wrapped inside the hundreds of windings of copper wire that tried to strangle its newfound captive.

"Incredible," Butelios said, grunting with effort as he prised the fugitive from prison before handing the coin back to me.

I was grateful for the admiration in his voice, and even more so that he had the foresight to stand behind me and catch me as I fell. Diadera approached. She stared at me for a moment and then reached out a finger to touch the shadowblack markings around my eye. *Not bad*, she said, through that strange connection we shared.

Told you I had it all under control.

I passed out after that.

36

The Hero

I drifted in and out of consciousness for the next few minutes, glimpsing the world through snatches of sights and sounds that came and went before I could make sense of them.

"What's wrong with the boy?" Ghilla asked. Having a girl clearly younger than myself continuously refer to me as "boy" was starting to bother me. I would've told her as much but neither my mouth nor my brain were working all that well.

Diadera took it upon herself to speak on my behalf. "He's exhausted. Ten days ago Tournam and Butelios found him half dead in the desert. They had Azir make a road, but he was too weak to go all the way through shadow, so they dragged him up the mountain."

"Then the moron tried to escape," Tournam added.

"And *then*," Diadera went on, "Kellen nearly got himself killed helping us fight the stygian in the abbey, only to have one particularly ungrateful idiot—" she turned her gaze on Tournam—"decide it was a good idea to interrogate him before he'd even had a decent sleep or a proper meal."

I could get used to having someone speak up for me for a change, rather than use my every infirmity as an opportunity to detail my long list of flaws. I looked up at Diadera, enjoying the way the long locks of curly red hair framed those weird freckles of hers. For some reason I found them appealing. More so than staring at the insides of my eyelids anyway. My vision went blurry as I felt myself fainting again.

"Let's get him back to the abbey," Suta'rei said. "Come on, Butelios. Azir's got a shadow path open for us, but you're going to have to carry him."

"Not yet," the big man said, his voice close to my ear. He was still propping me up, and now he gave me a gentle shake. "Kellen needs to see what he's done."

"Let the poor bastard sleep, Butelios. He needs food and rest." Oddly, that little shred of compassion came from Tournam.

I would've made an effort to make a smart-ass reply, but Butelios wasn't having any of it. "No, he needs to see." He gave me another shake, less gentle this time. "Come on, Kellen. Wake up."

Tournam tried again to intervene on my behalf. "Why is it so important he—"

"Because he's not like you. Open your eyes, Kellen."

Butelios's grip on my shoulders became too painful to ignore. As much from irritation as curiosity, I did as he asked, blinking until my eyes found their focus.

A few yards ahead of me, the families who'd been bound in Tas'diem's copper blood noose stood there, holding on to each other. They seemed hesitant about Diadera and the others, as if they had to force themselves not to shy away. But me they stared at with a kind of... I don't know. Maybe gratitude? I'm not used to people feeling that around me, so it's hard to be sure.

"They would have died," Butelios said quietly in my ear, "these people who wanted nothing more than to live in peace. Because they gave sanctuary to people like us, the war coven sent Tas'diem to kill them, unaware that he himself was shadowblack."

"What's your point?" I asked.

"Had you not been here, my friend, the mage likely would have killed us, and even had we survived, we never would have heard their cries nor been able to free them from his trap." His grip on me eased up a little. "Fifty strangers you saved today, little spellslinger. Maybe you're more of an Argosi than you would have us believe."

The villagers were still watching us. I had no idea who they were, or if they understood a thing Butelios had said. It didn't matter. One by one they made a sign with their right hands, touching each of their fingertips first to their mouths and then to their hearts. A couple of the little ones couldn't quite seem to get the gesture. Their parents kept showing them until they got it right.

I should have felt something then. A burning pride, perhaps? The warm glow that comes from knowing that for once I'd gotten something right? But I couldn't enjoy any of it. I just kept thinking how much I wished Ferius was there to see that for one brief moment I'd come close to being a proper Argosi.

"I think he's had enough admiration for one day," Diadera said. She gave me a wink. "Don't let it go to your head, Kellen. Makes your face look all funny."

A laugh escaped my lips. "Shut up, Reichis."

I hadn't meant to say that. Diadera's mockery reminded me so much of the squirrel cat that for an instant I'd...I'd forgotten. And in that forgetting, I'd stopped reminding myself not to feel his absence.

Diadera looked at me, head tilted. "*Reichis?*"

She hadn't been there when Tournam and Butelios had found me in the desert. She didn't know what I was talking about. Reichis was just a name Butelios had said back at the abbey.

I needed something clever to say—some way of shifting the conversation to give myself time to put the walls back up before it was too late. But I couldn't. Despite how hard I tried to stop myself, still my next words came out in a string of sobs. "He was a squirrel cat. My business...My friend, damn it. I think...I think he's dead."

Any normal person—especially one who'd just faced death at the hands of a mad mage—would've laughed their heads off or at least told me to pull myself together. But Diadera took hold of my hand. "I'm sorry, Kellen. Do you want to tell me about him?"

"No. I want to..." I pushed away from Butelios so I could get away from Diadera. I couldn't stand to have her see me like this. The villagers were watching me too, no doubt wondering why someone who'd beaten a shadowblack mage was now weeping like a lost child. "I need to find Reichis. That's my job. That's how it's supposed to be between us." Anger welled up inside me. "Instead I ended up in that stupid abbey, and then I came here thinking I could run off to find him, only I'm still probably hundreds of miles away from where he died, and even if I could get back to the Golden Passage, I'd have no way of finding him in the desert."

"Says who?" a deep voice asked.

I turned around to see Butelios standing behind Diadera, and with him the rest of the shadowcasters.

"The abbot may not like it, but shadowcasters go where we want, boy," Ghilla said quietly, conspiratorially.

The kid, Azir, asked Butelios, "Can you cry me a trail to follow?"

The big man nodded. "I'll find a way."

"Well?" Diadera asked me. "How about we go track down that squirrel cat of yours?" The genuineness of her smile and the glint of wetness in her eyes took me by surprise. I'd come within a hair's breadth of abandoning them all, and now...I knew enough about the abbey and its rules to know they'd be putting themselves at risk for me. The abbot played at being kindly, but underneath the smiles and jokes I doubted there was anything but iron and steel. If he found out...

"I should do this on my own," I said at last.

Tournam, who'd been nothing but a pain in my arse until now, put a hand on my shoulder. "Quit being a martyr, cloud boy." More gently, and without a trace of irony or sarcasm, he said, "You're one of us now, Kellen. We go where you go."

"Do you really cry?" I asked Butelios. "Or do they call it that because the shadowblack is seeping from your eyes?"

The two of us were on our knees, facing each other. The sun had drifted below the trees, the villagers gone now that they'd buried their dead and retreated to their homes to mourn. I was cold and it took an effort not to shiver. Diadera and the others, like me, waited on Butelios. "It is both," he replied. "The shadows emerge from behind my eyes, but I must cry to bring them forth."

"So you have to—"

"It's easier if you don't talk. Focus your thoughts on the squirrel cat."

"Right. Sorry." I glanced up at the others, expecting to find them all laughing at me. They weren't. Only Tournam smirked, proving that while he might be on my side, more or less, he was still an arrogant jerk. "Do they have to be here for—"

"Tell me about your friend," Butelios said. "What was he like?"

"I thought you wanted me to shut up and 'focus my thoughts.'"

"That was before I realised you were incapable of silence. Close your eyes and tell me about Reichis. Encompass his being in a single word."

Describe *Reichis* in one word? How was I supposed to do that? Thief? Liar? Murderer? Friend? He was all those things. Reichis was a wild beast who'd never submit to anyone, a terror to anyone who crossed him—including me. He was the exact opposite of what a familiar was supposed to be, and I had the bite marks on my arms

201

and ankles to prove it. He refused to do what he was told. He didn't make my magic any stronger. And he never, ever let me down. Reichis was all the things I'd been raised to despise and yet had proved to be the one thing I'd needed most.

One word. What a stupid way to try to encapsulate someone who would never let themselves be bound by anyone or anything. Reichis would have threatened Butelios with elaborate mutilations just for asking. Then he'd have looked up at me and said, "How about we ditch these losers, Kellen? Let's sneak back into that stupid abbey and steal all their stuff."

One word?

Soul.

Reichis was the soul I wished I'd been born with.

A soft, almost inaudible sob brought me back to the present. For once it hadn't come from me. I opened my eyes. Butelios was still watching me, black tears drifting from his cheeks to swirl in the air before aligning themselves in a path that led off to the south-east, over the cliff and across the empty air. Azir kicked off his shoes and stamped on the cold ground. The darkness slid from the skin of his feet, stretching out and fragmenting as it led into a distant fog.

Butelios gripped me by the shoulders and lifted me to my feet. "Come," he said, cheeks red from tears no longer black. "I will take you to your friend. I will show you where his shadow awaits you."

37

The Golden Passage

I followed the others through Azir's shadow passage. When we neared the end of the black road, they each took up a position, readying their abilities for whatever dangers awaited us. Tournam's shadow ribbons weaved in a figure-eight pattern in front of him. Diadera stood next to him, her swarm of black freckles darting above like angry wasps seeking out their target. Ghilla coughed up a cloud of smoke that hardened into a shield at the front of our line "You see anything out there, girl?" she asked Suta'rei.

My fellow Jan'Tep closed her eyes, revealing the blackened lids. Her brow furrowed, and the markings from her eyelids floated away, coming together like the wings of a butterfly before darting out into the fog at the end of the onyx road. "It appears to be deserted," she said after a few seconds. "Which I suppose makes sense for a desert. Something could still be hiding out there though." Her fingers twitched into the shape of an ember spell, reminding me that in addition to her shadowblack abilities she was also a proper mage.

"Let's hope so," Tournam said with a grin. "After that last debacle with a damned mage I need something to take my aggression out on." He gave Diadera a jab with his elbow. "How about you?"

She returned his smile. "Oh, definitely."

With their myriad abilities they made a formidable team, and yet Tas'diem had beaten them all, stringing them up like animal carcasses with his shadowblack tendrils. The six of them had so much raw power compared to the paltry collection of tricks a spellslinger like me could bring to bear. Why had one crazed mage—no matter how powerful—been able to ensnare them so easily?

They rely on their abilities, I realised then, remembering how the lessons Ferius had taught me—each and every one of them—came down to thinking your way out of trouble instead of using brute force. Ferius had no magic, only her training, her tricks and her daring. The thing about a good trick, though, is that it lets you use an opponent's strength against them, rather than relying on your own. Tournam, Ghilla, even Diadera, always drew on their shadowblack first, as if it were a compulsion. *No*, I realised then. *It's panic*. For all their bravado and banter, the shadowcasters lived in a constant state of fear, always betting their survival on the very thing that made them outcasts, never taking the risk to rely on their wits or on each other.

"Kellen, are you ready?" Butelios asked. The big man's oily black tears were returning to his face, sliding up his cheeks and back into his eyes. It made for a disconcerting sight.

"We need to go now," Azir said, jaw tight and his young forehead lined from strain. At his feet the onyx road was beginning to fragment. "The abbot's sent us on too many missions lately. I can't hold the road much longer."

"Well then," Tournam said, slapping the boy hard on the back, "here we go!" He gave a defiant laugh as he leaped off the shadow path and into the fog.

"Wait," I said. "What if it's a trap?"

Diadera looked back and grinned. "Kellen, we do this kind of thing all the time, and today was the first time we've ever been caught in a mage's trap. It won't happen twice." She winked and asked, "Nobody's luck is that bad, right?"

She'd stepped through the fog before I could warn her that my luck was precisely that bad.

If you've never spent the night in the open desert then you haven't seen the sky as it's meant to be seen. An endless expanse of sand surrounds you in every direction, its perfection broken only by the occasional patch of scrub you can barely make out in the dark even if you're looking for it. No distractions, precious few sounds. Your eyes go skyward, drawn to the thousand glimmering points of light, whose combined beauty fills even the most jaded mind with unimaginable awe.

On the worst night of your life, you still couldn't help but look up there and wonder if perhaps those stars were winking at you, welcoming you into their presence. Until of course you remember one thing.

The desert is a liar.

"There's something over here," Ghilla called out.

My eyes hadn't adjusted to the darkness yet, so it was hard to make her out from the other five. Azir was the same height as her, but he was kneeling a little way behind me, still catching his breath from the effort of bringing us here. I walked over to the girl. She was staring down at her feet. "This musta taken a whole lotta work, eh, boy? What you call this then?"

Three concentric rings had been traced in the yellow-gold sand, the largest about five feet in diameter, so perfectly formed that I instinctively stepped back to avoid disturbing them. Ghilla was marring the outermost circle by standing on it. Had one of my old spellmasters been there to witness her disrespect, she'd've gotten an earful of outraged insults and threats of dire punishment.

Even for me—an outlaw with no love for his people—it was an effort to stop myself from pushing her aside. Inside the circle, a long sequence of complex sigils filled nearly every inch of the space.

"It's a spell circle," I said. "This particular kind is a sequencing wheel. It holds spells within the shapes in order to trigger a series of conjurations one after another."

"Is it dangerous?" Ghilla asked, dragging the toe of her boot along one of the sigils, crossing it out.

"Not without a Jan'Tep mage to supply the magic."

My clan favoured pure tactical magic rather than rituals, the latter being considered overly elaborate and of limited use, given how much preparation they required. I looked around for Suta'rei. If her clan still performed things like abnegations—which were themselves a form of ritual magic—this stuff would be more familiar to her than to me. I spotted her about thirty yards away, staring off at the horizon. "Could you come here, Suta'rei?" I called out.

I wasn't sure if she'd heard me, but soon she nodded and walked over. Though she maintained her usual Jan'Tep composure, her eyes were wet. "What's the matter?" I asked.

"Nothing. What do you want?"

I pointed down at the circle on the ground. "Any idea what this was for?"

She seemed surprised when she saw it. "How did that get here?"

"Imagine someone drew it, girl," Ghilla said with a snort.

One day I'd really have to find out something about Ghilla's people—like who they were, and why they insisted on referring to their elders as "girl" or "boy."

Suta'rei knelt down and examined the circle. "Remarkable." She pointed a slim finger at the lines in the sand. "Look how stable they are, even with this breeze. The sand everywhere else is shifting about, but the lines remain pure." She crossed one of them out, and the sand fell away, breaking the line. "This was sand magic."

"Well, it's sand anyway," Ghilla scoffed.

"No, you little twit. Sand *magic* gives dominion over time. The reason the sand doesn't move until we touch it is that the mage who prepared this circle forced it to remain within a single instant in time. Thus it retains its form unless someone changes it."

Diadera came to stand with us, Tournam following close behind. "Sounds like a lot of work," she said. "What was the point?"

Suta'rei's eyes scanned each sigil within the inner circles. "There are three different spells involved." She pointed at a quadrant of linked glyphs. "Look, see here? These are part of a tracking incantation." Her brow furrowed. "Quite a simple one."

"Who's it trying to track?" Diadera asked.

Suta'rei's finger touched another set of sigils, then pointed up at me. "Him. The mage was looking for Kellen."

"Well, they must've been disappointed," Tournam said, arms across his chest. "No Jan'Tep spell can pierce the abbey's veil, so Kellen's in the clear."

"You're wrong, Berabesq," Suta'rei said. "Like all your people, you misunderstand the true nature of the universe. There is no force, no power—" she looked up at the sky—"no *god* that the fundamental magics cannot unwind." Ignoring his angry glare, she returned to the markings in the sand. "In fact, look at the way the grains of sand here have changed colour, turning from yellow to silver. It appears the mage *did* find Kellen's location. This second set of sigils holds a messaging spell, and it, too, was completed."

"The abbot won't be happy to hear that," Azir said, coming over to join us.

"What about the rest of the ritual?" I asked, pointing to the third ring.

Suta'rei shook her head. "The final spell was never completed."

"How can you tell?" I hated admitting to Suta'rei how ignorant I was of my people's magic.

She passed her hand over the final set of sigils, swearing as if flames had burned the palm of her hand, before crashing it down on the sand and destroying the markings. "These ones were meant to kill you."

I experienced an all too familiar stab of fear mixed with anger. "How? The circle is meant to sequence the spells one after the other. If the tracking spell managed to locate me, then why wasn't the killing spell triggered?"

Butelios spoke, his deep voice carrying even though he was a fair distance away, and we all turned to see him staring down at a mound in the sand. "Because someone killed her first."

38

The Shadow Play

There wasn't much left of the woman who'd come to murder me, but the sight of her bones put a knot in my stomach. Usually when someone wants to finish me off they do it up close—often after a long speech rhapsodising my many real or imagined crimes. This time however, had the final spell been invoked, I would've died never having seen the face of my executioner.

"What makes you so sure this body belongs to the mage who cast the spells?" Diadera asked. "For that matter, how can you tell the corpse is even Jan'Tep?"

A fair question, since there wasn't a shred of clothing or flesh left on the body. The pelvic bone and jaw indicated the deceased was female, but beyond that? In the desert it doesn't take long to reduce a body to bones and bits of hair. Carrion eaters are plentiful, and once they've had their due the sandstorms scrub clean whatever's left.

Suta'rei knelt down and tapped the bones of the dead woman's forearms. "See these faint horizontal striations that travel from the radius to the ulna and back again? The discolorations?" She held out her own right arm and pulled up the sleeve of her coat to show the metallic tattooed bands that began just past her wrists. "Over time the special inks our people use to imprint our bands seep beneath

209

skin, muscle and sinew. Eventually the markings appear on the bones."

I'd never known that. Once again Suta'rei had shown me how little I knew about my own people. Was this simply because my self-imposed exile had begun before I'd been fully inducted into the secrets of our magic? Or was my clan in some way primitive compared to hers? Were my father's ambitions to become mage sovereign of the entire Jan'Tep nation being met with serious debate by the other clans, or were they laughing behind his back?

"Jan'Tep magic is more than just skin deep, eh?" Tournam chuckled, shaking me from my thoughts as he held up the dead woman's wrist and dangled her arm.

Suta'rei shot him a sour look. "That which is real often provides physical evidence of its existence. Unlike the superstitious nonsense some call 'faith.'"

"You'll find plenty of evidence of God's power in the afterlife, heathen."

"Speaking of the afterlife," Diadera said, pushing Tournam out of the way, "can anyone tell me how long this mage has been dead?"

I knelt down for a closer look. Of all of us, I'd probably spent the most time out in the desert. Tournam and Azir were Berabesq, of course, but their people tend to live inside magnificent cities, not out in the kind of desolate expanse you find in the Golden Passage. "The bones are scoured clean. Even with scavengers and the hot sun, that takes at least a month."

"But we only rescued you a week ago," Tournam said.

I bristled at the word *rescued*, but let it pass. "Then it had to be a sandstorm. A big one." I stood back up to examine the terrain in all directions. Other than the spell circle, kept in place by magic, the desert was a pristine carpet of sand. That in itself provided a timeline. "Couldn't have hit more than a day ago."

Ghilla looked up at me, eyes suspicious as always. "How can you tell, boy?"

"Look around you, *girl*. This whole area is too smooth. Undisturbed. If you were to come back here tomorrow you'd find animal tracks, bits of debris and other signs of life."

Which means I've come a day too late to find out what happened to Reichis.

"Hey," Diadera said, taking my hand. She pulled me close and reached out a finger to touch my shadowblack. I flinched like I always did, but she refused to let go. *It wasn't your fault*, she said, sending her thoughts through the connection we shared. *Better that you live with the guilt than have died with your misplaced loyalty intact.*

I pulled away, breaking contact. I wasn't ready to let go of either my guilt or my debts to Reichis, not by a long shot. But an idea was forming in my mind. I turned to Butelios. "Those tears of yours— can they show me what happened to Reichis?"

He almost winced at the suggestion, the furrows on his brow deepening, making him look older than he was. "Not alone, I'm afraid." His gaze went to Suta'rei. "I would need an alacratist. We would have to..." He let the rest drift away unspoken.

The reluctance on Suta'rei's expression as she looked back at Butelios—the way she wrapped her arms around herself—spoke volumes about how unpleasant she found the prospect of doing what I'd asked. After almost a minute she nodded her assent. "If we must, then let us be quick about it. The intimacy this calls for is not something I..." It was her turn to leave something unsaid.

Despite the good-natured smile Butelios put on, I had the sense he was stung by her reticence. "This is not my favourite way to pass the time either, I assure you." He approached her until they were so close that had he bent down or she tilted her chin, their lips would have touched. He reached out to her, but Azir grabbed his arm.

"Wait," the boy said. "The abbot doesn't like it when you—"

"The abbot isn't here," Tournam said, cutting him off. He grabbed Azir's shoulder and lowered himself until they were eye to eye. "And no little busybody is going to tell him. Not unless he wants to wake up in the middle of the night to a most unpleasant thrashing."

The boy's lip trembled. He couldn't hold Tournam's gaze, but he didn't back away and I kind of admired the way he stood his ground.

Tournam continued. "If a Jan'Tep mage has tracked Kellen to the Ebony Abbey, then we need to know if she told anyone else before she died. If she shared that information with the war coven, they might be able to—"

"He's right," Diadera said. "I'm sorry, Kellen, but this is too important." Without giving me a chance to protest, she turned to Butelios. "We need to see what happened after the mage discovered Kellen's location. If you still have the strength after that, then you can attempt a second search for the squirrel cat."

Butelios was still facing Suta'rei, gazing into her eyes even as he spoke to me. "I'm sorry, my friend, but she's right. There are children at the abbey. We must think of them."

"Then let's get on with it," Suta'rei said, shivering.

The big man nodded his agreement, then bowed his head. Suta'rei leaned her own face close to his until their cheeks were touching. The awkward intimacy of their embrace was uncomfortable to watch. When their shadowblack markings came into contact, Butelios began weeping shadow tears as he had before. They drifted up into the air above the pair, circling like a floating crown. Suta'rei closed her eyes, revealing the pitch-black lids. The markings peeled away from her, joining together and flittering up high until they found Butelios's tears, which began to spin and dance around the elegant black moth. The strange procession hovered over to the dead mage's spell circle.

"Step back," Suta'rei commanded us.

Diadera tugged on my shoulder. I followed her and the others a few feet away. Once the spell circle was clear, Butelios's tears and Suta'rei's moth began to cast shadows upon the ground, like cutout paper puppets held in front of a candle to project their shapes against a wall. The shapes began to move, and a remarkable scene unfolded before our eyes, like watching a Gitabrian stage play on the Bridge of Dice, only here the actors were shadows.

The dead mage's silhouette sat cross-legged inside her ritual circle. Suta'rei's shadow moth fluttered its wings, and I could make out the barest whisper of the mage's incantations. Even before the first circle of sigils in the sand took on an eerie glow, I recognised the syllables she was repeating over and over.

"*Saret'kaveth. Saret'kaveth. Saret'kaveth.*"

The floating compass. Not the first form that I'd used the night before, which carries a tiny object from one person to another, but the second—the one from which the spell derives its name—which traces the path back to the sender.

"What is the girl holding in her hand?" Ghilla asked. The others had seen it too: a tiny sliver of darkness floating an inch above the silhouette's upturned palm, so black you could see it even against the mage's shadow.

Suta'rei kept silent, maintaining her focus on the link she shared with Butelios to unveil these past events. The others probably didn't know what they were looking at. But I did.

Anguish and disgust fought over which would take me first. They both lost to a despair so deep it made my bones ache. *Shalla, how could you do this to me?*

"What is it?" Diadera asked, holding on to my arm. I guess I'd stumbled in the sand. I couldn't bring myself to answer though. If I did, I'd reveal myself to be exactly what Tournam had accused me of earlier: a Jan'Tep spy.

Shalla hadn't asked me for an object touched by Reichis so she could help him. She needed something *I'd* touched so that she could track me to the Ebony Abbey. The moment I'd sent the onyx shard through shadow, she must have used conventional magic to divert it to a member of my father's war coven—someone close enough to the Golden Passage to seek out the traces left by the shadow road Azir had made when he'd helped Tournam and Butelios rescue me. Even that wouldn't enable the mage to pierce the veil surrounding the Ebony Abbey though. For that, they needed something bonded to me. Something made of shadow itself. The onyx shard.

My sister had sold me out to curry favour with our father.

"What's the mage doing now?" Azir asked, pointing to the silhouette that was now shifting the positions of its hands. The second ring of sigils in her spell circle ignited.

"She's revealing the location of the Ebony Abbey to the leader of the Jan'Tep war coven," I replied.

"How do you know?" Azir asked.

"I just do."

"Hells…" Tournam swore.

"Yeah."

I should tell them it's my fault, I thought. *They have a right to know who destroyed their sanctuary.*

"It doesn't matter," Diadera said defiantly. "The abbey's too far away for them to bring their posse or coven or whatever they want to call it. They can't hurt us."

"They can if they devise a way to create a bond between each of them and each of us," Suta'rei said, still locked in her strange embrace with Butelios. "That is how this mage intended to kill Kellen."

The third set of sigils in the circle came to life, the silhouetted figure of the mage weaving back and forth in a kind of sleepy ecstasy as her arms formed the final somatic shapes. I recognised the spell immediately. Silk and iron magic, mixed with a little blood and a trace of ember. She was going to kill me with a thought dagger.

Take an idea—barely more than a passing fancy, really, but something vile and disconcerting—then drive it deep inside the mind of your enemy, powered by silk magic to keep it alive and imbued with iron magic so it can't be removed. The sliver of thought spins inside the brain, over and over, relentless in its destruction, until the victim is capable of conceiving nothing other than what the thought commands. Usually that demand is to tear yourself apart. It's less a form of execution and more a kind of message for everyone else to witness. It would be an excellent way to kill everyone in the abbey, with no need for the posse to travel there themselves.

"Why didn't Kellen die?" Azir asked. "If the mage had a way to reach him, why couldn't she—"

Suddenly a new shape appeared and I nearly fell backwards. This one was smaller, maybe two foot tall, and leaped out of nowhere at us.

Diadera caught hold of me. "It's just another shadow shape, Kellen, part of what Suta'rei is seeing in the past."

"It's Reichis," I whispered under my breath.

The squirrel cat's silhouette landed on that of the mage. His back paws began tearing at the flesh on her back. Thin strips of shadow flew from her form, as if he were picking her apart piece by piece.

"Damn," Ghilla said. "That boy's got spirit in him, don't he?"

"All the spirit in the world," I said, the words catching in my throat.

The shadowy form of the mage spun around, trying to grab at the phantom squirrel cat. She fired some kind of spell at him which I couldn't recognise because it appeared only as a blast of blackness. The whole scene became blurry, as though a breeze were blowing it apart. "Hold it together, damn it," Suta'rei said.

Butelios was struggling. "They fought a while," he said. "Minutes. Maybe hours. I can't tell. It's all moving too fast now."

The scene was disappearing in a fog. I could no longer make out what was happening. "Please!" I yelled out. "Please tell me what happened. Did he—"

"Be quiet!" Butelios shouted. It was the first time I'd heard him express that much anger.

Out of the corner of my eye I saw Suta'rei holding him tighter. "You can do this, northerner. Just hold to the shadow a little longer."

The fog slowly tightened again, the silhouettes taking shape once more. "The woman," Butelios said, "this is how she died."

The mage's silhouette had fallen to her knees, hands struggling to get hold of Reichis's smaller form as his paws gripped the front of her collar, his teeth buried in her neck. With a sudden tug she tore him off her, but he came away with something soft and wet in his mouth. Drops of shadow dripped from his jaws. He had torn out her throat.

The mage dropped to her belly. She managed to crawl just a few feet before she lay still right in the spot where her skeleton awaited us in this world.

"He saved you," Ghilla said, her voice filled with a kind of awe, and for once not calling me "boy."

Diadera left me to put a hand on Butelios's arm. "You can let go know. It's okay."

"No!" I said. "What happened to Reichis? Please, I need to know!"

"Hold on a moment longer," Suta'rei said, her arms tight around

Butelios's chest. It wasn't clear to me if she was offering him support or preventing him from breaking contact. "I can see the rest now."

On the ground near us, the shadow form of Reichis walked on three legs. One of his front paws dangled. Broken. He stumbled, picked himself up, then kept moving. Each step grew slower, more laboured. I followed him, wishing he were really there, that I could say something to him, make promises I could never hope to keep. The squirrel cat's shadowy form led a few more steps before collapsing on a small mound of sand and fading into nothingness.

"What happened?" I asked. "Please show me what happened ne—"

I turned to see that Suta'rei and Butelios had separated. She was shaking her head over and over. The big man was crying still, though these were no shadow tears. "Look," he said to me.

I stared down at the mound of golden sand where Reichis's shadow form had fallen, and only then did I understand. I dropped to the ground and dug at it with my hands, scattering the sand as fast as I could. It didn't take long before I found the bones.

39

The Bones

"They're so small," I said. "It can't be him."

None of the others bothered to contradict me. They saw what I saw, and knew just as well as I did that these had to be Reichis's remains.

Squirrel cats are small-boned creatures. Stripped of meat and skin and fur, emptied of that indomitable spirit, what was left looked like the skeleton of a house cat. None of Reichis's bravery and brashness, his thieving nature and loyal heart, remained.

I was too scared to even touch the bones for fear they might crumble into powder and disappear into the storm beginning to rise up around us.

"You should speak to him," Diadera whispered. She held on to my arm as though worried I too would drift away into the swirling winds. "Tell him what he meant to you."

Why do people suddenly become so stupid the minute they want to console you? Dead was dead. Reichis was gone, lost to me forever because he couldn't stop himself from trying to save me even after I'd left him behind.

Desperate to escape the flood of grief that was already up to my neck and rising steadily, I considered Diadera's words—not because I believed it would do any good, but because they gave me the excuse to retreat into suspicion and callous insight. She spoke with a high Daroman accent, and displayed any number of their mannerisms—even her courtly flirtations. The Daroman culture takes death very seriously; theirs is an imperial people, and so rank and ancestry are recognised in manifold ways. Rituals. Parades. Solemn vigil. Grand oratory.

But they don't talk to the dead.

Which meant Diadera wasn't who she pretended to be.

So many lies. Hers. Mine. How were any of us not crushed under the weight of them? I looked into those pale green eyes of hers that pulled me in every time I saw them. She must've known her suggestion would reveal to me that she wasn't Daroman, yet she'd made it anyway. "Why?" I asked.

She answered both sides of my question at once. "Because it will ease your grief."

A hand pressed down on my shoulder. Butelios. "In the north we sing for the honoured dead. I will sing for Reichis, if you will allow it."

"I don't have any incense with me," Tournam said, his voice quieter, gentler than I would've thought possible for him. "But I know the sacred prayers by heart. Ask me and I will entreat God to grant your friend entry into his domain, to let him sit astride his shoulder as he gazes down upon us."

One after another they made similar offers. Azir. Suta'rei. Ghilla. All our peoples have ways of dealing with death. None would make me feel any better.

I removed my shirt and spread it on the ground next to the little mound. I picked up the desiccated bones one by one and carefully wrapped them in the linen fabric, finally rolling it up into an awkward bundle. I left behind a playing card, dark red, like blood. A debt had been paid, even if not by me. I shivered. It gets cold at night in the desert.

"We have to go now, Kellen," Diadera said. "The abbot needs to know what we've learned." She gestured to the bundle under my arm. "We can find a place to bury your friend back at the abbey."

I pulled away before she could take my arm. Diadera still thought I was going back with them. Neither she nor any of the others had worked out how a mage in the desert had been able to pierce the veil protecting the Ebony Abbey's location. What I needed to do now was keep my mouth shut, let Azir conjure up his road back to the abbey and then jump off it once the others were too far ahead to come back. It was a good plan. Simple. Sensible.

"It's my fault," I said.

I've heard it debated whether the most common cause of death among outlaws isn't getting killed by enemies, like most people think, but suicide. Maybe both sides have it right.

Diadera misunderstood, and made another attempt to console me. "Kellen, you didn't—"

"I'm not talking about Reichis!" I shouted back at her.

Idiot. Stop talking. Just keep breathing, survive one more day, then another, then another, until you find a reason to live. I couldn't though. The rest came out in a flood before a saner part of me could prevail. "I mean, not *just* Reichis. The mage got that onyx shard from me. I sent it to my sister and she must have given it to my father. His name is Ke'heops, lord magus of the House of Ke and the man plotting to become mage sovereign of the entire Jan'Tep people. He's also the leader of the war coven. In fact, the whole thing was his idea, so when he arrives at your gates and kills everyone you love, you'll know it was because of me."

I could see the shock registering on each of their faces. However inconsequential I was to the world, I'd nonetheless developed something of a reputation over the past couple of years. So had my family. The abbot didn't seem like the type of guy to take someone in without first finding out who they were, but I guess he hadn't told the others. Or maybe, despite the way I'd treated them, they'd wanted to give me a chance to prove myself.

"Why?" Ghilla asked. She looked hurt—as though until this moment she'd looked up to me and I'd suddenly disappointed her. The irony was almost funny.

I looked at Tournam, expecting the violence would start with him. He was watching me, eyes locked on mine. Then he shook his head. "What a bitch."

"What?"

"Your sister. What a lousy thing to do." He gestured to the bones rolled up in my shirt. "I'll bet you asked her to help the squirrel cat, right? And she sold you some line about how she needed a piece of your soul or his to cast some big spell to save him?"

I couldn't manage an answer to that. I was still expecting his shadow ribbons to wrap themselves around my throat and squeeze the life out of me.

"Something bonded to both you and the squirrel cat *would* be necessary," Suta'rei said. "Healing spells are based on blood sympathies, and those require some token bound to the recipient."

Diadera stood next to me. "Which made it that much easier to deceive Kellen."

"Are you all out of your minds?" I demanded. "Did you not hear what I said? It's my fault the posse knows the abbey's location! By all the ancestors, how have you people survived this long?"

Tournam gave me a punch in the shoulder. "Not by trusting our relatives, that's for sure." He chuckled. "Man, for an outlaw, you sure are gullible."

Before I could respond, Azir tugged at my arm. He pulled up the right leg of his trousers, revealing an ugly scar several inches long running halfway around his shin. "My father did this. He thought that if he cut off my legs, no one would ever find out I had the shadowblack. It still hurts when I walk."

"My brothers got to me," Ghilla said, lifting up her hair to reveal a circular patch of bare skin and an indentation at the back of her head. "Those boys thought they could drain the demon from my skull."

"You see what idiots you heathens are?" Tournam asked, opening his coat and pulling apart his shirt to reveal the scars of long-healed burns all over his chest. "Everyone knows you can only banish demons with fire!" His burst of laughter set off the others, and soon they were mocking each other's wounds, boasting about how only their people—*their* families—knew the secret to banishing devilry from the world.

How could they laugh at this? How could anyone find humour in being betrayed by the people who nature itself dictated should love them? I began to walk away, heading off deeper into the desert.

"Hey," Azir said, running to catch up with me. "Where are you going?"

"Don't know for sure," I replied. I hoisted the bundle under my arm a little higher. "Maybe I'll take Reichis's bones back to the forest where his people died. Bury him there."

I heard the shuffling sounds of the others following us. I turned to find them exchanging glances, but none of them dared deny me. Azir persisted though. "Where will you run to then, Kellen?" He pointed to the vast, empty desert before us, the first hint of early morning light tracing the horizon. "What's left for you out there?"

"Bounty hunters," Suta'rei said. "Hextrackers like that mage your familiar saved you from. An entire war coven. Every one of them hungry to make a name for themselves by slaying a shadowblack."

"Religious zealots," Tournam added. The softness in his voice made it sound like a confession.

Diadera came ahead of the others, standing close to me as she placed her hands on my chest. "The abbey is your home now, Kellen. And we're your family. Maybe not the one you chose, but the one waiting for you."

Ghilla came and gave me a gentle kick in the shin. "We ain't so bad, boy. You'll see."

What do you do in the face of something you've never earned but always wanted? I held the bundled shirt with the bones inside it under my arm tightly, as if doing so was somehow an act of resistance against their kindness. It didn't work though, because after a few moments my traitorous mouth opened, and I said, "Take me home."

A king rules not for himself, but for his people. Thus can he not be bound by conscience, but must instead be guided by every deed necessary for the survival of his realm.

—*Platitude frequently used by arseholes to justify their actions*

40

Across Shadow

Ferius Parfax once told me that grief is considered perverse by the Argosi. "Don't bring the dead back to life. Won't change the past, the present, nor the future."

If you're wondering how any of that makes grief "perverse," I'd asked that same question.

"Life is for the livin'," was her terse reply. "Losing yourself in grief over folks you can't help just means abandoning those you can. An Argosi focuses on the road ahead, kid. Never the one behind." From there she'd gone on to describe the seventh form of *arta forteiza*—resilience—and a number of exercises designed to enable an Argosi to set grief aside. The whole idea had struck me as cold and callous at the time. Now, though, I wished I'd paid more attention.

Reichis.

The bundle of his bones felt far too light under my arm. I held tight to it as I followed the others along Azir's onyx road, looking behind me every few steps in case something had fallen out from the rolled-up shirt. There was nothing there though. Nothing but shadows.

Diadera and the others spent the journey debating how best to inform the abbot that his abbey's most precious secret—its location—had been revealed to the Jan'Tep posse. The entire war coven would be searching for a fast ship by now, already mapping out the ways that seventy-seven mages could manipulate breath and iron magic to reduce a voyage of months to mere weeks.

All thanks to me.

Well, to my entire family really.

My father had assembled the posse to further his political ambitions. No doubt my mother had lent her considerable support; she'd always had more respect than him among the other clans. But it was Shalla who'd been the key to all this. She'd tricked me into giving her the means to locate the abbey. In return, she'd abandoned my friend in the desert to die alone.

I had forgotten the obvious truth that had always governed both our lives: there was nothing my sister wouldn't do to earn our father's praise. *I hope I never see you again, Shalla, because if I do, one of us will die, and I don't know if I have it in me to kill you.*

"Your scheme will only make things worse!" Suta'rei insisted to Tournam, the irritation in her voice pulling me from my dark musings.

"Why not?" he argued, the heels of his boots clacking against the glassy fragments that made up Azir's onyx road.

"Because, unlike you, the abbot isn't a fool. He's made a study of Jan'Tep magic and he'll know there's no such thing as a 'really big sort of mind-reading spell' that somehow searches the thoughts of millions of people at once to find out if any of them happen to know where the abbey is."

"Then what's your answer, girl?" Ghilla asked.

"Maybe we're all jumping at shadows," Diadera suggested. "I mean, what if the spell actually failed? Just because that mage *thought* she'd tracked Kellen, doesn't mean it worked. Maybe the posse doesn't even know where..."

I ignored the rest of the floundering discussion. They were

grasping at straws, all their brave words and clumsily constructed plans masking something troubling underneath that played across their faces.

Tournam's jaw was clamped so tight that you could see him anxiously grinding his teeth even as he insisted that he could "handle the abbot." Ghilla made some snide remark about how Tournam would likely start by licking abbot's boots and then move northward until he was kissing his arse. For all her brash words though, you could hear the slight tremor in her voice.

Diadera, putting on that sly, courtly pose of hers, claimed she could sway the abbot to forgive me. Suta'rei snorted at that suggestion and offered her own theory on just what Diadera's diplomatic efforts would entail. Like the others, she too exposed a nervous tic, through the way she blinked too often as she spoke.

They're afraid, I thought absently as I trudged along behind them. *Afraid of what the abbot might do. Afraid of being cast out from the abbey.*

Everything was "us" and "them" with these people. You were either a shadowblack fighting to survive in a world that hated you, or you were one of the countless enemies coming after them. The shadowcasters were a pack, of sorts, bound together by need and sometimes desire, but not by the bonds of friendship. Even when they fought together, they never really watched each other's backs.

"Azir's hurt," I said, the only one to notice the boy's shambling gait. He looked even more exhausted than I felt, which was saying something.

"He's fine," Tournam replied. "Just needs to toughen up, right, kid?"

Azir looked straight ahead, his entire being concentrating on the flakes of shadowblack that fell from his feet, growing and thickening to form the road ahead of us. "Path feels wrong today," he mumbled. "Too heavy."

Suta'rei and I both looked back, but there was nothing there.

Butelios put a hand on the boy's shoulder. "You are tired. There is no shame in that. To navigate through shadow as you do...You are a marvel, Azir."

Tournam butted the big man out of the way, sweeping aside the comforting hand. He gave Azir a light swat to the back of the head. "The kid's lazy is all. We've been too easy on him and now he's gone soft."

"Why must you pick on the boy endlessly?" Suta'rei demanded, barely catching her balance as she stepped forward to confront him. "Does it make you feel strong to bully him so?"

"Azir and I are Berabesq," Tournam replied. "You know nothing of our ways, Jan'Tep, so best you keep your heathen mouth shut."

"How about everybody shuts up?" Diadera said, her eyes on the road ahead. She had noticed the same thing I'd seen: the path was becoming narrower. Weaker. The fragments that made up its surface looked clumsily pieced together now. Fragile. Like they might not be able to take our weight.

A wind picked up all around us like the beginnings of a sand-storm. When we'd first entered shadow, there had barely been a breeze. Now we were being buffeted by it, and I gripped the bundle under my arm tighter for fear a sudden gust would snatch it from me.

"Somethin' bad is shakin' itself awake," Ghilla muttered. "Don't want to meet no spirit that lives here."

"Maybe you should rest," Diadera suggested to Azir. "Relax for a few minutes. We're not in any rush."

He shook his head, straggly hair moving with it. "Have to keep going. Don't want to get lost."

Hard to imagine getting lost on a road that travelled straight as an arrow, but I remembered what Diadera had said: the onyx path only *appeared* straight. Our eyes simply couldn't see the way it twisted and turned through multidimensional geometries. We might be hanging upside down at that very moment.

"We're almost there," Butelios said, pointing to the shimmering black fog a few dozen yards ahead of us.

"Road still feels too h-h-heavy," Azir said, though it was hard to hear him over the wind. It was the first time I'd heard him stutter.

Again I looked back, expecting to find some demonic presence stalking us, but though the onyx path that stretched behind us bobbed up and down uneasily, like a ship battered by the waves, there was no one there.

"Kellen, come on." Diadera beckoned me on. The others had already slipped through the fog. "No big demons or monsters after us. Azir's just tired. We're almost home, safe and sound."

Safe and sound.

A part of me almost wished there *had* been a devil on our heels. Safety meant there would be nothing to distract me from the endless grief waiting to swallow me whole.

Diadera grabbed my hand and pulled me through the fog with her, back to the abbey where it turned out grief was going to be the least of my problems.

41

On the Brink

I'd never really understood the term "the brink of war" before. In the Jan'Tep histories, the words seem to denote a very specific, entirely rational moment in time when the heads of a clan, perched upon thrones built high up on the pillars that rise above the council room, would gaze at each other and ask, "My fellow Lords Magi, we stand now *on the brink of war*. Shall we say yea or nay to mayhem and bloodshed?"

Here, though, the brink of war meant something entirely different.

The seven of us had stepped out from the fog to find the same mountaintop as we'd left, with the same chill in the air and crunch of snow on the ground. From the western edge of the abbey grounds we'd walked through covered cloisters, all of us silent save for the clacking of our heels on the black flagstones as we approached the training grounds. It was there that the first tangible sign that something was wrong greeted us.

The square was stuffed to the gills, as if every single inhabitant of the abbey had congregated there. Rows upon rows of monks stood on guard, black robes flapping in the breeze, the markings on their skin coming to life as they heeded the shouted commands of one of their brethren at the front.

"Banders, strike!" he bellowed, and a dozen monks sent their shadowy ribbons to lash out at a line of dummies made of wood and straw.

"Foggers, strike!" came the next command, and the second row stepped forward to open their mouths wide as I'd seen Ghilla do, each projecting billowing black fog from their mouth that enveloped and strangled several unfortunate bales of hay.

"Guess the abbot stepped up the training," Diadera said, unconvincingly.

I'd witnessed some of the training the day before, but not involving so many people, and not with the manic intensity that consumed them now. Tournam grabbed at a monk's shoulders. "What the hell's going on here, brother? Why are you all—"

The monk shrugged him off, ignoring his question and going back to slinging spiked balls of shadow at a target twenty feet off.

"Out of the damned way!" a woman shouted, almost running me over with a cart laden with more mundane weapons, such as pole arms and crossbows. She rolled the cart towards the other side of the square, where those without abilities were being yelled at to find a weapon suited to them.

The crash of earthenware smashing on the flagstones behind us sent the square into a near-frenzy. The shadowblack banders spun and sent their ebony lashes to kill the attacker. The old man whose only crime had been trying to carry one too many jugs of water came within a hair's breadth of losing his life.

They're terrified, I thought. *And they're turning that fear into a cold, deadly determination.* These people weren't just practising. They were readying themselves to kill.

That, I learned then, was the brink of war. Not so much the moments before battle, but rather the time when all thoughts of peace are abandoned, when every man, woman and child accepts that death is imminent and killing far preferable—killing without question, without hesitation and, above all, without mercy.

The Ebony Abbey was on the brink of war.

A deep voice thundered across the square. The monks attacking their wood and straw training dummies froze mid-strike to turn and see the abbot striding towards us—towards *me*. That's when I realised the thing he'd been shouting had been my name. "You lousy traitor," he growled, barrelling up to me, hands clenched in what certainly appeared to be preparation to strangle me. "I should've killed you the day you turned up here. Should've thrown you off the roof of the tower and saved us all a lot of grief."

Butelios tried to get between me and the abbot. He failed though, because there wasn't any space there. "My Lord Abbot, this wasn't Kellen's fault. He was betrayed by his—"

The abbot grabbed him by the front of his coat and threw him aside—an impressive feat considering Butelios was just as big as he was. "You think a drowning man gives a damn whether the drunk who pushed him overboard did it on purpose?"

He stared at the seven of us, daring any of us to answer. Abruptly he turned on his heel. "All of you, follow me." Without looking back, he swung his arm to point right at me. "Make sure he doesn't get away."

Tournam and the others shuffled out of the training square in the abbot's wake, exchanging looks of confusion and concern. I bent down to lend Butelios a hand before turning to follow. Diadera lagged behind with me. "It's going to be all right, Kellen. He'll yell at you a while and give a big speech about how shadowblacks either fight together or die alone. When he's done I'll get him to calm down so we can figure out what to do next." She squeezed my hand. "He won't send you away. I promise."

Regrettably, she turned out to be right on that score.

It wasn't until we'd traversed the entire length of the abbey and the abbot motioned for us to pass through the front gates that our destination became clear. I was expecting this to lead to some form of ritual exile, but then he followed us out himself and marched us towards the cliff's edge, where we met the first victim of the war to come.

The monk's black robes had been pierced by a gleaming cord of silvery light that now held him aloft, spearing his body to anchor itself deep into the rock face. The other end soared in an arc far into the distance, over hundreds of acres of sparse trees, fading into the clouds above the great ocean. Even without knowing what the cord was, we knew where it led. Somewhere back on my home continent of Eldrasia, Jan'Tep mages from the posse had launched a first, tentative thread of magic, like fishermen casting their lines into the water. They probably hadn't been expecting to snag such a big trout on their first try.

The dead man's corpse bobbed and weaved in the air, impaled on that thin rope of pure magical force.

"Brother Dyem?" Tournam asked.

The abbot gave a hoarse chuckle. "You want to talk about bad luck? Dyem was Caleb's brother, the unfortunate bastard whose demon took him over two days ago. Came out to grieve by himself, just standing there, minding his own business, when that light descended on him. Poor guy must've wondered if it was his brother's spirit coming to greet him."

Suta'rei approached the glimmering strand that spanned the

thousand miles between the abbey and those who would destroy it. "This is a spell bridge—more precisely, the first strand of one." She caught my gaze. "If they can summon more..."

I saved her the trouble of finishing that sentence. "The posse will be able to cross the bridge. They'll have a way to invade the Ebony Abbey."

"And it won't take them months or even weeks," Suta'rei added. "The spell compresses distance, achieving in physical space what Azir does through shadow. Once the bridge is complete, reaching the abbey will be a matter of hours, requiring no more effort than a pleasant stroll along a brightly lit avenue."

I had a hard time envisioning an onrushing horde of Jan'Tep mages with blood-lust in their eyes and magic flaring from their metallic tattooed bands as being on a pleasant stroll.

A spell bridge. A damned *spell bridge*. I'd only ever seen pictures of them in books. My old spellmasters had described them as purely theoretical conjurations—fascinating to think about, but utterly unfeasible. The number of Jan'Tep mages required to risk their magic and their lives in such an endeavour far exceeded those paltry few willing to sacrifice themselves.

I guess your scheme to be crowned mage sovereign must be coming along swimmingly, Father.

"How long will it take them to finish the bridge?" Diadera asked.

Suta'rei bent down to examine the gleaming silver rope more closely. Brother Dyem's corpse jiggled on the rope as though excited to see her. "It's hard to predict. A spell bridge over such a distance shouldn't be possible. It's not just the magic required, but keeping the strands stabl—"

A flash of light shattered the distant clouds and arced like a falling star over the ocean and the acres of forests towards the abbey.

Suta'rei was kneeling right beside the first strand. It didn't take a genius to figure out where the next would strike.

I threw myself at the tall girl, knocking her out of the way. The two of us rolled along the ground as shards of rock exploded all around us. Too late I realised my clumsy leap had brought us to the edge of the cliff and she was now sliding over the precipice. My left hand clung desperately to the collar of her coat as I dug the fingers of my right into the dusty ground. Most of her weight was now over the edge, and she was dragging me down with her. Just as I felt myself losing my grip, pain exploded as someone grabbed hold of my wrist so tightly I thought the bones would snap. The abbot, his lips tight in a grimace that was either strain or disgust, hauled us back over the rough ground to safety. "You don't get away that easily," he said to me.

I caught my breath and rose to my feet, rubbing at the bare skin on my torso that was now covered in dirt and scratches from scraping over the rocks. Reichis would've laughed his head off, pointing out that skinbags without proper fur should probably *wear* their shirts instead of using them to carry dead animal bones.

"Kellen…" Suta'rei said. Her hand was on my arm, which struck me as an unusually intimate gesture for her. "I'm so very sorry."

"It's nothing," I said. "Just a few…Oh."

She wasn't talking about the scratches on my chest.

Reichis.

I ran back to the ledge. When I'd grabbed Suta'rei, I'd had to let go of my rolled-up shirt. The way she was looking at me meant she must've seen it go over the side. I peered down, praying the little bundle had gotten caught on an outcropping, but all I saw was a rope of pure crimson light, sparks erupting from the rock face where it embedded itself next to the silver one.

"How are they doing this?" Diadera demanded, directing her

ire at the abbot. "You told us this place was safe, shrouded against Jan'Tep magic! How did the war coven pierce the veil?"

"They had help." He came to tower over me, his broad shoulders and muscular frame making me feel even smaller as I stood there shirtless, wearing a hat too big for my head that had somehow stayed on even as the last remains of my business partner had tumbled into the abyss. The abbot thrust his fist out at me and I flinched, expecting a punch to the gut, surprised when none came. He opened his hand, and there, resting on his palm, lay a tiny sliver of shadow. "This belongs to you, doesn't it?"

I nodded.

"It wasn't Kellen's fault," Azir said. "His sister tricked him into—"

The abbot ignored him. "It's ingenious, you know. All my life I've been perfecting the veil that surrounds the abbey, searching through every book on Jan'Tep magic, every history of their ways, making sure none of their spells could pierce it." He closed his hand over the sliver, clenching so hard a trickle of blood oozed from his fist. "Turns out all they needed was a shard of pure shadow bonded to someone inside the barrier."

A third cord of light broke through the air, driving deep into the cliff face, this one shimmering gold. It too bonded with the others, the bridge now just under a foot wide, sparks of raw magic glittering across its surface, curving away into the distance to span two continents.

"How many more strands do they need?" Butelios asked Suta'rei.

"I cannot give you a precise number," she replied, "save to say that to come this far, the bridge will need a great many strands to support it, perhaps one for every mage in the war coven."

"They'll have to rest though, right?" Diadera asked. "A spell like this must take its toll on them?"

Suta'rei nodded. "The coven will need time to recover. Perhaps a day."

"A day," Azir repeated, looking lost in thought, eyes blurry as if he couldn't quite focus. "I can make another couple of trips, try to get—"

"You can't take more than a few people at a time into shadow," Tournam said, for once not taunting him. "It won't be enough."

"Then we fight," Ghilla said.

"We'll die," Suta'rei countered. "Neither our numbers nor our abilities will be enough against the war coven."

While the others grasped at straws, the abbot's eyes were on me. Was he waiting for me to do or say the thing that would give him an excuse to kill me? Nobody wants to see themselves as a murderer— even the *actual* murderers I've met. Much easier to find some rationale to justify the killing, maybe even make it look heroic. But the abbot was doing more than that: he was waiting for the others to run out of ludicrous plans to make things right. He was testing their loyalty.

"Everybody, get out of here," I said.

"Kellen, don't," Diadera warned. Our shadowblack markings didn't need to touch for me to know that the look she was giving me was a question: *Are you trying to get yourself killed? Has grief driven you mad?*

I was glad our markings weren't in contact , because I didn't have a good answer. "Just go," I repeated.

Even Ghilla looked scared for me. "Why, boy?"

I took a step closer to the man who, for the first time since he'd dragged us out here, looked almost happy. "Because the abbot and I are going to have a little chat."

42

The Pebble

The Argosi Way of Water holds that there's always at least one path that circumvents impending violence. With arta loquit and arta precis—the talents of eloquence and perception—a wanderer can discern this path so long as they listen without preconception and speak without provocation.

"You should run," I said.

He looked surprised. I guess he'd been expecting me to plead for my life. The stuff of shadow began to emerge from beneath his robes, oozing out from his collar and the cuffs of his sleeves. His markings moved differently to those of the others. Unlike Tournam's whipping ribbons, Diadera's buzzing fireflies or Ghilla's black fog, the abbot's shadows were liquid. They floated in the air, beads of black oil dancing in clear water. The effect was mesmerising, conveying both power and grace.

"There's this thing that happens to shadowblacks sometimes," he said, the ebony beads drifting around him as he spoke, "when our demons are just beginning to overwhelm our minds. I'm told it's like the crest of a wave crashing down on us. Some find the strength to resist, some let the darkness take over. Still others—" he let the words hang there a second, pointing a finger at me—"become suicidal. Is that what's happening to you, Kellen of the House of Ke?"

I didn't appreciate his use of my family name. I felt a profound urge to slap the smile off his face.

Stop. Quit thinking like a squirrel cat, damn it. Use arta siva for once. Be charming.

"You should run now," were the words that came out of my mouth.

So much for my arta siva.

"And why would I do that?"

Fair question. Sometimes my mouth gets ahead of my brain, and the rest of me is forced to catch up. Truth be told, I had no idea why I'd said he should run—that is, until I noticed the pompousness of his gaze, the preening movements of his shadows and, above all, considered the manic preparations for war he'd made in response to the spell bridge. All of those combined told me something about him that he'd kept hidden from his followers.

"You're bad at this," I replied at last.

I barely saw his eyes widen before his shadows enveloped me, swallowing me up like quicksand. Every inch of my body was covered, turning the world black. When I tried to breathe, his shadows filled my mouth, keeping me even from wasting the last of the air in my lungs to scream. I tried to rip and tear the stuff from my body, but it was like pulling at rubber.

My throat spasmed. I'd been breathing out when he attacked, and already I felt myself becoming lightheaded, the muscles of my legs giving way. Then, just as abruptly, the shroud left me. I landed hard on my knees, gasping for breath, trying to rub away the last traces of his shadows from my skin even though they were already gone. The abbot waited patiently.

His display of power only confirmed what I'd suspected. "You're... an...amateur." It was hard to speak, but I couldn't afford to let him get in a reply; there was too good a chance it would be paired with a second attack. "You prance around your fortress like some battle-tested warrior, this god-like figure leading his people to peace and safety, but you don't have a clue, do you?"

He was watching me now, eyes narrowed. I think he knew I was neither crazy nor suicidal. I've no doubt he could see how scared I was, yet I was talking back to him in a way his brethren and students never would. "Enlighten me," he said.

"My father's bringing seventy-seven mages to this abbey. These aren't half-baked spellslingers like me or even adepts like Suta'rei. They're proper war mages. Hell, I'll bet most of them are lords magi. They'll burn everyone here to ash with ember spells, rip their internal organs apart with iron magic. They'll have silk spells and sand spells and some will even bring blood magic. Those people you have frantically training in the square will die without ever seeing the face of their enemy."

The abbot's blobs of shadow took on the shape of a dozen spears, which arrayed themselves around my head like a crown of swords. "They'll have to get past me first."

I shook my head, carefully though, so as not to impale my own eye. Reichis would laugh his little...*No. Stop thinking about Reichis. Stop hearing Ferius's voice. Stop wishing Nephenia were here. It's down to you now.* "Ke'heops is a master strategist. He won't try to impress you or terrify you with his power." I gestured to the strands of light piercing the corpse of the dead monk. "If he launched that spell bridge, it's because he knows beyond a shadow of a doubt that he's going to win once he reaches the other side."

The abbot said nothing, his eyes losing focus as my words broke through his certainty, his determination that he had to be right, all the way to the core of his being.

"You've got to run," I said. "Take your people and scatter as far and wide as you can. Pray that once my father's razed the abbey to the ground and he's won the glory he needs to be crowned mage sovereign, his posse will get bored and go home."

His next words were so quiet, I wasn't sure he even meant for me to hear them. "Do the Jan'Tep ever tire of killing shadow- blacks?" The tremor in his voice convinced me he'd break then, fall to pieces right in front of me. Instead he turned to gaze at the spell bridge, and off into the distance where the strands of light disappeared into the horizon. "I could beat any of them, you know. Any one of those bastards out there hunting our kind for pleasure or principle or whatever the hell they think gives them the right. Even with just Diadera and the shadowcasters beside me. I sometimes think I could take on the whole lot of them alone."

"Religious zealots often think that way. They're almost always wrong."

The abbot walked over to the massive black stone arch that housed the gates into the abbey and stood in front of a damaged section on the left side. He stared at it, as if doing so might make it disappear. Without looking back at me, he motioned for me to join him.

I approached slowly, painfully aware that convincing him he couldn't win wasn't the same thing as persuading him not to kill me. Then I saw what he was staring at, and my caution was replaced by confusion. When stone breaks, it wears away from the edges or comes apart where the mortar weakens. Here, though, the damage came from dozens of tiny, jagged lines spreading out from a central flaw, like a spider's web or the cracks in a pane of glass after it's been struck by a pebble, almost like Azir's onyx road after he'd...

"Ancestors..." My gaze left the arch, travelling past the gates and into the rest of the abbey. The unnatural, almost impossibly elaborate architecture, the ornate, fantastical towers, the perfectly smooth stone avenues and covered cloisters. Ever since I'd first come here, I'd wondered how they'd quarried so much of this peculiar black stone and got it to the top of a mountain. The answer was simple: they hadn't.

"Something troubling you?" The abbot was doing a lousy job of hiding his self-satisfied smile.

"This place," I said, choosing my next words carefully, "you created it."

"Well, I suppose I can take some credit for its construction, but—"

"No, I didn't say you built it or designed it or oversaw the people who did. I mean, you actually *created* it. This whole abbey, it's…" Just saying the words made me wonder if I was going crazy. "It's made from your shadows.."

"Come on now," he said, spreading his arms wide. "Look how big this place is What kind of man—nay, *god*—could ever create such a wonder?"

"Show me," I said.

He held his hand flat about an inch from the damaged section of the arch, closing his eyes tightly. At first nothing happened, but slowly, ever so slowly, the material lost its solidity, turning into a thick, viscous black liquid. The abbot brushed it with his hand, and the cracks disappeared. When he stood back up, the stone repaired, its texture that of solid rock once again.

"Incredible," I said out loud, though I hadn't meant to. I'd seen all sorts of mages who could manipulate matter before, and recently had almost died at the hands of a bloodshaper, but this? Creating an entire fortress from shadow? "This mountain… It's an oasis of shadow, isn't it?"

"Took me half my life to find it. The abbey stands at a nexus between a dozen planes of shadow, Kellen. In this place I have greater control over my shadows; I have more power." He gestured past the gates, to the people beyond as they went to and fro, frantic activity the only thing keeping them from blind panic. "Yet you still don't believe it's enough to defend them from a Jan'Tep war coven, do you?"

I considered the question for a moment, then lifted up my right leg and tugged off my boot.

"What are you doing?"

"There's a little rock in here that's been biting into the sole of my foot." I shook the boot until the pebble fell out into my palm. Keeping it there, I put my boot back on.

He raised an eyebrow. "Comfortable now?"

I didn't answer. Instead I watched his eyes, waiting for the moment when he blinked. The instant he did, I flicked the tiny rock at his face. It hit dead centre on his forehead.

He wiped away at the specks of dust left behind, even as the floating beads of his shadowblack became wickedly curved black blades encircling my neck. "You're too late," I said, fighting to keep my voice steady. "You're already dead."

"Dead? You think some peb—"

"It wasn't a pebble. It was a crossbow bolt. An arrow. A spear. Maybe just a sharp rock. You didn't see it coming, so it hit you, simple as that. Strong as you are, you're still human, and everybody blinks."

He chuckled then, though there was no joy in it. "You really are spectacularly good at pissing people off, aren't you?"

"What I'm good at is surviving against people with more power than I'll ever have."

His eyes met mine, held them. "With all those Argosi tricks of yours, if I asked you to kill Ke'heops, could you do it?"

The question took me aback. "It wouldn't save the abbey. Someone else would—"

"That's not what I asked." The abbot took a step closer to me, his gaze tracing the winding black markings around my left eye. "Your grandmother cursed you with the shadowblack. You may well die from it before ever learning her reasons. Your sister left your squirrel cat to die alone in the desert, even as she tricked you into giving away the secrets of the abbey."

He grabbed my forearm and held it up to the fading light, the sigils that marred the tattooed bands for sand, silk and blood glaring back at me. "Your parents took away your magic—no doubt to protect your father's ambitions. At every turn your family has betrayed you." He let go of my arm. "And now Ke'heops comes here, to destroy this place, this sanctuary for people like you and me. So I ask you again, Kellen, with all they've taken from you, will you not use your remarkable cunning and those Argosi talents to finally rid the world of your father?"

I stood there, enduring the abbot's scrutiny, smothered by the litany of offences he'd levied against my family and the unthinkable, inevitable question to which they led. Truth was, for a long time now I'd been asking myself if, when the day came, I'd be able to kill my father. The answer always came back the same. "No."

"Because he's cleverer than you or because you wouldn't have the nerve?"

"Does it matter?"

"I guess not." He turned away from me to walk inside the abbey gates. "Have you ever wondered why, with all their tricks and daring deeds, there are so many places the Argosi aren't welcome, Kellen? Why they aren't folk heroes and legends? It's because for all the good they do, they never take a side." He resumed his march into the abbey. "They never finish the job."

43

Constellations...

The abbey grounds were all but empty by the time I made my way back inside the abbey walls. The throngs of monks, craftspeople and their families had gone to bed after exhausting all their frantic energy on preparations for a war most of them would likely never see. Mages rarely feel the need to face their enemies head on. Once here, the coven would launch spells of ember and iron, destroying this place and turning all within it to ash.

That thought followed me as I climbed the stairs of the abbot's tower up to the third-floor guest room. It was pretty much the last place I wanted to be, but whatever else happened, I couldn't keep walking around without a shirt. So I washed myself in a basin of water someone had courteously left there, dressed in the closest thing I had to fresh clothing and set about cleaning my weapons. The steel cards Ferius gave me only work if the balance is perfect and the edge is as sharp as a razor. I wiped them off, one at a time, and polished each one until it gleamed in the light coming through the room's tiny slit of a window.

My powder pouches were empty, and there wasn't anything I could do about that. It was only by dumb luck that I still had my five castradazi coins. Back in that village—I didn't even know what country it was in—I'd had to pull open the stitch in the fold of my other shirt to remove the warden and fugitive coins. Afterwards I'd put them all in my pocket. Now I took them out one by one and polished them as I had the cards. I doubted it would make any difference to their effectiveness, but by that point I was clutching at straws, searching for anything that might distract me from despair and grief.

Eventually, however, I ran out of things to clean, and found I couldn't bring myself to stay in that room. I guess I'd gotten used to sleeping outside over the past couple of years. I wouldn't have said I liked it, but for some reason I always felt a bit lost if I couldn't see the sky. So I walked down the three flights of winding stairs and out the tower. It must've been long past midnight. The glassy surface of the stones reflected a thousand stars lighting up the courtyard. I leaned back to look up at the night sky and nearly lost my balance. There's something profoundly disorienting about staring at arrangements of stars different from the ones you're used to. Had I come to this continent by boat, I would've adjusted to its constellations. Instead I'd been brought here through shadow, where time and distance held no real meaning, and now I felt utterly lost.

There were no bodies left in the courtyard. Either the abbey's inhabitants had finished whatever funerary rites their loved ones had required, or perhaps the possibility of imminent invasion had made such rituals a luxury no one could afford. I hadn't even had time to wonder whether Reichis would've preferred to be buried, cremated or simply have the bones of his skeleton arranged together in a suitably terrifying pose. Probably that last one.

Tears started to slide down my cheeks.

I shouldn't have to say goodbye, I thought, weeping from bitterness as much as sorrow. *Life ought to be more than just losing the things you love one after another until you have nothing left.*

I wiped the sleeve of the shirt I'd taken from my pack over my eyes. It was shabby from too much wear and had a hole in the front. Reflexively I stuck a finger through and rubbed at a sore spot underneath, immediately finding the tiny ridge of a cut that had healed months ago, but still ached. *Ancestors, I'm only seventeen. How can I have this many scars? Am I really supposed to feel this old already?*

Exhaustion overwhelmed me, and I was forced to lean back against one of the columns holding up the roof of the cloister running alongside the square. The cold, hard surface bit through my threadbare shirt. By my count it had been two days since I'd eaten a solid meal, and almost a year since I'd had a good night's sleep. As more tears came, I counted myself lucky that the courtyard was empty, so for once there was no one to witness me cry.

"I used to weep too," a voice said from behind me, so close that I stumbled forward and felt myself begin to fall.

Ancestors, forget my other questions and just answer me this: why do you hate me so?

Big hands took hold of my shoulders, keeping me upright before gently turning me around. I looked up to find Butelios looming over me.

"Are you all right?" he asked.

"Just great," I replied, managing not to sob or sniff—a real victory for me by this point.

"You don't need to be ashamed," Butelios said. "It's just you and me here."

"I said I'm fine."

I wasn't though. I couldn't seem to muster any strength. If his hands had let me go right then, I'd've fallen at his feet. Butelios seemed to be aware of this, and kept holding me up, watching me. His eyes were brown, and surprisingly warm, I thought. It was strange to have another guy looking at me that way.

"Are you about to kiss me?" I asked.

"Do you want me to?"

"No," I said, too quickly. "Sorry, I'm not…I mean, it's not like I'm…Look, I just—"

He smiled out of one side of his mouth. "Are you this bad around girls too? Or is it only boys that leave you flustered?"

"It's everybody," I said, more defensively. "Especially when I'm exhausted and I can't be sure who here wants to kill me and who wants to bed me."

Butelios propped me up a little more until he was sure I wouldn't fall back down, then released me and stepped back a pace. "Better?" He didn't wait for a reply before adding, "What do you suppose it says about you that the moment anyone tries to show you the slightest kindness you assume they must want to sleep with you?"

I hate people saying insightful things about me when I'm too tired to think of a clever comeback. "Go to hell, Butelios."

He laughed and slapped me on the back. "No doubt I will, friend. But in the meantime, let's go have a little fun, all right?"

"Wait, what? I mean, I just told you I'm not—" I stopped myself. A test. The bastard had just given me a little test to prove his point.

"Come on," he said, his arm around my shoulder both leading me down the path towards the training square and keeping me from falling on my face. "There's a ritual we shadowcasters perform after every mission."

"What's that?" I asked.

"We get drunk enough to forget how close we came to dying."

44

...and Consolations

Celebrating has never really been my strong suit. It's possible this is because I haven't had much practice at it, given my life has been a long string of failures interrupted by occasionally tripping over destiny and unintentionally doing the right thing. Ferius had tried to teach me how to find the joy in being alive. Too bad she never covered what you're supposed to do when your best friend is dead and you've unintentionally destroyed the lives of four hundred innocent people. Maybe that was a more advanced lesson in the ways of the Argosi.

I tried to shake off such dark and bitter thoughts as Butelios led me through the cloister to the light of a roaring fire and the sounds of laughter.

"Do it again, boy!" Ghilla screamed with delight as she flew through the air out over the cliff-edge, tethered by Tournam's shadowblack ribbon around her ankle. His right arm was outstretched towards her, guiding the ebony force. The only thing that kept him from being yanked over the edge by Ghilla's weight was Butelios rushing to his side and hanging onto him. The big man's support was especially helpful given Tournam was using his other hand to hold the flask from which he kept drinking.

"Idiot," I muttered to myself.

"Kellen?"

I turned to find Azir standing behind me. I hadn't heard him coming, which made me wonder if the shadowblack markings on his feet allowed him to move silently. More likely I'd simply been lost in my own thoughts.

"I'm sorry about your squirrel cat," the boy said. "He must've loved you a lot to give his life fighting that mage who was trying to kill you."

"Nah. He just really hated the Jan'Tep."

Azir looked up at me with that expression that says, I can't tell if you're morbidly flippant or on the verge of breaking down in tears so I'm just going to smile politely. I fumbled for something poignant to say and barely achieved banal. "He was a good business partner."

The boy nodded as if what I'd said made some kind of sense. Unruly dark hair flopped down over his eyes the way mine always did. I had to stop myself from reaching a hand out to sweep it back like my father used to do when I was young and he still liked me. "Are you okay?" I asked, noticing his pallor and the way he swayed back and forth on his feet. He couldn't have been more than twelve or thirteen, but looked just as exhausted and world-weary as I felt.

"Navigating shadow takes a lot out of me. I don't usually make two trips in one day." He glanced back at the fire. "I'm going to go back to the others now, Kellen. You should come join us. Ghilla's going to tell one of her spirit stories. They're the scariest things you'll ever hear."

"In a minute," I said.

He held my gaze for a second. Just long enough to make it clear he knew I was lying, before he turned and headed off to the crowd around the bonfire.

I found a low wall to sit on and spent a while watching them all, feeling like a spy, wondering why I hadn't left this place already. A few of the younger students from the abbey were pleading with Tournam to let them hang out with him and the others. The Berabesq was making a show of evaluating each in turn, but it was obvious he was going to say yes. Several of the monks were there too—men and women whose stern black robes were distinctly at odds with their drunken demeanour. There's something unsettling about watching religious aesthetes making out with each other. "What the hell kind of place is this?" I wondered aloud.

"A truly dark and terrible domain," Diadera said, coming up behind me. Clearly I wasn't at my most observant, because she'd surprised me even though I'd been trying to spot her ever since I'd arrived. She handed me a leather flask. "Drink," she commanded.

I've never liked being told what to do, so I tried to give it back to her. "Not if it's the same stuff that's got the rest of you acting like fools."

She took a swig from the flask, then tossed it back to me, forcing me to catch it. "Drink."

"I told you, I don't—"

She took my arm and leaned against my shoulder, then gestured with her free hand at the crowd by the fire. "You are wise to resist my offering, young spellslinger. See what foul and sacrilegious acts these would-be demons perform." The mocking tone was at odds with the remarkably convincing formal speech she'd slipped into. "Witness the abhorrent gall with which they choose not only to suffer a sickness of their own making—one that will surely destroy them if some fine Jan'Tep mage does not get to them first—yet do they also conspire to steal brief snatches of solace on their way to their rightful doom."

"Funny. You're not afraid of the posse that's coming here?"

She dropped the act. "I'm terrified, Kellen. We all are. That's why everyone here but you is doing the only sensible thing left to do in this situation." She pressed the flask into my stomach. "Drink."

I flipped open the stopper with my thumb and leaned back to find out what was so magical about this stuff. The taste of warm peach tumbled down my throat, smooth at first, then delivering a kick that would've had me falling on my arse if I hadn't been so very determined not to embarrass myself in front of her.

"Well?" she asked. "Has the uncontrollable urge for licentiousness taken you over yet?"

I took another swig before saying, "Fine. I get it. I'm an idiot."

She took the flask from me then leaned up on her toes and whispered into my ear. "No, you're just a very sad boy who badly needs to learn to have fun."

"Maybe you've forgotten, but my friend is dead and there's a war coven led by my own father coming to kill all these people! Maybe this *isn't* the best time for—"

"This is *exactly* the time for those things," she said, not giving an inch of ground. She nodded towards the others. "You think they're being childish and irresponsible? Even before we came back to the abbey, we were all convinced we were going to die at the hands of that lunatic Tas'diem. No. Worse than that. Do you have any idea what he would've done to us if you hadn't tricked him like you did?"

In fact I had no idea what Tas'diem's intentions were, but I could imagine they weren't pleasant. Diadera tapped a finger against the shadowblack freckles on her cheeks. "How are we supposed to live with this disease, Kellen, fighting every day to hold on to our souls even as the abbot makes us go out there to risk our lives protecting the same innocent, upstanding people who want to see us dead?"

"I didn't mean..." I prised her fingers from my arm. They were digging into the muscle painfully. "Look, I'm sorry, all right? I'm just not used to all this."

Over near the fire, Tournam's black ribbons held Ghilla high up in the air on a throne made from his shadowblack while she regaled the others with some sort of ghost story. He finally settled her back on solid ground and she gave him a playful punch on the arm before running off to join some of the younger ones. A woman in monk's robes sauntered over to embrace Tournam, pressing her lips to his. A second monk—this one a man—joined them. Tournam let go of the woman and began kissing him. Strange behaviour for a Berabesq elite. The religious class of his people frowned on such behaviour, usually expressing their disapproval with the crack of a whip outside a temple.

"It's *kissing*, Kellen," Diadera whispered in my ear. "Are you really that bothered by it?"

I took the flask back from her and drank again, mostly because I wasn't sure what to say. Finally I tried, "I couldn't care less, to be honest."

"Liar." She put her hands on my chest. Every nerve lit up, silently begging her not to take them away. "I can feel the tension in your muscles," she said. "Watching the others having fun, seeing people letting their guard down, it really bothers you, doesn't it?" She sounded genuinely curious.

Ferius Parfax, one of the best liars I'd ever met—mostly because she could do it without actually telling an untruth—had taught me the "time-honoured art of confabulation," so it wasn't as if I couldn't come up with a way to get out of answering. But she had also warned that while it's sometimes necessary to deceive others, an Argosi never, ever deceives themselves.

"We're going to figure this out, Kellen," Diadera said, mistaking my hesitation for concern about the spell bridge. She leaned into me. "You, me, the others... We'll find a way to hold off the posse."

"What good will I be? I'm not an inspiritor like you or an alacratist like Suta'rei. Whatever abilities I might have had, my grandmother made sure to lock them inside me when she banded me in shadow."

"So?" She turned me around to face her. "Aren't you supposed to be an outlaw?"

"What's that got to do with it?"

"I'd always heard outlaws were good at picking locks." She reached up a hand and traced the black lines circling my left eye. "You just have to figure out how to turn the dials. Until then…" Her hand slid down my cheek, my shoulder, my arm. Her fingers intertwined with mine. "Kissing's really not a bad way to pass the time." A few of the shadowblack freckles on her cheeks drifted from her face to dance in the air between us. "I've heard that physical affection between those attuned to the same ethereal plane can be rather astonishing."

The flickers of firelight glinted off her lips. I could smell her breath—the hint of wine and cloves from the drink. Her cheeks were pale without the freckles, and the green of her eyes seemed even brighter than usual. The liquor had worked its way from my belly to my brain and was getting ready to take over. *In about three seconds you're going to kiss Diadera*, my mind informed me. *Then you're going to lose yourself in anything and everything she offers, because, right or wrong, for however long it lasts, it's going to feel a lot better than loneliness.*

Her face was close to mine, the tips of our noses brushing against each other as our lips slowly but surely began to bridge the gap. She wasn't forcing the issue, but waiting for me. All I had to do was lean in, just a fraction of an inch more, and all this pain would disappear.

Suddenly I was floating a foot above the ground, only this wasn't a metaphor for finally kissing Diadera. Strong hands were lifting me up. Annoyingly familiar ones. "Are you all right, Kellen?" Butelios asked, still holding me off the ground. "I saw you falling and felt compelled to provide assistance."

"Butelios, you arse!" Diadera said angrily. "Put him down!"

"The boy's exhausted," he replied, flipping me over so that he was now carrying me like a child in his arms. He ignored the shadowblack fireflies buzzing around us, apparently unconcerned for his safety or my pride. "Also, he's drunk. You can corrupt him tomorrow, if that's what he desires when he's sober."

With that, he turned and carried me back through the cloisters to the abbey towers, leaving me completely unsure as to whether I should beat him senseless or thank him.

45

The Price of Sleep

Being bounced along in the arms of a guy no more than a year or two older than you are has to be one of the more humiliating experiences a young man can be dealt in life. So it says something that I was so exhausted that the first word out of my mouth as Butelios carried me through the cloisters was, "Comfy."

The big man grinned down at me. "Well, I'm not going to hold you like this all night, so enjoy it while you can."

I gazed blearily ahead, towards one of the towers at the far end of the abbey. "Where are you taking me?" I asked.

"To my bed."

"Oh."

Oh...

"Listen," I said, aiming for a serious tone but slurring the word atrociously. I guess I was pretty drunk by then. "I'm not sure if I mentioned this before, but I'm not...I don't sleep with men."

He gave me a thoughtful look before asking, "Have you ever tried it?"

"No! I mean...No, it's just, I prefer women."

"Ah." Another thoughtful look. "How many?"

"What?"

"How many women have you slept with?"

"Well, none so far, but..."

He paused, standing there beneath the arch at the end of the cloister. "Then how do you know?"

"Know what?"

"That you prefer sleeping with women. If you haven't tried it with either, then how do you know? Maybe you'd like men better."

"I..." My brain—never all that quick in such matters to begin with—was at a considerable disadvantage from too little sleep and too much liquor. Butelios's logic seemed unassailable. "Look," I said finally, "if it's all right with you, I think I'm going to trust my instincts on this one and try it with a girl first." Like an idiot, I added, "If that's okay."

He bit at his lower lip, still standing there, still holding me in his arms. "Oh."

Not knowing what to do, I patted his arm awkwardly. "I'm sorry, Butelios."

He nodded, but didn't speak. His lip started to quiver a little. I felt his arms shake. I honestly thought he was about to cry when all of a sudden his mouth opened wide, his head fell back and he let out the loudest, deepest, most rumbling roar of laughter I'd ever heard.

Loud enough that it got my brain working again. "You're screwing with me, aren't you?"

He stopped chortling just long enough to say, "'Screwing' with you? No, Kellen, that's not screwing. Are you sure you don't want me to..." But he couldn't even get the jibe out because by then he was bent over double with laughter and I had to get my feet down before he dropped me.

By the time he had himself under control, tears were streaming down his cheeks. "Ah, Kellen Argos. I have decided that you and I are going to be good friends." He clapped me on the shoulder, and had to then grab on to keep me from stumbling from the force of the blow. "Yes, I think we are proper friends now."

In the brief moment of silence that followed, I could just hear the sounds of the others back by the fire. I wondered how Diadera had decided to celebrate, given my abrupt departure. "You've got a funny idea of friendship, Butelios."

He caught me staring back the way we'd come. "You mean Diadera? I believe you will thank me for my intervention soon enough."

The small part of my brain whose job it is to keep me from getting myself killed even when I'm tired flared to wakefulness. "Why would you say that? Does she mean me harm?"

"No, Kellen. Diadera likes you—a great deal, from what I can see, though I'm not such an expert in these matters." He gave me a gentle push and resumed walking to the tower.

"Then why was it so important to stop us from...from whatever she had in mind?"

He didn't answer at first, and we walked in silence to the entrance of one of the towers. He pressed a hand to the door and swung it open. We'd wound our way up a staircase to the second floor before he stopped and said, "Diadera knows how sad you are, Kellen. She can see it filling you up inside, drowning you in sorrow. She just wants to make you feel joy instead."

His sideways explanations were beginning to annoy me. "What's wrong with a little joy?"

He opened the door to a modest room with a simple bed and a small desk. "This is my chamber," he said. "You will sleep, and I will stand guard outside. I will weep tears of shadow for you, for what you have lost, and on my oath they will keep any who wish you ill from gaining entrance."

"Is someone planning to attack me?"

Not that you haven't given people plenty of reason to.

"No one in the abbey means you harm, and it wouldn't matter if they did. I will guard you."

"Then why—"

"Diadera is wrong, Kellen. With my tears I have seen into the shadows that bound you to your friend. I know what Reichis meant to you. You don't want to feel happy right now. You want to feel safe."

Safe.

The word sounded foreign to my ears, like the name of a place others had described to me but which I'd never seen myself. When was the last time I'd felt safe?

For a long time I stood there watching Butelios, searching his face for signs of deception. He tolerated my scrutiny without flinching or shying away. After a while I walked past him, into his room, my every step slow and unsteady, as if my body was finally accepting that it needed sleep so badly that simply falling to the floor would be a welcome release. I collapsed onto his bed and heard the door begin to close behind me. Before it shut and I lost myself in slumber, I managed to say, "Thank you, my friend."

46

The Visitor

I slept like the dead. No dreams, no nightmares, no strange encounters with my sister. After almost two years of living as an outlaw, of never—*ever*—feeling safe enough to do more than doze in fits and starts, each punctuated by a sharp spike of terror at every unexpected sound or unwanted thought, I truly, deeply, slept.

For about two hours.

Something soft brushed against my lips. Even unconscious, several possibilities presented themselves. Most pleasant among them was that Diadera had snuck in to venture further down the road we'd barely set foot on earlier that night. Butelios had said his tears would protect me from anyone who wished me *harm* after all. He hadn't specified what would happen if someone wanted to slip into bed with me. Unless he'd decided to... *No.* Though I'd only known him a couple of days, there was something about him that made me trust him.

Hell, even outlaws have to have faith in people once in a while.

That silky sensation against my mouth was still there, gently teasing me back to consciousness. Not someone's lips though, more like sleek cloth. Not a gag or robe either, but a swathe of something smooth settling over the bottom half of my face. I reached up to brush it away. My fingers touched the fabric, and suddenly it became

262

hard as iron. It was as if molten ore had been poured over my face and made to cool instantly, becoming rigid. Impenetrable.

I thrashed around in a panic, desperate to tear off the iron muzzle but unable to get a grip on it. A forearm pressed down on my chest just below my neck. Strong, but not heavy or thick. Most likely a woman. Guessing where my assailant's face must be, I reached up to tear at it. My fingers met a surface too stiff and smooth to be skin. A mask then. I slid my hand lower, aiming for her neck, only to have jaws clamp around my wrist. Jaws with big teeth. I tried to pull away, but the creature held on, not crushing my bones, but biting just hard enough to make it clear that was a distinct possibility should I keep resisting.

"Relax, Kellen," a voice whispered. "You're perfectly safe."

Safe? That word had thus far failed to fulfil its promise.

The flicker of a small flame chased the darkness away, emanating from what looked to be a wick stuck to the end of my assailant's forefinger. She brought it closer to her face, revealing a crimson lacquer mask that glistened in the dim light, its features twisted and terrifying. Thick ridges over the brows narrowed downward as the gruesome smirk of its mouth slowly contorted into an ever wider and more horrific smile. People who tell you to relax should not come wearing Mahdek funeral masks. "It's only me, silly," she said.

Calling me "silly" would normally have meant my sister, Shalla, but she would never use the words "*only* me" when referring to herself.

The creature holding my wrist in its teeth gave a faint barking laugh, and in the dim light I made out a particularly ugly-looking dog that wagged its short, ungainly tail for my benefit. "Ishak?" I tried to say. The metal apparatus over my mouth turned the name into an incoherent mumble. That didn't stop me from looking back up at the Mahdek mask and asking, "Nephenia?" in a barely intelligible garble.

"I'm going to remove the ironcloth now," she said. "It might feel weird, so don't move, and please don't scream."

She was doing a terrible job of reassuring me. The finger with the flaming wick came closer, though I didn't feel any heat even when she traced a circle around my lips. The oddest part was that I could feel her touch even through the solid gag. The next thing I knew, an almost weightless length of silk lay across my face. Had it always been that way and some charm had fooled me into thinking it was rigid?

Ishak released my wrist and I removed the cloth before pushing myself up to a seated position on the small bed. Nephenia slid a finger across the surface of her mask and it fell away into her hand as a simple red scarf. "Panahsi taught me how to spell ironcloth back in Gitabria," she explained, stuffing the scarf into the pocket of the leather pack she carried over one shoulder. "His way of asking my forgiveness for having used that sleep spell on me, I suppose." The way she said it made me doubt the gesture had quite done the trick.

"Nephenia, how on earth did you...?" The question died on my lips then, becoming irrelevant as I realised just how badly I'd missed her all these months. Despite my precarious hold on consciousness and sanity, I leaped to my feet. This proved to be a mistake when my balance failed me and I found myself tumbling into her. Only when she'd caught me did I realise that at some point in my two hours of peaceful slumber I'd gotten too warm and had slipped off my shirt and trousers.

"You really aren't shy about your body, are you?" she asked with a smirk that Ishak echoed with a barking laugh.

This was not, regrettably, the first time I'd presented myself naked before her. I scrabbled for my clothes, blessedly finding them right there on the floor. Despite my embarrassment, the second I was dressed I grabbed her in both arms, holding onto her more tightly than was proper in the circumstances, but far less so than I wanted to. She hugged me back. "I've been worried about you," was all she said.

A dozen clever retorts came to mind, each one, I felt, a witty rejoinder suited to the occasion. My attempt to be charming failed when none of them came out. Instead it was a wracking sob that made my ribs hurt. "Reichis is dead," I cried. "He died alone in the desert. He was trying to protect me."

She started to pull away, but I held on. For a few seconds she relented, then gently pushed me off her. I teetered on stiff legs and fell back down on the bed. For one small instant I'd experienced joy at this unexpected reunion, so much so that all the obvious questions had seemed irrelevant. But that momentary happiness only served to let out my bottled-up grief, and now I couldn't seem to force it down again. "Why are you here, Neph?" I asked, my voice flat and lifeless.

She unslung her pack from her shoulder and placed it down on the bed beside me. I watched numbly as she unbuckled the strap at the top and pulled the drawstrings open. The little wick attached to the tip of her forefinger continued to provide light, but not enough to see inside. "Ishak and I thought you might want this," she said quietly.

I reached inside the pack, wondering which of my things I'd forgotten when I'd left Nephenia and Ferius outside Gitabria all those months ago. My fingers found something unexpected though: a soft, warm body lay curled inside. My hands drifted along damp fur. A low, rumbling snore vibrated the tips of my fingers. I kept searching until I felt the small head and then a fuzzy muzzle. Without warning, sharp teeth bit into my skin. I recognised that bite.

"*Reichis?*"

47

The Promise

Never in my life had I been so desperate to believe something I knew couldn't be true.

"How?" I demanded, practically shouting. "How is this possible?"

"Shh!" Nephenia hissed. "I'd just as soon not get captured in a nest of shadowblacks." She pushed back her spiky dark hair to show me a silver bell attached to her ear. "I brought a hush charm with me, but it's only so effective."

A nest of shadowblacks. It was strange hearing the reflexive Jan'Tep prejudice coming from Nephenia. Of course, I'd felt it, too, until I turned out to be one of them. "How did you get past Butelios?"

She removed a round piece of glass from her coat pocket, about three inches in diameter. When she held it up in front of me, I was suddenly looking at an empty room. "Mirror charm," she explained. "Sand and silk magic. Doesn't make you invisible so much as trick the target into seeing their surroundings as they were before you got there." She stuck it back in her pocket. "It would've worked just fine were it not for those weird floating black tears." She shivered. "Grossest magical wards I've ever seen."

"What did you do to Butelios?" I asked. Nephenia hated sleep spells, so that only left something more violent, and possibly permanent.

"Nothing. When his tears touched us, he decided we were okay. He's still keeping watch outside." Her expression changed a little. "I wasn't sure whether to trust him, but—" Ishak interrupted with a little bark and she patted his head. "Yes, dear. You're an excellent judge of character."

I had a thousand questions, but asked none of them. My entire being became focused on two simple tasks: first, making sure this wasn't a dream, and second, proving to myself that what should be impossible was actually real. As surreptitiously as I could, I pinched my arm hard enough to make me wince.

Okay, let's call that a pass.

Once the animal inside the pack had bitten me, it had gone right back to sleep. The feel of those teeth had been so familiar, and yet the far more logical explanation was that this *wasn't* Reichis. Maybe Nephenia had gotten confused and found some other squirrel cat in the desert. Maybe she wasn't really Nephenia at all and this was a prank for which I would later ensure rivers of blood would be spilled by those responsible. Slowly, tentatively, I reached back into the pack.

Nephenia put a hand on my arm to stop me. She only had three fingers, but she held on tight. "You shouldn't wake him," she warned, but at the look on my face she relented. "Just be careful. He's still very weak."

As though I was holding a bubble of soap between my two hands, I removed the squirrel cat from the pack and set him on my lap.

He feels too small. Too light.

"Why is his fur so wet?"

"He has a fever," Nephenia explained. "And he's lost a lot of blood. We've been bringing his temperature down with weakweed, giving him as much water as he can take, but he was so far gone when we found him, Kellen. The dehydration alone was enough to kill him."

"But how can he be here? Alive?" I couldn't take my eyes from the strange creature snoozing on my legs. He barely looked like a squirrel cat any more, never mind one as tough and full of life as Reichis. My desperate need to find out the truth set me babbling like a fool. "I found his bones. I brought them here to the abbey, but then when that bolt of light appeared I had to grab Suta'rei and my shirt went over the cliff and I couldn't—"

"Kellen?" Nephenia asked, staring at me as if I'd gone mad. "What on earth are you talking about?"

Focus, I commanded myself. *Concentrate. You can't make sense of what's happening until you start talking sense yourself.* "In the desert... The Golden Passage. I was there just hours ago."

"I know. I saw you."

"You were there? But–"

She raised an eyebrow. "Kellen, how do you think we got here?"

Okay... Okay... So she was there in the desert, using a charm of some kind so we didn't see her. Then when Azir made his road through shadow, she must've followed.

"Azir said his road was too heavy. Tournam and the others thought he was just—"

"I know, Kellen. I just told you Ishak and I were there—remember?"

The hyena gave a confirming bark.

She smiled and gave him a scratch behind the ear. "Yes, dear, you were very clever." She turned her attention back to me. "Now, what we *couldn't* hear was what you all were saying back in the Golden Passage. The shrouding charm I was using there blocks the sound in both directions. So would you please tell me why on earth you dug up that wildcat's bones?"

"Wildcat?"

"The mage's familiar. I thought you must be planning some kind of tracking spell, but of course you never sparked your iron band, so I couldn't understand why you'd... *Oh*..." She inched closer, careful not to disturb the furry bundle in my lap, and wrapped her arms around me. "Oh, Kellen, I'm so sorry. You must've thought the bones were Reichis's."

Ishak gave a little yip, to which Nephenia replied with a stern look. "He's *not* a halfwit. He was just sick with worry and..." She paused. "Help me out here, Kellen. How, in the name of our ancestors, could you possibly confuse a wildcat's skeleton with that of your own familiar? You didn't notice that they have completely different tail bones?"

"Different...?"

Okay, this was unfair. I looked down at the apparently not-dead squirrel cat curled up on my lap. "Suta'rei's shadows, they showed me what happened. I saw Reichis crawling away from the mage. He collapsed right where we found the bones."

Ishak tilted his head, staring at me curiously. He gave a series of little barks that of course I couldn't understand but I felt sure were meant to convey that I was an idiot.

"Reichis went to eat the wildcat's remains," Nephenia explained. "Ishak figures he must've finished eating the dead mage's eyeballs and found her ears too chewy."

A chuckle escaped my lips then, and with it some small portion of the grief I'd been carrying. I looked down at Reichis, who was still busily snoring and excreting a rather unpleasant-smelling sweat on my trousers. I lifted him up in my arms and held him to my chest. Resting my head against his wet fur, I whispered, "Tell me it's really you, partner. Tell me you're alive so you and me can raise all kinds of hell on everyone who dared cross the brave, heroic squirrel cat and his faithful—if somewhat dense—human sidekick."

A sleepy chitter came from the warm fur. I pulled my head away and saw a pair of black beady eyes blinking up at me. He chittered a second time.

"What's that?" I asked.

Again he made the sound, and again I couldn't make out what he was saying. The noises coming from his mouth formed no words in my mind. It was no different than hearing Ishak's barks or the squawking of the birds outside the window. "Reichis?"

Nephenia put a hand on my shoulder. "Kellen..."

"Why can't I hear him?"

"He...Reichis died, Kellen."

"That makes no sense. He's right here! You—"

"Stop," she said, the three fingers of her hand pressing into my shoulder. "Just stop and listen, okay? I know you want answers, and I promise I'll give them to you, but we don't have much time."

"Time for what?" I was still staring at the ball of fur in my arms, who'd gone back to sleep.

Nephenia urged me to set him back down on my lap and then took my hands in hers. "Shalla made me swear to get you out of here, Kellen. That was the deal. She'd keep Reichis alive long enough for me to find him, and in exchange I had to come take you from this place."

"You're lying," I said. The very mention of my sister sparked a burning rage deep in my guts. "Shalla tricked me into sending her the means to find the abbey so she could help my father destroy it. She betrayed me."

Nephenia gave me a look that was equal parts sympathetic and scolding. "Kellen, she's Shalla. What did you expect? She's been manipulating everyone around her since before she could speak in complete sentences." She sighed. "But she does love you. That part is incontestable."

I needed to steady myself, to shed just enough of the warring emotions inside me to think clearly again. *Breathe in nothingness*, I told myself, the way Ferius had a hundred times before. *"Can't hear your mind tellin' you what's true and what ain't if your ego keeps shoutin' over it."*

A few breaths later I said, "Tell me exactly what happened."

"It was about a week ago," she began. "Ferius and I were buying supplies near the Daroman border. I was picking loaves of bread when all of a sudden your sister's face appeared in one of the crusts." Nephenia shuddered. "I may never eat bread again. Anyway, Shalla said you'd reached out through shadow and that your 'stupid nekhek familiar' was in trouble. She was keeping him alive with blood magic, but the spell was taking too much out of her. She couldn't keep it up much longer."

"How was that even possible? Not two days ago Shalla told me she needed something connected to Reichis in order to heal him from a distance."

Nephenia shrugged. "To me she said something about having a piece of his fur she'd found in your family's home."

"But Reichis and I haven't been there in almost two years. Where would she have..." *Of course.* Shalla hadn't suddenly discovered a scrap of Reichis's fur just in time to save him. She'd found it ages ago, back when the squirrel cat had first rescued me from my father's study and kept it in case it would ever be useful to her. She hadn't needed the shard of shadow I sent her for him. That part was all a ruse.

Breathe. Just keep breathing, slow and steady.

"Go on," I said at last.

"That's pretty much all there is to it. From the moment you first contacted her through shadow, she had me racing on every horse Ishak and I could buy, borrow or steal to get to the Golden Passage before it was too late."

"What about Ferius?" I asked. "Is she...?" I realised part of me was expecting her show up then, kick in the door and offer up her usual frontier philosophy and Argosi nonsense. But the door stayed shut, and no such pronouncements came.

Nephenia looked down. "Ferius, she... She wanted to come, Kellen. So badly. But she couldn't. Shalla's demands were specific, and the Argosi don't allow themselves to be..." She seemed to be struggling to find a nice way to end that sentence.

"The word you're looking for is 'blackmailed.'"

Nephenia's hands curled into fists, the pair of missing fingers on each one making them look even deadlier. "Shalla made me swear an oath not to interfere in the war coven's work. I've vowed to do whatever it takes to get you out of here alive, Kellen. That's it. In exchange..." She nodded down at Reichis, and some of the anger went out of her. "She saved his life, Kellen. The spells she used, they were hard on her, but she kept him alive as long as she could."

I thought back to that night—was it only a day ago?—that Shalla had magicked me into her dream. The blood dripping from her hands... *She was risking herself to help Reichis, to give Nephenia time to find him.*

I hated my sister. I loved my sister. I had no earthly idea how to feel about my sister.

"Why can't he talk?" I asked.

"He was already so far gone when I got to him, Kellen. I think his heart had stopped more than once. Shalla's spells kept bringing him back, but something... The bond between you, I think it's gone now. Ishak can still understand him a little, but he says Reichis is different. Quieter."

Very carefully I lifted him back up to my chest and held him there, resting my head against his fur to hear the flutter of his heartbeat. "I don't care if he can't speak to me any more," I said, determined to make those words true. "Reichis is alive. You saved him and that's all that matters."

Nephenia watched me hold him for a while, then she reached up a hand to my face, her thumb very gently wiping a tear from my cheek. "It's hard not to love you sometimes, you know that?"

I could've been okay in that moment. If that had been my whole life, sitting there on that little bed with Reichis in my arms and Nephenia telling me I was hard not to love—hell, even with Ishak making funny hyena faces at me—I would've been okay with how my life had turned out.

Except life doesn't work that way.

"Neph…" I began.

"Don't," she said, taking her hand away.

"You don't even know what I'm going to say."

She took Reichis from me and set him on a little bundle of blankets inside the main body of the pack. Now that he was semiconscious, I would've expected him to bite and claw at anyone trying to stick him in a bag. But he just made sleepy noises and nestled himself deeper into the blankets. Nephenia closed up the pack and carefully slung it over her shoulder. "I'm getting you and the squirrel cat out of here, like I promised." She motioned for the hyena to hop off the bed. "Ishak scouted a village about five miles from here. We'll hide out there until we can book passage on a ship. Whatever is going on between the Jan'Tep and the shadowblacks is going to have to play out on its own."

"There are children in the abbey, Neph."

"Then tell their families to take them and go. Seventy-seven mages are coming to destroy this place, Kellen, and nothing you or I or anyone else can do will stop them." She motioned for Ishak to hop off the bed. "Once your father has his grand victory, he won't care about a bunch of kids and their fam-ilies hiding out in the mountains."

"They won't leave. The abbot won't back down and his people won't abandon him."

She removed the scarf from her pack and tossed it across her face. It moulded itself to the shape of her skull, once again hardening into the fearsome features of a crimson Mahdek funeral mask. "Then they'll die alongside him." I saw her hand slip into the pocket of her coat. "But I won't let you die here with them."

"Wait! Stop!"

She hesitated, but I knew that in about two seconds she was going to decide the only way to save me was to knock me out and drag me out of the abbey. For someone who used to be so shy and retiring, she'd turned into a real hard-ass. More importantly, knowing Nephenia, she'd probably spent every spare minute constructing an array of charms to break us out of here whether I was willing or not. "I'll come with you," I said, putting up my hands in the traditional Jan'Tep gesture of submission to show I wasn't preparing any somatic gestures for spells. "We'll leave the abbey."

Even through the red lacquer of her mask I could tell she was suspicious. "You'll come to the village with me?"

I shook my head. "You said your oath was to get me out of the abbey. Fine. Let's get as far away from here as humanly possible." I gave her my most reassuring smile, which is what I do nowadays when a truly terrible plan is taking shape in my head. "Let's go home."

48

The Long Road

"I can't believe I stopped the abbot from killing you," Tournam said, glaring at me as the eight of us struggled not to slip off the uneven surface of Azir's onyx road.

"You have a better plan?"

"*Plan?*" Ghilla scoffed. "You call this a plan, boy? We go walkin' right into the crocodile's waters."

"Will they torture us?" Azir asked, shuffling his feet into the empty space ahead of us, shadows flaking off from the bottom of his feet to form the glassy fragments of the road only fractionally faster than his steps. He was tired, and scared, and no one his age should've had to go through this. "If they capture us, I mean. Will they torture us before they kill us?"

"Nobody's getting caught and nobody's getting tortured," I replied.

"Kellen's right," Suta'rei said, eyes closed as she walked next to Azir. The butterfly wings of her ebony markings fluttered as it flew ahead of us, tracing the path of the Jan'Tep spell bridge through shadow so that Azir could follow. "Our people do not dirty their hands or their dignity with the debased punishments favoured by lesser nations."

"See?" I said. "Nothing to—"

"No, they will instead conjure silk magic to shatter our minds, leaving us drooling wrecks with our own broken fingers tearing the flesh from our skulls to scratch at the bone beneath in a futile attempt to extract the spells driving us mad."

"Nice friends you've made," Nephenia whispered, adjusting the strap of her pack. It took everything I had not to keep reaching inside to check on Reichis, to stroke his fur and plead with my ancestors to restore the bond between us so the squirrel cat could tell me how stupid my plan was, how ugly these other skinbags were and just what a mess I'd gotten myself into without him.

"How much f-f-further?" Azir asked. He was shivering, not from cold or even fear, but from the crippling exertion of navigating us through shadow. His whole body looked hollowed out with the effort of holding the road together. Whatever limits his ability had, he'd gone beyond them even before I'd convinced him and the others to accompany me on this dubious venture.

"You've got this," Tournam said, putting a hand on the boy's shoulder. "One foot after the other."

Azir shook off his hand. "I'm fine."

Ghilla looked back at me, as she'd been doing periodically since we left. It wasn't because she wanted assurances. No, she'd just lock eyes with me to show that, unlike Azir, she *wasn't* scared, and that when all this turned out to be a scam on my part, she wanted to be the one to kill me with that strangling black fog she coughed up on demand. In response, I made sure to pat the pouches at my sides, now full again thanks to the two bags of red and black powders that Nephenia had brought with her. A gift from Ferius.

Ghilla wasn't the only one revealing their thoughts with every glance or glare. The countless hours my Argosi mentor had made me spend in every cheap, dirty watering hole on the continent, studying the unintended revelations of a stranger's gaze—"*Folks talk with their eyes, kid. They don't mean to, but they do. Just gotta learn to listen is all*"—turned out to actually kind of work.

Suta'rei wanted to know if I really did have a way to circumvent the insurmountable threat of seventy-seven war mages. Azir wondered if today was the day his young life would end. Butelios wanted reassurance that the price he'd pay for supporting me wouldn't be the trust of his friends.

Tournam's sly glances back mostly seemed intent on Nephenia, and whether she might be single, and if so, might she be interested in a well-muscled Berabesq narcissist with a self-satisfied smile and an ego so big he didn't notice the way she had to stop herself from flinching every time she saw the shadowblack markings on his arms. I guess no matter how far you travel, you can't shake the prejudices of your upbringing.

But of all of them, it was Diadera who watched me the closest, and whose furtive glances I found the most difficult to interpret. There was so much there to see. She was worried. She was angry. She was confused. Most of all . . . she looked hurt.

For all that she'd pretended our near-encounter at the bonfire had been careless fun, it was the thing she'd said when I'd first arrived at the abbey that kept coming back to me: "*I've never met anyone whose shadows are so close to my own.*" Had that meant more to her than she'd let on? Was the flirtatious Daroman courtier act that I kept interpreting as some masterful manipulation actually just a mask for . . . loneliness?

"Focus," Nephenia whispered to me. She grabbed my arm and held me back a moment while most of the others forged ahead. "You're free to fall for any girl you want, Kellen, but Ishak and I are risking our lives to rescue you. If we end up dead as a result, I'm going to consider you a very bad friend."

"I'm totally focused," I said.

I'm also in love with you.

The thought came unbidden and unexpected. I was utterly unprepared for it.

I'd convinced myself a while back that my feelings for Nephenia had just been a childhood infatuation—the kind everyone has about that one girl you grew up so near to and yet you knew you could never touch. But fantasies are considered futile distractions for a mage. To a spellslinger, they can be deadly.

I *wasn't* in love with the girl I used to pine over in class when we were kids though. *I'm in love with this daring, clever and slightly terrifying woman with two missing fingers on each hand whom I walked away from months ago but who risked everything to save a cantankerous squirrel cat from dying alone in the desert because she knew that if he had, my soul would've broken in half.*

"Kellen? Is something the matter? You're looking at me funny."

"I'm fine. Just working through the details of my devastatingly brilliant plan."

Ishak gave a bark. Nephenia translated it with nothing more than a raised eyebrow before she went ahead. I felt a hand on my shoulder and heard Butelios say quietly, "Still convinced you prefer girls? Boys are vastly less complicated, my friend." He walked past me, but for a brief moment I caught him watching Diadera with a tenderness I wouldn't have expected. Had he been protecting me last night when he kept me from tumbling into bed with her? Or had he been looking out for her as well?

You should've tried harder to convince that Argosi you met up north to make you her teysan, my big friend, because you are just as annoyingly mysterious as any of them.

"Stop!" Suta'rei called out.

I ran ahead to catch up with the others, who were now bunched around Azir. His onyx road came to a fractured end in front of him. "What's wrong?" I asked.

He shook his head, and sweat flicked off his brow. "'M'okay," he mumbled. Tournam was now holding the boy's shoulders, keeping him upright so he could continue summoning the road without having to support his own weight.

Suta'rei's eyes were closed again, her head lilting this way and that as her black butterfly fluttered in the distance. "I can see their encampment now. It is as you surmised, Kellen. They are amassed near an oasis in the Jan'Tep territories." Her voice caught in her throat. "I've never seen so many master mages in one place before."

"Wh-wh-wh..." Azir had to stop to catch himself, standing on one foot, the other about to step into empty space. "Wh-where should I g-g-go?"

They all looked at me. "Can you take us just a little further?" I asked. "Maybe a mile or so away from the camp?"

"He's obviously exhausted," Nephenia said. "Can we risk it?"

Ghilla gave a snort. "You don't know nothing about shadow-walking, do you, girl?"

Nephenia looked at me. "Did that child just call me 'girl'?"

"Focus," I replied.

"I can do th-th-th..." Again Azir paused, taking a slow, wheezing breath. "I can do this. Another mile is just a step." To prove his point, he lifted his foot and set it down a little to the right, stamping it on the emptiness. Suddenly a dense fog came up from his heel, like black steam. Just beyond it I could make out a thinly forested slope. He walked through, and the rest of us followed. A moment later he collapsed in the tall grass.

"It's okay," Tournam said, lifting him up in his arms. "He's just not used to so many trips so close together."

"Where are we?" Nephenia asked. "We need to get our bearings if we don't want to get caught unawares."

Suta'rei whispered something to Ghilla, who looked thoughtful for a moment, then nodded. Then the black wings of Suta'rei's shadowblack butterfly separated, each one covering one of Ghilla's eyes. She bent over and coughed noisily. I thought she was throwing up, but what came out was a small pool of shadowblack. On the ground at our feet it took shape, becoming a miniature rendition of a mountain between two valleys, with little rivers and forests.

"We're here," Suta'rei said, pointing to a spot near the base of the mountain. "In the southern end of the Jan'Tep territories, near the Berabesq border. Near my home." She didn't sound happy about it.

The first rays of the morning sun had been glinting off the abbey's black cobblestones when we'd set off. We couldn't have walked for more than an hour in shadow, yet now it was full dark, the moon hanging brightly overhead. At some point I needed to find out how all this shadow travel worked. Assuming I lived long enough.

"What now, cloud boy?" Tournam asked. He gave us all a grin. "Time to go kill some mages?"

"Only if you want to die," Suta'rei said. "They'll have protective wards in place. We won't get within a hundred yards without being struck by lightning or bursting into flames."

"Make camp as best you can," I said, pushing through the brush to what looked like a reasonable path up the mountain. "I'll be back in a couple of hours."

"Where are you going?" Diadera asked. "You heard Suta'rei's warning. If you get too close, those mages will kill you without a second thought!"

"No, it's like she said—they'll capture me and use silk spells to rip my mind apart for any secrets I have about the abbey. Then they'll make me torture myself for a while just in case I was able to resist some part of the spell, but mostly just for fun. *Then* they'll kill me."

"Then why would you—"

I started the long walk up the mountainside, saying only, "Because I've got my own spy on the inside."

49

The Informant

The ground was mostly loose shale, which made every step precarious. The sense of impending doom was only magnified by the possibility that any second now I might walk into a hextracker or chaincaster. Suta'rei was right that the posse would have set wards around their encampment, but mages are paranoid by nature. Any number of them might also have set their own traps to give themselves advance warning of an attack.

That, of course, was critical to my plan.

See, I didn't *exactly* have an ally inside the war coven. I mean, what are the odds that out of seventy-seven mages even one of them would be working with an itinerant spellslinger? What I *did* have, however, was a sister who thought I was a bumbling reckless idiot.

Two years of surviving as an outlaw with no end of enemies at my back had done nothing to convince my family—especially Shalla—that I was anything other than a clumsy, ham-fisted boy who couldn't cast a proper spell if he fell down the stairs and his hands happened to twist into the right somatic shape. My sister was all too aware that I'd gotten myself tangled up with the Ebony Abbey, and since no sane person would *ever* try to sneak into a war coven's encampment, she'd be absolutely convinced that I would do exactly that, and would thus set wards further out than the other mages to alert her when I came.

See? Simple.

"My, my," a feminine voice said soothingly. "What have we here? Has the rabbit come to hunt foxes?"

A strange lightness came over my bones, and soon I was floating a few feet off the ground, the earth having apparently lost interest in me. I found myself turning head over heels, very slowly, like a porcelain doll being examined for flaws. I drifted helplessly for a few seconds until the face of a slim young woman came into view. "You're not Shalla," I said, which made me sound precisely as stupid as I now felt.

Long, lustrous hair an impossible azure colour travelled down past stunningly high cheekbones to drape over a blue gown that shimmered as if it were made of sapphire. Her steps as they approached were slow, unhurried and, most troubling of all, a few inches off the ground. Now, if you're wondering about the virtue of a spell that lets you walk less than a foot in the air, the answer is that it kept the extended train of her dress from touching the dirt and scrub. All in all, it struck me as a lot of effort to make just to look stylish.

"There's a prize, you know," she said, turning her hand just a little and causing me to rotate upside down. With her free hand she reached out a finger and tapped the markings around my left eye. "First shadowblack kill will be awarded a seat beside the mage sovereign at his coronation."

You would think at a time like this, having just been captured and with a great deal of agony in store for me, I'd have better things to do than defend the dignity of my lousy family. Maybe the blood rushing to my head was addling my brain. "First of all, lady, if anyone's going to be sitting next to the mage sovereign, it's going to be

Bene'maat. His *wife*. Not some tarted-up flying floozy who goes off to war wearing a ballgown."

Tarted-up flying floozy? Did I really just say that? Ferius Parfax, what have you done to me?

"Second," I went on, determined to do better on my next volley, "Ke'heops just happens to be my father. So I suggest you release me at once before I get irritated and inform him that you assaulted his favourite son."

I'm his *only* son of course, and the word "favourite" has no place in our relationship whatsoever. Also, why was I sticking up for my mother? She'd helped him when he counter-banded me, stealing any chance I'd ever have at sparking anything other than my breath band.

The mage's glittering eyes—which were a dazzling blue, of course—widened with surprise. "*You* are Kellen? Son of Ke'heops?"

I nodded, which is actually harder to do upside down than you'd think.

She clapped her hands excitedly. "Excellent! That means I also win the prize for eliminating the black stain from the House of Ke. I've always wanted a sanctum of my very own!"

A *sanctum*? My father had placed a bounty on my head that would pay for an actual mage's *sanctum*? Evidently ours was a richer family than I remembered. Also, apparently he hated me even more than I'd thought.

"Well, come along," she said, beckoning me with her finger. Powerless to resist, I started floating in her direction.

"Could you turn me right side up?" I asked. "I'm getting a headache."

She stopped and sighed theatrically. "I suppose it can't hurt."

Very slowly I began to rotate in the air. I let my hands drift closer to the pouches at my belt, now full of the red and black powders and thankfully sealed up tight. In about three seconds I was going to be upright. I would unbuckle the straps, flip open the tops and blast this cheerful, elegant psychopath to the very same hell she no doubt had planned for me.

"Oh wait," she said, and turned to face me. "That would let you use that pathetic powder spell of yours, wouldn't it?" She gave me a self-satisfied smirk. Usually my best chance with mages is that they think spellslingers are so weak they're not worth defending against. This one twisted her hand and I went spinning, over and over. I couldn't tell which way was up until I vomited and the results fell back down on me. By the time she stopped I couldn't see straight, never mind aim. "There. That's better, isn't it? Shall we go now, or are there any other threats about your dear papa you'd like to mention?"

I threw up again. I tried to get some on her, but I missed. Even that small and petty act of vengeance was denied me. "I shouldn't have brought up my father," I admitted. "Ke'heops wouldn't lift a finger to save me."

"Oh, poor little Sha'Tep boy, so full of his own sorro—"

"My sister, on the other hand, is going to kick your ass."

"Shalla? That little daddy's girl?" The mage laughed. It was a very pretty laugh, as maniacal giggles go. "Your sister runs after your father like the tail on a puppy. It's all very amusing. There's a running joke among our people that Shalla wags every time Ke'heops takes a shit."

My people aren't known for their clever witticisms.

My captor came a little closer, floating a few inches higher so we were eye to eye. "Don't you think that if she were looking for you, that little milksop would have appeared before now?"

Truth be told, during the course of this encounter I'd become fairly certain that I'd critically misjudged both my situation and

Shalla's inclination to protect me. I'd just kind of assumed that as soon as I came close enough, a warning spell she'd have put in place would alert her to my presence and she'd come running. But I'd forgotten one of the most important things about Shalla, which I took some small pleasure in revealing to my captor: "The thing about my sister is...she likes to wait for just the right moment to make an entrance."

The mage stared at me, those unnaturally blue eyes narrowing as my words seeped through all her self-congratulatory pronouncements. Her hands came up in the first somatic gesture for a shield spell. "*Soma'eh'pa—*"

She dropped like a discarded sack of grain, the lovely azure of her gown making a pretty, though not very practical, silk bed as she landed on hard shale ground.

The air before me shimmered as a second young woman stepped out from a remarkably refined obscurement spell. Golden-haired, with skin that bordered on the luminous, she looked taller than when I'd last seen her. Her garments were an elegant rendition of a war mage's silver-banded leather armour that kept her arms bare to show off her six sparked bands. She gave me that look of hers that said I was, as always, utterly predictable.

Which was true, I suppose, except that there was an excellent chance I was about to kill her.

50

The Camp

"Hello, Shalla," I said, waiting until the slow rotation of my body in the air got me upright again.

"Brother." She invested the word considerable disappointment. Her contempt, however, was reserved for the woman lying unconscious on the cold ground. "Look at her in that preposterous gown. Why Father allowed Essa'jin to be part of the war coven when better mages were refused I will never understand. And air walking? It's just so pretentious."

Better mages? So Father denied her a place in the posse.

"Maybe she has other attributes Ke'heops admires," I suggested, thinking back to the eagerness with which Essa'jin had spoken about the chance to be seated next to him at the celebration for the slaughter of the Ebony Abbey.

Shalla's cheeks flushed. An angry glare came to her eyes. "Forgive me, brother, it seems I forgot to remove the—what did you call her again?—the floozy's binding. And here you are floating in the air, quite helpless." She made a somatic gesture with her left hand and suddenly I was falling, barely managing to avoid crashing head first onto the shale by rolling over my shoulder.

My sister was distracted by her petty victory, and I was back on my feet. *I could do it,* I thought. *She's a thousand times more powerful, but I'm a split second faster and she won't be expecting it.*

I hadn't come here to kill my sister, and truth be told, it wouldn't help. If there was any hope of averting this war, Shalla would play a crucial role. But the anger I felt, the betrayal that she'd tricked me and used me once again, was overpowering. But my hands were shaking now, and that, added to a question I shouldn't have cared about but somehow couldn't stop myself from asking, contrived to save her life. "Is it true what Essa'jin implied? Has Ke'heops set our mother aside?"

"Oh, don't play the prude, Kellen," Shalla snapped, though I noticed she turned away from me so I couldn't see her eyes. I followed my musical training and let her be the notes while I provided the silences. "Mother knows how much Father loves her," she said after a time. "Whatever sacrifice she makes, she does so for our family and our house. As we all do."

"Except me." I was goading her, because that, too, is part of our relationship, and if she tried to use a spell to punish me, in that instant my hands would stop shaking. Again she tried to keep quiet, and in such silences one can one almost hear the workings of my sister's brilliantly manipulative mind. I should've kept my mouth shut, but she always did get the best of me. "Shalla, what is it you th—"

She spun back to me, and the sullen girl was banished as the devious schemer took to the stage. "Maybe you *have* been serving our family, Kellen. All this time." She took my hands in hers, squeezing them tight. "Please, brother, let me speak."

The word "please" being so rarely part of Shalla's vocabulary, I confess it had a certain spellbinding effect on me. "Fine. Say your piece."

She gave me a smile—like the one you give a puppy when it rolls over on command. "A dangerous and daring mission, brother. A young Jan'Tep mage, travelling the world, learning the secrets of our enemies and unwinding plots against our people, reporting only to Ke'heops himself."

I pulled my hands away. "Have you lost your mind? I *left* our people, remember?"

"A brave sacrifice, and one necessary to keep the mission secret even from our clan."

"Mages from our clan have been trying to *kill* me!"

"That just makes it even more brave."

I rubbed my fingers against my temples. Her preposterous story was literally giving me a headache. "Shalla, in case you somehow hit your head and forgot the past two years, I have actively worked against our clan. I've foiled every Jan'Tep plot I could, and refused to obey every order our monster of a father had the nerve to issue to me!"

"Have you?" She winked at me and began to stroll around me and the unconscious Essa'jin as though we were sculptures in a sand park. "You did uncover a Sha'Tep rebellion and execute their leader, did you not?"

"Ra'meth—not I—killed our uncle."

She shrugged. "Who remembers such insignificant details? You then prevented Ra'meth from arranging a duel in which he would have murdered our father. You ended the machinations of a rogue spellslinger in the borderlands."

"Dexan Videris was working for our clan's lords magi!"

"Perhaps at first, but then he betrayed our trust. And you made him pay for it."

"I'm not your damned enforcer!"

"And let's not forget how you discovered the secrets of the Gitabrian mechanical bird and destroyed it and the woman who dared create it." She twirled theatrically. "But even after such wondrous feats, our young Jan'Tep hero was not done. He did the one thing no mage has been able to do: found the Ebony Abbey so that the threat of the shadowblack could be wiped out once and for all!"

"You do recall that *I* have the shadowblack, right?"

Shalla came over to me and tapped a finger on the markings around my left eye. "And here, the greatest sacrifice of all: a child, banded in shadow by his grandmother—one of the great mages of our clan. Because she was mad? No, because in those final hours before the shadowblack took her, she realised there was only one way our people could find the source of this evil and wipe it out forever."

"Not one word of that is true, you realise?"

"Perhaps not." She patted my cheek playfully. "But, for an exile, one could argue you've been awfully useful to our people, don't you think?"

This is why it's dangerous to engage in a conversation with my sister about anything more momentous than the weather or what to eat for dinner. Listen long enough and you'll start to think she might have a point. "What is this really about, Shalla?"

She looked up at me with those pale blue eyes of hers, so full of certainty and affection. The manipulator had taken her bow and now the yellow-haired girl who loved her brother returned. "Kellen, if you've secretly been working for our father all this time, then there's nothing stopping you from coming home. You could take your place at Father's side! He's going to be crowned mage sovereign very soon. Imagine, for the first time in three hundred years, our people will have one ruler to lead our nation to greatness!"

I would've dismissed her glorifying exuberance, but underneath it I heard a desperate plea; an almost hysterical need for me to go along with this pretence. The anger that had brought me so close to killing her fled. I understood now what this was all about, just as I understood why she'd used me to find the Ebony Abbey. Nephenia's words echoed back to me: "*She's been manipulating everyone around her since before she could speak in complete sentences. But she does love you. That part is incontestable.*"

"Kellen...Brother, please," she said, taking my hands in hers, "you have played the outlaw far too long. At long last you must choose a side."

It became clear to me then that Shalla was trying to avoid saying something that should have been obvious to both of us: my life would soon come to an end. My father had run out of ways to avoid my death. If he'd tried to avoid it at all. Now my sister, her pleading with him no longer effective, had concocted this one last scheme to save me—to give Ke'heops the excuse he needed to grant me clemency.

It was, as these things go, a rather generous offer, which made what I did next feel all the more dirty.

"You shouldn't worry about me, Shalla. Worry about that collection of deluded half-wits sitting at the top of the mountain, thinking they're going to somehow travel a thousand miles to wipe out an army of trained shadowblacks in their own fortress. They haven't got a chance."

She looked at me wide-eyed, then slapped me. "Are you completely insane, brother?" She pointed to the top of the mountain. "There are more than seventy war mages up there! They'll have the spell bridge finished in a matter of hours! And when they do, they will storm across it and destroy every black-marked fool in that awful place."

I chuckled. "Shalla, first off, I know our people. You can't get seventy-seven mages to agree to anything. Odds are there are a dozen or so adepts up there with maybe a full war mage or two for show. And besides, a spell bridge spanning a thousand miles? It'll break the instant someone sets foot on it."

"Kellen, this is real. This is happening. You've got to—"

"Have fun playing war coven with the other children, Shalla. One day, when you grow up and see a little more of the world, you'll stop being so easily fooled by sparking bands and big talk. Until then, let's just say I'll believe all these grandiose claims when I see some proof."

I started to turn away, but she grabbed my face with both hands, her fingertips pressing into my temples. *"Hateth'eka, maru'pasha, sovei'e'khan!"*

My vision blurred, my head swam. I started losing control of my body and for a second I worried I'd gone too far and now she was going to incapacitate me. But being right has always been of particular importance to Shalla, and soon the silk spell took hold and I saw what she wanted me to see.

I was walking through the encampment, past glorious pavilions and floating palanquins. Sha'Tep servants were preparing meals and feeding fires. I felt awkward—as if I were too short all of a sudden. Then I realised it was because I was seeing through Shalla's eyes—watching her memories. "This was an hour ago," she said, her voice distant.

"I never argued that our people weren't experts at travelling in excessive comfort," I replied, speaking with her voice—which was especially disconcerting.

"You're a fool, and I can't save you unless you pay attention!" The ambling journey continued, past the main camp and towards a sheer cliff down one side of the mountain. There, facing the empty air like a true army, stood all but one of the seventy-seven mages my father had assembled. They held their arms out in front of them, and magic glistened like sweat on their forearms. My breath turned to ice as I finally understood how they would be able to create a spell bridge that spanned the distance between two continents.

The tattooed metallic bands on each and every one of them were extending out from their forearms like ribbons—the way Tournam and some others had learned to do with their shadowblack. They stretched out into the distance, travelling hundreds of miles as they wound around each other, over and over, becoming strands of rope, and those ropes binding together to form the bridge. The colours of iron, ember, blood, breath, silk and sand magic all mixed together, a dance of shimmering light so beautiful I would have cried at the sight of it had I not known its purpose.

"It's incredible," I said, because it was important that Shalla hear my admission.

"So you understand?" she asked, so excited she didn't notice my right hand had drifted into the pocket of my coat. The silk spell began to fade and my eyes took in the mountain slope once again, and my sister standing there with desperate hope that the brother she loved would soon return home.

"Thank you, Shalla," I said.

I kissed her on the forehead, like one does a child. She hated that, and opened her mouth to scold me. That's when I stuffed a leaf of weakweed between her lips. Nephenia had brought some to keep Reichis's fever down and I had reckoned it wouldn't hurt to have a little at my disposal.

At first Shalla just stared at me, eyes wide, the leaf hanging out of her mouth. Most of the time weakweed just removes a mage's ability to bring the essential forces into their body. But if you take it just after casting a spell, it also renders you unconscious.

I caught Shalla before she could fall, and laid her gently near a tree. I removed the leaf from her lips and placed it between Essa'jin's. It wouldn't do for the other woman to wake before Shalla did.

I should have run then, but I didn't. I found a few pieces of wood and some twigs for tinder. I used my powders to light a fire so she wouldn't get too cold. I doubted the courtesy would earn me much forgiveness. "I'm sorry, Shalla," I said, because it seemed important to speak the words aloud.

I'd never doubted my father's ability to convene a war coven. He's always been the sort of man that others instinctively want to follow, even if they resent him for it. What I'd needed to know was how the bridge worked, and what weakness—if any—it might have. Ke'heops must be in dire need of a quick victory to construct the spell bridge from his own mages's bands.

And while the Argosi consider revenge even more perverse than grief, there was a cruel but appealing symmetry to what I was going to do to my father's prized war coven.

51

Discord

"You can't be serious!" Nephenia repeated for the third time. She hadn't given me the chance between either of the other two to explain, so I wasn't quite sure what the point of the third was other than to give her a reason to poke me in the chest even harder. For a girl with two missing fingers, she really knows how to hurt you with the other three.

"What's the problem, girl?" Ghilla asked. The others had the sense to stay out of it, but whatever culture whisper witches come from, they have precious little sense of self-preservation. "We get some of these metal inks you Jan'Tep are so fond of, go back to the abbey, and then 'counter-band'—whatever that is—the ribbons coming from the war coven. They lose their powers forever and we don't have to worry about getting slaughtered. We win."

"The whole world wins," Tournam added, leaning against a tree while watching us argue. His eyes spent a lot more time on Nephenia than on me. "You can even stay with us, lovely. Find you some nice black eye make-up and make you an honorary shadowblack."

"I'd rather be dead," she replied, which was unusually callous for her.

"Well, the rest of us *will* be dead," Diadera said, striding up to Nephenia until they would have been nose to nose, had Diadera not been a couple of inches shorter. "Seems you lost some of your brain along with those fingers."

Nephenia ignored her and delivered her pronouncement to all of us. "I'm not going to let you destroy the lives of seventy-seven mages. Counter-banding them is like cutting out half their soul."

The others shuffled about, unsure what to make of this. Suta'rei wouldn't meet my eyes. She, more than any of the others, understood the perfidy of what I was suggesting. Butelios didn't look happy about it either.

Diadera, on the other hand, positively loved the idea. "When we're done taking half their souls, I'll find a way to scrape out the other half. Jan'Tep have been murdering my kind for centuries." The black markings of her freckles flew up from her cheeks and began to swarm in the air between the two of them. "Want to see why?"

This was getting out of hand, but Neph gave a flick of her fingers that I knew meant I should back off. "I wondered how long it would take you to threaten me," she said to Diadera. "I could see it in those little dirty looks of yours, same as I see the lust in that moron over there." She gestured to Tournam.

"Hey, what did I do?" he asked, only now taking an interest in the conversation.

Diadera's firefly freckles drifted closer to Nephenia. "Guess you should've done something about it before now, charmcaster. Because if you try reaching into your coat for one of your little trinkets, my shadowblack will tear you to pieces."

"Are they fighting over Kellen?" Tournam asked Ghilla. "Because that's just—"

"Shut up, Tournam," I said.

Something odd was happening or, rather, something that should have been happening *wasn't*. Ishak, who on any other occasion when someone dared threaten Nephenia would bare his teeth, was sitting a few yards away, staring disinterestedly into the distance.

He's not worried about her. Which means . . . Oh, crap. Neph, what are you doing?

She offered Diadera a smile I recognised at once. It belonged to a certain Argosi who was perpetually teaching people how to get in trouble. "Check your right pocket."

"You're bluffing," she said. "I would've known if you put something there."

"Then go ahead and attack me with those filthy bugs that follow you around."

Diadera tried not to take the bait, but after a few seconds she reached into the pocket of her long leather coat. Her hand came back with a small metal object fashioned to look like a miniature spider. She tried to shake it off, but Nephenia whispered a single word under her breath and all of a sudden the tiny metal arms became glued to Diadera's palm. "I'd leave it be," she warned. "The instant the arms lose contact with your skin or I say the word, you'll feel a light pinprick. Things will go badly for you after that."

Ghilla came stalking towards Nephenia, her mouth open, the shadowblack markings filling her throat ready to blow strangling fog. "Shouldn't mess with my girl, Jan'Te—"

Nephenia gave a whistle and all of a sudden a scream came from the back of Ghilla's head. The girl grabbed frantically at her own hair, trying to find the source. "I wouldn't," Neph said. Then she turned to face the others. "Listen up, morons. I'm an exiled Jan'Tep charmcaster with no clan and precious few friends. I'm a pretty girl with a valuable talent and that makes me a target all over this continent. I've dealt with plenty of scumbags who thought they could take advantage of me. So if any of you wants to take your shot, I promise you'll soon find out why none of the rest succeeded either."

"You planted charms on us?" Azir asked. He looked as if his feelings were genuinely hurt.

"Nothing that would ever hurt you, or you'd ever notice," she replied. "Unless you gave me no choice." She turned to me. "Come on, Kellen. Time for us to get out of here."

"What? I can't! I told you, there are children at the abbey!"

She shrugged. "I told you before—if you really cared about those kids, you'd get them the hells away from that awful place. As for these shadowblacks you've taken up with?" She gestured towards Diadera and the others. "I've set the charms to each release their spell once I'm a mile away from them. But if they come looking for me? Well, if I have to choose between a bunch of shadowblacks and our own people, it's no choice at all."

"Typical Jan'Tep," Diadera said, though I noticed she wasn't coming any closer.

"What's happened to you, Neph?" I asked.

She didn't answer, and I wondered if maybe I'd missed the obvious: six months had passed since I'd last seen her, and while that may not sound like a lot, every step on the long, hard road of an outlaw changes you. Had life as an exile turned Nephenia cold-hearted?

No, I realised. *It's made her smart. And cunning.*

"I thought you were different," I said. "Your uncle mistreated you. Your own brothers took two fingers from each of your hands, but here you are, still parroting the same Jan'Tep prejudices about how the life of a shadowblack isn't worth protecting."

She stared back at me, eyes narrowed. I'd never met Nephenia's uncle, but I knew for sure she didn't have any brothers, so what she did next would tell me where we stood. "Says the guy who left his own sister unconscious halfway up a mountain."

Okay, so we're in business.

"To be fair, it was only a quarter of the way up, on the eastern slope, so she'll get plenty of sun if she's still there in a few hours." Having gotten that out of the way, I tapped a finger on the markings around my left eye. "Will you do me the same courtesy when these grow a little too big and you decide my soul's not worth saving?"

"I'd hoped we could find you a cure, Kellen. Before it was too late." She unslung the pack with Reichis in it and placed it on the ground between us before backing away towards the trees. Ishak got up and loped alongside her. "Guess it was too late before I even met you."

I let her have the last word. When she was gone, I picked up the pack and checked on the squirrel cat. He was still sleeping, but his fur wasn't as slick with sweat as it had been earlier. *Hang on, buddy. Another day of this insanity and I promise we'll find you a nice bath and a cartload of butter biscuits.*

Tournam came to stand beside me. "Thanks so much for introducing your friend to us, Kellen. She was a big help."

"She is Jan'Tep," Suta'rei said. "You can no more ask her to feel sympathy for a shadowblack than ask a mother to empathise with the snake she finds in her child's bedroom."

"Oh?" Tournam asked. "And you being one of them, is that how you see us? As monsters?"

Suta'rei closed her eyes, the black markings that covered her lids like the entrances into dark, empty tunnels. "It's how I see myself."

52

The Inks

"So how does it work, boy?" Ghilla asked.

I took off my coat. "You do realise you're the youngest one here other than Azir, right?"

She grinned. "Yeah, but I got me an old soul."

As I rolled up my shirtsleeve, I pointed to the glyphs on my forearm. "You see these symbols?"

"Jan'Tep bands. Who cares?" But she and the others huddled around me.

I focused my will on the breath band. It was dark enough out that my pathetically dim sparking was noticeable. "This is what happens when a mage draws one of the fundamental forms of magic into themselves."

"We know how Jan'Tep magic works," Diadera said. "We've all seen Suta'rei do it, and it's not like most of us haven't been hunted by one of your people at one time or another."

"Look at the second band," I said, showing them my ember band.

Butelios pushed through to look at it closely. I got the sense maybe this was new for him, which was too bad, because it meant his first real encounter with Jan'Tep culture was going to involve seventy-seven war mages. "Those marks," he said, pointing at the copper glyphs in my ember band while being careful not to touch. "They look...wrong."

"What do you mean?" Suta'rei asked. "You know nothing of Jan'Tep banding."

The big man shook his head. "I don't know. They just look... hurtful."

"They're called inverted glyphs," I explained. "Part of what we call counter-banding. It stops me from ever using those forms of magic."

"What happens if you try?" Azir asked, coming closer. "I mean, really hard?"

A good question. Since counter-banding is known to be irreversible, I'd never bothered to test it. "Probably nothing," I said, but for the hell of it, I poured my will into the band. Nothing happened at first, but that wasn't a surprise. People think of exerting will as if it were like concentrating really hard. My old spellmaster used to joke that new initiates always looked constipated, because they confused exerting will with clenching their buttocks. It's different, though. Hard to explain—which is why it can take years to learn. Sparking a band requires not so much trying to push or pull at something with your mind. The way of the Jan'Tep is the way of mastery. Control. Dominance. You don't bend the magic to your will; you demand that it bend before you. That requires, among other things, believing it's possible.

For the first time since before I'd left my people, I made myself believe I could be a mage. I sent my will pouring through the bands for iron, ember, silk, sand and blood, probing for one that would submit to me. Nothing at first, but when I returned to ember I began to feel a kind of itch, not unlike the one I'd felt the day I'd first sparked my breath band. At that tiny glimmer of hope, I doubled and redoubled my efforts. Had my old spellmaster been there, he would've been proud—and surprised—at how perfectly and utterly I exerted control over the ember band. And then it happened. The itch became something else—something that both burned and froze me all at the same time, that hurt so bad I dropped to my knees.

"Kellen!" Diadera said, grabbing at my shoulders. "What's wrong? Tell us what to do!"

"There's nothing you can do," Suta'rei said, an uncomfortable tightness in her voice. "This is what it means to be counter-banded."

I released my will and the pain began to fade. No magic had come to me, not any I could use anyway.

"Does it still hurt?" Azir asked.

I shook my head. I couldn't bring myself to speak.

"Then why are you crying?"

"Leave him be," Suta'rei said.

Tournam—probably still annoyed that Nephenia had failed to fall for his charms—was less sympathetic. "What's the big deal? You knew you were counter-banded before, right? So you're never going to be a big mage like your daddy. Get over it."

Suta'rei put a hand on his chest and gently pushed him away. "He just learned that had his parents not counter-banded him, he could have been an ember mage."

"I'm sorry, Kellen," Diadera said. She knelt beside me and put a hand on my left cheek, her fingers touching the markings around my eye. *Do you need some time alone? I can get the others to leave for a while.*

No, I replied silently through our shadowblack connection. *We don't have time.*

Tournam was right. Nothing had really changed. I couldn't use ember magic before and I still couldn't. It was just that little flicker I'd felt—that tiny promise that something more could have been there had I not been counter-banded. It brought back all the broken dreams I'd thought I'd left behind me.

Diadera probed deeper through her touch. *Maybe this is a sign, Kellen. Maybe it's time to finally put those things away. To stop being part Jan'Tep mage, part Argosi, part everything except the one thing you are: shadowblack.* She leaned over and kissed my cheek. The warmth of her lips against my skin, the feeling of being so close, not just physically, but bound together somehow. It was confusing and intoxicating. I wanted more.

I rose to my feet and shook myself off. *A few hours ago you decided you were in love with Nephenia. Now you're getting hot and bothered over Diadera. Figure out who you are before you ruin someone else's life.*

"I'm okay," I said to the others. "The pain was a good reminder."

"A good reminder of what?" Tournam asked.

I pointed to the bands on my forearm. "The members of the war coven are forging the bridge from an ethereal connection to their own bands. If we start counter-banding the threads of the bridge that are attaching themselves to the abbey, those mages will feel what I felt, only I'm guessing a dozen times worse."

"Now *that* I'd enjoy seeing," Tournam said.

Butelios looked less certain. "Might not such an attack leave your entire people without their most powerful protectors?"

I was struck by his compassion for those who'd happily see him dead, and again wondered at how different he was from the others, but right now I had more immediate issues to deal with. "With luck we won't have to counter-band many of them. No mage who witnesses it happening to their fellows is going to stick around. They'll withdraw their magic and the bridge will come apart before anyone can cross it."

Diadera, Suta'rei, Tournam and Ghilla all shared a glance, keeping it from Butelios and Azir, which confirmed something I'd begun to suspect about this little group. I had more pressing concerns, though. "How far are we from the central Jan'Tep territories?" I asked.

Suta'rei pointed to the east. "About two hundred miles. Why?"

I turned to Azir. "Can you make a road to get us there? There's something I need from my father's home."

The boy looked stricken. "I'm...I'm really tired already, Kellen, and if I have to get us back to the abbey, then—"

"We don't need banding inks, if that's what you're looking for," Suta'rei said.

I turned to see her removing vials from her pack that I recognised immediately. "What are you doing with—" I stopped myself, because I already understood why. When Suta'rei had fled our people, she must've brought the inks with her. She knew one day the shadow-black would start to take her over. She'd end up like that crazed mage we'd fought a couple of days ago. Before she lost the will to fight back, she'd remove some of what would make her a danger to others.

"It's my duty," she said to me, quietly, as though the fear and misery in those words was something only the two of us could share.

Tournam punched me in the arm. "Looks like we'll have a fair fight for once. Knew you'd come through, cloud boy."

The gesture was friendly, but the nickname only reminded me that the sasutzei had been dormant since the first fight in the abbey. I wasn't sure if she was even still in my right eye any more. *Wherever you've gone, you crazy wind spirit, I hope you find a better travelling companion than I turned out to be.*

We stayed there a little while, giving Azir as much time to rest as we could. Ghilla wondered why we couldn't just use the spell bridge, since it would've been faster. Suta'rei gave an exhaustive and rather morbid account of what would happen to us the moment the mages sensed intruders on their bridge, which put an end to that discussion. Eventually Azir stood up, closed his eyes and forced a shadowblack road into existence. The lines on his pale face made him look as if he was burning up something inside him that could never fully be replenished. Tournam had to carry him as we travelled, the muscles on his arms shaking as he held Azir upright the entire way, so the boy's feet could create the road ahead of us without him having to support his own weight.

I followed the others. None of them watched me to see if I might betray them or questioned my loyalty. They'd watched Nephenia abandon me, so to them I was shadowblack through and through now. With each passing step, I wondered if I'd ever be anything else.

53

The Soulbinder

By the time we returned to the abbey a kind of giddy optimism had infected the others. Tournam announced to anyone who would listen that we'd brought the means to defeat the Jan'Tep posse. The abbey's inhabitants, thirsty for salvation, drank up every tiny drop of hope he offered them. In the desert, so many become fooled by mirages that you often find corpses with sand in their mouths and smiles on their faces.

I'd expected the abbot to be dubious about what we'd learned, if not enraged at us for having left the abbey without his consent. Instead he was jubilant, practically bellowing with joy as he pounded a heavy fist on the desk inside the private room atop his tower. Sheaves of paper went flying, many covered in sketched fragments of my shadowblack markings. He leaped up from his desk and hugged each one of us. "If ever I'd hoped for proof that the world can be just, that this place we've built matters, and that the gods—assuming there are any—can love even a pack of reprobate shadowblacks like the seven of you, this is it!"

"It's only a theory right now," I warned him, uneasy at just how far there was to fall from the heights of his exuberance.

"It's a damned certainty!" He snatched up half a dozen sheets from the desk before hauling us out of his office and down the spiral stairs.

It wasn't long before we were outside the abbey's gates and at the cliff's edge where the spell bridge had first appeared. The sight of it was daunting. Ten feet wide now, the smooth surface shimmering as the ribbons of light from which it was made danced in the breeze. They became solid as stone when you touched them however, and that was enough to bring Tournam and the others back down to earth.

Not so the abbot.

"Jan'Tep bands," he said, kneeling on the end of the bridge to peer at them. "You're sure?"

Though the ribbons of raw magical force shifted and became entwined around each other in constant flux as they fought to warp the very laws of physics, the strands were stable where they had anchored themselves into the cliff face. There you could easily make out the distinctive colours and textures of the six forms of Jan'Tep magic: iron, ember, breath, blood, silk and sand. All of them were represented, each individual band stretching a thousand miles to the forearm of its owner. Ghilla produced a short, sharp blade from inside the sleeve of her coat and stabbed it into one of the bands, then made a show of listening to it before shaking her head. "Too bad. Would've been nice to hear one of those boys scream."

"It's not the actual band," I said. "It's more like a tether to the mage's ability to summon the six raw forms of magic."

"But the connection *is* there?" the abbot pressed. "The individual mages are tied to them somehow?"

I nodded. "The bond between a mage and their bands is more than just the metallic inks on their skin. Those are just the physical aspects, infused by years and years of an initiate's training in each form of magic. In theory, if we imprint counter-glyphs on the strands of the bridge, we'll disrupt their ability to draw on those forces."

"It'll hurt them too, right?" Azir asked.

He'd insisted on coming up the tower with us, despite Tournam's urging that he get some rest. But the boy looked withered, his skin pale and his lips almost blue. He couldn't walk unsupported and he shivered uncontrollably. The demands of so many trips had broken him. I'd expected to see a look of eagerness in his eyes—that he *wanted* to hurt the enemy who would ruin his home and had, perhaps, already ruined his life. Yet all I saw was concern. "Maybe we could just do it a little," he said. "Just enough to make them go away."

"Have you forgotten who we're talking about?" Diadera asked, her tone icy.

"I h—"

"Azir is right," Butelios said, coming out the gates. "Mercy can deliver greater victories than brutality."

"That's the exact opposite of how life works, boy," Ghilla said.

I'd wondered why Butelios had disappeared when we'd first come back. Now he handed me a small packet of folded cheesecloth. "You haven't eaten in some time, my friend. If you are to save all our lives, you should at least have a little food in your belly."

In fact Nephenia had forced a few strips of dried jerky into me, but I was touched by the gesture. When I opened the cloth, I broke out laughing.

"Do you not like them? I merely thought they'd be a convenient—"

I unslung my pack and set it on the ground next to me before waving the contents of Butelios's package in the air. A sniffing sound was soon followed by a little black muzzle pressing against the narrow opening at the top of the pack, followed by growls and a rather frantic attempt to chew his way through the drawstrings tying it closed. Loath to lose my fingers, I tugged the pack open and then dropped half the contents of Butelios's packet inside.

"Spirits!" Ghilla swore at the noises that followed. "How long since you fed that thing?"

"Nephenia wasn't neglecting him," I replied, "but she didn't have any butter biscuits to hand."

"He sure seems to like them," Azir said, edging a little closer.

Reichis's furry face appeared out of the pack and he growled at each of us in turn, blurry little eyes darting in all directions for his intended prey. "Here," I said, holding out the remaining biscuits. "Guess you're feeling better, eh?" It was all I could do to keep the desperate sense of relief from turning me into a weeping mess.

For his part, the squirrel cat ignored me, focusing all his attention on devouring the butter biscuits. He even shook one in his mouth several times as though trying to break its neck before gulping it down. When he was finished he gave a final sniff in the air and, apparently satisfied there were no more butter biscuits within range, tucked himself back in the pack and set to snoring loudly. I knelt down to close up the top. "Hope you're planning on being more help than this when the fighting starts," I whispered.

"If you're done playing with your pet," Diadera said, "there are seventy-seven Jan'Tep out there and I'd like to see every single one counter-banded before they take their first step on that bridge."

"What?" Butelios asked. "Surely we need only perform the procedure on a few." He turned to me. "You said once the first were afflicted, the others would abandon the spell."

"No mage would ever risk losing his magic forever just to hold a bridge together," I said, but now my attention was on Suta'rei. She'd begun to set out a tray of burning braziers with pools of molten metallic inks in copper dishes. She studiously avoided catching my eye.

Why won't she look at me? She's . . . ashamed. But why? I felt the first stirrings of an itch in my left eye, presaging one of my shadow-black headaches. *No, damn it! Not now. I need to figure out what's happening here.*

I started towards Suta'rei, but she turned away from me. "You're not planning on giving the posse the chance to run, are you?" I asked.

She made no reply, only exchanging a glance with the abbot. He was staring at the pieces of paper he'd brought with him from his desk. *Suta'rei already knows the reverse sigils for counter-banding a mage. What is on those pages that she could possibly need?*

The sensation around my left eye changed. Now it felt as if some-one were pinching the lids. I blinked in response, and for just an instant I was looking right at the pages in the abbot's hand. *No, not looking at them . . . I'm seeing into them somehow.* They were sketches like the ones he'd taken at the cauldron of the unique patterns my grandmother had inscribed around my eye, but he'd altered the designs. Before I could see more, the strange vision fled me.

"Kellen?" Diadera asked. "Are you all right?"

I blinked again, trying to peer deeper, but nothing happened. I poured my will into the markings around my eye, trying to force them awake the way I would the breath band on my forearm. Again, nothing. What had triggered my shadowblack? What thought had enabled me to see so clearly for that brief moment?

Questions. I'd been asking myself questions. *That's what awakens the markings . . . Not force of will. Not magic.* I remembered then how highly the Dowager Magus of my clan had prized clever questions—how they'd been the key to breaking the mind chain that impris-oned her. *My shadowblack must work the same way . . . the ability can only be unlocked by asking the right questions.*

A hundred of them formed in my mind, all shouting for my

attention. They weren't the right ones though, because all they produced was a sharp pain in my eye. *Focus. Find the right one.* I let all the clues and details I'd been ignoring until now arrange themselves in my mind, each one like a little sigil stone bearing a dozen different questions I'd failed to see before. I knocked them over one at a time like dominoes until there was only one left, and upon it a single question: *why would the abbot be so interested in my shadowblack?*

"Ancestors…" I said out loud, as I once again became aware of my markings. They weren't pinching or burning any more, but twitching, turning, like the dials on a lock.

"Kellen?" Diadera asked again. I think her hand was on my arm, but it felt distant, like a soft breeze. Her voice was faint—an echo from somewhere far away. "Something's happening to you…"

Even without being able to see myself, I knew the twisting black lines around my eye had changed. No longer were they the dials of a lock, binding the shadowblack inside me; instead they were like… lenses that shifted and adjusted themselves as my gaze went to the abbot. *No, not to him. Inside him.* In the past, when the attacks came, people and places would become terrifying, warped distortions of themselves. Now I saw with perfect clarity, bearing witness to the secrets buried beneath the abbot's lies.

"Incredible," I heard him say, but nestled between those syllables lay other words, inscribed in shadow. They were scrawled all over the skin of his face too, and carved into the flesh of his hands. They told tales of pain and fear, of blood and vengeance. It would have taken a lifetime to read them all. I didn't need to though, because the answers I was looking for were written elsewhere, in the furtive movements of the one person who still refused to meet my gaze. Suta'rei continued placing her instruments and adjusting the flames beneath the braziers, slowly, precisely, carefully, because that's how you have to move when your hands are shaking. "Those aren't the inks for counter-banding, are they?" I asked, though I could already read the truth in the trembling of her lips. "You're preparing the abnegation ritual."

She froze. Her eyes finally met mine and there I saw, plain as day, letters written in ink the colour of shame as they desperately spelled out a single word: *duty*.

I flipped open the tops of the pouches at my sides. "Step away from the bridge, Suta'rei."

"Whoa," Tournam said, coming to stand between us. "Everybody calm down until we figure this out."

"Don't you get it?" I asked. "The abbot's been lying to you. He's not trying to destroy the spell bridge. He *wants* the posse to come here."

"But why?" Azir asked. "Why would he—"

I ignored him, keeping watch on the abbot in case he made a move. Of all of them, his shadowblack was the most dangerous. "You lied to me back at the cauldron," I said. "All those drawings you made, all that nonsense you spouted about figuring out how to unlock my bands, it was a ruse to hide the real reason you've been so fascinated with my markings ever since I got here. You wanted to learn how to band others in shadow."

He shrugged, betraying not the slightest hint of worry, nor did my shadowblack reveal any within him. "If there were more of us in the world, maybe our enemies would think twice before trying to hunt us all down."

Azir, unsteady on his legs, stumbled as he tried to make his way to the abbot. "But, sir, what if they don't want to be shadowblacks?"

"Stay out of this, you idiot," Tournam warned. Even without my markings shifting to focus on him, I could easily interpret the confusion on his face. He knew a fight was coming, and now he was trying to decide whose side to take. I saw the same question written in the expressions of Diadera and Ghilla too.

"Everything changed when Suta'rei told the abbot about Tas'diem and what he'd done to those villagers," I said, hoping that if the rest of them could just see how far gone he was, they'd force him to abandon his plan. "He's going to imprint the patterns my grandmother used to bind me in shadow directly onto the strands of the spell bridge. He'll infect every mage in the posse with the shadowblack."

"So what, boy?" Ghilla asked. "Maybe once they know what it's like, livin' as we do, they'll stop huntin' us."

"Don't you understand? Once he's banded them in shadow, the mages won't be able to break their connection to the abbot. He won't have to carve the abnegation sigils into their flesh the way Tas'diem did; he'll burn them right into their very souls. He'll force his will upon them, make them kill each other, and when that's done…"

"When I've finished doing what's needed to protect this abbey, I'll drain each and every one of those bastards dry." He shook his head ruefully. "I wonder, Kellen, is it hard for someone who wraps themselves in petty notions of Argosi frontier philosophy to witness the simple truth of how wars are fought?"

"You don't have to do this." I turned to Suta'rei. "You swore you'd never become like Tas'diem, but what you're doing now is no better. Banding them in shadow and inflicting the abnegation ritual on them is worse than murder."

"Leave the girl alone!" the abbot shouted, the anger in his voice failing to hide his true meaning. *Pay attention to me*, it said. *I'm in charge here.* "Tell us, Kellen, with those newfound enigmatist abilities of yours, can you see your own role in all of this? After all, if you hadn't been so desperate to rid yourself of the shadowblack, you might never have come here in the first place, and I never would've learned the secret to binding others in shadow. And if you hadn't gone to spy on your own people, we wouldn't have discovered how to exploit the spell bridge."

"You lousy son of a bitch." Stupidly I tried to rush him, but Tournam caught my shoulder and threw me back.

The abbot walked over to Suta'rei and took a long silver banding needle from her. Pure shadow oozed from the markings on his hand, winding up the narrow shaft to become a single glistening drop at the sharpened tip. "You accused me of being a religious zealot before, Kellen. Maybe I am, but my faith is in my people, and my religion is whatever it takes to keep them safe." He knelt by the spell bridge, and with the end of his banding instrument began to trace the first glyph onto some unwitting mage's soul.

There was a roar, and Butelios shoved Tournam out of the way to get to the abbot. "No! I will not allow this abomination! I can't let y—"

Without so much as a word, without the abbot even turning to look at him, a tendril of shadow whipped out from the cuff of his robe and slammed Butelios against the gates. The big man slumped to the ground, unconscious, a thin trail of blood following the back of his head down the bars.

"Get him out of here," the abbot commanded Tournam and the others. "If you can bandage up his wound, fine. If he tries to resist, drop him over the mountainside." When no one moved he turned to face them, righteous fury painted over the features of his face. "This is war, not some courtly game with polite little rules! Every day you people come to me, crying about your fears, about being exiled by your families, about being hounded by Jan'Tep bounty hunters. 'Protect us,' you plead, over and over and over again." He raised up the silver banding instrument, filling it once again with his shadowblack. "Well, this is how it's done."

For a moment, just a split second really, I thought the others might turn on him—that this daring, charismatic leader who had no idea how crazy he sounded had gone too far. But as I looked from Tournam to Suta'rei, to Ghilla, and finally to Diadera, I could read only their desperation to believe his words, the depths to which they were swayed by his rationalisations and enthralled by his promises to protect them. I'm not sure I've ever felt quite so alone as I did then.

Without warning, the twisting black lines around my eye shifted again, returning to their usual patterns as the world once again buried itself in lies. Apparently I'd reached the limits of this "enigmatism" of mine. I guess uncovering the truth and knowing what to do with it are very different things. *What am I supposed to do now, Grandmother? What purpose drove you to give me this gift that no sane person would want?*

I slid my hands into the powder pouches at my sides and faced the abbot. "You know, when we first met I said you were old, dumb and weak. What I should've said is that you're old, dumb and dead."

The abbot went on with his banding, the black oil of his markings sliding down his wrists to provide the ink. "You want a duel then, Kellen? Want me to set down this instrument so we can see if the outlaw spellslinger can outdraw the big, bad tyrant?"

"I can't think of anything in the world I want more."

Diadera came close to me. "Kellen, you're angry, and you have every reason to be concerned about the abbot's plan, but please, just lis—"

I pushed her away. "Don't you touch me." She was in the way of my shot, and with Tournam, Ghilla and Suta'rei already moving into position to protect the abbot, the angles were too tight. If there had ever been a moment when I could have won this fight without hurting these people who, despite everything I'd done, had offered me a place among them, it was long gone.

"I warned you, Diadera," the abbot said, still facing the bridge. "Soon as he showed up, you started making eyes at him, but I told you Kellen wasn't the sort to seek out comfort or solace. No, that boy wears his markings like a Daroman marshal's badge, as if being an outlaw was some kind of noble pursuit."

"It could have been real," she said, though I wasn't sure if she was talking to me or the abbot or herself. She was coming towards me again, those pale green eyes of hers promising we could still fix this, that it wasn't too late. But by then my mind was too busy racing through every possible way out of this situation to think about the road never travelled.

Wait till she's close. Slip to the side, heel behind her knee, arm around the throat. A steel card at her neck. The others will hesitate, so push her towards the banding braziers. When the abbot and Suta'rei move to protect them, pull powder and fire. Tournam's the fastest with his bands, but Azir's the most valuable. Grab him and throw him towards the cliff so their attention is focused on saving him. Ghilla doesn't care about anyone else, so she'll be preparing to spew shadow fog. What do I do then?

Diadera was inches away now. "Please," she said. "You're one of us."

Faster, damn it. Put all the pieces in play. Pull out every gambit you know.

I call myself a spellslinger, but at heart I guess I'm just a con artist. Like my father once said, everything is tricks with me. The problem with tricks, though, is that sometimes the most devastating trick is the one that's been played on you.

Diadera reached up a hand to touch my markings. I looped my

arm around it, catching her in a joint lock. Had she really come to me with some plea to get me to see reason, I would've had her. Problem was, she hadn't. The shadowblack freckles from her cheeks flew into mine, burrowing deep under the skin, and in so doing, revealed an ability Diadera had kept hidden from me until now. I felt consciousness leave me as she took control of my mind, leaving no room for me inside it.

Guess everyone's a soulbinder these days.

54

The Apology

To say I awoke an hour later would be imprecise. I was never asleep, not really. Diadera's freckles had somehow infected my own shadow-black, giving her control over my body, because apparently the world needed of one more esoteric means of stealing a person's freedom.

I was seriously starting to wonder if maybe magic was just inherently evil.

That aside, given that Diadera had played the inside of my mind like a badly tuned guitar, I was confident she knew I was now conscious, so I didn't bother trying to hide it. Instead I sat up on the bed and watched her through the bars. The green eyes that stared back at me were no longer as bright, as if even they had been dimmed by the shadows lingering between us.

"I'm sorry," I said.

She looked surprised. "You're sorry? For what? You're the one stuck in a cell, Kellen."

"Yeah, but I've been in lots of cells before."

"So?"

"So, you've got to figure I must be pretty good at breaking out of them by now."

"I wish that were true this time." She sounded sincere. It made it hard to hate her. Almost.

I leaned back against the wall. The glassy black stone felt slick and unnatural now that I knew it was all part of the abbot's shadowblack. How much of this stuff could exist in one person's body? Did he take more of it from people who died here? When they were taken over by demons, did he kill them only so that he could draw the shadowblack from them later?

I allowed those and about a dozen other morbid questions to occupy my thoughts for a moment while I checked on Reichis. He was still inside the pack, sound asleep, crumbs of butter biscuits strewn over his fuzzy little muzzle. "Some help you were," I said. "Where was all that tough-guy squirrel cat talk when I was being dragged here in preparation for the gallows?"

"I won't let anyone kill you," Diadera said. "I promise."

I wiped off a few of the crumbs from Reichis's face. He bit me. I found it oddly reassuring. "If you believe that, Diadera, then I'm even more sorry for you."

"Stop saying that! Stop telling me you're sorry. You don't know anything about me."

I closed the top of the pack. "Really?" I walked over to the bars and reached a hand through the gap. I was surprised that she let my finger touch the shadowblack freckles on her cheeks. *You're a lot like a friend of mine.*

No, you only think that. You're like all the others. I show you a few carefully selected fragments of who I am and you think you see the whole picture. You don't. You never even looked past the obvious, even when I . . . Even when I wanted you to.

People who take over your bodies and lock you in cells have no business playing on your guilt. Still, it worked on me. As my sister is fond of reminding me, deep down I'm a sucker who'll sell his own soul for the chance to be loved. *Do you want to know what I see in you?* I asked.

I could feel the muscle in her cheek tighten. *You think because you're an enigmatist now you can break into my mind? Go ahead and try.*

An odd sincerity suffused her thoughts, as if some part of her really did want me to force her to reveal herself. I removed my hand and instead took hers, placing her fingers against my own markings so that she would know I wasn't unlocking them. It felt important to show that what I said next came from me, and not some supernatural insight given me by the shadowblack. "This friend of mine..." Despite my current predicament, a smile came to my face. "She's like you in so many ways. She loves to tease, because that's how she tells you that you're okay—that she doesn't see you as broken or less worthwhile than anyone else. She's bold too. I swear, the more dangerous the situation, the bigger the swagger in her step. The more scared she is, the more brazenly she talks."

"Sounds like she's hiding something."

I let that slide. Diadera was leaning close to the bars now, the red curls of her hair so close I found myself longing to touch them. "She's got hair like yours too, which I imagine is pretty rare."

"Red hair's not that uncommon."

"It is among the Mahdek."

She froze like a deer who's just smelled the hunter and heard the twang of the crossbow but can't yet feel the wound and is frantically trying to figure out which way to run. "Why would you say that?"

"I didn't know at first. I knew something was off though. The whole Daroman act—that was too perfect. Every gesture and mannerism, every syllable uttered in the most scintillatingly pure High Daroman accent? You've obviously travelled, and no one who travels keeps their accent that pristine."

"Not many would've picked up on such subtleties. Your Argosi friend teach you that?"

I shrugged. "Some, but that only told me you were hiding

something. In the end, it all came back to that day in the abbot's tower when I first arrived. You came to find me outside his office."

"I remember. So what?"

"You hated me."

"Hated you?" she laughed. "I practically threw myself at you."

"Yeah. That doesn't happen to me a lot. People tend to find me kind of off-putting until they get to know me. After that they usually want to murder me, but you didn't need to wait that long. Tournam even said the next day that you were supposed to kill me."

She hesitated, but her eyes didn't look away at all. "He told me you were Jan'Tep. I swore a long time ago that Suta'rei would be the only one of your people I'd tolerate. So I came to seduce you. Get you to come with me out to the cliff side. A lot of people when they first come here, when they see a demon emerge from someone who has the same disease as them, they just walk right off the edge of the cliff. No one would've questioned it."

Tournam. Diadera. Ghilla for sure. How many of these people had wanted to murder me on sight?

"So what happened?" I asked.

Diadera's fingertips traced the winding black vines around my eye. *This. I'd never met anyone whose markings were from the same ethereal plane as mine. For a second, when I touched them, I didn't feel . . .*

"Alone," I said out loud.

She nodded, taking her hand away. "Your Mahdek friend—has she told you what it's like? To wake up every day and know that your people are gone? That they were killed, brutally, horribly, and that no one shed a tear for them?"

"I'm sorry."

"Stop saying that! I don't need your pity."

"No, I don't mean about being Mahdek." I stepped back from the bars. "I don't know what it's like to lose your people. I only know what it's like to have your own people hate you, hunt you and want nothing more than to see you dead."

"Then you should want to see them suffer!" She gripped the bars so tight the flesh of her knuckles drained of colour. "The Jan'Tep despise shadowblacks, Kellen! Hate them as much as they hated my people, and you know what they did to us! Even that friend of yours, the three-fingered girl with the hyena, she ran away from you the moment she saw the rest of us and realised what you were destined to become. They aren't your people any more, Kellen. We are. You should want to see the Jan'Tep wiped from the face of the earth!"

"I do," I admitted. "Some days I want it so much I almost wish the demon inside me would take over."

"Then side with us! Promise to work with the abbot and—"

I shook my head. "The problem is that I keep thinking about that friend of mine. Ferius Parfax is her name. Saved my life, then proceeded to make a giant mess of it. Craziest person you could ever meet. Despite everything she's seen, every ugly thing the world's shown her, she gets up every morning and tries to save it. Not just that—she does it with joy. With *joy*, Diadera. Every step, she walks the Path of the Wild Daisy. Can you imagine such a thing?"

There was silence between us for a while, then finally Diadera said, "She sounds amazing. I wish I'd met her."

"You still could."

"No."

"One thing I've learned walking the long roads, nothing's ever too late unless you choose to make it so." Wow. Ferius would've been proud of that one.

"This woman, this Ferius, who you say saved your life? The abbot saved mine. He taught me to take all my rage and helplessness and turn it into strength. Instead of living in fear of the shadows, I use them to protect the people I care about. Instead of hiding from my enemies, I make them hide from me."

"Sounds noble. I can't believe no one's written a song about it."

She didn't take the bait. "My life is going to be short, and my death more awful than most. I can't afford to wait for love or friendship or any of the lies people tell to make themselves feel better. But I can still find pleasure, and purpose, and take whatever comfort those give me for as long as I can."

"Even if it means helping the abbot perform the abnegation ritual on his enemies? Can you really live with that?"

Without looking away from me, she opened her coat and began unbuttoning her shirt, just enough that I could see the top of the markings she'd cut into her skin. "Oh, Diadera . . . why?"

"Because I chose my side, Kellen. When the fighting starts, if things are going badly and my sacrifice means the abbot can hold off those Jan'Tep monsters even one minute more? I'll give him my shadows, and slip into whatever death awaits me with a smile on my face." She stepped away from the bars. "I'm sorry if that disappoints you."

"No, Diadera. I'm sorry."

A small smile appeared on her lips. "How many times do I have to tell you to stop saying that? I don't want your pity, Kellen."

"It's not pity. I'm just wishing you could've known real friendship, just once." I looked back at the travelling pack sitting there next to the bed, and listened for a moment to the snores and grumbles that emerged. "He steals my stuff, he bites me and now he can't even speak to me, but even now just being near him makes me feel better."

"That's not friendship, Kellen. That's called having a pet."

"Shh," I whispered. "He can hear you, and he's probably hungry for eyeballs right about now." I came back to the bars, knowing the risk, but needing one last time to feel that strange connection with her that I would likely never share with another human being. *If you'd had the chance to know Reichis properly, you'd have learned the most important thing there is about friendship.*

I could feel her probing, trying to push deeper in my mind. I let her, but only down the path I set for her. *You'd do anything for him,* she thought.

That's what I've been trying to tell you, Diadera. No matter how bad things get or how badly you disappoint them, real friends never, ever abandon you. Even when they have to pretend to do so.

Too late her eyes went wide as she finally understood. Her shadowblack freckles flew up into the air, the swarm seeking out the threat that had been there all along. Diadera just hadn't been able to see it for the simple reason that she couldn't imagine it.

The blow came quick, and she slumped down to the floor. Red curls slipped between the bars, as if some small part of her were trying to reach the other side.

"How long have you been here?" I asked the darkness.

"Since before she brought you in," Nephenia replied, stepping close to the bars so I could see her. Ishak padded along next to her.

"How did you get back to the abbey?"

Nephenia gave a rather inelegant snort. "You would think after the first time they'd be on guard for it, but Azir was so exhausted and the others so full of themselves at having the means to defeat the posse that nobody noticed when we trailed you through shadow a second time." She pulled a tiny glass ball from her coat and broke it against the lock on the cell door. I heard a click and it swung open.

"You didn't need to use up one of your charms," I said. "My soto-castra coin could've done it."

"We don't have time for that. Besides, I made the charm months

324

ago. The spell wasn't going to last much longer anyway." Ishak gave two little barks. She patted his head. "Yes, dear, I'll tell him."

"Tell me what?"

"When we got back to the abbey, I wasn't sure where to hide or what to do. Ishak surmised you'd end up in a cell eventually so we might as well come and wait for you here."

"You took your sweet time in freeing me."

Nephenia looked down at Diadera's unconscious form. "I . . . I figured you had things that needed to be said."

It's funny how someone can know you better than you know yourself. All the while I'd thought I was playing it glib, spinning things out with Diadera to give Nephenia time to find me. Turns out she was just giving me time to say goodbye.

"You have a plan?" Nephenia asked. "Because from what I heard sitting here, it sounded like your crazy abbot friend is up to something awful. So unless you have some idea about how to stop everything from going to straight to seven hells . . ."

I went over to grab my pack. As I got there Reichis crawled out, stretched himself twice, farted and then wandered past the open cell door to clamber on top of Ishak's back, sitting there like a bizarre little furry cowboy. He chittered something in the hyena's ear.

"What did he say?" I asked.

Ishak yipped a few times. Nephenia's brow furrowed. "He says he's not sure. It's hard to make sense of the squirrel cat any more."

"Oh. I guess tha—"

"But he's pretty sure Reichis says you having a plan means we're all screwed."

Well, at least my business partner was as perceptive as ever. I held out a hand to Nephenia. She looked down at it, one eyebrow raised. "Are you trying to hold hands with me, Kellen?"

"No. But I assume you have something for me?"

She watched me steadily, trying to keep her features impassive, but not entirely able to keep a hint of a smile from creeping onto her face. "Why would I have something for you?"

"Because after you left, you went to make sure Shalla was okay."

"You know I hate your sister, right?"

"Yeah, but you went anyway, because you knew I wouldn't want to leave her alone and undefended like that. And once she woke up and the two of you went through your usual litany of threats and accusations, then she no doubt started up on how I was making a terrible mistake and had a responsibility to support my family and—"

The smile became a grin. "And how terribly angry Papa was going to be."

"Then she'd tell you it was your duty as a Jan'Tep—even an exiled one—to get a message to me."

"Shalla would never trust someone like me with such an important missive."

"Of course not. That's why she gave you something that would let her communicate with me here in the abbey."

Nephenia reached up and pinched my cheek with the three fingers of her hand. "How is it you're so cute and yet everyone still wants to kill you?"

She let go of my cheek and withdrew something from the pocket of her coat. "You were half right. Shalla did give me something for you, and it is a means of far-talking." She handed me a playing card. "Only it doesn't reach your sister."

The card was beautifully illustrated and disconcertingly familiar. A picture of an elaborate crown held aloft by wooden hands, an offering made to the only one worthy of such a gift. The title beneath it read: "The Crowned Mage."

"Looks like Daddy wants a word," Nephenia said.

55

The Negotiation

Why is it that however far I travel, I never seem to be able to get away from my father? No matter how much I might have looked up to him as a child, I'd always been closer to my mother. Yet I hadn't spoken to Bene'maat for almost two years. Not a word since I'd left home. I couldn't help but wonder if that wasn't by Ke'heops's design.

"Hello, Father," I said.

The image on the card had already come to life, strong, carefully manicured hands reaching down to take the crown and place it on his head. No doubt that was his favourite part. "Kellen. I see you've once again found new and interesting people with whom to conspire against your own family."

I smiled back at him, then flung the card against the dungeon wall, breaking the connection.

"Feeling a little irritable?" Nephenia asked.

I walked over to pick up the card. "Just setting a few ground rules for this negotiation."

It took a minute or two before the spell inside the card could breach the gap between us once again. My father didn't look amused.

"Don't say an ancestors-damned word, Father," I warned before he could express his outrage. "I'm going to talk and you're going to listen. Understand?"

He was still for so long that it wasn't at all clear that the spell in the card was still working. "Speak then."

That told me a lot. My father would never suffer the indignity of me taking control of the conversation unless he already knew he was in trouble. "I assume you've started seeing the effects of the abbot's shadow-banding?"

Ke'heops nodded. "Seven mages—men and women of good houses—began to show the signs. They turned their magic against us." The illustrated jaw tightened. "I had to end them."

"Well, you should probably abandon the bridge. Live to fight another day."

His drawn lip curled. "How little you understand of the ways of the world, Kellen. We are halfway to the abbey. If we turn away now, after I have promised our people a victory, I will never be crowned mage sovereign." He held up a hand. "And before you dishonour yourself and me with more clever remarks, know that such a defeat will keep our people weak and servile for a hundred years. Changes are afoot, Kellen. The world moves towards a deadlier war than any of us have ever seen. Maps will be redrawn. Would you see your homeland reduced to scattered fiefdoms beholden to greater nations?"

I was completely comfortable with that idea. Nonetheless I asked, "Will you risk losing every one of your mages over this fight?"

"Yes. I will send every last one of them to their deaths if needed. There are two kinds of leaders men seek, Kellen. Those who rule best in peace, and those who rule best in war. Even you must understand the times we live in. I will lose many—perhaps most—of my mages, but if just a few of us survive, we will reach the other side of the bridge and destroy the Ebony Abbey forever. Our people will mourn our dead, but they will do so with a pride long denied them."

"And what about Shalla?" I asked. "Will you be so sanguine when she dies?"

"Your sister is forbidden from fighting in the battle. She has remained behind at the encampment as I commanded."

I did him the courtesy of pretending that was remotely possible. Shalla was a stickler for rules, except when it came to protecting her family. She would no more allow Ke'heops to come to this death trap without her than she would allow me to die here alone. I wondered what she would do the day she was forced to choose between us.

"There might be another way," I said.

My father gazed back at me without any expression at all. No doubt he thought he was hiding his true feelings from me. But two years of learning the Argosi ways had taught me that even the absence of emotion can be a sign. In this case, it told me my father very much hoped I might have the answer to his problems. Considering how little faith he had in me, that meant he was truly desperate.

"I'll stop the abbot from shadow-banding more of your mages. You'll be able to bring your forces across the bridge."

"How?"

"None of your business." I wasn't just being belligerent either. If my father knew *how* I was going to do it, he'd find a way to turn that to his advantage. "In exchange, you're going to let the children here go free."

"Children? You mean shadowblacks?"

I nodded. "And their families. Most of these people are just trying to live their lives in peace. They don't have Jan'Tep magic, nor do they have any shadowblack abilities. They're just suffering from a curse that our own people brought to the world. If demonic forces ever take hold of them, someone will kill them easily enough before it becomes a problem. Let them go find peace for whatever time they have."

"No," my father said—too quickly, which meant I knew he was thinking about it. "To allow so many to go free would diminish my victory."

"Not nearly as much as having your asses handed to you by a bunch of lunatic monks—which is exactly what's going to happen unless you do things my way."

He looked at me through the frame of the card. "Your way. What is *your* way, Kellen? Where do these petty acts of interference and defiance lead? Has the Argosi so addled your mind with her frontier philosophy that you believe an outlaw spellslinger can alter the natural course of history?"

I didn't of course. I doubted all the Argosi with all their talents could stop whatever continental war was coming. But there's a reason Ferius taught me arta valar before she taught me how to fight. "Just watch me," I said.

The surface of the card rippled just a bit as he snorted. "Very well. Stop the abbot's atrocity before I lose any more of my mages and I will give you an hour to remove the children. Once the battle begins in earnest though, anyone left will die in fire and thunder. I will allow no trace of the Ebony Abbey to remain standing."

"I've a feeling that won't be a problem."

"Then it appears we have an agreement and, with it, duties we must each fulfil."

I hesitated, only now understanding how alike the abbot and Ke'heops were. "Father..." I wasn't even sure how to ask the question, but still I forced the words out. "Have you ever...Have you or Mother ever performed the abnegation ritual on our clan's enemies?"

He was silent a long while, just watching me. I feared I already knew the answer, and he was simply waiting for me to come to that conclusion myself. "No, Kellen, I would never carry out such an abomination, even on my enemies. There was a time when I might have considered it, but not so long ago I committed an act almost as depraved, and the memory has haunted me ever since."

"What?" I asked. "Which crime could possibly have caused the mighty Ke'heops's to question his duty?"

I saw the lines of the card settle back to their static form as he closed the spell, but not before I heard my father say, "I counter-banded my own son."

56

The Gates

Nephenia, Ishak, Reichis and I ran up one flight of stairs after another until we finally found ourselves inside a hallway in one of the largest of the abbey buildings. We sprinted outside and across the courtyard, past monks readying for war, innocents preparing themselves for the worst and children playing in naive ignorance of what was coming. By the time we were approaching the abbey gates, I could already see the damage the abbot had done to the once gleaming spell bridge. The bright colourful Jan'Tep bands were intermixed with thorny black vines that twisted around them, tearing at them. Sparks of red and gold, silver and blue, grey and yellow shattered the night sky as their essence fought against the black seeping inside them. The abbot was working fast.

"Come on," I said, heading for the gates.

Reichis, seated atop Ishak's back, kept chittering, as he had been the entire time since we'd left the dungeon. Periodically the hyena would translate for Nephenia and occasionally she'd start to convey his commentary to me.

"He says—"

"I know exactly what Reichis is saying. He's saying this plan is terrible, I'm going to get us all killed, and this is what he gets for agreeing to be the business partner of a weak-kneed skinbag."

Nephenia grabbed my arm. "That's fantastic! I thought you couldn't understand his words any more."

"I can't. The little bugger is just predictable, that's all."

Reichis gave a lengthy snarl.

I leaned into his face. "No, you're *not* going to eat my eyeballs. You know why? Because if I'm dead, then you'll be all alone, with nobody to find you baths and butter biscuits. Face it, Reichis: it's you and me against the world, just like always."

Ishak gave a loud bark. Nephenia just glared at me. That too I could translate without magical assistance. "I know you're risking your lives too. It's just...Look, can you all hold off hating me until *after* we stop these lunatics?"

Neph glanced at the hyena, who then turned his head to look at Reichis. Finally he gave a little yipping sound. "Fine," Nephenia translated. "But afterwards you're going to be making some *spectacular* apologies."

With that negotiation settled, the four of us ran through the gates to face what we'd known all along would await us there. It occurred to me then that I might never need to make those apologies.

57

The Casualty

We'd expected trouble, of course. The abbot, for all that his methods had taken a dark turn, had spent years earning the devotion of his followers. That isn't easy to do. He'd have monks with him—banders or foggers or whatever else they called them—guarding him as he worked. I'd be a fool to think the shadowcasters wouldn't be there too. By now, their paths chosen, their loyalties decided, they might even be spoiling for a fight. What I hadn't foreseen was that the first casualty would already be waiting for us.

"He's dead," Tournam said. He was kneeling on the ground, holding Azir's still form in his arms. There was no blood, no broken bones. Only the palpable emptiness in the boy's lifeless gaze.

There was an odd stillness in the air, as though the death of an innocent had become a wall separating the two sides, holding us back from committing further violence. For his part, Tournam wasn't even looking at us, though I knew he was speaking to me. "It wasn't a wound or a spell or anything. Just too many trips in too short a time. Too much fear of being found, of being captured by the posse. Fear takes its toll, you know. It weakens the spirit." He shook his head over and over. "Dumb kid. I kept telling him he had to grow up. Stop being such a child."

"I'm sorry," I said. "He...I think he looked up to you."

Tournam rose to his feet, still carrying Azir's body. "He hated me. Thought I was a bully. I guess he was right, but I was just trying to toughen him up, you know? I thought if he could just stay strong a little longer, get a couple more years in him, he'd be okay."

A group of four monks, along with Suta'rei and Ghilla, stood between us and the abbot. We'd have to get past them to stop him infecting the spell bridge any further.

"What would Azir have wanted?" I asked Tournam. "If he were still here, what would he tell you to do?"

The Berabesq's eyes finally turned to me. "He'd have said we were going too far. He'd have begged me to listen to you, to think about what we were about to do before it was too late." He walked to the edge of the cliff, stepping up onto the outcropping of rock near the bridge. "But Azir isn't here any more." He lifted up the body over his head and threw it over the cliff. Though we knew there would be no sound when it finally hit the bottom, still we were silent for a while.

"Tournam, where is Butelios?"

He nodded to where he'd disposed of Azir. "Rolled him over the side. He was still unconscious. I don't think it hurt."

"You damned—" I stopped. Anger would do me no good now, and unlike Tournam, I would do what Butelios would have wanted me to, look for a path to peace.

The other shadowcasters were watching me. Ghilla had grown on me, despite the threats and calling me "boy" all the time. Suta'rei was a fellow Jan'Tep, yet so different from me that I'd hoped that by getting to know her I might understand my people better. And Diadera, whom I heard come running up behind us. Nephenia had warned me this might happen, but her shadowblack would've gotten her out of any restraints once she woke up, and neither of us felt right about using magical means to bind her. There'd been more than enough of that lately. Besides, there had been a small, foolish part of me that still hoped that once we were all together again I could reason with her and the other shadowcasters. Make them see that this catastrophe couldn't be allowed to continue.

But pain and loss can be like kindling when it sits atop enough anger, and Azir's death had lit a spark.

"Do you understand now, Kellen?" the abbot asked, rising from the bridge. Evidently he wasn't done lecturing me, nor did he intend to leave the killing to the others. "The Jan'Tep are a disease. Even when they don't murder us with their spells, their mere existence takes any hope of peace from our lives. I can't let them get away with that. Not now when I have the means to protect us from them."

I could have told him that his words almost perfectly mirrored my father's, that expecting death at every turn had become his excuse to become no better than those he despised. I didn't though. Sometimes being right doesn't make a bit of difference.

"Well?" the abbot asked, removing his robes. The shadowblack markings all over his body practically shimmered in the air, as though aroused by the prospect of violence. "You've wanted to duel me ever since you got here. Now you finally get your chance."

My eyes went from the abbot to Diadera, then Tournam and Ghilla next to him, and finally to the monks arranging themselves as they awaited the order to attack. Nephenia was poised for a signal from me. She knew as I did that there was no good way for this to end. Shadowblack monks were going to kill Jan'Tep mages. Jan'Tep mages would slaughter shadowblack monks. All that was left was for Nephenia, Ishak, Reichis and me to try and keep the fires of hate from spreading so fast that a bunch of children and their families who'd had no say in this, no power to affect any of it, would be caught in the flames.

All that was left was to fight.

58

Bridge Dancing

Of the four of us, only Nephenia had any real magic of consequence. Despite having lost two fingers from each hand and being therefore unable to make the somatic forms required of Jan'Tep high magic, she was one hell of a charmcaster.

She opened with an iron box with a caged storm inside that released bolt after bolt of lightning everywhere, sending shards of rock at our opponents. Next she threw flecks of steel from a small jar onto the ground. They skittered along the flagstones like tiny rats, crawling up the robes of one of the monks to gnaw at his flesh before he could stab her with his shadowblack ribbons in the first exchange of blows. As he fell, his tendrils swung wildly, and had Ishak not tackled her to the ground, Nephenia would've found herself knocked over the cliff's edge.

Reichis focused on sneak attacks, biting into the neck of an opponent then leaping off into the air, spreading his limbs wide so his furry flaps could catch the wind. He'd disappear for several seconds, before reappearing on the other side to find a new opponent. He fought as he always did: furiously, bravely, recklessly. But he was smaller now, thin from fever and ancestors-knew-what-else he'd faced in that desert. He wouldn't be able to keep this up for long. None of us would.

Any second now, Ghilla would envelop one of us in her choking fog, or we'd be engulfed by Diadera's swarm of shadow- black fireflies. Tournam's ribbons, like those of the other monks, could tear us apart. We couldn't match strength for strength, so we had to find a subtler way to victory.

"Come here, you gutless bastard!" the Berabesq shouted, wiping at his eyes. I'd tossed a handful of black powder at him. Of course, it hadn't had any effect. A moment later his shadowblack ribbons had grabbed hold of my wrists and ankles, preventing me from fighting back. I felt my arms and legs being pulled from their sockets. "Nothing clever to say, cloud boy?" he demanded.

I opened my mouth, but no words came out. Instead I spat a mouthful of the red powder into his face. Though my hands were bound, still I managed to form a clumsy version of the shape as I uttered the one-word incantation. A sudden burst of fire set him screaming. The flames weren't enough to kill him, but he was soon blinded from the burns and out of the fight. It was a cruel and dirty trick to pull on someone who for one brief moment in time had tried to be my friend.

Another of the monks sent his shadow tendrils at me, but by then I'd already pulled one of Ferius's razor-sharp steel cards from my pocket and launched it spinning towards him. It sailed right through the narrow gap between two of his black ribbons, lodging itself deep in his cheek. It was maybe the best card throw I'd ever done, and Ferius wasn't even there to see it.

Ghilla had snuck up behind Nephenia and was about to smother her with her shadow fog, when a boy called out, "Wh-where should I g-g-go?"

It was Azir's voice and everyone froze when they heard it. Ghilla turned to see Ishak behind her. He barked a second time with the dead boy's voice. "Wh-where should I g-g-go?" Even I was surprised.

It took me a second to remember that Azir had spoken those words yesterday when we'd journeyed through shadow to reach the war coven's encampment. The hyena had the ability to mimic anything he heard. To use a dead boy's voice was an even crueller trick than the one I'd played on Tournam, but I guess war doesn't leave much room for decency.

With Ghilla distracted, Nephenia whipped a strip of silken fabric across the younger girl's mouth and uttered a three-syllable incantation. Suddenly the cloth turned rigid, clamping itself to Ghilla's mouth as it had to mine the night before.

Another dirty trick. Another victory for our side.

By my count, the fight had been going on for less than a minute. We could probably hold out for another thirty seconds. The problem with tricks and deceptions is that once the enemy's seen one, you can't use it again. I'd once asked Ferius what she'd do when she finally ran out of tricks. Her answer hadn't reassured me.

"Look at you," the abbot said, stalking towards me. "Fighting your own kind."

"Story of my life," I said.

I was near the edge of the cliff. I'd managed to work my way around so I was close to the bridge. About a third of the strands were black now, infused with shadow from the abbot's seemingly limitless reserve of whatever stuff it was that existed at this portal between our plane of existence and those of the many voids. I leaped off the rocky outcropping and onto the bridge itself. It felt solid beneath my feet.

Diadera met me there. "How are you doing this?" she asked. The swarm of her freckles darted between us as if waiting for the command to strike. "You've barely got any abilities. Your friend is outnumbered by people with more power. It's just the two of you and a couple of animals out here. How are you winning?"

"Do you remember that day I first came to the abbey, when that demon was killing monks left and right in the courtyard? That was the first time I saw you and the others fight. Even then, I could see something was wrong. You know how to use your abilities to attack together, but not how to protect each other. That's why Tas'diem took you all so easily."

She was coming closer, watching my hands to see what trick I'd try to use on her. "The shadowcasters did just fine before you got here, Kellen. We'll be just fine after I've thrown you off this bridge."

I backed away a step, keeping my hands up so she could see I wasn't holding anything. "You're wrong, Diadera, and I so wish I could make you see that. Underneath all the missions and drunken parties and whatever else you do together, these people aren't your friends. Not the friends you need anyway."

She shook her head. "I can't believe the things that come out of your mouth sometimes, Kellen." Her shadowblack freckles went up high, preparing to dive down on me. "What good will you be to your friends when you're dead?"

"Let's find out together."

I sprang at her. For an instant she looked stunned, but then brought her swarm to attack me. I'd seen what those tiny bits of shadowblack could do, so it took everything I had to keep my eye on the target. Just before the swarm reached me, a blast of wind sent them spinning away. Over by the cliff's edge Nephenia was waving a small triangular fan. It looked a little silly, but the resulting wind was so powerful that even outside the direct line of its effect, I had trouble staying on my feet. Diadera got hit harder and stumbled. She was close to the edge of the bridge, already losing her balance. I ran over and grabbed hold of her wrist with one hand, keeping her stable while my free hand threw a steel playing card through the air that hit the abbot before his shadowblack ribbons could get a grip on Reichis. The squirrel cat seemed oblivious to the threat, instead attacking the neck of a man who'd gotten hold of Ishak. The hyena leaped away, landing on the last monk before he could get to Nephenia.

Diadera looked stunned, watching all of this unfold. I pulled her back onto the bridge, holding her close to me. "Me, Reichis, Nephenia and Ishak, we take care of each other, Diadera. That's why we can fight the way we do. That's what you and Tournam and Ghilla and the others never learned. That's how Tas'diem was able to capture you, and that's why you're going to lose now."

She didn't fight back or yell at me. She didn't even deny my claims. Oddly, what she said was, "We should've been looking out for Azir."

Suddenly she flew out of my hands, snatched away by the abbot's ribbons. He settled her down next to him. "You're wrong, Kellen. I look out for my flock. I guard them. That's all I've ever wanted to do."

"Then protect them now," I shouted back. "Get them out of here. Run to the coast and take a ship. Use your abilities to hide the vessel as it journeys somewhere far from this place. My father's mages will content themselves with destroying the abbey. That's all they've ever wanted, to declare victory and show the world how brave and powerful the Jan'Tep are."

My words were wasted on him. All the things I'd said about my father were just as true of the abbot. He was sick and tired of a world that looked down on those with the shadowblack. More than wanting to protect his people, he wanted to prove that they were better than everyone else.

"You're a fool if you think that posse will ever stop hunting us," the abbot said. "And a damned fool to think I don't know you've been positioning yourself on that bridge to run across and warn them. I'm going to kill you now, Kellen of the House of Ke. Not because I want to, but because it's the right thing to do. Then I'll finish what I started, and those mages will serve me from now until the day their souls are eaten alive by whatever demons have a claim to them."

He raised his arms, and a wave of shadowblack oil rose up high above me, blotting out the sun. He held it there, just a moment, so I could see my doom coming. "Even after all you've done, Kellen, you're one of my people. My flock. Come back to us. Swear you'll fight alongside me and I'll give you the one thing the Jan'Tep never will: forgiveness."

It was, considering the circumstances, a rather generous offer. My reply was a whisper, too soft for him to hear, but he got my meaning. His hands balled into fists and came crashing down, bringing the wave of shadows down with them, only to be met by a screaming white cloud that billowed from my right eye.

Suzy threw herself against the shadowblack, her chill freezing it solid before she shattered it into a thousand onyx shards that fell before me. But something was wrong. Instead of returning to my eye, her cloud drifted away into the open sky. I felt the tiniest breeze against the skin of my cheek, and heard a sigh I knew meant farewell.

"Goodbye, Suzy," I whispered back to her. "Hope the next guy proves to be less trouble than I was."

"Looks like you're finally out of tricks," the abbot said. He came to stand before me on the bridge. "It's over, Kellen, and I'm sorry."

"Me too," I said, and took the card from my pocket.

The abbot gave a weary smile. "You think you can hurt me with a sharpened steel card when I'm ready for you? Go ahead. Throw it."

I spun it at him. He caught it neatly in the air. That's when he noticed that the card was made of paper, not steel. That's when he saw the face of his enemy for the first time.

"Hello, Lord Abbot," Ke'heops said. "I understand you took time out from poisoning my mages to amuse my son and allow us time to complete our crossing. You have my eternal gratitude, which I will presently convey to you in person."

The abbot threw down the card. "You lousy son of a bitch," he shouted at me. "You never expected to beat me. You were just slowing me down. Giving your father time to kill the ones I'd banded so he could finish crossing."

It was then we all heard the roar of dozens of mages running across the bridge, the first syllables of incantations for spells both wondrous and foul whispering on the wind.

"I'm sorry," I said to the abbot as I ran past him to make for the abbey gates. "But I'm told this is how wars are fought."

59

The War

It was madness after that. Mayhem and slaughter and the endless screams of the dying. We didn't take a side, but that didn't mean we escaped the battle. Nephenia, Ishak, Reichis and I fought back to back, moving inch by inch through the chaos to try to reach the families in their homes.

For all the training the abbot had given his monks, they broke ranks just minutes after meeting their enemy on the field. It was probably the one thing that saved those wretched few who'd survived. Splitting away to barricade themselves behind crumbling walls and the remnants of fallen towers enabled them to use their shadowblack abilities to pick off a few careless mages not watching their flanks. But no one could doubt the power imbalance. The end would come soon, which left us very little time to keep this massacre from becoming a wholesale slaughter.

"Where are they all?" I asked as we ran in and out of the smaller apartments within the abbey's residences. We'd been searching for almost an hour and had so far collected only a few of the abbey's civilians.

"They must be hiding," Nephenia replied. "Which is what we all need to do. It's not safe out there."

It's not safe anywhere, I thought as we ran outside to scramble past the shattered remnants of a covered cloister. The destruction would only get worse. A quarter of the war coven weren't even hunting monks. Instead they cast iron and ember spells to bring down buildings and punch holes in the curtain wall. My father wanted to see the Ebony Abbey levelled to the ground, and that's exactly what his forces would deliver.

We reached the courtyard, which was blessedly empty save for a few of the dead and dying. The monks having been quickly routed, there was no ground for them to hold. "Down here," I said, lifting up the grating that I knew covered the entrance to the sewers.

"What are you doing?" Nephenia asked. "We need to get these people through the abbey gates. Your father—"

"My father agreed to allow me one hour to round up as many civilians as I could and get them through the gates." It wasn't nearly enough time, which was, of course, his intent. He and a dozen of his mages would, after having ceremonially executed the abbot and his personal guards, await us on the spell bridge. I doubted those members of the war coven my father had kept from joining their gleeful comrades in the carnage inside the abbey would be happy standing around waiting on a bridge whose glimmering beauty had been marred by the twisting ebony vines, knowing that each dark strand represented a fellow mage who'd been poisoned with the shadowblack and subsequently executed by the soon-to-be mage sovereign.

But that was my father's problem. Mine was that my hour was about to run out, and we only had a half-dozen families with us. "You have to hide them while I go looking for more," I told Nephenia. "Otherwise—"

"If you're looking for passengers," a coughing voice called out from the sewer tunnel below, "then I believe we have a few down here eager for a voyage to just about anywhere."

Before I could even descend to see who was there, the first of them climbed the ladder and crawled out onto the cobblestones, wheezing from the dust and filth filling up the tunnels from all the destruction above.

"How many are there?" Nephenia asked.

"I don't know. I don't want to block their exit and slow them down."

One after another they came, numbers swelling until the courtyard was half full. Mothers and fathers hauled what few personal belongings they could while bigger children shuffled alongside, leading the littler ones by the hand or carrying babes in their arms.

"Ancestors..." I said, but not because of the growing crowd, but because of the beaten and bloody young man in torn robes who came up last, who, the families informed me, had found them and brought them to safety. He climbed up the ladder and stepped out into the courtyard, wiping a hand over the dust and grime from a bald head and face pale beneath the dried blood, save for the twisting markings that ended in black teardrops on each cheek, and wearing an idiot's smile so bright it made you want to kiss him. Even if you weren't into boys.

"Butelios?" I shouted, grabbing his arm to keep him from falling back down into the sewer. "How come you're...? Tournam told me he'd thrown you over the cliff!"

The broad grin became a frown. "I know. I was awake, merely pretending to be unconscious. Of course, by the time Tournam had me in his ribbons, it was too late to do anything but play dead and hope for the best. I do wish people would stop throwing me over cliffs though. I believe you started this trend, my friend."

"That still doesn't explain how you survived."

"Ah. Well, it turns out there's a rocky shelf about ten feet down the cliff, should you happen to reach out desperately enough to grab hold of it. There's even a bit of a ledge from which to sidle over a few feet and then climb back up on the other side of the gates. Oh, by the way—" He reached into the pocket of his robe and took out a torn and filthy piece of rolled-up cloth. "I found this on the ledge."

It was my shirt, and, sure enough, wrapped inside were even a couple of wildcat bones that hadn't fallen out. Reichis chittered, Ishak barked and Nephenia started to translate. "Don't bother," I said. I went over to where Reichis sat on the hyena's back. "Look, I'm sorry I confused what are obviously disgusting, misshapen wild-cat bones for squirrel cat bones, which as any remotely educated person knows are sleek, perfectly formed works of art that evoke the wonders of nature. Now, do you want a souvenir or not?"

After a certain amount of hissing and growling, Reichis took the shirt from me, sniffed it, removed what appeared to be a rib and then tossed the rest on the ground. That problem solved, I turned to another, much bigger one. "How many people are here with you, Butelios?"

"Just the children and their families."

"I'm seeing a lot of people here who don't look related," Nephenia said. "So will the war coven."

"And I," Butelios said, looking at them, "see a great many people who did not ask for war, cannot fight one and need our help." He turned to me. "Kellen, these are all the ones I could find in time. There are still a few hiding inside the abbey, too scared to come out when I called. Some are children."

Nephenia picked up Reichis and handed him to me. "You go make things work with your father. I'll take Ishak and start trying to round up anyone else I can." She turned to the hyena. "And you are going to be cute and cuddly for a change in order to help me convince the young ones not to run away from us." She turned back to me and pressed something into the palm of my hand. I looked down to find a tiny lodestone attached to a string. As soon as I lifted it up, the lodestone swung towards Nephenia. "I've charmed it to seek me out. I'll find a safe place to hide the children, and you can join me later."

If anywhere in this hell hole can be called safe, I thought, but I put the charm in my pocket.

"Kellen," she said, looking at the horde I was about to lead through the abbey gates. "With Ke'heops...be the man you want to be, not the petulant son who thinks he deserved a better father."

"You're starting to sound like Ferius, you know that?"

She kissed me on the cheek. "You say the nicest things sometimes."

With that, she and Ishak took off past the throngs of terrified children and their parents who were waiting for me to tell them whether they were going to live or die. "Okay," I said at last, turning to head back through the abbey gates to the spell bridge outside. "Let's go see what sort of mood the future mage sovereign of the Jan'Tep nation is in."

60

Renegotiation

My father, as it turned out, was in a magnanimous frame of mind when we found him with his personal guard of a dozen war mages standing in their brightly coloured armour upon the spell bridge.

"You may choose half," he said, walking with me further along the bridge to keep our discussion private.

"*Half?*" I nearly sent Reichis flying from his perch on my shoulder, which earned me a hiss and a nasty nip on the ear. I barely noticed. All my anger was reserved for my father. "Has that crown been pinching your skull too tightly? We had a deal!"

So far my attempts at being lovable were going swimmingly. I swear, if I ever saw Ferius again I was going to have her revise every single lesson in arta siva I'd ignored the first time around.

Be charming, I reminded myself.

"These people are no threat to anyone," I said quietly.

Ke'heops had remained remarkably composed during my entreaties, but now his mouth twisted into a look of disgust. "They are shadowblack and the conspirators who shelter their kind. No, Kellen, I gave you an hour and you exceeded that. I agreed that a modest number of innocents could pass unharmed and you bring me this misbegotten horde. I will not have you embarrass me in front of mages who risked their lives on this mission and who have lost

349

comrades to the abbot's foul machinations. Now make your choices from among this rabble, or I will choose for you."

"You'd murder them in cold blood?" I demanded. "Why am I even asking? Of course you—"

Stop. Don't make it personal.

Butelios shuffled past the dozen mages of my father's honour guard, offering them friendly smiles as he went. "Kellen?" he whispered to me when he was close enough. "We need to do something quickly. Our charges grow more fearful by the second. I'm afraid they might bolt or worse yet try to storm the bridge. If that happens..."

I looked back to the clifftop at the end of the bridge where two hundred skittish souls looked very much like horses trapped in a barn that's beginning to catch fire. If they tried to rush the bridge, my father's mages would have all the excuse they needed to slaughter them. "Go back and keep them as calm as you can," I said to Butelios. "This won't take much longer."

"It certainly will not," my father said, overhearing. "I won't stand out here all day debating with you while the rest of my war coven does all the fighting within the abbey. Make your choice, Kellen."

Think, damn it. He's your father, not some raving lunatic. Reason with him.

I struggled to come up with some rational point of principle with which to persuade the mighty Ke'heops to do something so fundamental to human decency that merely trying to explain why it was the right thing to do seemed impossible. Nor could I think of any flattery or personal offering that would sway him to my side. This was a day of reckoning he'd promised his war coven, and they wanted blood. Most of them, in fact, looked like they'd settle for mine. The pompous, preening jackasses in their preposterously ornate mages' armour and...*ballgowns?*

Even as the tiny details and clues began to rearrange themselves in my mind, I felt the subtle shifting of the shadowblack rings around my eye. I banished the question before they could unlock.

Pretty sure I don't need help with this particular mystery.

"Kellen?" my father asked. "Have you made your—"

"A moment if you please, Father."

Don't make it personal? No. Make it entirely personal.

"You look well, Essa'jin," I said to the woman in the sapphire dress with the unnaturally blue eyes and somewhat preposterous azure hair.

She glided towards me, floating a few inches above the bridge's surface, though I noticed her steps seemed less practised than when I'd first met her, outside the war coven's encampment. "Son of Ke," she said. An interesting mode of address, as it's one conventionally used as a reminder of duty to one's house. "A nekhek," she said, noting Reichis on my shoulder. "I see you have found company worthy of your stature. Is his health … that is to say, he appears to be a most ill-favoured animal."

"They're an ugly and ill-tempered breed," I replied, ignoring the squirrel cat's angry chitters, "though this one in particular has had some difficult times of late. Fortunately help came from an unexpected source, and I am grateful for it."

"Yes, well, whatever," she said, visibly uncomfortable. "As you say, an ugly creature."

I smiled at that, and at the fact that Reichis, for once, didn't hiss back. "Truer words were never spoken. You, on the other hand, continue to be the most beautiful woman ever to bear the title of mage. I am glad to see you here. I wanted to apologise for my untoward behaviour when we last met."

"For what?" she asked.

"When you said you would sit next to my father, I insulted you, and so beg your pardon. Truly, Ke'heops would be lucky to have you at his side, even more so than my mother, Bene'maat, who after all, has always been a bit—" I leaned in to whisper conspiratorially— "second rate."

Essa'jin's eyes blazed. "You prattle like a child, and seek to mock me." Before I could deny it, she held out a finger. "Utter one more veiled insult to me and I will send such nightmares as will cause you to prise your eyes open with spikes for fear of falling asleep."

I gave her a short bow. "I'll take my leave then."

My father was looking at me curiously when I rejoined him. "You know Essa'jin?"

"Very well, in fact. Now, I know you're keen to get inside the abbey and finish destroying it, so just let these poor souls pass and we won't delay you any further."

"Have you gone mad? I told you—"

"Yes, yes. Choose half. Only I think I'd rather you made the choice."

He shook his head, visibly disappointed in my gambit. "You think I won't do my duty? Kellen, I will execute each and every one myself if that what is required."

"And to avoid looking weak in front of your mages?"

"In order to show that the commands of the mage sovereign will be obeyed! Damn it, boy, can you not understand the simplest principles of leadership?"

"Oh, I understand them fine. Once you give an order, it's important for everyone to see it's carried out. Like, for instance, the command you gave forbidding your daughter from joining the war coven." I leaned in a little, though it wasn't necessary given how far the others were from us. "I hope you haven't been ogling Essa'jin as you both crossed the bridge, Father, because that would be entirely shameful."

"Don't be..." His eyes went wide, first with surprise, then with a kind of despair to which he was clearly unaccustomed and, I confess, kind of fun to watch.

"Choose, Ke'heops. One way or another your troops will see one of your iron-clad dictates bend just a little. Either out of compassion for the innocent, or because you can't even tell when your own daughter is masquerading as a floating fashion disaster in an ugly blue dress."

His jaw tightened, and the effort it cost him not to turn and look at the girl in blue was visibly painful to him. "You would use your own sister against me?"

It was hard not to laugh at that, but I managed it, mostly because the question actually made me sad. "It's what we do, you and I, isn't it?"

61

The Path of Tears

Twelve very angry mages stepped aside so that what no doubt appeared to them as a horde of vicious shadowblacks could escape across the very bridge those same mages had risked life and magic to construct for the sole purpose of exterminating their kind once and for all. Of course, to anyone who wasn't insane with bloodlust and drunk on their own self-importance, those who passed were frightened souls forced to leave the one place that had promised them safety in exchange for an uncertain future back on the continent they had fled to get here in the first place.

"Without the abbey, this land is too harsh," Butelios said, standing with me on the spell bridge. "Better they return to the continent of their birth and build new lives there."

"How much of a life can it be?" I asked, the weight of everything I'd learned at the abbey crushing any sense of triumph I might have felt at getting these innocents away from the battle. "Even if they escape their enemies, the shadowblack itself will always find them."

Butelios shook his head and smiled. "You had more in common with Diadera and the shadowcasters than I ever did, my friend. Like them, you are convinced that the shadowblack is a curse. But what if those demons we fear come not from some darkness beyond our control, but from the darkness we allow to infect our own thoughts?"

He tapped his chest. "I *choose* to believe that the shadowblack can be something different. Something good. Do you know why?"

"I have a strange feeling you're going to tell me."

"Your grandmother banded you in shadow, denying you the future you'd hoped for. Yet in so doing, look—" he gestured back to the families—"you became the one person who could save all these people." His gentle gaze went to the winding black markings around my left eye. "Diadera was right. They truly are like the wheels on a lock."

"Yeah, only I'm not even sure how they work, and I have no idea why my grandmother banded me with them."

He squeezed my shoulder. "A fascinating mystery—one would think a proper enigmatist would feel compelled to solve it one day."

I smiled then, not because I shared his optimism, which was, by any standard, completely preposterous, but rather because of the way he'd spoken, how familiar it was, and how even now I couldn't help but feel clever at having figured it out at last.

"You're going with them?" I asked.

He nodded. "I am... known to many of them. They trust me."

"As they should," I said, genuinely meaning it. "Though I think if you're planning to lead them on this exodus, they ought to know your proper name, wouldn't you agree?"

He looked at me quizzically. "My name?"

"My first morning in the abbey, after you and Diadera had kept Tournam from killing me, you told me the story of an Argosi who'd come to your city in the north. You said you begged her to make you her teysan but she refused."

"What I said was true," he insisted. "The Path of Skyward Oaks denied me several times in fact, yet she never sent me away either, no matter how long or how far I followed her. And then, after some seven years in her company, I realised something."

"Seven years? What was it you only figured out after seven years?"

He tried to look solemn, but a second later his composure broke into a wide grin. "The Argosi *never* agree to teach another, just as their *maetri* never agreed to teach them!" He broke out laughing and without warning he grabbed me in a bear hug, nearly dislodging Reichis. "I am glad we met, my friend. You brought me more hope and laughter than such times as we live in should ever afford."

He let me go to set off across the spell bridge, following the mass of people to whom, I suspected, he would need to devote the rest of his life. "Wait!" I called out. "You still never told me your name. That's hardly fair."

He stopped. "If I tell you, will you yourself finally admit to being an Argosi once and for all, and cease the little jokes and jibes you make to hide the truth from yourself as much as from the rest of the world?"

"I . . . I guess I've never felt right calling myself one."

The man I'd come to know as Butelios turned and said, "Then know that the Path of Joyful Tears will always greet you as a fellow Argosi."

I smiled back at him, unsure why that small kindness meant so much to me. "And the Path of Endless Stars will always be grateful for it."

62

Vengeance

Inside the Ebony Abbey chaos and slaughter were gradually giving way to patient, methodical destruction. Barely a third of the massive curtain wall remained standing, most of the cloisters had crumbled to the ground and all but two of the towers had collapsed. None of which reduced my anxiety when the lodestone Nephenia had given me swung like a mad pendulum in all directions. It wasn't a defect of the device itself; there was simply too much wild magic in the air for such a fragile charm to function properly.

"Can't you use that legendary nose of yours to find her?" I asked Reichis.

He gave no reply, not even a chitter. Maybe he couldn't even catch a scent amidst all the smoke and carnage. "I really wish you could talk to me," I said as I ran down one of the covered cloisters. Bolts of ember magic were blasting from all sides, chasing the brief flickers of shadowblack from those few monks still fighting back or just fleeing for their lives.

Reichis gave a sudden growl and I looked up to see one of the last remaining towers toppling towards us. I ran as fast as my legs would carry us, knowing it wasn't nearly fast enough. My passing thought was, *This is probably not the worst way to die, considering the options I've been presented with lately.*

A thousand tons of stone collapsed on top of us, only to stop mere feet above my head. They weren't frozen in place—but continued their fall so slowly that I could walk between them.

"Would you mind getting a move on?" Shalla asked, her voice strained. "This is...not as easy as it looks."

I made my way through the gentle snowfall of crumbling black rock. "Iron magic?" I asked.

She grabbed me by the arm and took me about a dozen yards away from the wreckage before allowing it to all come crashing down on the courtyard. "Sand, silly. I slowed time down around the falling tower. No one mage is powerful enough to hold back that much weight using iron magic."

"Not even you?" I asked, lending as much fake surprise to my voice as I thought was believable. Then, to add insult to insult, I threw in, "By the way, have you misplaced that lovely sapphire dress? Also, please tell me that was part of the illusion and you haven't left poor Essa'jin at the base of that mountain wearing nothing but her undergarments."

She stuck her hands on her hips. "Are you *determined* to make me cross with you, brother?"

I grabbed her and pulled her into the longest embrace of our lives. "Always," I said softly.

Our reunion was short-lived. I heard a shout and let go of Shalla to pull powder from my pouches. Two Jan'Tep mages were coming towards us, calling her name.

"My Lady Shalla!" the shorter, stockier of the two called out, only to groan as tracks of blood trickled down from his matted brown hair. He clung to a taller man like a dying leaf to a rotted tree branch. I could see the short one was a tribulator from the way his iron and blood bands glowed, but their light flickered. I thought he didn't have long to live.

"Ore'jieq?" she said. "You need help!" She turned and called into the din around us, "I need a fleshbinder here now!"

"He insisted on bringing you word directly, my lady," the taller man said.

"Word of what?"

Ore'jieq's eyes went soft. He opened his mouth to speak but then coughed. In any other situation I'd've said he was being a little dramatic, but given what appeared to be his impending death I figured I should let that go. "Your father," he said, so quietly it wasn't until he repeated it that I could be sure. "Your father...I was next to him when one of the black towers fell. My brethren dug us out, but Lord Ke'heops, he...He's asked to see you."

The glow of Shalla's victories fled, leaving her pale as the dead. "Oh, no...Ancestors, please no! Where is he?"

Ore'jieq gestured eastward. "At the other end of the abbey. The remnants of the shadowblacks have amassed there. It'll be a fight to break through, my lady, but I will do my best to assist you." He tried to take a step, but even with the taller one holding him, his knees buckled, threatening to take both of them down.

"Stay here, Ore'jieq," Shalla ordered. To the taller one she said, "Get one of the healers for him, Shoth'arn, now!"

"But, my lady, you'll need—"

The glyphs of the tattooed bands on her forearms gleamed so bright it became impossible to look at her. "I need nothing."

I tried to take her hand. "I'll come with you. I can—"

She shrugged me off, pushing her will through the iron band around her right forearm to send me stumbling back. "You'd only be in the way."

Shalla left me standing there like an idiot, unsure of what I should do. Ke'heops had brought all this hell upon the world, but he was still my father. If he was really dying, shouldn't I be by his side?

Would he even want me there, given our last encounter involved me blackmailing him?

I would've wrestled with the question longer, but it occurred to me then that Shoth'arn wasn't calling for any healers, and Ore'jieq seemed to be making a remarkable recovery. The two were watching me, smirking, waiting for me to figure out the obvious. Ore'jieq wiped a hand across his forehead. The blood came away clean, with no sign of any wound underneath. "A worthy performance, wouldn't you say, Shoth'arn?"

The other mage chuckled. "We might've been half-decent actors, were it not a degrading profession suited only to the basest of fools."

"Not the basest," Ore'jieq corrected. His iron and blood bands were gleaming brightly now, solid as the sun above a dry desert. "The basest of fools call themselves spellslingers and become traitors to their people."

"True," Shoth'arn agreed. His iron and ember bands sparked. "Then they become dead."

I backed away, hands in front of me to show I wasn't readying an attack. "Ke'heops made an agreement with me, a covenant. He's mage sovereign, his word is—"

"His word may well become law," Shoth'arn said, looming over me, "when this battle is over and he is crowned. Until then, he is merely a clan prince."

"Not *our* clan of course," Ore'jieq said.

"No, indeed. And you, Kellen of the House of Ke, traitor to the Jan'Tep, you are nothing more than—"

A new voice finished the sentence. "My son."

A sudden burst of lightning blinded me, then, just like that, Shoth'arn and Ore'jieq were gone. A second before, the two men had been stalking towards me, somatic forms twitching along their fingertips as they prepared to blast me to pieces. The next, all that was left of them was two small mounds of ashes.

Ke'heops, prince of my clan, soon to be mage sovereign of my entire people, stepped towards me. As he did, the screams of battle around us, the smoke and fog and stench of blood, all of it faded from my mind, as if the war itself parted before him. "You saved me?" I asked.

"They disobeyed my command. As I have attempted to teach you on more occasions than I can count, there must be consequences for disobedience to one's lord."

My knees were shaking. Hell, my entire body was shaking. "You should've dropped something on them or used some other secondary force. Any half-decent silk mage will be able to trace the spell that burned them back to you. Can't imagine their clan will be too happy when they find out you killed two of their finest."

Ke'heops stopped, and smiled at me negligently. "Really? Is that your professional political assessment, Kellen?" He shook his head. "You never seem to understand how these things work." He knelt down and scooped up a pile of Ore'jieq's ashes in his hand. "I want our people to admire me, to respect me, perhaps even to love me." He rose and blew the ashes into the wind. "But none of those things will matter unless they also fear me."

Well, *I* certainly feared him. Problem was, some small part of me, maybe that trace of arta valar that insisted on popping up at times like these, sent a chuckle past my lips.

"Something amuses you?" Ke'heops asked.

"It's just I've never heard you so succinctly describe your parental philosophy before."

He considered that for moment. "Clever," he said at last, almost as a sigh. "Always so determined to be clever. Tell me, Kellen, what does that wit of yours tell you I'm going to do now?" He made a show of glancing around us. "There is no one here to stop *me* from killing you. No one who will second-guess *me* if I go and find every one of those shadowblack children and their families you blackmailed me into granting passage across the bridge." He took another step, now so close I could smell the warmth of his breath, the scent of the oils he'd used on his skin since I was a child. It felt perverse that I found it somehow reassuring.

"You won't go after the children," I said. "Matter of fact, I expect you'll let a few of the remaining stragglers slip through your ranks too. Not many of course, just enough."

"Enough for what?" he asked.

I looked around at the remains of the Ebony Abbey, at this place that could have been a haven of peace, a school, a community, a lifeline for those who so badly needed it. Now it would be a shrine to violence and hatred. "You had a great victory here, Father. The kind of victory that soon becomes legendary. You did what no Jan'Tep leader has done in three hundred years."

He tilted his head, still watching me. "I haven't heard a reason not to *complete* that victory."

I shrugged. "If you eradicated every last shadowblack, what would there be left for our people to fear? What was it you said to me earlier? 'There are two kinds of leaders men seek: those who rule best in peace, and those who rule best in war.' I don't think you see yourself as someone people flock to in times of peace."

He stared at me long and hard with eyes so cold and unfeeling it was everything I could do not to cower before him and beg forgiveness. Only when he was sure I would continue to deny him that small, simple pleasure of fatherhood did he smile and ask, "Is this what the Argosi call 'arta precis'?"

"It's as close as I get to it, Father."

"And what does this talent of yours tell you about your own fate?

After all, I don't need you to scare anyone for me." He reached out a hand and got his answer when I flinched, absolutely convinced I was about to become a third pile of ash next to Ore'jieq and Shoth'arn. His expression softened and his hand touched my cheek. "Perhaps you still have something to learn from your father after all."

It's possible there was something I could've said that would have brought us closer together, but even had my enigmatist's markings revealed it to me, I wasn't ready to say it.

He took his hand away. "I won't kill you, Kellen. There's no need now. As you have noted, I have won the victory our people needed. Soon I will be crowned mage sovereign."

"Is that the only reason you haven't killed me, Father?" I asked.

I could see in his face that, like me, he hesitated to say the words out loud. But maybe he was a better man than I am because finally he shook his head. "No, Kellen, that is not the only reason. You live because, as I have tried to tell you many times, I am your father and I love you."

Without waiting for a response, perhaps not trusting what I might reply, he turned and walked away, striding towards the last bitter hours of the battle. I managed to find my voice in time to call out to him, "But that's not enough, is it?"

He stopped then. I couldn't say for sure, but I would've sworn his shoulders sagged just a little. "No, it's not. You live because you have been useful to me, Kellen. Useful to our house. Even when you rebel, even when you resist, even when you try your very best to spite me, your every act has been precisely what I needed, even if it hasn't always been what I desired." He turned back and looked at me, just for a second, his eyes narrowed as though he were trying to make sense of me. "Our fates are something of a mystery, aren't they?"

63

The Mahdek

Reichis and I set off in search of Nephenia again, but we couldn't find her. The lodestone had stopped working entirely, and all I could do was hope that she'd either made it out of the abbey already or was holed up somewhere safe—something I ought to be considering myself, given how many of my father's mages probably still wanted to see me dead.

"Kellen!" a voice shouted.

I looked up to see Diadera coming towards us. Her shadowblack freckles surrounded her, ready to strike at her command. Apparently it wasn't just the Jan'Tep I had to worry about.

"Don't come any closer," I warned, reaching for my powders. "I don't know how you survived the posse, but quit while you're ahead. I don't want to hurt you."

"I came to—"

I didn't get to hear what she was going to say next. Reichis growled so loud the roar in my ears was overwhelming. He sprang down from my shoulder to the ground and then raced towards Diadera. "Reichis, no!"

My warning came too late. Everything happened far too quickly after that. There was a mage behind Diadera—that's what Reichis had seen. The squirrel cat leaped up, back legs barely touching her shoulder before he launched himself at the mage. A scream of pain tore through the air as the squirrel cat's claws tore out the man's eyes. He lashed out, fingers contorted into a first-form ember spell that made flame burst from his hands. Reichis screamed as his fur started to burn. I ran for him, fast as I could, but it wasn't enough. The mage was hanging on to him, determined to burn him alive.

Diadera struck out with her shadowblack, the tiny sparks of shadow stinging the man's face. He let go of Reichis and fell to the ground screaming. Still I kept running, throwing myself on the squirrel cat to put out the flames. He scratched me bloody trying to get away. Fire has always made him crazy. Finally it was out though, and the mage who'd attacked us lay dead a few yards away, the white bone of his skull showing through the ruins of his face as Diadera's fireflies returned to her cheeks.

I checked over every inch of Reichis's fur for any remaining smouldering bits. He wasn't too badly burned, all things considered.

"He saved me," Diadera coughed. She was standing over us. "Why would he do that?"

"He…" I was about to tell her the truth—that Reichis was probably protecting *me* or that his usual bloodthirst for Jan'Tep mages, especially their eyeballs, had taken over. "We look after each other," I said instead.

She smiled and knelt down next to us. It was then that I saw that the whites of her eyes were gone, replaced by a red mess of burst blood vessels. She put a hand on her forehead as if she were checking a fever. "That mage, he touched me. Right here. Why would he do that? It doesn't even hurt."

"Oh, ancestors, no…" I reached out to catch her as she tumbled forward.

"Kellen?" she asked. "Why can't I see?"

Iron magic. In his blind panic, the mage had summoned a gut

sword or some other iron spell that compressed an enemy's internal organs. The bones of the skull are usually too thick for iron magic to penetrate, but there'd been no distance between them. He'd put his hand right on her forehead. He'd crushed her brain.

I laid her down as gently as I could, glancing around for anyone else who might attack. "It's okay," I said. "You just need to rest a minute."

She must've known I was lying, but still she played along. "Weird not being able to see. Is the squirrel cat all right?"

"He's fine," I said. "You saved his life. Now he owes you all the butter biscuits and dead rabbits on two continents."

She didn't laugh. Instead she reached out a hand. "Help me sit up. I don't want to lie here like this."

I did, though I had to prop her up with my shoulder to keep her from falling back. She spread her hands. "Can I hold him, just for a moment?"

"I don't think that's a good—" I started to say, but Reichis crawled up onto her lap.

She stroked his fur, and it turned from dark grey with red stripes to golden. It was a remarkable gesture of respect, coming from him, but she couldn't see it. She petted his head, and I saw she was tracing a finger around the ridge of one of his eyes over and over. He didn't seem to mind, but an itch in my shadowblack markings told me something was wrong. I grabbed him away from her.

"Kellen?" she asked.

"What were you doing to him, Diadera?"

"I was...Is it raining?" Blood was dripping from her eyes down onto her cheeks, which were pale now because her shadowblack freckles had disappeared from her face.

I looked down at Reichis's muzzle, horrified by what I found there. "How...? Diadera, what have you done to him?"

She pulled at the collar of her shirt, tearing off the top two buttons to again show me the abnegation marks she'd carved into her skin. "You were so alone without him," she said, the deep sorrow in her voice at odds with the girl who'd only hours before told me she had no use for friendship or other illusions. "Even when you got him back, I could tell it wasn't the same." She reached out a hand blindly, taking mine when she found it. "I don't want you to feel alone, Kellen. Now you don't have to."

I pulled away, rising to my feet and holding onto Reichis. Without me to hold her up, Diadera fell back against the cobblestones, her head landing with a soft thump. Blood oozed from her ears. "You had no right!" I screamed at her. "This isn't what I wanted, damn you! I would never want—"

"Quit shouting, Kellen," Reichis chittered, clambering up to my shoulder. "The crazy girl is dead. Let's ditch this lousy dump before we end up in the same condition."

For the first time since I'd left him in the Golden Passage, I'd understood everything he'd said, and while I had no idea how it worked, the cause was as plain to see as the shadowblack markings around Reichis's left eye.

No one can love you until you first love yourself.

—*Things girls say to you when they don't*
like you that way

64

Farewell

The muddy ground sucked at the heels of my boots like grasping hands trying to pull us down into the muck with the dead. Memories are like that too. They tug at you, holding you back. "You're not ready to move on," they whisper. "Just stay here a while longer. It'll all make sense soon, I promise."

Memories are liars.

It's something every Jan'Tep initiate learns in their training. Magic requires true envisioning—maintaining esoteric geometry in your mind with flawless accuracy. Those sharp lines and curves with their precise colours and textures are utterly unlike the lazy finger painting of past remembrances.

That time your spellmaster first told you that one day you might become a great mage? Remember the hint of a smile on the left edge of his mouth? What about his hair? Do you recall if any strands were out of place? How about his right hand—were the fingers just dangling there? Or were they slightly curled?

You won't remember such things of course, which means you remember nothing. You're simply recreating the images, the words, the events themselves, fashioning them to suit how you think you might have felt at the time. Memory is like everything else in the world: the further away you are, the harder it is to see. Only hours had passed since the battle at the Ebony Abbey, yet even now I knew my recollections were flawed.

Two armies fighting a war of spells and shadowblack magic. Black ribbons darting everywhere, grabbing at steely-eyed mages whose metallic tattooed bands shine like strips of starlight as they pierce the encroaching darkness. Chaos and blood. Shouts calling for violence, screams begging for mercy.

In my mind, endless hordes of mages and monks clashed like the waves of two oceans fighting for dominance. In reality though? My father had led fewer than fifty men and women over that bridge; the rest had died before they'd reached the other side. The abbey had housed perhaps four hundred souls, half of whom we'd helped escape. Others fought, of course, but probably almost as many died simply trying to flee. Any Daroman soldier would've told you this was nothing more than a skirmish. No real war at all, merely the first drops of rain in a bucket that was eager to hold so much more.

Ferius, in one of her rare moments of candour, once told me that the Argosi believed hidden forces within the great nations were driving us towards a continental war—conflict on a scale that not even the most battle-hardened Daroman general has ever seen. The Argosi were going to prevent it, Ferius had said, with the same certainty with which she places her bets in a game of cards. I'd found her swagger reassuring then. Now it just seemed like childish petulance.

Darome. Berabesq. Gitabria. The Seven Sands. The Jan'Tep territories. They were moving inexorably towards war—one so violent and bloody that I doubted there would be anyone left to remember it, even poorly. Maybe that's why wars keep happening; they kill off so many people it becomes easy to forget what really happened, and all that's left is to make up stories about it.

"So they're really not coming?" Reichis asked.

He was perched on my shoulder, as he had been for the past hour, while I trudged through the cloying mud. It would take us all night to walk to the nearest village from the remains of the abbey. From there, days or weeks to reach the coast. Then I'd have to find some way to buy our passage on a trading vessel—assuming any were crossing the narrow ocean between this place and our own continent of Eldrasia. We would see no one but strangers for months. Ke'heops had brought down the bridge the moment his own forces had withdrawn, knowing, I am sure, that I was still on the Obscarian side. I guess he considered this to be a suitable fatherly punishment for my actions, or more likely, my attitude.

"Nephenia's going west," I replied. "Wants to see the world past our own little piece of it."

Was that what she'd said? It was hard to be sure, even though it had only been a couple of hours since I last saw her. That tiny lapse in time was enough for me to question whether things had gone the way I remembered.

"It's a big world, Kellen," she'd said with a grin, only I wasn't sure now if she'd been smiling. Her lips might have been a thin, strained line across her mouth.

"I could go with you," I said. "Reichis always likes finding new things to kill. Besides, I've heard the Shan make the most incredible steel weapons. Maybe I'll buy a sword and then sail to Tristia and learn to fence or something. Or we could go south and visit the Peaceful Lands. I've never been quite sure whether the name is supposed to be sincere or ironic, so maybe we should pick up the swords first. And butter biscuits. I don't think Reichis will embark on a sea voyage unless he's got a big supply. We could find stuff for us too, of course. I mean, what foods do you like these days? All that travel with Ferius—has she tried to make you eat weird snails and things yet? She used to do that to me all the time. I was never sure if..."

Had I really babbled on like that? I'm almost positive I didn't say half those things, no matter how clearly I remembered saying them. I couldn't have though, because I distinctly remember Nephenia putting a hand on my cheek.

"Goodbye, Kellen," she'd said.

That part had happened for sure.

"What? You don't want me to come with you?"

It's not like I expected us to become lovers or something. It's just...Maybe somehow everything that had happened would make sense if it ended with Nephenia and me together. Foolish? Pathetic? Maybe, but I'd challenge anyone to see what I had seen and *not* grasp at some small shred of hope that life might not all be hell.

I think Nephenia had removed her hand from my cheek, because she reached out a finger towards the black markings around my left eye. I'd flinched.

A test.

"Why do you do that?" I'd asked. "Why do you think it's okay to humiliate me like that?"

"Because I keep hoping that one day I'm going to touch those markings and it's not going to bother you. Maybe you'll have stopped thinking of yourself as defective."

"So what? That doesn't change the fact that I care about you. Nephenia, I lov—"

In my memory, she shook her head over and over and over. "You can't love someone until you love yourself."

"Well, I'm pretty sure I can, because—"

She cut me off. "Kellen, don't tell me how you feel about me. Tell me how you feel when you close your eyes and it's just you there."

I didn't even try. I've never been suited for honesty. My talents are in deception, trickery and, most of all, distraction. "You make out as if the shadowblack was just some blemish that embarrasses me. It's not. It's real and it's deadly and most of all it ruins the lives of everyone around me. And before you shake your head at me, Nephenia, remember that I saw how disgusted you were when you saw Tournam and Diadera and Azir and the others. I saw how you looked at me when I was with them. I *saw*."

I can't remember the expression on her face then, which is strange, since I'm positive I was looking carefully. "I wasn't disgusted by their shadowblack markings, Kellen; I was disgusted by how they revelled in them. Couldn't you see that? When you came to this awful place, didn't you notice how excited they all were by the power they could wield? Didn't you realise it was the same look of hunger, of desire, that every Jan'Tep initiate has when they discover they can use their magic to wield power over those without? How could you not have seen that?"

I hadn't had an answer then. I didn't have one now. Whatever clever retorts had been trying to work their way through my brain had faded to nothingness when Nephenia had pulled me close and briefly pressed her lips against mine. One kiss. A reminder? A promise? Another test?

"How come you get to kiss me whenever you want, but I never feel like I can kiss you?"

"Because you won't risk being rejected, so instead you keep hoping some lucky accident will make it happen for you. Falling in love isn't the same as tripping into it, Kellen." Her fingers brushed my hand. "Besides, you have no idea how often I've wanted to kiss you only to stop myself at the last second."

"Why stop yourself?"

She smoothed the hair away from my face, her fingers lingering on my cheek. "Because I think I love you Kellen, but I won't know for sure until I meet the man you're going to be once you finally get tired of being the boy you once were."

She kissed Reichis's fuzzy head too, just above the ridge of his left eye. He growled at her. "Don't be like that. I think it looks cute." And then she and Ishak left, and that was that. The strange girl with the three-fingered hands who'd thrown everything aside to come and save me had walked out of my life again.

Either I was unimaginably inept at love, or the whole thing was just another con game.

"You got a mirror?" Reichis asked, shaking me out of my thoughts.

I turned my head to discover he'd worked his way to the top of my pack and was digging around inside, sticking his butt in my face. "Do you mind? What would you need a mirror for anyway?"

He hopped up and spun himself around to face me. "I want to see what my markings look like. I bet they're fierce." He leaned his muzzle towards me, so close all I could see was a patch of fur. "Come on. They're cool, right?"

"Cool?" I stopped walking, letting the mud get a stronger hold on my boots as I stood there. "Are you out of your mind? *Cool?* Reichis, you've got the shadowblack now! Do you have any idea what that means?"

He looked troubled. "You're saying they *don't* look cool?"

"Reichis, there's a damned portal on your face that's connected to an etheric plane that will slowly feed on your worst, most vile thoughts. Those markings will only get bigger over time, and eventually those thoughts will become a demon who will take over your entire being."

By this point he'd flipped around again and was digging in my pack.

"Are you even listening to me?" I demanded.

He came back up with a butter biscuit in his mouth. Apparently at some point in the midst of all the people dying and buildings falling, either he or Ishak had managed to loot the abbey stores of its supply of biscuits. "Sorry, what?"

"I was trying to explain to you that you've got—"

"I heard you. Vile thoughts. Demon. Big, ugly, evil thing. One day I'll get transformed into one?"

I nodded.

Reichis pulled the butter biscuit out of his mouth. "I'll become this monstrous killing machine that terrorises everything in its path?"

"Most likely."

Reichis sat down on his haunches on my shoulder. He took a bite from the biscuit and chewed noisily for a while, then said, "Cool."

"You're an idiot," I said.

He closed his paw into the squirrel cat equivalent of a fist and rapped it against the top of my head. "Is being a whiny little skin-bag a symptom of the shadowblack?" he asked. "Because that would explain a lot."

Before I could reply he wriggled back into my pack. "We should've brought more butter biscuits," he said, digging around frenetically and tilting me off balance. "Also, why are you wasting valuable butter biscuit space in your pack with this letter?"

"What letter?"

He re-emerged and held a creased and dirty envelope between his paws. "It says, '*To Kellen the idiot skinbag, from some other idiot skinbag.*'"

Reichis can't read. Thankfully.

I took the envelope from him. The only thing on it was my name, written in a hand almost breathtakingly elegant—at odds both with the sorry state of the envelope and with the temperament of the person who'd sent it. "It's from Ferius," I said, tearing it open. "Nephenia must've slipped it in there."

"Well?" Reichis asked. "What does it say?"

65

Two Letters

Kid,

I must've written this letter a dozen times since that night out on the Gitabrian border when you took it in your head to leave. I wrote a new one when the girl (who insists I call her "Nephenia"—have to rid her of that habit) nearly got me and the hyena killed running into a burning building. No screaming kids inside, you understand—just the fool who'd set the fire.

Anyway, I wrote a different one a few weeks after that, when we came across the Path of Whispering Willows. You ain't met her yet, which is to the good, because when she talks she makes no sense, and she talks all the time. Who can get any peace with all that nonsense frontier philosophy rattling around you all the time?

Wrote a couple more letters a month ago after we had a fine time with a Jan'Tep bounty hunter. Fella thought he could set a trap for me to get to you. I ask you, kid, what is it about a little magic that makes a boy so foolish? Made him take one of my debt cards in exchange for not whoopin' him like he deserved. Maybe he'll find some wisdom in it. Kinda doubt it though.

Well, after all that, the girl (Nephenia, I mean) sees your sister's face in a loaf of bread and tells me we've got to run off to the Golden Passage to rescue a squirrel cat. Felt as dumb as it sounds. Still, glad we got to the little fella in time. You should've seen the trail of bodies he left behind. Me and Nephenia got into a fight after that. We have a lot of those. Worst teysan I ever had—never questions the Argosi ways like you did, just nods her head like she understands and then goes off and does the opposite. I tried to tell her you'd chosen your path and that you're near as good getting yourself out of trouble as you are getting into it. But she took off anyway. Hope you understand why I couldn't come. It's not the Argosi way. Still, since I couldn't seem to stop writing and rewriting the same letter over and over, I reckoned I'd best have her give this one to you. I threw out all the other ones, except the first, so you'd see that all my wandering thoughts eventually came back to the same place.

To you.

I took the second letter out from behind the first, my fingers fumbling with it awkwardly. I hadn't been prepared for the strange intimacy of seeing words written in the hand of my mentor. The joy of holding something she had made just for me only sharpened the terrible reminder that she was a thousand miles away, that I might never see her again, and that it had been my choice that had made things so.

"You gonna read the rest or what?" Reichis asked.

"Don't know," I replied. "Haven't decided yet."

"Read it out loud. You'll feel better."

"Why would I feel better reading out a private letter in front of you?"

The little bastard bit my ear, and hung on to it while murmuring, "Because then I'll stop doing this."

"Fine," I said, and read the second letter to him.

Kellen,

It's morning here on the Gitabrian border. Been sitting here a while now, waiting for the sun to rise up over those hills. Waiting for the girl to stop crying. Funny how tough she is on the outside, how soft on the inside. Gotta teach her how to switch that around. Person's got to be weak in the skin and strong in the bone. Like you.

Bet you're shaking your head right now, telling yourself how bad you are at everything, how scared you are of everyone. That's okay. It's your way, I guess. I've been Argosi a long time now, and we learn not to mess with another's ways. Still, though, there's one more trick I reckon I should've taught you. One lesson I can still give that maybe won't pull you off your path.

It goes like this:

Since the moment I watched you leave (you didn't think you really snuck out on old Ferius, did you?), I've been waiting for your absence to hit me. You and me, we've travelled a long while together (by Argosi standards anyway), and, well, I ain't shy to say it. I love you, kid. Don't know when it happened. You ain't my kin and there ain't nothing about us that's alike. Somewhere on those long roads we rode together, though, you became something I never had and probably never will have again. Don't rightly know what the word is for it, but it's something special all right.

So how come I ain't missing you yet? How come I ain't shedding tears like rainwater the way the girl keeps doing? Hopping up and down about how you could be in trouble, and maybe we could catch up to you, and maybe there's some nonsense Jan'Tep tracking spell that'll let us find you? How come I don't feel that knife of loneliness—that feeling I didn't even have a word for until I got used to you being around—slipping through my ribs?

Maybe it's because I'm still hearing your voice in my head. Complaining. Questioning. Arguing. I take out a smoking reed from my waistcoat and I can feel your eyes on it, wondering if I smoke too much but not saying it. I watch that sun rising and I feel that hope you always get that maybe today we won't have to fight our way out of another mess. You know what's funny? The Argosi don't have hope. First thing we learn is to get rid of hope, same as we rid ourselves of grief. An Argosi has to be sharp. See things true, not the way we want them to be or the way we fear they might become. Gotta stay clear.

Well, I guess I can't be that way no more. Got you in my head. It's early hours yet, maybe you'll fade away, but somehow I don't think so. I think maybe you're a part of me now, and maybe I'm a part of you. Maybe you're out there, looking for some nonsense cure for those marks around your eye, and you've run into a little trouble (nothing you can't handle, of course), and you'll feel me there with you, reminding you to dance, not fight. Play music instead of talking. Listen with your eyes instead of staring. Maybe, if I keep hearing you talk to me, it means you're hearing me talk to you too, giving you what advice I have to give, but maybe more often just reminding you of what you already know in that great big messed-up heart of yours.

That's the lesson, Kellen. Those who know love, even for a little while, are never really alone.

That's the thought I'll be holding on to. Like I said, the Argosi don't waste time on hope.

But I sure hope I see you again some day, kid.

Ferius Parfax
Three parts gambler, two parts Argosi, and one part Kellen of the House of Ke.

I folded the two letters and put them in my pocket, not trusting its safety in my pack given Reichis's lack of sentimentality about such things.

"Ugh," he groaned, sniffing at my face. "You cryin' *again?*"

"I'm not crying," I lied.

He sniffed again. "Yes, you are. You're blubbing like a little skin-bag baby begging for his mama's milk because he's too weak and whiny to go kill a rabbit. Matter of fact, I think you cry even *more* than skinbag babies. I mean, if I were to count the number of times I've watched you whimper, Kellen, why it's more than all the rabbits in the whole. . ."

He went on like that, not at all concerned about hurting my feelings or even if I were paying attention. I suppose it was inevitable. We'd been apart for far too long, and then our bond was broken and I couldn't understand his insults. So now he was making up for lost time.

An idea came to me then. Not a world-changing, grand- destiny sort of idea, but the kind that would make the next few hours of walking go by a lot smoother. "Oh, the crying," I said, interrupting him, "that's just the shadowblack."

He tilted his fuzzy head and looked at me. "The what now?"

"The shadowblack. It makes you cry."

"*Cry?*"

I nodded. "Like, constantly."

"*I'm* not crying," he growled. "I *never* cry."

"Oh, not at first. But you'll feel it soon enough. Come tomorrow you'll be crying all the time."

"What? But I'm a squirrel cat! My kind don't—"

"Just over some things," I said, lending my voice a tone of reassurance. "Like, getting punched or stabbed won't make you cry."

"Of course not. I never—"

"Mostly things like sunsets."

"Sunsets?"

I nodded. "Don't watch sunsets. Especially if they're beautiful. You'll start tearing up right away. Oh, and pretty flowers can set you off too."

"*Pretty flowers?*"

"And rabbits."

"Wait . . . *Rabbits?*"

"Yep. Rabbits are worst of all. I can't see a thing when there's a rabbit around on account of my eyes are so watery. It's not so bad though."

"Not so bad? I *eat* rabbits, Kellen. I kill rabbits. I *murder* rabbits."

I paused a moment, allowing Reichis's growing discomfort to build to almost fever pitch. "Well, maybe you wouldn't have to kill them any more," I suggested. "Maybe you could make friends with them instead."

"Make friends with *rabbits?*"

"Yeah, like, you know, be nice to them. Snuggle them. Petting rabbits always makes me feel better."

I could practically feel his fur grow cold against my cheek as he sat there on my shoulder, speechless for once. I resumed my march through the boggy ground towards the nearest village.

"Kellen?" he asked a little while later as the sun was coming up over the horizon.

"Yes, Reichis?"

"We gotta find a cure for the shadowblack. I mean, like, really gods-damned fast."

"You sure? I mean, it's a big world, and we may have to travel all of it before we find a cure."

A low growl started in his belly and worked its way up his throat until he snarled in my ear, "Then walk faster, arsehole."

Yeah, this was going to be a fun trip.

The story continues in...

QUEENSLAYER

Book FIVE of the Spellslinger series

Keep reading for a sneak peek!

Acknowledgements

The Ways of Shadow

I make it a rule not to explain all the details of magic systems within the books themselves, because doing so is a bit like listing the names of every street in a city or what foods the characters ate each day. However I do get asked about the various systems of magic in the *Spellslinger* series, so I thought I'd share a few notes on shadowcasting here, along with some rather important practitioners of those darkest of arts who helped bring *Soulbinder* to you.

Enigmatists: Unravellers of Secrets

We think of mysteries as ideas without form, yet still such enigmas cast shadows upon the world. Enigmatists like Kellen must find the right questions to ask, and in so doing infuse those questions with their shadows, giving them a momentary connection to the secrets they seek to unravel. Unlike alacratists, who perceive that which is or was, enigmatists peer into that which might be.

The wonderful and patient Felicity "Fliss" Johnston spent countless hours venturing into shadow with me as we searched for the essence of *Soulbinder*. Kim Tough read the earliest draft, chapter by chapter, always coming back with her masterful blend of insight, honesty and supportiveness. Eric Torin, as he has for every single one of my books, cast a light on those areas of the story where I'd failed to explore deeply enough. Christina de Castell, with her unique insight, helped me escape from the shadowy bands into which I'd gotten myself knotted.

Alacratists: Witnesses of the Past and Present

The etheric planes from which the shadowblack emerges have no rules of space or time, and thus alacratists can use their markings to perceive the shadows of people and places from a distance or even in the past, and then project them for others to see.

Talya Baker brought her unparalleled copy editor's eye to the novel, not only helping me improve the prose. but also scrutinising everything from the castradazi coins to which arm each Jan'Tep band should be on. Melissa Hyder once again proofread the novel, hunting down typos and inconsistencies that would otherwise have gone by unnoticed.

Praemandors: Wielders of Shadow Bands

The markings on a shadowblack's body can become deadly weapons in the hands of a praemandor, for only they can control the twisting black ribbons and turn them into deadly lashes. Every writer needs a few praemandors to keep them in line . . .

Wil Arndt and Brad Denhert read early versions of the opening and whacked me with shadow ribbons until I spotted the places where more depth was needed. Jim Hull of narrativefirst.com kindly pushed me to face some of the structural inconsistencies of Kellen's journey. I breathed a sigh of relief when Simone Hay informed me that *Soulbinder* was her second-favourite book of the series. As promised, Simone, Kellen got a lousy shadowblack ability. Nazia Khatun gave the book the squirrel cat seal of approval, without which the book would surely have been cursed to linger in shadow forever.

Acknowledgements

Inspiritors: Awakeners of Sentience

The shadowblack isn't simply a form of energy; it is potential life devoid of consciousness. Inspiritors like Diadera infuse shadow with fragments of their own spirit, lending them form and purpose. A talented inspiritor can literally bring an idea to life. Of course, Diadera could only do this in the form of her firefly freckles, but I've met a number of other inspiritors who create remarkable wonders.

One of my favourite parts of the publishing process is witnessing the cover design process unfold. My editor Nivia puts together a brief and Lauren Panepinto transforms it into a compelling new image. My thanks as well to Gleni Bartels for transmuting the text into the beautifully finished book you hold in your hands.

Perplexors: Concoctors of Confusion

Sometimes called "foggers," those like Ghilla have the ability to bind shadow to their very breath, summoning a fog of pure shadow that can confuse their enemies, or even tear them apart. Of course, they only do it for the very best of reasons . . .

Someone has to mesmerise publishers into believing in my books, and no one could do it better than superstar agents Heather Adams and Mike Bryan. Without their faith and determination, *Spellslinger* would never have seen print. Of course, then someone has to convince people to read it, and I'm grateful to Tina Mories, Nicola Chapman and Felice McKeown for their efforts to spellbind readers into giving the series a try.

Imperiasters: Architects of Shadow Forms

Only a very few can transmute the stuff of shadow into pure physical form the way the abbot could. Imperiasters bring their unfathomable will to bear as they bring to life permanent structures that could never have existed otherwise.

Acknowledgements

One of the scarier things authors have to worry about these days is the strength, durability and commitment of publishers. Mark Smith turned Bonnier Zaffre into a powerhouse, and Jane Harris leads its children's and YA division to one success after another. Yet with all that going on, they've always been willing to meet with me, to discuss books and my career. Best of all, they tolerate my entirely inappropriate sense of humour.

Iterantors: Travellers of the Onyx Roads

Shadows can stretch any distance yet require no physical mass. For this reason, iterantors can create roads through shadow that enable them to travel across continents in mere hours. Of course, the vaster the distance, the greater the chance of getting lost. It is for this reason that the true talent of iterantors is not simply the creation of paths, but the ability to safely navigate infinite avenues of confusion and danger to the one true destination.

The fabulous Bonnier Zaffre sales team—Angie Willocks, Nico Poilblanc, Victoria Hart and Vincent Kelleher—have travelled through countless shadowy realms to bring *Soulbinder* to bookstores everywhere. Of course, Ruth Logan and Ilaria Tarasconi travel even further afield to get the *Spellslinger* series to countries all over the world. When they do, it's the incredible translators who perform the most amazing spell of all: taking a story, with all its idioms and stylistic quirks, and making it enchanting in a completely different language. At last count, *Spellslinger* is published in thirteen languages, which is just about the most amazing thing that can ever happen to an author.

Lamentarists: Trackers of the Shadowblack

Shadows in the presence of strong emotions create echoes of those sorrows, fears or joys. Lamentarists like Butelios have the rare ability to pick up those emotions even across great distances, to experience them and then to weep shadow tears that will lead to their source.

Acknowledgements

Butelios is probably my favourite new character of the series. (Ouch! Damn it, Reichis, I said *new* character!) I've had occasion in my life to encounter people with that otherworldly generosity of spirit—people driven to seek out things they love and share them with others rather than aggrandising themselves. It's why I enjoy meeting book bloggers, librarians, booksellers and readers of the series. You make being a novelist the best job in the world.

You can reach me at www.decastell.com and @decastell on Twitter. I'll always be happy to hear from you.

Sebastien de Castell
August 2018
Vancouver, Canada

extras

meet the author

Photo Credit: Pink Monkey Studios

SEBASTIEN DE CASTELL is the author of the acclaimed swash-
buckling fantasy series, the Greatcoats, and the Carnegie
Medal–nominated *Spellslinger*. His debut novel, *Traitor's Blade*,
was shortlisted for the Goodreads Choice Award for Best Fantasy, the Gemmell Morningstar Award, the Prix Imaginales for
best foreign work, and the John W. Campbell Award for Best
New Writer. He spends his time writing, traveling, and going
on adventures. Visit him at www.decastell.com.

if you enjoyed
SOULBINDER

look out for

QUEENSLAYER

Spellslinger: Book Five

by

Sebastien de Castell

Kellen and Reichis have just finished fighting a duel in the desert when Kellen inadvertently smears blood on the Daroman flag—an act of treason for which the marshals have no choice but to arrest him.

Just before he's put before the queen to be executed, Kellen is given a strange piece of advice from one of his fellow prisoners: kill the Queen and he'll be given clemency by those who take power. But when Kellen comes face to face with the eleven-year-old monarch, he realizes she's vastly smarter than he expected—and in a great deal more danger.

1

Snow and Copper

Shush, shush, shush, whispered the snow, soothing as a man holding his hand over your mouth while he sticks a knife in your liver in the middle of a crowded street.

There were seven of us in this particular crowd, shivering on this frigid plateau high up in the border mountains. Merrell of Betrian, the man I'd planned to kill stood behind Arke'tan, the mage he'd hired to kill me first. A few yards away stood two bored Daroman marshals we'd found on guard near the border. They'd graciously offered to oversee the duel (which is to say, threatened to arrest us unless we paid the overseeing fee). That just left the tall, graceful eagle that was Arke'tan's familiar and the short, nasty squirrel cat who passed for mine. Oh, and me, of course.

"You're gonna get it now, Kellen!" Merrell hooted at me from across the fifty yards stretch of snow-dusted ground that separated us. "Arke'tan here's a real mage. Ain't no fool, neither, so your little spellslinger tricks ain't gonna work on him."

"Yeah, you're right, Merrell," I shouted back. "My tricks only work on fools."

Merrell swore, Arke'tan smirked, and the two marshals chuckled. Neither the bird nor the squirrel cat paid any attention. They were focused on each other. Me, I was thinking that maybe Merrell wasn't the biggest sucker shuffling about trying to keep his toes from freezing off that day.

I thought I'd been running him down. I thought I'd been racing after him to keep him from crossing the border into the Zhuban territories where he knew I wouldn't follow. I thought I'd been chasing after a dumb, pug-ugly wife beater who'd tried to cheat me at cards. Turns out that was all wrong.

Merrell was a lot wealthier than he'd let on. He was also a lot better connected, too, because however much money I thought he had, I was surprised it was enough to hire himself a full-on war-mage. My people don't usually do contract work for borderland hicks.

Looking at Arke'tan was like staring into a distorted mirror of myself. I was a few days shy of my eighteenth birthday and unlikely to see twenty. Arke'tan looked to be in his early thirties, head of a notable Jan'Tep house with wealth, power, and a long, glorious future in front of him. My hair is what's politely referred to as "manure coloured," his gleamed like platinum and gold in the sunlight. I was lean from hard living and a life on the run, he had the muscular build of a soldier.

"I like your armour," I shouted across the swirling patch of snow that lay between us. Shining, form-fitting plates linked by silk threads guarded his chest, arms, and legs. "It's very... golden. Matches your bird."

"It is an eagle, boy," he replied, smiling up at the hunter flying in lazy circles through the air like a buzzard anticipating his next meal. "A bird is something that flitters around before you shoot it for food. An eagle makes you his dinner."

He pointed absently towards me. Unlike him, I didn't have any armour, just my leather coat and riding chaps to keep myself from getting scraped up every time I fell off my horse. "I like your hat," he said, nodding at the Daroman frontiersman hat I wore to keep the sun off my face, and off the black marks around my left eye. "Those silver glyphs going around the brim are...cute. Do they do anything?"

I shrugged. "The man I stole the hat from said they'd bring me luck."

Arke'tan smiled again. "Then he overcharged you. This fool has paid me rather a lot of money to end you, but I would have done it for free had I known you were Shadowblack. I'm going to send a bolt of lightning straight through that filthy left eye of yours."

The bird...eagle, rather, let out a caw for emphasis, as if it understood the conversation. "You think the bird knows..." I began.

"Of course he knows what you're saying," Reichis chittered in reply, then added, "idjit." The squirrel cat means "idiot" when he says that, but we'd been in the borderlands for a few months, and he'd taken to talking like a gap-toothed frontiersman. "The eagle's his familiar. Whatever that overgrown skin-bag hears, the bird hears."

I glanced down at Reichis, who looked a little ridiculous holding his paw just above his eyes to shield them from the harsh sunlight reflecting off the snow and ice so he could scowl at the mage's eagle. If you've never seen a squirrel cat before, imagine a drunken god had gifted a slightly tubby two-foot-tall cat with a big bushy tail and furry flaps running between its front and back legs that enable him to glide down from tree-tops and sink his claws and teeth into his chosen prey—which is pretty much everything that moves. Oh, and then that same god gave his creation the temperament of a thief. And a black-mailer. And probably on more than one occasion, a murderer.

"I bet that guy's eagle doesn't call him 'idjit,'" I said.

Reichis looked up at me. "Yeah, well, that's probably because I'm not your familiar, I'm your business partner. *Idjit.*"

"You think that's going to make a difference in about five minutes when the marshals tell us to draw and that eagle snatches you up and rips out your entrails?"

"Point," Reichis said. He patted me on the leg. "All right, so you're a genius, kid. Now go blow this guy away so we can eat that ugly-lookin' bird for supper."

I let my hands drift down to the powder pouches at my sides. Merrell nearly fell on his arse and the two marshals instantly had their crossbows aimed at me in case I was about to cheat the duel, but Arke'tan ignored the gesture entirely.

"He ain't afraid of you blasting him," Reichis said. Well, he doesn't really speak—he makes squirrel cat sounds—but the nature of our relationship is such that I hear them as words.

"Right," I said. "Intransigent charm shield?"

"Gotta be."

I peered across the gap between us and Arke'tan. I couldn't see anything on the ground. I'd picked this spot intentionally because it's pretty damned hard to keep a circle intact when all you can draw it in is ice and snow. I couldn't see anything, so that left only one logical possibility.

"Say, fellas? You all mind if we move just a few feet to the right? I've got the sun in my eyes here and we can't have an unfair duel, right?"

The older of the two marshals, Harrex I think his name was, shrugged his bony shoulders and nodded towards Arke'tan.

The mage just smiled back and shook his head. His eagle did a little dive towards us and turned up just a few feet away from my face.

"They got here early and laid down copper sigil wire under the snow then poured water on it and waited for it to turn to

401

ice," I said to Reichis. "Guess you were right that we should've camped out here last night."

"Idjit."

Harrex pulled out a sundial and held it out in front of him. "Well, gentlemen, I reckon we're just about there. In a minute it'll be mid-morning and marshal Parrius here will start the countdown from seven. You both know the rules after that?"

"Kill the other guy?" I offered.

Reichis glared up at me. "That your plan? Make jokes until that mage can't blast us on account of he's laughing too hard to speak the incantations?"

"Might be our best shot. No way I'm going to be able to blast through that shield."

"So what do we do?"

I looked over at Arke'tan and watched the smile on his face widen as he stood there, calm as could be, waiting for the duel to begin.

"Seven!" marshal Parrius shouted out.

I looked down into Reichis' beady squirrel cat eyes. "How about we switch dance partners?" I suggested.

"Six!"

"You're saying I go after the mage?" Reichis had a smile on that little fuzzy face of his. He might be greedy, he might be a liar, a thief, and a blackmailer, but the little bugger loves to fight, and he's got a death wish the likes of which you've never seen.

"Five!"

"Don't screw around, Reichis. You know what to do."

"Four!"

Reichis gave a little shake. His fur changed colour from its usual mean-spirited brown with black stripes to pure white, making him almost invisible against the thick carpet of snow. I flipped open the metal clasps on my pouches.

"Three!"

Arke'tan brought the fingers of both his hands together in a kind of steeple shape. I knew the somatic form, even if I couldn't cast the spell myself. I winced at the thought of what it would do when it hit me.

"Two!"

Arke'tan winked at me. The eagle pulled around from his last circle to get ready to dive after Reichis. The squirrel cat got down on all fours and pressed his back feet against the snow, digging in for leverage.

"One…" Parrius said, a little too much enthusiasm in his voice for my taste.

Well, this was going to be one for the poets. Although I suppose it would only be interesting if I won, since the "tale of the incredibly powerful war mage who killed a completely unknown spellslinger with barely enough magic in his hands to light blast powder" didn't sound particularly epic.

There's usually only two ways to lose a duel: end up on your knees begging for mercy, or on your back waiting for your ancestors to collect your corpse.

"Begin!"

I was about to discover a third option that was even worse.

2

Fire and Lightning

The first tiny blue sparks of lightning formed around Arke'tan's fingers just as the eagle began a downward dive to kill Reichis. I could almost taste the electricity in the air that preceded the bolt and I prayed that Arke'tan was just arrogant enough to want to follow through with his threat. I jammed my hands into the pouches at my side, letting the forefingers grab some of the red and black powders that awaited there even as I dove to the ground. I watched the lightning bolt tear past where an instant ago it would've hit my left eye. Good aim.

Reichis was kicking up a tiny snowstorm behind him as he raced toward Arke'tan screaming "Die, you stupid pigeon!"

The eagle was just about on Reichis when I threw the powders up in the air in front of me as my right shoulder hit the ground. Inert and innocent as babes on their own, the two powders had a hatred for each other that created a deadly explosion on contact. The magic's not in the blast, you see, that's just the effect of the powders themselves. The magic's in the hard part—aiming the direction of the blast, and not blowing your own hands and face off in the process. My hands each formed the necessary somatic shape: bottom two fingers pressed into the palm, the sign of restraint; fore and middle fingers pointed straight out, the sign of flight; and thumb pointing to the heavens, the sign of, well, somebody up there help me.

extras

"*Carath Toth*," I said, uttering the two word invocation. Only the first one was needed, strictly speaking. Toth was a bounty hunter who'd tracked Reichis and me a few weeks ago. Now my powder was suffused with his blood, and saying his name gave the spell a little extra kick.

A blast of red and black fire, the flames intertwined like black snakes, followed the direction of my forefingers as they shot out at the eagle, leaving a haze of smoke in their wake. I missed the birds heart but got one of his wings, sending him careening into the ground a few feet away from Reichis. The squirrel cat didn't stop to look, though. Just kept those little legs pounding towards his goal.

"Shadea!" the mage screamed, his hands unconsciously relinquishing the somatic shape for his next spell. *Hurts when your familiar gets hit, don't it?* I thought maliciously. I had nothing against the eagle, you understand, but he was trying to kill my business partner.

Arke'tan aimed his second blast just as I was getting back to my feet, forcing me to dive again, this time flat on my stomach. I felt the electricity pass just over my head and I knew I wasn't going to evade a third bolt.

Reichis bridged the gap towards the war mage and gave a feral growl as he leaped up into the air. Arke'tan nearly fell back despite the fact that there was no way in hell the squirrel cat was going to be able to breach the shield. But the shield wasn't the target. The instant Reichis hit the ground he started digging ferociously, tearing through snow and ice to where the fragile circle of copper wire holding the spell must be buried.

Arke'tan was just starting to figure it out when I fired another shot at his familiar.

"*Carath Toth*," I said.

"No!" Arke'tan screamed. He fired a different kind of spell this time, some kind of blessing or protection that enveloped the eagle and dissipated my blast into airy red nothingness. *Nice trick*, I thought.

"Now!" Reichis growled to me.

I saw the crease in the snow where he'd been digging. That was my opening. But I wasn't in the right line to send a bolt through the hole in the shield.

"Damn it," I said, as I got to my feet and ran towards Arke'tan.

I saw him look down at the ground, his hands forming a new and ugly shape this time. His eyes went from the hole to Reichis, and then up to me. He aimed the spell towards me. *Too soon, damn it, too soon.* I wasn't in line with the gap yet.

"*Carath Moron!*" I shouted at the top of my lungs, aiming my fingers at Arke'tan as if I'd really been casting the spell. Reflexively he changed the configuration of his fingers and formed a transient shield. A mistake, since I hadn't actually fired and his warding would only last a second without copper to anchor it. Arke'tan's mouth went wide as he realized I'd tricked him. I was now in line with the gap in his shield. The "moron" part wasn't necessary, but when you're an outlaw with a price on his head, you take your fun wherever you can.

With the opening in the shield now visible as a stuttering shimmer, I whispered, "*Carath Toth*" one last time. The powders slammed against each other in the air. Aiming down the line of my fingers, I sent the explosion through the gap before Arke'tan could get another warding spell up. The bolt took him square in the chest and right through the decorative plating of his armour. For a second the war mage remained standing, ignorant of the fact that his body now lacked the vital organs necessary for life. The blast had left a hole big enough for me to

406

see right through him, to where Merrell was kneeling behind his champion. I walked towards him as the mage's body figured out what had happened, and fell to the ground.

If that all sounds too easy, it wasn't.

Besides, we're still not at the part where I screwed everything up.

if you enjoyed
SOULBINDER

look out for

THE FIFTH WARD: FIRST WATCH

by

Dale Lucas

A member of the Yenara City guard has gone missing. The culprit could be any of the usual suspects: drug-dealing orcs, mind-controlling elves, uncooperative mages, or humans being typical humans.

It's up to two reluctant partners—Rem, a miscreant who joins the Watch to pay off his bail, and Torval, a maul-wielding dwarf who's highly unimpressed with the untrained Rem—to uncover the truth and catch the murderer loose in their fair city.

Chapter One

Rem awoke in a dungeon with a thunderous headache. He knew it was a dungeon because he lay on a thin bed of straw, and because there were iron bars between where he lay and a larger chamber outside. The light was spotty, some of it from torches in sconces outside his cell, some from a few tiny windows high on the stone walls admitting small streams of wan sunlight. Moving nearer the bars, he noted that his cell was one of several, each roomy enough to hold multiple prisoners.

A large pile of straw on the far side of his cell coughed, shifted, then started to snore. Clearly, Rem was not alone.

And just how did I end up here? he wondered. *I seem to recall a winning streak at Roll-the-Bones.*

He could not remember clearly. But if the lumpy soreness of his face and body were any indication, his dice game had gone awry. If only he could clear his pounding head, or slake his thirst. His tongue and throat felt like sharkskin.

Desperate for a drink, Rem crawled to a nearby bucket, hoping for a little brackish water. To his dismay, he found that it was the piss jar, not a water bucket, and not well rinsed at that. The sight and smell made Rem recoil with a gag. He went sprawling back onto the hay. A few feet away, his cellmate muttered something in the tongue of the Kosterfolk, then resumed snoring.

Somewhere across the chamber, a multitumbler lock clanked and clacked. Rusty hinges squealed as a great door lumbered open. From the other cells Rem heard prisoners roused from their sleep, shuffling forward hurriedly to thrust their arms out through the cage bars. If Rem didn't misjudge, there were only about four or five other prisoners in all the dungeon cells. A select company, to be sure. Perhaps it was a slow day for the Yenaran city watch?

Four men marched into the dungeon. Well, three marched; the fourth seemed a little more reticent, being dragged by two others behind their leader, a thickset man with black hair, sullen eyes, and a drooping mustache.

"Prefect, sir," Rem heard from an adjacent cell, "there's been a terrible mistake…"

From across the chamber: "Prefect, sir, someone must have spiked my ale, because the last thing I remember, I was enjoying an evening out with some mates…"

From off to his left: "Prefect, sir, I've a chest of treasure waiting back at my rooms at the Sauntering Mink. A golden cup full of rubies and emeralds is yours, if you'll just let me out of here…"

Prefect, sir… Prefect, sir… over and over again.

Rem decided that thrusting his own arms out and begging for the prefect's attention was useless. What would he do? Claim his innocence? Promise riches if they'd let him out? That was quite a tall order when Rem himself couldn't remember what he'd done to get in here. If he could just clear his thunder-addled, achingly thirsty brain…

The sullen-eyed prefect led the two who dragged the prisoner down a short flight of steps into a shallow sort of operating theater in the center of the dungeon: the interrogation pit, like some shallow bath that someone had let all the water out of. On one side of the pit was a brick oven in which fire and coals glowed. Opposite the oven was a burbling fountain. Rem thought these additions rather ingenious. Whatever elemental need one had—fire to burn with, water to drown with—both were readily provided. The floor of the pit, Rem guessed, probably sported a couple of grates that led right down into the sewers, as well as the tools of the trade: a table full of torturer's implements, a couple of hot braziers, some chairs and manacles. Rem hadn't seen the inside of any city dungeons, but he'd seen their private equivalents. Had it been the dungeon of some march lord up north—from his own country—that's what would have been waiting in the little amphitheater.

"Come on, Ondego, you know me," the prisoner pleaded. "This isn't necessary."

"'Fraid so," sullen-eyed Ondego said, his low voice easy and without malice. "The chair, lads."

The two guardsmen flanking the prisoner were a study in contrasts—one a tall, rugged sort, face stony and flecked with stubble, shoulders broad, while the other was lithe and graceful, sporting braided black locks, skin the color of dark-stained wood, and a telltale pair of tapered, pointing ears. Staring, Rem realized that second guardsman was no man at all, but an elf, and female, at that. Here was a puzzle, indeed. Rem had seen elves at a distance before, usually in or around frontier settlements farther north, or simply haunting the bleak crossroads of a woodland highway like pikers who never demanded a toll. But he had never seen one of them up close like this— and certainly not in the middle of one of the largest cities in the Western world, deep underground, in a dingy, shit- and blood-stained dungeon. Nonetheless, the dark-skinned elfmaid seemed quite at home in her surroundings, and perfectly comfortable beside the bigger man on the other side of the prisoner.

Together, those two guards thrust the third man's squirming, wobbly body down into a chair. Heavy manacles were produced and the protester was chained to his seat. He struggled a little, to test his bonds, but seemed to know instinctively that it was no use. Ondego stood at a brazier nearby, stoking its coals, the pile of dark cinders glowing ominously in the oily darkness.

"Oi, that's right!" one of the other prisoners shouted. "Give that bastard what for, Prefect!"

"You shut your filthy mouth, Foss!" the chained man spat back.

"Eat me, Kevel!" the prisoner countered. "How do *you* like the chair, eh?"

Huh. Rem moved closer to his cell bars, trying to get a better look. So, this prisoner, Kevel, knew that fellow in the cell, Foss, and vice versa. Part of a conspiracy? Brother marauders, questioned one by one—and in sight of one another—for some vital information?

Then Rem saw it: Kevel, the prisoner in the hot seat, wore a signet pendant around his throat identical to those worn by the prefect and the two guards. It was unmistakable, even in the shoddy light.

"Well, I'll be," Rem muttered aloud.

The prisoner was one of the prefect's own watchmen.

Ex-watchman now, he supposed.

All of a sudden, Rem felt a little sorry for him...but not much. No doubt, Kevel himself had performed the prefect's present actions a number of times: chaining some poor sap into the hot seat, stoking the brazier, using fire and water and physical distress to intimidate the prisoner into revealing vital information.

The prefect, Ondego, stepped away from the brazier and moved to a table nearby. He studied a number of implements— it was too dark and the angle too awkward for Rem to tell what, exactly—then picked something up. He hefted the object in his hands, testing its weight.

It looked like a book—thick, with a hundred leaves or more bound between soft leather covers.

"Do you know what this is?" Ondego asked Kevel.

"Haven't the foggiest," Kevel said. Rem could tell that he was bracing himself, mentally and physically.

"It's a genealogy of Yenara's richest families. Out-of-date, though. At least a generation old."

"Do tell," Kevel said, his throat sounding like it had contracted to the size of a reed.

"Look at this," Ondego said, hefting the book in his hands, studying it. "That is one enormous pile of useless information. Thick as a bloody brick—"

And that's when Ondego drew back the book and brought it smashing into Kevel's face in a broad, flat arc. The sound of the strike—leather and parchment pages connecting at high speed with Kevel's jawbone—echoed in the dungeon like the crack of a calving iceberg. A few of the other prisoners even wailed as though they were the ones struck.

Rem's cellmate stirred beneath his pile of straw, but did not rise.

Kevel almost fell with the force of the blow. The big guard caught him and set him upright again. The lithe elf backed off, staring intently at the prisoner, as though searching his face and his manner for a sign of something. Without warning, Ondego hit Kevel again, this time on the other side of his face. Once more Kevel toppled. Once more the guard in his path caught him and set him upright.

Kevel spat out blood. Ondego tossed the book back onto the table behind him and went looking for another implement.

"That all you got, old man?" Kevel asked.

"Bravado doesn't suit you," Ondego said, still studying his options from the torture table. He threw a glance at the elf on the far side of the torture pit. Rem watched intently, realizing that some strange ritual was under way: Kevel, blinking sweat from his eyes, studied Ondego; the lady elf, silent and implacable, studied Kevel; and Ondego idly studied the elf, the prefect's thick, workman's hand hovering slowly over the gathered implements of torture on the table.

Then, Kevel blinked. That small, unconscious movement seemed to signal something to the elf, who then spoke to the prefect. Her voice was soft, deep, melodious.

"The amputation knife," she said, her large, unnerving, honey-colored eyes never leaving the prisoner.

Ondego took up the instrument that his hand hovered above—a long, curving blade like a field-hand's billhook, the honed edge being on the inside, rather than the outside, of the curve. Ondego brandished the knife and looked to Kevel. The prisoner's eyes were as wide as empty goblets.

Ingenious! The elf had apparently used her latent mind-reading abilities to determine which of the implements on the table Kevel most feared being used on him. Not precisely the paragon of sylvan harmony and ancient grace that Rem would have imagined such a creature to be, but impressive nonetheless.

As Ondego spoke, he continued to brandish the knife, casually, as if it were an extension of his own arm. "Honestly, Kev," he said, "haven't I seen you feign bravery a hundred times? I know you're shitting your kecks about now."

"So you'd like to think," Kevel answered, eyes still on the knife. "You're just bitter because you didn't do it. Rich men don't get rich keeping to a set percentage, Ondego. They get rich by redrawing the percentages."

Ondego shook his head. Rem could be mistaken, but he thought he saw real regret there.

"Rule number one," Ondego said, as though reciting holy writ. "Keep the peace."

"Suck it," Kevel said bitterly.

"Rule number two," Ondego said, slowly turning to face Kevel, "Keep your partner safe, and he'll do the same for you."

"He was going to squeal," Kevel said, now looking a little more repentant. "I couldn't have that. You said yourself, Ondego—he wasn't cut out for it. Never was. Never would be."

"So that bought him a midnight swim in the bay?" Ondego asked. "Rule number three: let the punishment fit the crime, Kevel. Throttling that poor lad and throwing him in the drink... that's what the judges call cruel and unusual. We don't do cruel and unusual in my ward."

"Go spit," Kevel said.

"Rule number four," Ondego quickly countered. "And this is important, Kevel, so listen good: never take more than your share. There's enough for everyone, so long as no one's greedy. So long as no one's hoarding or getting fat. I knew you were taking a bigger cut when your jerkin started straining. There's only one way a watchman that didn't start out fat gets that way, and that's by hoarding and taking more than his fair share."

"So what's it gonna be?" Kevel asked. "The knife? The razor? The book again? The hammer and the nail-tongs?"

"Nah," Ondego said, seemingly bored by their exchange, as though he were disciplining a child that he'd spanked a hundred times before. He tossed the amputation knife back on the table. "Bare fists."

And then, as Rem and the other prisoners watched, Ondego, prefect of the watch, proceeded to beat the living shit out of Kevel, a onetime member of his own watch company. Despite the fact that Ondego said not another word while the beating commenced, Rem thought he sensed some grim and unhappy purpose in Ondego's corporal punishment. He never once smiled, nor even gritted his teeth in anger. The intensity of the beating never flared nor ebbed. He simply kept his mouth set, his eyes open, and slowly, methodically, laid fists to flesh. He made Kevel whimper and bleed. From time to time he would stop and look to the elf. The elf would study Kevel, clearly not simply looking at him but *into* him, perhaps reading just how close he was to losing consciousness, or whether he was feigning senselessness to gain some brief reprieve. The elf would then offer a cursory, "More." Ondego, on the elfmaid's advice, would continue.

Rem admired that: Ondego's businesslike approach, the fact that he could mete out punishment without enjoying it. In some ways, Ondego reminded Rem of his own father.

Before Ondego was done, a few of the other prisoners were crying out. Some begged mercy on Kevel's behalf. Ondego wasn't having it. He didn't acknowledge them. His fists carried on their bloody work. To Kevel's credit he never begged mercy. Granted, that might have been hard after the first quarter hour or so, when most of his teeth were on the floor.

Ondego only relented when the elf finally offered a single word. "Out." At that, Ondego stepped back, like a pugilist retreating to his corner between melee rounds. He shook his hands, no doubt feeling a great deal of pain in them. Beating a man like that tested the limits of one's own pain threshold as well as the victim's.

"Still breathing?" Ondego asked, all business.

The human guard bent. Listened. Felt for a pulse. "Still with us. Out cold."

"Put him in the stocks," Ondego said. "If he survives five days on Zabayus's Square, he can walk out of the city so long as he never comes back. Post his crimes, so everyone sees."

The guards nodded and set to unchaining Kevel. Ondego swept past them and mounted the stairs up to the main cell level again, heading toward the door. That's when Rem suddenly noticed an enormous presence beside him. He had not heard the brute's approach, but he could only be the sleeping form beneath the hay. For one, he was covered in the stuff. For another, his long braided hair, thick beard, and rough-sewn, stinking leathers marked him as a Kosterman. And hadn't Rem heard Koster words muttered by the sleeper in the hay?

"Prefect!" the Kosterman called, his speech sharply accented.

Ondego turned, as if this was the first time he'd heard a single word spoken from the cells and the prisoners in them.

Rem's cellmate rattled the bars. "Let me out of here, little man," he said.

Kosterman all right. The long, yawning vowels and glass-sharp consonants were a dead giveaway. For emphasis, the Kosterman even snarled, as though the prefect were the lowest of house servants.

Ondego looked puzzled for a moment. Could it be that no one had ever spoken to him that way? Then the prefect stepped forward, snarling, looking like a maddened hound. His fist shot out in front of him and shook as he approached.

"Get back in your hay and keep your gods-damned head down, con! I'll have none of your nonsense after such a bevy of bitter business—"

Rem realized what was about to happen a moment before it did. He opened his mouth to warn the prefect off—surely the man wasn't so gullible? Maybe it was just his weariness in the wake of the beating he'd given Kevel? His regret at having to so savagely punish one of his own men?

Whatever the reason, Ondego clearly wasn't thinking straight. The moment his shaking fist was within arm's reach of the Kosterman in the cell, the barbarian reached out, snagged that fist, and yanked Ondego close. The prefect's face and torso hit the bars of the cell with a heavy clang.

Rem scurried aside as the Kosterman stretched both arms out through the bars, wrapped them around Ondego, then tossed all of his weight backward. He had the prefect in a deadly bear hug and was using his body's considerable weight to crush the man against the bars of the cell. Rem heard the other two watchmen rushing near, a flurry of curses and stomping boots. Around the dungeon, the men in the cells began to curse and cheer. Some even laughed.

"Let me out of here, now!" the Kosterman roared. "Let me out or I'll crush him, I swear!"

Rem's instincts were frustrated by his headache, his thirst, his confusion. But despite all that, he knew, deep in his gut, that he had to do something. He couldn't just let the hay-covered Kosterman in the smelly leathers crush the prefect to death against the bars of the cell.

But that Kosterman was enormous—at least a head and a half taller than Rem.

The other watchmen had reached the bars now. The stubble-faced one was trying to break the Kosterman's grip while the elfmaid snatched for the rattling keys to the cells on the human guard's belt.

Without thinking, Rem rushed up behind the angry Kosterman, drew back one boot, and kicked. The kick landed square in the Kosterman's fur-clad testicles.

The barbarian roared—an angry bear, indeed—and Rem's gambit worked. For just a moment, the Kosterman released his hold on the prefect. On the far side of the bars, the stubble-faced watchman managed to get the prefect in his grip and yank him backward, away from the cell. When Rem saw that, he made his next move.

He leapt onto the Kosterman's broad shoulders. Instead of wrapping his arms around the Kosterman's throat, he grabbed the bars of the cell. Then, locking his legs around the Koster-man's torso from behind, he yanked hard. The Kosterman was driven forward hard, his skull slamming with a resonant clang into the cell bars. Rem heard nose cartilage crunch. The Kosterman sputtered a little and tried to reach for whoever was on his back. Rem drew back and yanked again, driving the Kosterman forward into the bars once more.

Another clang. The Kosterman's body seemed to sag beneath Rem.

Then the sagging body began to topple backward.

Clinging high on the great, muscular frame, Rem realized that he was overbalanced. He lost his grip on the cell bars, and the towering Kosterman beneath him fell.

Rem tried to leap free, but he was too entangled with the barbarian to make it clear. Instead, he simply disengaged and went falling with him.

Both of them—Rem and the barbarian—hit the floor. The Kosterman was out cold. Rem had the wind knocked out of him and his vision came alight with whirling stars and dancing fireflies.

Blinking, trying to get his sight and his breath back, he heard the whine of rusty hinges, then footsteps. Strong hands seized him and dragged him out of the cell. By the time his vision had returned, he found himself on the stone pathway outside the cell that he had shared with the smelly, unconscious Kosterman. The prefect and his two watchmen stood over him.

"Explain yourself," Ondego said. He was a little disheveled, but otherwise, the Kosterman's attack seemed to have left not a mark on him, nor shaken him.

Rem coughed. Drew breath. Sighed. "Just trying to help," he said.

"I'll bet you want out now, don't you?" Ondego asked. "One good turn deserves another and all that."

Rem shrugged. "It hadn't really crossed my mind."

Ondego frowned, as though Rem were the most puzzling prisoner he had ever encountered. "Well, what do you want, then? I can be a hard bastard when I choose, but I know how to return a favor."

Rem had a thought. "I'm looking for work," he said.

Ondego raised one eyebrow.

"Seeing as you have space on your watch rosters"—Rem gestured to the spot where they had been beating Kevel in the torture pit—"perhaps I could impress upon you—"

Ondego seemed to appraise Rem honestly for a moment. For confirmation of his instincts, he looked to the elf.

Rem suddenly knew the strange sensation of another living being poking around in his mind. It was momentary and fleeting and entirely painless, but eminently strange and unnerving, like having one's privates appraised by the other patrons in a bathhouse. Then the elf's probing intellect withdrew, and Rem no longer felt naked. The elfmaid seemed to wear a small, knowing half smile. Her dark and ancient eyes settled on Rem and chilled him.

She knows everything, Rem thought. *A moment in my mind, two, and she knows everything. Everything worth knowing, anyway.*

"Harmless," the elfmaid said.

"Weak," the stubble-faced guardsmen added.

The elf's gaze never wavered. "No."

"You don't impress me," Ondego said, despite the elf's appraisal. "Not one bit."

"No doubt I don't," Rem said. "But, by Aemon, sir, I'd like to."

The watchman beside Ondego leaned close. Rem heard the words he whispered to the prefect.

"He did get that brute off you, sir."

Ondego and the big watchman continued to study him. The elf now turned her gaze on the boisterous prisoners in the other cells. A moment's eye contact was all it took. As the elfmaid turned her stone idol's glare on each of them, they fell silent and withdrew from the bars. Bearing witness to the effect the elf's silent, threatening stare had on those hard, desperate men made Rem's skin crawl.

But, to his own predicament: Rem decided to mount a better argument—he certainly couldn't end up in any more trouble, could he?

"You're down two men," Rem said, trying to look and sound as reasonable as possible. "That man you were beating and the partner he murdered. Surely you can give me the opportunity?"

"What's he in here for?" Ondego asked the watchman.

Rem prepared himself to listen. He was still trying to reason that part out himself.

"Bar brawl," the stubble-faced watchman said. "The Bonny Prince here was casting dice with some Koster longshoremen. Rolled straight nines, nine times in a row. They called him a cheat and he lit into them."

It was coming back now. Rem remembered the tavern. He'd been waiting for someone. A girl. She hadn't shown. He'd had a little too much to drink while waiting. He vaguely remembered the dice and the longshoremen—two tall fellows, not unlike the barbarian he'd just tussled with in the cell.

He couldn't recall their faces, or even starting a fight with them...but he did remember being called a cheat, and taking umbrage.

"I wasn't cheating," Rem said emphatically. "It was just a run of good luck."

"Not so good," Ondego said, "seeing as you're here in my dungeon." To the guardsmen beside him: "Where are the other two?"

"Taken to the hospital, sir," the big man said. "Beaten senseless by the Bonny Prince here."

"And a third Kosterman, out like a light on my dungeon floor. What is it with you and these northerners, boy?"

Rem shrugged. "Ill-starred, I guess."

Ondego seemed to appraise Rem anew. Three Kostermen on their backs was bold, and he couldn't deny it. "Doesn't look like much," the prefect said, as if to himself, "but he can hold his own in a fight."

Ondego was impressed with Rem—no thanks to the stone-faced watchman laying that damned "Bonny Prince" label on him. Rem guessed that Ondego's grudging respect might work in his favor.

"I don't like being called a cheat," Rem said, "first and foremost because I don't cheat. Ever."

Ondego nodded toward Kevel, limp in his chair. "Neither do we," he said.

"So I see," Rem answered.

A long silence fell between them.

"Get him on his feet," Ondego said. "We'll try him out."

Without another word, the prefect left.

Rem looked to the tall man. He felt a smile blooming on his face, then suddenly felt the pain of his brawl the night before. A swollen, split lip; a bruised nose; at least one missing tooth, far back in his mouth; the taste of old blood.

The big man offered a hand and yanked Rem to his feet. Upright, Rem swooned for a moment, his vision briefly going black again before finally clearing.

"Don't look so pleased with yourself, my bonny boy," the stubble-faced watchman said. "You've no idea what you're in for walking the ward."

423

Follow us:

/orbitbooksUS

/orbitbooks

/orbitbooks

Join our mailing list
to receive alerts on our
latest releases and deals.

orbitbooks.net

Enter our monthly
giveaway for the chance
to win some epic prizes.

orbitloot.com